Bungay Castle

Bungay Castle
A Novel.

By Elizabeth Bonhote

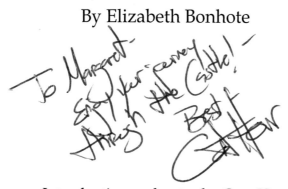

Introduction and notes by Curt Herr
Biography by Christopher Reeve

ZITTAW PRESS

Zittaw Press: *Bungay Castle*

ISBN 0-9767212-5-2
978-0-976212-5-3

Zittaw Press welcomes comments and suggestions regarding any aspect
of this reproduction—please contact us at customerservice@zittaw.com.

Library of Congress Control Number:

2006902278

www.zittaw.com

To Rich who laughs in his sleep...
and to Nancy, who at 73, swims with the manatees...

Bungay Castle *by Henry Davey from* Antiquities of Suffolk, *1827*

Contents

Acknowledgements

Special thanks to Richard Stockwell, Jim Perry, Linda Cullum and my graduate assistant Jessica Sobotka. I'd also like to thank Chris Reeve for his valuable information on Elizabeth Bonhote and supplying historical pictures of the actual Bungay Castle located in Suffolk England.

Introduction

Tomb with a View: The Restorative Power of Love in Elizabeth Bonhote's *Bungay Castle*

The book you are holding in your hands is not an excellent novel—it has not been a best seller in over 200 years—Long out of print and long forgotten, a bit tattered in places, even a bit musty—this novel is covered in cobwebs thicker than Spanish moss. Thankfully, however, Bungay Castle was built to last, and the novel, like its name sake, acquires strength when we look at its importance in terms of what it holds inside of its crumbling walls instead of its aged condition. Imperfectly structured, a victim of neglect and decay, *Bungay Castle* reveals it riches to those who journey beyond the massive front door of academic perceptions of excellence, for *Bungay Castle* is a rich and highly surprising novel well worth the wait and deserving of academic attention. *Bungay Castle* is a surprising read for it is a rare example among its contemporaries of female domestic Gothic novels. Examining Bonhote's use and reversals of the established gender codes of behaviour, *Bungay Castle* shines like a rare gem. It is a Gothic novel which surrounds its readers with positive feminist ideals—a very rare element in the genre. Skilfully blending the elements of classic fairy tales and romance in a Gothic setting, Bonhote reverses gender stereotypes in its heroes to create a world where men become the trapped maidens in the tower while insightful young women reject patriarchal prisons, explore their world with gusto and bravery while rescuing the innocent, virginal male.

(Be aware—this essay will give away many of the secrets that hide in the shadows of the castle's halls. To truly experience the novel as it was meant to be, read the novel first, and then come back to this introduction).

Gothic Light

Before introducing Bonhote's novel—it is important to understand Bonhote's unique placement as a female writer in the Gothic genre of eighteenth century popular literature. According to the Gothic writers before her, the Gothic novel contains several important themes. Stressing fear and suspense, the Gothic novel destroys rationality through the use of supernatural elements which questions the validity of logical thought and order. Gothic novels attack what readers held most dear: firmly established social codes, religion, the family, and the home. These novels threaten to destroy the equilibrium created in a life of domestic order. The domestic life is under attack and the home becomes a place of impending violence and imprisonment.

Contemporary scholarship has divided the gothic novel into two separate forms: Male Gothic and Female Gothic. These labels have nothing to do with the gender of the author—instead, the labels categorise the novels based upon plot structure and thematic elements. A novel that is labelled Male Gothic will contain a male's attempt to penetrate a typical female interior: the home, a room, a self (Punter 278). Men are frequently locked out of or away from female spaces and attempt to break into the domestic world they are isolated from: *The Castle of Otranto*, *The Monk*, *Frankenstein* and *Wuthering Heights* are classic examples. Stressing sexual violence, destroying established social taboos, and focusing on unexplained supernatural and horrifying occurrences, male Gothic fiction's main purpose is to lead the gentle reader into a world of terror and horror with little recourse of healing. Horror exists because the devil exists and once he has his eyes set on a victim, there is little chance of escape. Female Gothic, on the other hand, avoids the sensationalistic horrors and focuses more on social instabilities and inequalities. Unlike Male Gothic fiction, Female Gothic examines women who are locked inside—entombed with in a world of domesticity and unable to participate in the world they can only view through a tower window. Trapped within this confining interior, they are left to explore the little space they have—the walls of the fortress. The home is still a place of danger. However, through exploring the prison that entombs them, the women of Female Gothic fiction discover the tools needed to free themselves from the patriarchal prisons which hold them. Able to act within their social codes, the women in Female Gothic discover ways to create agency over their own lives while purging their homes of tyranny and lust represented by the antagonistic male figure. Thus, they are able to re-establish their homes as heaven of domestic bliss (Ellis xii). Stressing suspense rather than horror, any supernatural occurrences in Female Gothic novels are explained simply with logic and reason.

Easily overshadowed by the sensationalistic plots of Walpole, Lewis, and Radcliff, Bonhote's *Bungay Castle* is high in sensitivity and romance and light on terror and the supernatural: Gothic light. Bonhote rejects the violence, horror and dread of her contemporaries to focus on the domestic troubles of a singular family living in a somewhat romanticized Gothic situation. Unlike most Gothic novels, the fears and dreads in *Bungay Castle* are quickly explained—generally only a sentence two away—and may seem somewhat ridiculous to the readers of Lewis and Radcliff. The novel does contain the elements needed for the Gothic genre: thunderstorms abound, ghostly weeping is heard through the thunderclaps, secret passages encrusted with ancient cobwebs beg to be explored. However—the frights may appear a bit silly to contemporary readers of the novel: a large pie shakes with mysterious quivers and almost seems alive—but oh gosh, it is just the family's pet squirrel (who up to this point has never been mentioned in the text) hiding under the crust. While exploring the supposedly haunted subterranean passages below the castle, the frightening mystery turns out to be a cheerfully yappy puppy. And in a mock *Otranto* theme, a floating helmet is not the gigantic ghostly head of an angry patriarch seeking vengeance—it's just a little girl suited up to give her siblings a fright—nothing more.

However light on the frights and dreads, Bonhote's use of gender codes is surprisingly contemporary. The rise of the Gothic novel in the middle of the eighteenth century reveals a society firmly grounded in established codes of stereotype and gender behaviour. Entombed within the rigid confines of socially prescribed gender code behaviour, men are limited to two major roles: the fair hero or a variation of the overpowering ogre. Their goals are clear—protect the pure, while shielding the family name from danger—or—claim as much sex, money and power as possible and damn the consequences. For example, *Otranto's* Manfred violently stalks his dead son's fiancé through the subterranean passages of his ancestral home, only to horrifically murder his own daughter in a metaphoric act of rape with a sword. Women of Male Gothic fiction are reduced to even less; they become the protectors of their own virginity and without it, they are damaged goods, unworthy of life on earth. Antonia in *The Monk*, is perhaps the most extreme example of this idea. Abducted, raped repeatedly, and bleeding to death in the arms of her lover who arrived too late to save her, she is happy to die for she is no longer a virgin:

> She told him that had she still been undefiled she might have lamented the loss of life; but that, deprived of honor and branded with shame, death was to her a blessing: she could not have been his wife; and that hope being denied her, she resigned herself to the grave without one sigh of regret. (Lewis 327)

Locked within these limiting roles men and women are unable to see a view beyond the metaphoric walls that imprison them. Any deviation of these roles is met with suspicion and is usually dealt with a horrific punishment involving crypts, subterranean living burials, or deaths involving Satan himself.

At first glance, Bonhote relies heavily upon the male stereotype. Men are brave, strong, and, well...large. Robust and healthy—the good men of Bungay Castle seek to protect their families' honor, name, and fortunes. To heighten this theme, Bonhote's opening paragraph places the novel's castle in the middle of violent times.

> During the bloody period of the Baron's wars, when civil discord threw her fire-brands around, to lay waste and make desolate the fertile plains and fruitful fields of this long envied country; when the widow mourned the husband torn from her embraces, and the orphan wandered friendless and unprotected; when brother waged war against brother, and the parent raised his arm to destroy the son he had reared and cherished. (35)

Ironically, this is the most violent passage in the novel—and it is the opening paragraph. Bonhote clearly establishes the inherent dangers readily available in the outside and unprotected world. It is a world where accepted standards of a life of quality are destroyed: lovers are parted, fathers murder their sons and brothers fight to the death in civil strife. Clearly the male centered, phallocentric world is one that is unliveable. However, like a movie camera soaring over the bloodied battlefields, Bonhote slowly focuses her lens on a welcoming sight: the imperfect towers of Bungay Castle. As we approach and are invited inside its massive stone walls, we find a very different world of female sensibilities, for the inhabitants of this rare place live a life in great opposition to their masculine surroundings. They are protected from danger and living out their lives surrounded by fortress walls and domestic bliss: readers discover a complete family (an extremely rare element in a gothic novel and worthy of mention), and a merry band of men who enliven their days and nights with conversation and comradery. Indeed, even Sir Philip de Morney, patriarch of the family, finds solace and happiness inside of the castle's crumbling walls.

> And there for some years [he] found that happiness he had vainly sought in more enlivening scenes; and there he tasted those serene and contented pleasures he had been unable to procure in the world. ... He had every endowment of the mind for the true enjoyment of domestic life. (36)

Unconcerned with propagating more war, Sir de Morney is a rare figure in Gothic literature: a masculine leader who takes pride in his feminine side. Content to live in a world where his family is centre stage, he values his heart above his intellect.

Contrasting the kind patriarch is the Baron - rough, larger than life - he exudes masculine control while attempting to woo a woman many years younger than he: de Morney's young daughter Roseline. The Baron is the typical male tyrant found in most Gothic novels. A series of dead wives behind him, the Baron quickly becomes Bungay's Bluebeard. Repulsing his hoped to be bride with his overpowering ways and rough demeanour—his demand for her hand becomes more dreaded and more frequently threatening. Clearly establishing him as a demon lover, the once vital Roseline wastes away under his suffocating affections. Like the victim of a vampire's desire, she becomes pale, weak and listless while the Baron swells with growing masculine vigour. However—Bonhote does not allow the Baron to get away with his Gothic plans. Upon the discovery of his first born son Walter— believed to have died in childbirth—the Baron quickly transitions from the overbearing ogre to a kind and gentle grandfather with his child's best intentions at heart. He even releases his intended bride to the arms of his son with great dignity—holding the laws of love above all others. Clearly this is a man who understands the restorative power of love is stronger than muscular, physical or political force. Though they may be trapped within the gender codes of their society—both men have the ability to see the ramifications of their actions. They are able to rise above their gender tombs for a compassionate view of their families' futures.

Scooby-Doo and Nancy Drew Too: Female Gothic Fiction

Bonhote's central characters are the teenagers who reside in the walls of Bungay Castle. It is with these central characters, Roseline and Walter, that Bonhote fully establishes and strengthens her unique themes. Predating the Buffy clique, the Scooby gang and Nancy Drew, the teens of *Bungay Castle* may indeed be the original teen sleuths. Independent of the adults, the teen detectives explore their world with great curiosity. They question reason and logic while figuring out ways to navigate the restricting world of the adults without raising parental eyebrows. Additionally, Bonhote reverses the established standards of the prince rescuing the maiden in the tower. In *Bungay Castle*, this gender stereotype is dashed to pieces, for the male becomes Rapunzel who passively waits for his Princess Charming to rescue him. In a genre so focused upon the journey of male protagonists, it is inspiring to discover Bonhote's most significant character in not the eldest son, Edwin. Instead, Bonhote focuses our attention upon 16 year old Roseline, the novel's heroine.

Roseline is a rare female character in Gothic fiction for she does not follow the stereotypical behavioural patterns of most shrieking, passive Gothic women. Though entombed within patriarchal dominant forces, she contains the rare ability to see beyond the walls that enclose her: a tomb with a view. Brave, insightful, resourceful, Roseline recognizes the need to have power over her own identity and future. As the narrative begins, Roseline wakes during a terrific thunder storm to hear faint groans, rattling chains, and distant sobbing from some remote location far below the castle's floors: classic Gothic elements. Rather than passively scream like her friend Madeline, Roseline urges her to be quite and composed. "Edwin would ridicule our childish fears and the rest of the gentlemen would laugh at us" (47). Roseline clearly understands that in order to have agency over her own life, she must also have the respect of men. Fear, intimidation and childish imagination would destroy that respect. Seeking answers to the mysterious unearthly noises, Roseline is the first character in the novel to express "a strong desire to explore the secrets of her habitation" (57). In Jungian terms, Roseline's castle is her world—and she clearly has strong desire to explore both. "I am totally unacquainted with many parts of this castle," she tells Madeline. "I have two or three times wished to explore its secret passages, look at the dungeons, and visit all its subterranean contrivances, but have been forbidden by my father" (47). Roseline's desire demonstrates her strong feminist characteristics. She wishes to see the inner workings and secrets of the castle- clearly a male world. Her brother, Edwin, promised to show her the castle's security on a secret tour of the "immense strength of [its] fortifications" (47). Ignoring the typical desire to explore the riches of the light filled rooms and lofty turrets, Roseline desires to explore the hidden male domain of the underground—intuitively understanding that she will uncover secrets that lie hidden in this dark phallocentric world. Taking her cue from Roseline, Madeline promises to toughen up so she too can join the exploration. Practicing insightful subterfuge, Roseline agrees to Edwin's promise of a subterranean tour in order to dive into the mysteries of her world. Though he is leading the Scoobies through the castle's lower depths, Edwin does not lead them to any answers—that is Roseline's job. Though she is guided by a male, Roseline is the only one who truly takes notice of her surroundings while her brother is oblivious. Bonhote makes it very clear the Roseline is an important addition to the exploration party. "Happily was it for the party that Roseline had not only a greater share of prudence and understanding than most of her sex, but likewise more fortitude than is usually their portion" (60). It is only through Roseline's insight, curiosity, and strength that they find the answer to the midnight wailings. Through her fortitude, Roseline saves Walter from death, restores him to life, and enables him to achieve what had been robbed from him from birth: his title, his wealth, his family. Thus, Bonhote's heroine is a rare figure in Female Gothic fiction. She desires knowledge beyond her castle's walls, understands how to manipulate the male dominated codes that entrap her, and is able to retain the role of lady while rejecting patriarchal prisons.

Dude Looks Like a Lady: Bonhote's Male Hero

Every independent maiden must have her man to rescue, and Roseline's man is Walter: the effeminate blonde young man imprisoned within Bungay Castle's endless dungeons. Walter's journey from feminized and infantilized male prisoner to Gothic hero encompasses many literary traditions. Classic romance, Bildungsroman, and high camp, Walter is the embodiment of both male/female and child/adult sensitivities. When he is first introduced, he is described with extreme feminine details.

[T]hey beheld an elegant young man ... wrapped in a striped-satin morning-gown which reached to his feet, with his hair hanging in graceful ringlets, and nearly concealing a face as pale as death, lying on a kind of couch, and to all appearance in the last stage of consumption. (73)

Weepy, consumptive, and resigned to his position, (a distant ancestor to Linton Heathcliff in *Wuthering Heights*), Walter is the ultimate passive victim. As he attempts to rise, the effort is too much and he sinks back on the day bed unconscious—a bad beginning for any male hero. Wrongly imprisoned by his evil Uncle's scheme, Walter's entire life has been literally subterranean. Uneducated, illiterate, and ignorant of the outside world, Walter never seeks answers to his imprisonment nor does he demonstrate desire for a better life. He has succumbed completely to the tyranny of the past. Unlike his rescuer, Roseline, who skilfully questions authority, Walter is resigned to his tragic position. Like a child, he passively waits for action to be taken from exterior sources rather than taking action himself; it is only through his interaction with Roseline, Edwin, and Madeline that Walter shows desire for a better life.

As Walter's journey progresses, his identity shifts and changes as Bonhote explores themes of entrapment and gender codes. Intuitively understanding his innocent position, Roseline, Edwin and Madeline conspire to save him by moving him out of the dark, hopefully, to healthier surroundings. Hiding him in an unused room at the top of one of the castle's towers, Walter's identity begins to shift. Placing him in a tower, removing his will, and making him the object of rescue, Bonhote has rewritten the Rapunzel tale with wonderfully feminist implications. Walter is still a passive victim and like Rapunzel, he sits in a window, long blonde hair trailing below him, while he waits for rescue—from a heroic woman. More significantly, however, is his appearance to those who see him from below. Knowing that the tower has been unused for decades, anyone who sees his unfortunate figure silhouetted in the window horrifyingly realizes they are seeing a ghost—(it is, after all, a

Gothic novel). Walter's character has been reduced to a shadow, a non-entity, a see through, nonexistent void. Ghosts are forced to repeat past actions; thus, this symbol is frighteningly appropriate. In the great distance he has travelled from dungeon to tower top, Walter is still a prisoner and still waiting for rescue—repeating the only actions he has ever known. By reducing Walter to a ghost, a symbolic state of identitylessness, Bonhote has created a ghost-like figure who is finally able to build an identity from nothing. Bonhote's symbol of the ghostly Walter represents his lack of a solid self and the ability to create selfhood from that void. Additionally, Walter's journey has never allowed him to actually touch the earth; he survived below the earth, and has been placed far above it—yet his feet have never been able to touch the actual surface of the day lit earth. Giving him a distant view far above the earth—a tomb with a view—Walter recognizes his desire to walk on the ground below him and the need for self creation outside of his patriarchally imposed prison. Walter now has the ability to see his world and is ready to create a stronger foundation of self.

Walter journeys from damsel in distress to brave hero during the course of the novel and changes not only his own life, but the lives that surround him as well. Throughout, Bonhote never allows us to forget that it is the world of men which creates destruction and the world of women which rescues and heals. For example, in the novel's climax, Roseline, though in love with Walter, is forced to wed the beast-like Baron. With only seconds to spare, Walter bursts into the church through a secret underground passage (thus mastering the subterranean world), and stops the wedding—dressed as a woman.

> The attitude, the expressive face of Walter, as he stood gazing on the [wedding] party, caught every eye, and excited universal admiration. His dress was scarlet, richly laced: in his hat he wore a plume of white feathers, fastened by a clasp of diamonds, his tall elegant form and fine-turned limbs presenting a subject for statuary, which few would copy in a stile (sic) that would have done justice to the original. (164)

Bonhote focuses the reader's attention on Walter's exterior—his red dress, his decorated hat, his jewellery. Rather than describing the physical and muscular structure of the typical male hero, his attire is more complimented than his bravery. This serves duel purposes. His outlandish costume removes any hint of masculine and physical threat—a red dress and diamond broach is not the attire of a threatening fighter. Furthermore, in this costume, Walter is not the figure of fear and threat—his costume is. He has been cloaked in someone else's clothing and it is her memory that causes the shock and fear, not Walter. The Baron does not fear Walter's strength or bravery, but instead, thinking Walter is the ghost of his dead first wife, the Baron mistakes him for someone else. Walter is dressed as his mother and once again, he is mistaken for a ghost—a figure more fearful than himself. His feminine costume and elegant pose render him a romantic and non-threatening hero with deep implications of lost love.

Walter's disguise is a reminder that female qualities are powerful antidotes to the destructive plans of men in Bonhote's world. It is only through the young women in the novel that action is taken to correct the tyranny of the past and to ensure a brighter future. As an agent of positive transition, Roseline influences Walter to seek control over his own future; thus, his disguise truly is the uniform of a hero. Dressed as his dead mother, Walter becomes a mirror of the painful past and a window into the future. When the Baron first sees Walter's surprise attack, he is an immediate reminder of the Baron's first wife and Walter's mother, Isabella. Upon seeing the frightening image before his eyes, the Baron melts—not from fear, but from the memory of a broken heart. This climax enables two transitions to occur. First, Walter transitions from the passive Rapunzel to Belle in "Beauty and the Beast"—a young independent individual who is capable of creating great transitions in men and offers sincere sacrifice. Like Belle, Walter finally understands how to manipulate the system that oppresses him in order to free himself from exterior controls while ensuring the happiness of future generations. Upon discovery of his lost son, the Baron transitions as well. Like the Beast who is shown true and sincere love (a feminine attribute), the Baron too becomes humanized. He sheds his masculine, destructive hide while Bonhote accentuates his female side. The Baron suddenly becomes paternal, intimate, personal, compassionate and emotional. He even sheds tears as he sees his son (and Isabella's double) for the first time. Transitioned by the power of regained familial love, the Baron relinquishes his hold upon Roseline. Walter and Roseline are soon wed and the Baron becomes the perfect grandfather, ensuring his son, daughter-in-law, their children and extended families a lifetime of happiness and protection.

As Bonhote's novel concludes, she reiterates the themes she created as we wondered the halls of Bungay Castle. Concluding with a traditional fairy tale ending, Bonhote stresses the importance of female qualities as heroic antidotes to destructive masculine forces.

> The hero and heroine of our tale retained the virtues of their youth, the gentleness of their manners, and the sweetness of their dispositions to the end of their lives; and, what may be thought more rare and more singular, they never lost their humility, tenderness, and unbounded affection for each other. (233)

In Bonhote's eyes, survival must contain an abundance of love, compassion and nurturance—nothing less.

Curt Herr
Kutztown University

Works Cited

Bonhote, Elizabeth. *Bungay Castle*. Ed. Curt Herr. Camarillo, CA: Zittaw, 2006.

Chevalier, Jean, and Alain Gheerbrant. *The Penguin Dictionary of Symbols*. Trans. John Buchanan-Brown. New York: Penguin, 1996.

Ellis, Kate Ferguson. *The Contested Castle: Gothic Novels and the Subversion of Domestic Ideology*. Chicago: University of Illinois, 1989.

Lewis, Matthew Gregory. *The Monk*. Ontario: Broadview, 2004.

Punter, David, and Glennis Byron. *The Gothic*. Malden, MA: Blackwell, 2004.

Biographical Sketch

ELIZABETH BONHOTE: 1744 – 1818:

"The darling child of sensibility" –this is how Elizabeth Bonhote sums up the character of her heroine, Roseline in the novel, *Bungay Castle.* The term "sensibility" came into vogue in the eighteenth century, and was used to describe refined emotions, delicate sensitiveness of taste, and a tender compassion for others. The author emphasises, both in this novel, and in other writings, that such feelings predominated in her own character, and argued that "refined sensibility" was one of the finest attributes a female could possess, even though it also entailed suffering. The word, no longer in current use, is now best remembered in the title of Jane Austen's novel *Sense and Sensibility,* (1811), which satirises not only the prevailing taste for sensational Gothic novels such as *Bungay Castle,* but also the trait of "sensibility" itself, especially when coupled with a lack of wisdom and commonsense.

Elizabeth Bonhote (*nee* Mapes), was born into a family of small-town grocers in rural Suffolk. As a rule, provincial tradesmen had little more education than was needed to write a bill, or count a tray of pork pies, and were certainly not known for possessing refined temperaments. Indeed, the trading classes are often pilloried in the popular novels of the time as vulgar and mercenary. So how did it come about that Miss Mapes grew up to acquire such a sensitive disposition and become one of the most successful female writers of the late eighteenth century — both a "darling child of sensibility" and a literary "Blue-stocking"?

The explanation seems to be that her father, James Mapes, (1714 – 1794) was disappointed in having no sons in the early years of his marriage. He therefore decided to provide Elizabeth, his eldest surviving child, with a better education than girls could normally expect in the Georgian period. James came from a family of grocers and confectioners, who, by the late 17th century, had established a prosperous business in the small market town of Bungay. Wealth increased his family's status, and he became a leading member of the community, elected a Churchwarden, and styled a "gentleman", very much a recognition of superiority in a period when class differentiations were firmly observed.

James Mapes married Elizabeth Galliard in c. 1740. It is pitiful to read through the parish registers and discover that at least three sons were born, all of them named James after their father, and none of them survived. Consequently, the parents' hopes and joys were pinned upon Elizabeth (or Eliza, as she was known), born on April 11th, 1744. A surviving son was eventually born, more than ten years later, but no infant is held in such tender regard as the first to survive, following a succession of heart-breaking disappointments.

So Eliza was treated as "special" from an early age, and her intelligence fostered. The education offered was usually limited, the curriculum restricted to reading, writing, and French, with the chief emphasis placed upon the more important feminine accomplishments of needlework, music and drawing.

Whatever her schooling may have comprised, Eliza supplemented it with extensive reading and grew up to become a well-educated and cultured young lady. She was particularly fond of English literature and Christian theology and seems to have had some knowledge of history and philosophy. In her guide to the education of the young, *The Parental Monitor*, published in 1788, she provides a list of authors she could personally recommend. It includes poems, novels, and plays by authors such as Young, Cowley, Burney, and Richardson, and Addison and Steele's *The Spectator*, a celebrated literary periodical of the period. She particularly advocates the reading of poetry, "for it will improve your ideas, captivate your attention, awaken and call into action your sensibility" (*The Parental Monitor*). Her sensitivity may have been partly inherited from her mother, but deepened as a result of her education, and her friendship with the Reverend Thomas Wilson and his family, whose Christian principles contributed towards her mature outlook and compassionate nature.

During her teenage years, Eliza spent much time absorbed in study, and it can be guessed that shyness and solitude contributed to a lonely adolescence. There could have been few in the small town community who shared her outlook and interests. Women were daunted by her unfeminine accomplishments and men were uncomfortable with a young lady who was better read and possessed a livelier intelligence than themselves. Her sensitive nature caused her to feel easily hurt by gossip or criticism, with the result that she preferred to remain chiefly in the company of her parents or the few friends who were of a congenial nature.

Women tended to marry at quite an early age in the Georgian period, but Eliza's disposition ruled out marriage as an easy option. The local lads were only too eager to acquire such a dowry as the wealthy grocer could provide, but Eliza looked askance at these suitors, for they lacked the culture and the conversation she craved. Her opportunities for an appropriate match were further restricted by the social conventions of the day, for, if the sons of shopkeepers were not good enough for her, nor was she considered good enough for the handsome sons of the gentry, the Windhams, Dallings, and Baispooles who owned country estates in the district. The young curates, too, were outside her sphere, for, reckoned to be of the same social standing as the gentry, they were eager to marry into those families that held the patronage of the large parishes to augment their stingy stipends.

So Eliza's opportunities for marriage were severely limited, not least because it was unthinkable that a young lady of such romantic sensibilities could marry for anything less than True Love. She therefore determined to brave her parents' groans, and her relatives' gripes, and wait until a man of dash and discernment came along. Meanwhile, she immersed herself in her literary interests, having determined to become an author herself.

This was a rash ambition, as she herself recognised. In one of her novels, (*The Rambles of Mr. Frankly*, 1772), she describes how a female authoress is condemned by men as a monster, by women as a fool, and how all her husband's misfortunes were imputed *"to his having a bookish wife"*. Even though a small number of women were becoming writers and gaining some degree of acclaim, they were often ridiculed for pursuing an unfeminine interest, "Amazons of the pen*"* as Samuel Johnson disapprovingly termed them (qtd. in *The Sign of Angelica*, 125). Attitudes must have been even more disparaging in a small rural town. It is therefore greatly to Eliza's credit that she persevered. Her whole career exhibits a single-minded determination to succeed, perhaps initially accentuated by her situation, finding herself at odds with the rest of her society, and unable to find a suitable marriage-partner.

Her earliest literary efforts were verses, which she continued to produce throughout her life. Some were published in the provincial newspapers that flourished in the period, such as the *Norwich Mercury*, the *Norfolk Chronicle,* or the *Ipswich Journal.* Two rare manuscript verses survive, the elegy on the death of her friend, Mrs. Wilson, signed "Eliza Mapes, 1770", when she was 26, and on the death of the Reverend Thomas Wilson in 1774. Other poems were written to commemorate national or local events, and she also composed addresses in verse for public recitation at the Bungay Theatre, which attracted large audiences during its three or four week summer season.

Her first more ambitious work was a novel, *Hortensia, or, The Distressed Wife,* published in 1769. Written in an epistolary form, influenced by Samuel Richardson, it dealt with the misfortunes of an unhappy marriage. It was published anonymously, which must have pleased her father, worried about attracting the kind of criticism that might affect his grocery trade and social standing in the town. James may have been secretly proud of his daughter's ability, but business is business, and in any case, writing a novel was no way to attract a husband.

Then, suddenly romance blossomed. Her parents must have breathed a sigh of relief. A marriage in prospect at last—now perhaps Eliza would lay her pen aside and settle down to become a dutiful wife as Providence had ordained for women, for she was nearly twenty eight. The suitor was Daniel Bonhote, a young attorney, who had arrived in Bungay to take up a position with the wealthy local solicitor, Henry Negus. His personal circumstances were respectable enough to please Eliza's parents, for solicitors commanded a handsome income, and their education and professional training accorded them higher social status than that of tradesmen. Furthermore, James Mapes would know Henry Negus well, as a prominent fellow member of the town community, and Negus could vouch for the good character and conduct of his new young partner.

But what attractions could the young gentlemen offer for the choosy Miss Eliza? He had been brought up in London, and had acquired all those social skills and graces that the capital could offer which were so sadly lacking amongst the country bumpkins of Bungay. In addition, it was revealed that Daniel was illegitimate, but of noble birth, and this delighted Eliza, for it made him seem like a hero from a romantic novel. And the interesting young man's father was no less a personage than Sir Joshua Vanneck, a wealthy London merchant, who owned the Heveningham estate, not far from Bungay. His eldest son and heir, Sir Gerard Vanneck, was to build one of the finest mansions in the county on the estate, only a few years after Eliza's wedding.

Daniel and Eliza were married in Bungay in 1772, and set up home in a smart Georgian house in the centre of the town. Eliza's social status was now envied, for she was not only a respectable wife, but had married into the aristocracy. To be connected with such an illustrious family as the Vannecks opened the doors of many drawing rooms that would otherwise have remained firmly closed to the daughter of a small-town grocer. Eliza's prayers had been answered, and the couple appear to have been very happy. In particular, Daniel did not insist that his bride should burn her books and write no more, as some husbands might have done. So, shortly after the marriage, Eliza, now with a prosperous partner and maids to manage the house was ready to publish her second novel, *The Rambles of Mr. Frankly,* in 1772. This was a moralising tale, influenced by Laurence Sterne's *Sentimental Journey* 1768,which had first introduced the themes of sentiment and sensibility to the reading public. Eliza's novel describes how Frankly learns contentment from observing the lives of various classes of people during strolls in Hyde Park. Differing in style from *Hortensia*, it has no plot, concentrating solely upon the wanderings and philosophical musings of its leading character. Immediately popular, it was subsequently translated into German at Leipzig and published in Dublin and Paris. It continued to sell so well that in 1797 it was reprinted with additions by the Minerva Press. With only her second novel, Eliza had scored a major success.

Despite her husband's support, Eliza's writing career was subsequently interrupted for a prolonged period following illness caused by pregnancy. Three children, Eliza, John, and Susan were born between 1773 and 1777. It was not until 1787 that a further novel was completed and published, *Olivia, or, The Deserted Bride*, a novel of domestic virtue inculcating sentiments "such as will serve to amuse the good, caution the undesigning, and make some impression on the profligate and vicious". During her convalescence, Eliza had also been planning another book, not a novel this time, but an educational guide which eventually appeared under the title *The Parental Monitor* in 1788. It was issued as a subscription edition, the 345 subscribers including aristocracy, clergymen, teachers and booksellers. The names of Sir Gerard Vanneck and his family appear among them, suggesting that they were not averse to having an authoress in the family, although it might have been a different matter if one of the legitimate heirs had presented Eliza as a prospective bride.

The text consists of a series of short moral essays, on a wide variety of topics, addressed to both girls and boys, and enlivened by illustrative stories and quotations from celebrated authors. Its tone throughout is tender, lacking the gloomy sermonising and threats of punishment that characterise some religious manuals of the period. Eliza's caring Christian attitude towards children and animals, the frail and the afflicted, represents a move away from the coarser and rougher elements of Georgian society, pointing the way forward to the more refined principles of the Victorian era. It is also her most influential book, and must have had an affect on both parents and teachers for several decades, for it ran to three editions, was published in Dublin, and posthumously in the USA.

She subsequently published three more fictional works, that reflected the contemporary taste for novels of family life, combining "a reaction against coarseness, preoccupation with conventional morality and a strong bent towards emotionalism" (MacCarthy, *The Later Women Novelists, 1744-1818*). They appealed to a growing female readership, catered for by the circulating libraries, and no doubt also to members of the Bungay Book Club which had been formed in 1770. Reviewed in periodicals of the day, *Darnley Vale, or, Emelia Fitzroy*,

1789, and *Ellen* Woodley, 1790, in particular, were favourably noticed in the *Monthly Review. Darnley Vale* is perhaps the best of the novels. Written with spirit and eloquence, featuring of course, a heroine of extreme sensibility, it deserves to be re-published as representing another aspect of the author's oeuvre, in contrast to the more sensational Gothic romance of *Bungay Castle.*

Apart from her husband, the other great love of Eliza's life was Bungay Castle. She had known the building from childhood, for her father's house and bakery stood only about twenty yards distance from the castle walls. It had been erected in c. 1165, by Hugh Bigod, Earl of Norfolk, a member of the Norman family who had assisted William the Conqueror with the conquest of Britain in 1066. Bigod was soon boasting that it was one of the most impregnable fortresses in the kingdom, but his insurrection with other local barons against Henry II caused the king to march an army to Bungay to capture the castle and organise its demolition. Hugh only managed to rescue it from complete destruction on payment of a massive fine of 1000 marks. Although partly rebuilt with a curtain wall, drawbridge and gatehouse towers in the 13th century, the castle was later allowed to fall into neglect, being described in a document of 1382, as "old, ruinous, and worth nothing a year" (Mann 29). It subsequently passed into the ownership of the Howards, Dukes of Norfolk, who continued to own it, off and on, for the next six centuries until finally, towards the close of the 20th century, the family presented it to the town of Bungay with an endowment towards its preservation.

The castle that Eliza was familiar with in the eighteenth century was a sorry sight, for it had fallen into the most degraded state throughout its entire history. From the 15th century it had continued to crumble into ruin, and buildings inhabited by poor families were gradually built up against its walls. In 1766 the site was acquired by Robert Mickleborough, whose main interest was in demolishing the walls to sell the stone and rubble as road building material. Eliza viewed this development with incredulous horror. Her imagination had woven fanciful stories about the ancient edifice, and its inhabitants, since infancy. The castle walls, however, were built of such massive proportions that the building proved difficult to demolish. The labourers it was said, broke many a pick-axe in the attempt. Mickleborough was eventually obliged to desist, but not before much damage had been caused to the central keep.

Fortunately, the two loves of her life, Daniel and the castle became united together, when, in 1791, the Duke of Norfolk offered the site for sale again. Daniel purchased it for his wife. What an extravagant and romantic gift! For what could they possibly do with it?

The building was uninhabitable, and the hovels attached to it housed some of the poorest families in the neighbourhood. True, there was a lofty house built between the castle gate-house towers, but it was occupied by a relative of the odious Mickleburgh, and so unavailable as a dwelling. Eliza was obliged to purse her lips in Christian resignation every time she encountered a member of the Mickleburgh clan, for apart from the damage they had inflicted upon the ancient edifice, their continued presence denied her the opportunity to dwell upon the site herself.

Despite these obstacles, it seems that Eliza was able to erect a summer-house somewhere on the spot, where she spent many a tranquil hour, day-dreaming about the ancient ruin and its fabled history. Nor were her day-dreams unprofitable. Very soon she determined to write a novel on that very theme, to create a real story instead of mere flights of fancy. And it was to be a departure from her previous works, a novel in the Gothic style, made popular by other female authors such as Clara Reeve (*The Old English Baron*, 1777), and Ann Radcliffe (*The Mysteries of Udolpho*, 1794).

Daniel had done well. The crumbling ruin became a minor gold-mine. Eliza's novel, *Bungay Castle*, produced in two volumes by the Minerva Press in 1796, sold well, and established her as one of the publisher's best-selling authors. The tale is a strange and somewhat incongruous mix, combining the glamour of the past and the thrill of the supernatural with her familiar themes of domestic life and morality. The book contains many of the requisite elements for a Gothic fantasy, together with colourful characters, engaging touches of humour and good dollops of the kind of virtuous moralising found in *The Parental Monitor*. Like the castle itself, the novel has been neglected and is now thankfully available for a new generation of readers more than two hundred years after its first publication.

It was the last novel she wrote. As middle age advanced, Eliza's life started to decline. Her supportive parents had both died by 1794, and her children had grown up, married, and left home. Daniel continued to enjoy a successful career, having been appointed under-sheriff of Suffolk in 1790, but for some reason he decided to sell the castle site back to the Dukes of Norfolk in 1800. Despite the problems it had entailed, its loss must have been a deep disappointment to Eliza, for she still retained dreams of inhabiting the site. Yet the publication of her novel had reawakened great public interest in the building, and it is sad that Eliza did not live to see the ugly hovels surrounding it demolished in 1841—"so that the towers now stand alone and look much more majestic than heretofore", as a local diarist commented.

Then in 1804, Daniel died, very suddenly in his 56th year, after a short illness. His death was a terrible shock, and it is likely that Eliza never recovered from his loss. His devotion to her is recorded in his will, in which he commemorates "the excellency of her head and heart." Her last publication, *Feeling, or, Sketches from Life: a Desultory Poem*, 1810, expresses the dejection and loneliness she felt without a loving partner to support her. She lived on for another fourteen years, finally dying at Bungay on June 11th, 1818, aged seventy four. She had been left a wealthy widow, and in her will she bequeathed dwelling-houses, her parents' baking-office and shop in Bungay, and approximately £3,500 in cash and annuities. Her family used part of the inheritance to provide five almshouses for the "widows of poor tradesmen", a worthy way of commemorating both their mother's origins and her Christian benevolence

No portrait of her survives, and little is recorded about her character other than the details she revealed in *The Parental Monitor*, indirectly in her novels, and in the introduction to *Bungay Castle*. In a dedication on the fly-leaf of one of her books, she termed herself "the Elegant Authoress". The description is both teasing and ambiguous, but it is pleasing to imagine that Eliza Bonhote was as elegant in her person, as in her prose.

Christopher Reeve
May, 2006.

Works Cited

Bonhote, Elizabeth. *Olivia, or, Deserted Bride*. London: William Lane, 1787.

——. *The Parental Monitor*. London: William Lane, 1788.

MacCarthy, B.G. *The Later Women Novelists: 1744 – 1818*. United Kingdom: Cork University, 1938.

Mann, Ethel. *Old Bungay*. London: Morrow, 1984.

Todd, Janet. *The Sign of Angellica: Woman, Writing and Fiction, 1660 - 1800*. United Kingdom: Virago, 1989.

A Note on the Text

The text of *Bungay Castle* is set from the first edition published by William Lane's Minerva Press in 1796. For the most part, Bonhote's original spelling and punctuation have been retained, though the printer's errors were corrected.

BUNGAY CASTLE:

A NOVEL.

BY MRS. BONHOTE.
AUTHOR OF THE PARENTAL MONITOR, &c.

IN TWO VOLUMES.

Astonished at the voice he stood amaz'd,
And all around with inward horror gaz'd.
ADDISON.

LONDON:
PRINTED FOR WILLIAM LANE,
AT THE
Minerva Press,
LEADENHALL-STREET.
M.DCC.XCVI.

TO

THE MOST NOBLE

CHARLES DUKE OF NORFOLK,

WHOSE URBANITY AND PHILANTHROPY
MUST EVER REFLECT
ADDITIONAL HONOURS
ON THE NAME OF
HOWARD:
BY WHOSE NOBLE FAMILY
BUNGAY CASTLE
WAS POSSESSED FOR MANY CENTURIES;
THE FOLLOWING PAGES
ARE RESPECTFULLY INSCRIBED
BY HIS GRACE'S MOST OBEDIENT,
AND VERY HUMBLE SERVANT,
ELIZ, BONHOTE.
Bungay,1797

INTRODUCTION.

CASTLE-Building appears to have been the passion of all ages; while some have been raising their fabrics on the most solid and lasting foundations, others have been forming them in the air, where the structure has been erected with infinitely less trouble, as their own invention led them to wish, and very pleasant, no doubt, was the delusion of the moment.

It is now the prevailing taste to read wonderful tales of wonderful castles; to recall them from the oblivion of ages, and represent them as the Novelist finds most suitable to the circumstances of his tale. In times like these, every book that serves to amuse the mind, and withdraw the attention from scenes of real distress, without inflaming the passions, or corrupting the heart, must surely be as acceptable to the reader as it may have been found pleasant to the writer, and should exempt the latter from the severity of criticism. Under the influence of this opinion, the Author of the following sheets has been tempted to send them into the world. She might, indeed, to evade the danger of having her work condemned, pretend to have found it in some recess of her favourite ruins, or to have discovered it artfully concealed in the bottom of an old chest, in so defaced and mutilated a condition, as to have rendered it a very difficult and laborious task to collect the fragments and modernize the language; but the writer of these pages has not been so fortunate; and, had she attempted to assert so marvellous a circumstance, she could not have expected any miss of fifteen would have been credulous enough to believe her.

The thought of publishing a novel, under the title given to these volumes, has long been her intention,—a thought which originated from her living within the distance of twenty yards from those venerable ruins, which still attract the attention of the stranger and the curious. Often in early youth has she climbed their loftiest summits, and listened with pleased and captivated attention to the unaccountable tales related by the old and superstitious, and considered as real by herself and her inexperienced companions.—In one place, it was said the ghost of an ancient warrior, clad in armour, took his nightly round to reconnoitre scenes endeared by many a tender claim. In another, a lovely female form had been seen to glide along, and was supposed to disappear on the very spot where it was imagined her lover had fallen a victim to the contentions of the times.

"Her face was like an April sky

Dimm'd by a scatt'ring cloud;
Her clay-cold lily hand, knee high,
Held up her sable shroud."

All these circumstances added strength to a romantic turn of mind, which acquired additional force from a love of reading the old romances, and this propensity for the marvellous was for some time indulged in the midst of scenes which afforded ample scope for the creative excursions of fancy. After having left her paternal dwelling many years, she is again replaced in it by some of those changes which so frequently occur in the progress of human life; and has purchased the little spot of ground on which stands the principal part of all that now remains of Bungay Castle, and which, though a mere heap of unconnected ruins are still so venerable as to excite, in the feeling and thoughtful mind, a sympathetic regret at the instability of human grandeur and the weakness of human strength.

Among these ruins, once the property, and, in all probability, the temporary residence, of the noble house of Norfolk, cottages are now built, and inhabited by many poor families, and those very walls, which perhaps sheltered royalty, are now the supporters of miserable hovels. Such are the awful effects of time, and the unaccountable revolutions it produces!

But, were it in the Author's power as much as it is her inclination, she would adorn their venerable remains with all the flowers of spring, and the tempting treasures of autumn should surround them. The jessamine and honey-suckle should clasp them in their embraces, and the tendrils of the vine and the fig-tree should encircle and decorate them with their luscious sweets. She would, on the loftiest corner of their remains, build herself a little hut, in which she could fit and contemplate the variegated scenes around. She would reverse the order of things, and render them as lovely and beautiful in age, as they were grand and magnificent before time had robbed them of those envied and valuable properties which it cannot restore.

Being again in the habit of spending many leisure hours in this favourite spot, endeared to her for bringing to remembrance the enlivening scenes of youth, and, having opportunities to pursue her sedentary amusements, she determined to accomplish her design, seeing no reason why Bungay Castle should not be as good a foundation for the structure of a novel as any other edifice within or without the kingdom. But, as so many ages are elapsed since this Castle was reared, and since time and death have swept away with ruthless hand almost every vestige of what it once was, she has to lament, and so perhaps may her readers, that she was furnished for this employment with no other materials than the scanty portion her own imagination afforded. She has borrowed some real names, and she hopes the characters she has introduced will be found neither disgusting nor unnatural. But, as Solomon so many centuries ago declared, there was nothing *new* under the sun, she cannot surely be condemned for not producing new characters, nor blamed if any contained in this work resemble those of the present day; and, though in the reigns of our first sovereigns, and many of their successors, the customs and manners of the people were somewhat different, she is convinced the world was in many instances just the same. The same virtues, vices, and passions, degraded or ennobled human nature; and, though delicacy, sensibility, and refinement might be less known, and not so frequently mentioned, they no doubt retained as proper and powerful an influence over the mind. Love too, that invincible and all-subduing passion, implanted in the heart of man from the beginning of the world, was as generally known and acknowledged by the king and the peasant, the hero and the coward.

This painfully leads to an observation, which, while it is humiliating, has too much truth for its foundation to admit of dispute, that, though the same vices which disgrace the present times were practiced in the earliest ages, more pains were then taken to conceal them from public observation, and the conduct, of which the modern fine gentleman of avouwed debauchee will now proudly boast, would then have been considered as sufficient to stamp the character with indelible infamy. By our unfashionable progenitors modesty was distinguished and admired as the most becoming ornament of woman; adultery was punished, and seduction held in contempt; the artful betrayer of unsuspecting innocence was pointed at by the finger of derision, and the victim of baseness compelled to conceal her shame either in the shades of retirement or the seclusion of a nunnery. We may justly lament, if we are not permitted to condemn, that in this respect the present age is not quite so sensitive, and may shed the tear of regret at being so often forced to look down with pity, when we meet, at almost every corner of our streets, the unblushing front of degraded beauty, and our ears are shocked with the execrations of profligacy from the lips that in early life had been taught to speak a language as pure as their own uncontaminated hearts.

The Author of these pages has not attempted to enter on the politics of the past or present times. Had she ever cherished such a design, the sentiments of one of the first[*] and most interesting writers this age has produced, would instantly have determined her to decline her intention, but she has ever thought that so heterogeneous a mixture was not likely

---

[*] Mr. Cumberland

to please the taste of many readers, and that a novel was never intended as a vehicle for politics, and any farther than it was necessary for the elucidation of the story. Firmly attached to her King, perfectly satisfied with our laws and constitution, and grateful to heaven for being permitted to live under so mild and just a government. In a country where freedom and plenty have hitherto taken their stations, and shed their most benign influence, she will ever remain contended to leave politics and the affairs of state to be settled by better, wiser, and more experienced heads.

Gentle reader, we will now enter upon a story, of whose origin you are informed. If any, who sit down to read it with minds tortured by mental or bodily diseases, should find a temporary relief from misery or languor, the Author will consider it as a luxuriant reward for her employment. If, on the contrary, they should be disappointed, or dissatisfied, she sincerely wishes they may meet a more agreeable entertainment from the next publication thrown in their way.

To the Reviewers she takes this opportunity of publicly making her acknowledgments for the liberality and candour they have invariably shewn to her former publications; and, though she has never had the satisfaction of being personally known to any one of them, she has for many years considered them as friends.

BUNGAY

BUNGAY CASTLE.

CHAPTER I.

DURING the bloody period of the Baron's wars, when civil discord threw her fire-brands around, to lay waste and make desolate the fertile plains and fruitful fields of this long envied country; when the widow mourned the husband torn from her embraces, and the orphan wandered friendless and unprotected; when brother waged war against brother, and the parent raised his arm to destroy the son he had reared and cherished; when every castle was kept in a state of the most guarded defence, lest it should be wrested from its owner by the ambition and enmity of his neighbour:—then it was that *Bungay Castle* reared its proud towers and battlements aloft; while its massy walls stood in gloomy and majestic grandeur, as if they could bid defiance to every design formed against them by man, and to the more certain influence of all-conquering time; so perfectly stupendous and strong was this once-spacious edifice, it was not only an object of desire to the proud and aspiring barons, but, it has been said, even to contending kings.[1]

The noble and loyal lord of this castle, being called upon to fill some important office in the service of the state, appointed Sir Philip de Morney to be governor during his absence, and never had he shewn the goodness of his heart and the excellence of his judgment more than in the delegation of his power and authority over so numerous a train of vassals and dependents to this his bosom friend.

Sir Philip de Morney was a bold and hardy veteran: he was grown grey in the service of his king and country; brave in the field, just, merciful, and benevolent, in his dealings with all his fellow-creature,— possessed of an abundant fortune, he accepted this important trust to oblige his friend, and promote the happiness of those to whom he knew he was attached;—fond of an active and useful life, he wished not to sink into indolence or obscurity, till the infirmities of age should render

---

[1] Bonhote's opening establishes two important elements in her text: First, offering happiness and refuge the outside world can not provide, Bungay Castle is a utopia where domestic life is highly valued. Secondly, as the novel progresses, this utopian quality is quickly disrupted as Bungay Castle transitions into a microcosm of the tempestuous outside world destroying the equilibrium Bonhote previously established. Additionally, Bonhote's novel is highly representative of the classic plot structure found in traditional fairy tales. Opening with domestic happiness, the novel soon develops the potential for familial and social unrest. The novel concludes with newly discovered strengths and regained domestic bliss for all who reside in Bungay castle.

him incapable of taking his share in the busy scenes of that important period, in which, though the pernicious doctrine of equality did not influence the minds of the vulgar against their lawful sovereign, or the rights of the subject, the ambition of the nobility, and the feuds and distraction of the contending parties, produced scenes of misery equally distressing, but happily not so extensive in their effects.

Into Bungay Castle he removed with his whole family, and there for some years found that happiness he had vainly sought in more enlivening scenes; and there he tasted those serene and contented pleasures he had been unable to procure in the world; though formed to make a brilliant figure on its great stage, he had every endowment of the mind for the true enjoyment of domestic life, uniting with the most unshaken courage the gentlest philanthropy. He had married at an age of thirty-five a lady much younger than himself, by whom he had several children, and looked forward with the hope of being the parent of a more numerous offspring, while, like the patriarchs of old, he lived respected and revered in the bosom of his family. Ah! little did he suspect the revolution ambition would one day make in his mind.

Lady de Morney was yet in the pride of life; her beauty unfaded, her spirits lively, and her mind in its full vigour; her person was lovely, her disposition amiable: sweetness, modesty, truth, and fortitude, were the inmates of her bosom, and gave additional graces to the ease and elegance of her manners: strictly exemplary in performing the important duties of wife and mother, no complaints were heard where she presided; no looks of discontent were seen on the countenance of her dependents: time was neither abused nor found a burden; her whole study and attention were employed to promote the happiness of her husband, and to superintend the education of her children; for the latter employment no one was more adequate than herself,—her own example serving more than precept to enforce the lessons of truth on the ductile mind of youth; her own gentleness made them happy, while her conduct convinced them of the value and dignity of virtue.

She considered youth and innocence as the most valuable of earthly treasures, and she was not more anxious to preserve the one in all its native purity, than to teach them how to enjoy the other with cheerfulness and gratitude: having stored their minds with virtuous precepts, best calculated to chain the attention, and which she hoped would lay the most solid foundation for securing their future happiness, she lived with her children in habits of the most soothing and perfect friendship, and very seldom was under the unpleasant necessity of assuming the stern authority of a dictatorial parent.

But, as no character on earth can be found without having some of the weakness and frailty of erring morality annexed to it, the author does not mean to present Lady de Morney to their view as being entirely faultless. She was vain of her high birth, being allied to nobility; and so partial to her eldest son, that she could scarcely suffer him to be out of her sight; yet her partiality originated from a circumstance so interesting and affecting to all who knew it, that, though it might by some be considered as a weakness, it was by none but herself condemned as a fault. When her son was in his infancy, she was seized with a fever of so malignant a nature, as deprived her for some weeks of her senses: during this distressing period of her delirium, and in the absence of her nurse, she one day snatched the infant from the arms of a young woman, his attendant, and, before any one was aware of her design, ran out of the house, and with almost incredible swiftness down a long gravel walk to the bottom of the garden, and threw him into a lake, by which it was bounded. By the fortunate and timely assistance of an old and faithful servant, who was luckily at work near the spot, and who had hastened to it on seeing his lady so unexpectedly make her appearance, the family were alarmed, and the child providentially, but with difficulty, saved.[2]

This incident, of which she was unguardedly informed, made so forcible an impression on the mind of this susceptible and affectionate parent, as she could not shake off: it created an additional claim upon her heart for every tender indulgence, and gave to every juvenile action and good quality redoubled value. He had in a manner been raised from death, rescued from a watery grave, into which her own, a mother's, hand had hurled him; and yet he loved her, as her fond and plaintive partiality led her often to imagine, better than the rest of her children. She would sometimes embrace this darling son, and, with all the enthusiasm of maternal tenderness, tremble at the horrid remembrance of having so nearly deprived him of an existence that added so much to the happiness of her own. To all her children Lady de Morney was an indulgent parent; but for Edwin she felt that indescribable fondness which not only threw a veil over his failings, but robbed her of that fortitude and energy with which she acted on all other occasions. So far

---

[2] This is perhaps the most perplexing episode in the novel. Unlike the myriad gothic occurrences which are quickly explained throughout the novel, Lady de Morney's attempted infanticide remains unexplained; however, in a novel that centres around gender politics and codes of behaviour, her murderous action can be interpreted as a reaction against the imprisoning limitations on women's roles. Attempting to kill her first born son is a clear rejection of her singular and only role: mother. Additionally, this is the only action that Lady de Morney takes through out the entire novel. Once her son is rescued from an early death, she becomes a passive observer rather than an active participant in his life. She silently relinquishes her role as mother to become a servant. As the novel progresses, the younger generations in Bungay Castle are more prepared to question the roles assigned to them in healthier and more productive ways.

from attempting to deny any request he made, it was her study to prevent his wishes. She would at times apologize to the rest of her children for the extreme affection nature had implanted, and which she could not help cherishing for their brother, but which she regretted as a weakness she was unable to conquer. This conduct served to reconcile the young people to a partiality which originated from so singular and awful an incident, and, so far from shewing either envy or regret, it seemed to endear their mother's favourite to their youthful and guileless hearts. Another circumstance, which equally helped to reconcile them, was the sweetness of Edwin's disposition, who as often availed himself of his mother's indulgence to gratify and make them happy, as he did to obtain any of her favours for himself.

In a situation from which thousands of her sex and age would have shrunk disgusted and affrighted, Lady de Morney was cheerful and contented. The rooms were Gothic and gloomy, but her husband and children enlivened every place they inhabited. She was at times surrounded by and exposed to dangers; but her beloved De Morney and his faithful people were ever near to protect and guard her. She was the wife of a noble soldier, and she had acquired a fortitude almost equal to his from the knowledge of his unfailing courage, which gained energy from danger, and redoubled ardour from difficulty.

The castle itself could boast few internal beauties, but her children, whom she saw playful as youthful fawns, and happy as health, innocence, and unbroken spirits, could make them, were treasures inexhaustible: they beheld the rough implements of war without terror or dismay, instructed by their father to consider them as the only ornaments fitted for a soldier. The young De Morneys were taught the use of arms as soon as they had learned to walk.[3]

Seldom were the Gothic gates of the castle unbarred to admit the social friend or gay companion to the festive board; seldom did the voice of mirth and jollity echo through the lofty rooms and vaulted passages; but a sweet serenity supplied their place, which, having lost during the absence of her husband, at an early period of her marriage, Lady de Morney now felt the full value of possessing; and, though secluded from the gaudy pleasures of court, she felt herself a gainer by the exchange in the balance of happiness.—Lady de Morney had a sister, who was placed by the Lady Gundreda as superior in the

---

[3] One wonders if the family is under that much of an outside threat that they must teach toddlers how to shoot firearms. Interestingly, this family detail is not limited to the males of the household for Bonhote refers to the children as the 'young de Morneys,' only one of which is male: Edwin. It becomes quite clear why Roseline becomes such a strong force in the novel's progression-she has been taught from an early age to take responsibility for her life and to protect those who surround her.

nunnery of Bungay; with her she spent many of her leisure hours: between them the tenderest friendship strengthened the endearing ties in which they were united by nature.

The abbess was a pious, but yet she was a young and interesting woman, of a benevolent and placid disposition; and, though she had voluntarily secluded herself from the world, she was not so much disgusted with its pleasures as she felt herself wounded by the severity of its disappointments.—Early in life, death had deprived her of a lover who had engaged her most animated and ardent affection, and with whom she had indulged the fond hope of being united in the indissoluble bands of Hymen; but adverse fate had ordained it otherwise, and those virtues and good qualities which had made him inexpressibly dear to her, rendered his loss the more exquisitely painful. With him the world lost all its power to charm, and she resolutely determined to fly that world for ever, and never to permit another lover to displace the sainted Henry from her heart; she therefore unreluctantly withdrew from the varying and busy scenes of life,—not to avoid temptation, but to be able to indulge, in the gloomy shades of a nunnery, the memory of a man, to whose worth and constancy she deemed no sacrifice to great. Time served to convince her of the wisdom of her choice; and, giving way to all the luxury of a pure but romantic imagination, she encouraged the consoling hope, that, if her regretted Henry were permitted to know what was acting in this lower world, his spirit would be gratified by the purity of her choice, and his heart convinced of the unabating strength of her affection. She often flattered herself that her Henry was deputed to watch her conduct, and would be the first to convey her to the bright regions of immortality; yet, though thus severely tried in the lessons of affliction, she troubled no one with a repetition of her sorrows; and, though she often wept in all the bitterness of anguish, her tears fell when no one observed them, and only to the ear of her sympathizing sister did she venture to mention a name so dear and so beloved.[4]

Young Edwin de Morney, whom we have already mentioned, was at this period in his seventeenth year; and, notwithstanding the unbounded indulgence of his mother, he had made a rapid proficiency in every part of his education. Nature had been equally liberal of her favours to his mind and person: his temper was good,—his manners and conversation those of the gentleman and the scholar, and, with all

---

[4] Lewis's *The Monk* and Shelley's *Frankenstein* are filled with tales of romantic souls who give their lives to the happiness of others upon losing happiness themselves. Locking herself away over a broken heart, the Abbess's action exemplifies and emphasizes the gothic and romantic authors' concern with the theme of sacrifice and lost love.

the interesting gaiety and natural cheerfulness of youth, he united a benevolent and susceptible heart.

His eldest sister, Roseline, was only one year younger than himself; her form was small, but symmetry itself; every limb so nicely turned, it would have been chosen by a statuary for the model of a Venus: her face was beautiful in the extreme; her eyes expressive and sparkling, and the smile which shewed itself was of that irresistible kind as caught the attention and won the heart; and it would have been difficult for a connoisseur in beauty to point out which feature it was that had the greatest claim to admiration, while the unfading and fascinating beauties of her polished mind, which was stored with all the graces the best education could bestow, or the most lively genius acquire, rendered her conversation as delightful as her manners were captivating. She played on the lute, and warbled her artless song in strains so sweet, as would have rivalled the daughters of Italy. Her heart, unwounded by the barbed thorn of affliction, and free from the entanglements of love, was like one of the first days of infant-spring, which, enlivened by the bright rays of an unclouded and all-cheering sun, serves not only to revive, but to embellish the whole face of inanimate nature, just bursting into life, and rendering all its sweetly modest beauties of redoubled value to those who had lingered through a dreary winter, in eager expectation of its approach. Lively as the birds which hovered round the turrets of the castle, she entered gaily into all the youthful sports of her brothers and sisters. To the little blooming Edeliza she was particularly attached; and, though she saw her as beautiful as herself, felt neither envy nor regret in the reflection. No modish complaints filled her with imaginary terrors, and, as she had known no sorrows, she thought it not only incumbent on her to shew her gratitude to heaven and her parents, but to soften, by every benevolent attention in her power, the miseries and misfortunes of others.

In those days, the education of young women was completed at a more early period than in the present; and, if the manners were not altogether so highly finished, or the mind so profusely decorated, or rather fettered, with innumerable, and, to too many, useless accomplishments, the time was undoubtedly more rationally employed, and the fair sex less exposed to the allurements of flattery and the dangers of temptation: though more retired in their habits, and reserved in their manners, they were neither less susceptible of the tender passions, nor less fervent or sincere in their attachments.

Roseline had formed an early friendship with a young lady educated in the Bungay nunnery, of which her aunt, fortunately for the young people, was the superior. This sweet victim of ambition was designed by a proud and haughty father for the monastic life, in order to enable him to provide more liberally for the rest of his children. She had not yet however entered on the year of her novitiate; but it was soon to commence, and, at its awful close, she was to bid a final adieu to that world, to which her heart had of late become too tenderly and anxiously attached. As it approached, time seemed to wing his flight with redoubled rapidity, and she felt a trembling dread that her fortitude, like a false friend, would forsake her in the hour of trial, and a trembling presentiment that the moment, which shut her from the society at the castle, would exclude her from every prospect of happiness; yet this repugnance to obey the will of her parents was new to her mind:—she dared not investigate the cause too nicely, lest she should find a subject for self-condemnation. She found, with painful regret, a troublesome guest was admitted to her bosom, and she was afraid, in attempting to become more intimately acquainted with its prevailing influence, she should permit the stranger to gain greater ascendancy.

The youthful Madeline, on her first entrance into he nunnery, had neither felt nor shewn any discontent: she had assumed the formal and unbecoming habit without a sigh, and yielded to the rigid rules prescribed with uncomplaining resignation; but, as time crept on with solemn and leaden pace, unrelieved by any of the innocent amusements of social life, only to repeat and bring forward the same dull round of gloomy and mortifying scenes, not only repugnant to the feelings of nature, but disgusting to the senses, she began to think and to complain to the bosom of friendship, that those fetters, put on by the rigid will of unfeeling parents, to be finally closed by the iron laws of bigotry and superstition, were unjust and galling, and the free-born soul of innocence and virtue drooped and pined beneath the sacred walls by which it was inclosed;—how cruel to make religion a pretext for such persecution and misery, and to counteract the designs of the Creator, who never formed his creatures for seclusion from that world in which he had profusely strewn so many blessings for the enjoyment of rational and social beings![5]

Roseline, by the urgency of her entreaties, frequently obtained leave of the abbess for Madeline de Glanville to visit at the castle. This

[5] Madeline's sub-plot accentuates Bonhote's theme of social intercourse as a prerequisite for a healthy and abundant life. Isolation from fellow humans only leads to disaster as demonstrated in many gothic novels especially noteworthy in *Frankenstein*. Many of these novels feature men and women who reluctantly give up their lives in the service of a higher power. Clearly Madeline is not called to the religious order. She is merely a commodity her father gives to the church so he has fewer mouths to feed. Lewis's *The Monk*, contains the most extreme example of a reluctant novice. Agnes attempts to heal her broken heart and hide from society by becoming a nun—while pregnant.

favour was the more readily granted, from her having observed with real regret some secret grief preyed on the mind of her young charge, which, though she could not help commiserating, she did not choose to mention. Those days, which the fair Madeline spent at the castle, were the happiest she had every known; while there, she was gay and cheerful as the youthful companions who studied to amuse and entertain her. The song, the dance, the lute, drove from her remembrance the gloomy nunnery in which she was condemned to waste and linger out her future life.

Sir Philip and Lady de Morney treated her with the tenderness and indulgence of parents; the friendship and affection between her and Roseline was mutual and sincere; for Edwin she felt, as she innocently supposed, the fond regard of a sister. All the younger branches of the De Morney family rejoiced to see her, and gladly assisted in rendering her happy; and when the hour arrived for the unfortunate Madeline to return to the nunnery, whilst she observed with secret gratitude the gloom it threw on the countenances of her friends, it gave additional pangs to the feelings of her own heart; her spirits instantly deserted her, and tears of unfeigned regret marked the sad moment of departure. When she re-entered her solitary cell, she would sink into a despondency which the austere rules of the order was not likely to conquer.

The inhabitants of the castle and its environs were in themselves a little common-wealth, which contained a vast variety of characters. Men of different nations were met together, and, by the unaccountable effects of accident, ambition, or necessity, brought into the same habits, and lived cordially together, serving one master; and, united by one cause and interest, the utmost harmony prevailed among them; for Sir Philip de Morney was a just and active governor; gentle as the lamb, and forgiving as mercy to the virtuous or injured,—but a terror and a stern master to the traitor or oppressor, whether friend or foe: he knew the importance of his situation, and how much the happiness of others depended on the careful and faithful discharge of those duties belonging to his high station, and intrusted to him by his noble friend the Earl of Norfolk; he therefore wisely and justly determined not to be biased nor misled, either by the partiality or designs of other men, nor to suffer any prejudice to gain ascendancy over his mind in the rewards he bestowed, or the punishments which guilt would sometimes compel him to inflict.[6]

---

[6] Bonhote accentuates Bungay Castle as a place of great unity among all who inhabit it. While the outside world rages in bitter conflicts as demonstrated in the novel's opening paragraph, Bonhote makes the reader very aware that life inside the castle is a commonwealth consisting of different nations and great unity. Through creating a perfect

CHAPTER II.

In the middle of a cold and inclement winter's night, when the wind blew with uncontrollable force, and the snow, rain, and hail beat with fury against the windows, every instant breaking some of the few panes which admitted a scanty light into the interior apartments, and threatened to demolish those of the state-rooms, while nature appeared to shudder at this unusual warring of the elements, the centinels on guard were alarmed by a loud rapping at the western gate, and the rumbling of a carriage, with the clattering of horses' hoofs was distinctly heard.[7] For some moments the people stood irresolute; at length one of the soldiers roughly inquired who it was wanted admittance at so unseasonable an hour, when only treason or treachery could be suspected.

A voice replied, "We are no traitors; we come with no hostile intentions, but have brought dispatches of the utmost importance to the governor, and must beg to be immediately admitted, as we are in danger of perishing from fatigue and the severity of the weather." This answer caused a general bustle; the governor was summoned, and the troops, lodged within the interior parts of the castle, ordered to arms before the gate was thrown open; nor were the strangers permitted to enter till their number was ascertained, and the soldiers prepared to oppose them, should they have any bad designs to accomplish by this strange and suspicious visit; but the alarm soon subsided, and the soldiers almost tempted to laugh at their own fears, when they saw a carriage draw up to the gate, guarded by about twenty men, out of which they took a person who appeared quite passive, and was so muffled up, that, in the hurry which was made use of to convey him into the governor's apartment, it was impossible to discover either his age or person. The governor, after reading the dispatches, withdrew

---

world inside of the castle's walls, Bonhote primes her reader for a greater loss when civil unrest finally finds its way inside.

[7] A frequently repeated motif in Gothic literature, threatening storms frequently bring mysterious arrivals- both natural and supernatural, spectral and human. De Willows and his men arrive in the middle of a horrific storm and Roseline first hears the mysterious subterranean cries during a violent storm. Shelley's Victor Frankenstein formulates his idea to create life through harnessing a storm's energy when he sees a horrific lightning bolt destroy his family tree. Conversely, he also kills the female being he creates during a storm as well. According to Jean Chevalier, storms are heavily symbolic. A theological symbol, storms can reflect the formidable and almighty power of God. While [a storm] may bring a revelation and new life, it can also be a manifestation of providential wrath (941). Storms can represent the creation of new life through rainfall; conversely, they are able to destroy and create death when excessive.

with the prisoner and two of the people, who appeared to have the command and direction of this mysterious expedition.—

Refreshments were ordered for the travellers, and beds made up for them in the barracks; but the governor had a long conference with the gentlemen before they separated. In the middle of the following night they departed from the castle with as much secrecy, and as little ceremony, as they had entered it, no one appearing desirous to develop the cause which brought them, or daring to ask any questions of the governor, in whose power alone it rested to satisfy their inquiries, as at this time civil commotions and private feuds between the contending nobles were continually arising to disturb the peace of society, and involve the nation in accumulating distresses; this strange visit was not only silently observed but in a few weeks scarcely recollected, even by those who had witnessed it; and the guards, with only silent shrugs and significant looks, thought it safest, wisest, and best, to perform with exact attention the discharge of their respective duties.

At this period of our tale, the joyous festival of Christmas was approaching,—a festival which our old-fashioned forefathers welcomed with every mark of grateful and benevolent hospitality; and its arrival was beheld with as much complacent and cordial hilarity by the rich and great, as it was with delight and impatience by the poor and needy. While the holly and mistletoe decorated the kitchens, and the innocent joke went round, as the blushing maidens received the compliments and good wishes of the season, the loaded tables served still more to exhilarate their spirits, and even the stranger and the beggar were invited to taste the good things they enjoyed.

The youthful inhabitants of the castle began to reckon with eager and high-raised expectation the days, the hours, and even the minutes, which must pass away before the lovely Madeline, who had obtained permission of the abbess to spend the Christmas holidays at the castle, could join their party. Various plans of pleasure were formed, which they hoped would be productive of such amusements as would amply gratify their own wishes, and those of their expected visitors; for Agnes de Clifford, who was a boarder in the nunnery, was to accompany Madeline, by whom and Roseline she was much beloved. She was a lively interesting girl, about Miss de Morney's age, and, next Madeline, held the highest place in her regard.

In reality, the young people at the castle were as much confined as those in the nunnery from any intercourse with the world, Sir Philip de Morney having a decided aversion to the introducing young people early into life; but by the urgent entreaties of his lady, he was now prevailed upon to relax from the strictness he had observed respecting his elder children, four of whom felt a wish for a more enlarged society;

and, as their father had no design of placing any of them in a religious retirement, it began to be time for them to know something of that world in which, in all probability, they must take an active part.

The holidays were spent in the utmost harmony; the festivity which reigned in every part of the castle seemed to have banished sorrow from its walls. The surgeon, captains, and lieutenants, were all of their parties, and the evenings generally concluded with a dance: their dependents were sometimes permitted to join the set, and the good priest, Father Anselm, who attended the castle, would gladly have been a partaker in their innocent amusements, had not the rigid rules of his sacred order forbidden such relaxations.

A few days before the young ladies were to return to the nunnery, Madeline was taken ill, and her disorder increased so rapidly, it was not only thought dangerous, but found impracticable to remove her with safety. For some weeks her life was despaired of, and, when immediate danger was over, she was left in so weak and languid a state, that air and exercise were pronounced absolutely necessary to effect a perfect recovery. This sentence was heard with secret delight by the suffering Madeline, as she was certain it would procure leave for her longer continuance at the castle, and the permission, when obtained, had more efficacy in restoring her, than all the medicines she had taken during her illness. Edwin and Roseline, much as they had suffered from the alarming indisposition of their loved companion, rejoiced that it had been productive of an indulgence they had almost despaired of gaining.

As the progress of her recovery was slow and precarious, many symptoms of a decline being visible, every one was eager and anxious to amuse the fair invalid, and none appeared more earnest in their endeavours than Hubert de Willows, captain of the guard, a young man, whose wit, vivacity, and unceasing good humour, and so strongly recommended him to the favour and protection of the governor, as had obtained him a constant invitation to his table, with a lively imagination, he had a turn for satire, so pointed, that, while it rendered him a most entertaining companion, kept many of his enemies in awe, and he had the merit of never shewing his talents at the expence of a friend, nor any worthy character; but he considered vice and folly as fair game, against which he levelled his attacks.

Arthur de Clavering, the acting surgeon, was allowed both judgment and humanity. The practice of physic and surgery was then but obscurely known, compared with the more enlightened practitioners of these days. De Clavering, however, patched up many a broken constitution. People lived as long, and had fewer diseases, than has been the lot of succeeding generations, but, whether this is owning to chance or folly, I leave wiser heads to determine.

Arthur de Clavering was rather an extraordinary character; his person was neither tall nor short; of a thin habit; had a countenance so pleasing, and eyes so penetrating, it was impossible not to be struck with him, as something beyond the common race of mortals. He had been abroad, had read much, was acquainted with both men and manners, had a plain and rather awkward address, was singular in his expressions, and formed his opinions with a justness and rapidity that astonished those with whom he associated; told a number of good anecdotes with a delicacy and humour peculiar to himself; public places and general society he avoided so cautiously, that he was considered as a misanthrope by those who did not know him intimately.

Lieutenant de Huntingfield was a humourous bachelor of forty: he professed himself an admirer of the ladies, and pretended to lament that the state of his finances would not permit him to take a wife to his bosom, and increase the ancient family of the De Huntingfields, which, he apprehended, if fortune proved averse to his accomplishing, would become extinct.

Among the rest of the officers was a Cambrian youth, who was a general favourite in the castle. Hugh Camelford was gay, high spirited, thoughtless, and extravagant; but with all so generous and good humoured, it was impossible not to be pleased even with his eccentricities; he rode good horses, gave good dinners, and was always in good spirits. De Clavering and Hugh Camelford were the best friends in the world. The doctor, as he was generally called, had once, during some indisposition, advised him to be bled; but the fiery youth would neither follow his advice nor submit to his entreaties: he was then threatened with death for his obstinacy.

"In Cot's cood time I am ready to die, (said the invalid;) but, if ever I lose one drop of my Welch bloot, put in the service of my country, may my coot name be plarted with the titles of poltroon and coward!"—He saved his Welch blood, and recovered, and De Clavering, though at first somewhat displeased, treated him as friend and brother ever afterwards.[8]

There was a still more singular character in the castle than any yet described,—Alexander Elwyn. He was placed there as a school for improvement in tactics and all the relative duties of a soldier: he had good connexions, and a genteel allowance, but was a miser at twenty. This sordid humour made him the butt of the garrison, and De Willows, with the rest of the officers, vowed to laugh him out of the habit as disgusting as it was unnatural and unnecessary.

---

[8] Camelford is from North Cumberland and Bonhote attempts to capture his heavy accent phonetically. Generally C's and G's are interchanged as are P's and B's and D's and T's.

In a few weeks Madeline was so far recovered, as to be removed into one of the state apartments for the benefit of air; and adjoining room was likewise fitted up for Roseline, to sleep near her friend during her confinement. They generally parted from their attendants as soon as the rest of the family retired. Being one night earnestly chatting over some occurrence that had afforded them pleasure, they were alarmed by footsteps under their apartment, and a low murmuring sound of voices indistinctly reached their ears. Madeline was a good deal frightened, but Roseline, who had great presence of mind, and more courage, made, or rather appeared to make, very light of the matter, telling her friend the rooms they occupied were, she knew, connected with some passages and offices belonging to the castle, and she doubted not but the noise proceeded from the people on duty. This, in some degree, abated the fears of Madeline, till, after a profound silence of half an hour, they heard a deep groan, followed by the rattling of chains; at the same instant one of the windows flew open with the greatest violence, and as instantly closed again, which was followed by the bell at the corner of the room ringing violently. [9]

Madeline gave a faint scream; Roseline jumped out of bed, and ran for some water, supposing she would have a fainting fit; but she gently put it aside, and with wild affright inquired what was the matter, and what could occasion the unaccountable noises they had heard. "The wind, and the people in some of the lower apartments, no doubt, (replied her friend;) therefore I beg you would not discompose yourself; if you do, you will compel me to disturb the family, and that I am afraid would displease my father; and, in all probability, Edwin would ridicule our childish fears, and the rest of the gentlemen would laugh at us."

This silenced Madeline, and Roseline continued: "I am totally unacquainted with many parts of this castle. I have two or three times wished to explore its secret passages, look at the dungeons, and visit all its subterranean contrivances, but have been forbidden by my father. Edwin did once promise to shew me how well we were secured from outward danger by the immense strength of the fortifications, and equally secure of a retreat, should the castle by attacked; but he cautioned me not to give a hint of his design, either to my father or mother, nor to drop a word of his intentions before my brothers or

---

[9] Though seemingly trivial to the contemporary reader, Bonhote employs an abundance of symbolic gothic occurrences in this paragraph - all of them clues which lead Roseline closer to her role as independent heroine. The groans and rattling chains indicate a painful imprisonment while the blown open window represents the need for escape from the restricting social world of the castle - within herself and the soon to be discovered secret prisoner. The ringing bell is Roseline's call to arms, an alarm awakening her from her slumber to call her to action.

sisters. Eager as I was to have my curiosity satisfied, your illness, my dear girl, and the pleasure we counted of partaking during your visit, drove it from my mind; but I will take the earliest opportunity of claiming my brother's promise."

"Defer your design of doing so till I am sufficiently recovered to accompany you, (said Madeline faintly,) and pardon the trouble my folly and weakness have occasioned you: this illness, I am sorry to find, has had as much influence on my mental feelings as on my bodily frame; but, if you will comply with my request, I will endeavour to be more courageous, and get well as fast as I can."

"Agreed, (cried Roseline;) you and I, my dear Madeline, have yet seen too little of life to be weary of it, and I trust our hearts are both too guiltless to have any fears of those supernatural appearances, of which superstition and ignorance give such improbable accounts."

"Yet I have heard strange tales of this castle being haunted, even in the retired recess to which my adverse fate has in all probability doomed me to spend my hapless days, and—"

"You are too much inclined to believe them, (interrupted her friend;) but, my dear Madeline, be assured of this,—if we had nothing more to fear from the living than we have to apprehend from the dead, we should be perfectly secure, and our lives would pass away in a more serene and placid manner than the turbulent wills of our fellow-mortals will allow. Hark! I am sure I hear the soft and distant sound of a lute. I never yet knew a ghost that had a taste for mortal harmony."

"I certainly hear music, (sighed Madeline;) from what place can it proceed?—Surely it must be—"

"The amusement, no doubt, of some one either on the ramparts or in the cells; for you have fluttered my spirits so much, I cannot determine from what part of the castle the sound can reach us: let us, however, rest satisfied, that no ghosts would trouble themselves to play a midnight serenade in order to terrify those who could never have injured them. Let us wait till you are quite recovered before we mention a word of the occurrences of this night: for, were my father to hear of our alarm, we should be instantly removed into other apartments, and should not then be able to accomplish our purpose of exploring the intricate recesses of this castle. Good night, Madeline; I hope the musician will not cease his harmony till he has lulled us to repose."

She then jumped into her own bed; but her spirits were not altogether in that composed and courageous state she wished her friend to imagine. She had heard strange stories of lights being seen, of ghosts gliding along the ramparts, of noises being heard; but, as she had not been told of a ghostly musician, she was inclined to hope it would, by some means or other, be explained to her satisfaction.

Till the rising sun, however, peeped over the hills which bounded the view from her windows, she could not rest; she then sunk into repose, and slept so soundly, that it was with difficulty her sister, Edeliza, could convince her that the family waited breakfast till she should be in the humour to join them. Madeline took her's in bed. Roseline hurried on her clothes, and Lady de Morney tenderly inquired if indisposition had prevented her rising at her usual hour. Complaining of not having slept till late satisfied all parties, and, after a gentle reproof from Sir Philip, and a joke from Edwin for hugging her pillow so long, the subject was dropped.

The next day was fixed for Madeline to join the family at dinner, for the first time since her long and alarming illness. De Clavering, De Willows, and Hugh Camelford, were invited to be of the party on this joyous occasion, and it was with the utmost difficulty that Edwin de Morney could conceal the rapture he felt in his bosom at the thought of seeing the fair nun once more among them. He had ventured, with the consent of Roseline, to make her several stolen visits, and in those moments of rapturous delight had discovered that Madeline de Glanville reigned sole mistress of his heart. Too young for the practice of deceit, too sanguine and inexperienced to think of the consequence of loving one devoted to the service of her God, he flattered himself the partial indulgence of his mother would enable him to conquer any difficulties thrown in his way, either by his father, or the designs of Madeline's parents had formed for her future destination. He likewise cherished the sweet hope that Madeline would not be averse to accept him a lover. His own heart had taught him to read the language of the eyes, and in her's he saw, or thought he saw, joy sparkle at his approach, and a soft sadness over-cloud them at his departure.

The party met at dinner. Madeline entered the room, leaning on the supporting arm of Edwin, and followed by Roseline. Never, in the full bloom of youth and health, had the fair invalid looked so inexpressibly lovely. A faint blush tinged her cheek upon receiving the congratulations of the company on her recovery. The doctor humourously declared he was entitled to their thanks for the resurrection of their friend.

"A resurrection, methinks, it is in reality, (said de Willows;) for the mortal seems to have put on immortality, and to have brought down from heaven the beauty and form of an angel."

"Hey day! (cried Sir Philip;) why, good people, you all seem to be taking vast pains to make my sweet nun believe a language you yourselves do not seem perfectly to understand. That we are all glad to see her restored to us I hope and trust she believes; but our congratulations must convince her, notwithstanding your high-flown compliments, that she is a mere mortal, like the rest of her sex."

"Not exactly like some of them, (said the doctor;) for, if she were, De Willows would not look at her as if he had a mind to seize the precious morsel from mother-church."

This sally produced a hearty laugh from all but Edwin and Lady de Morney, who, seeing the conversation was become distressing to her young friend, summoned them to sit down to dinner.

"In Cot's name, (cried Camelford,) let us obey orders, for I feel myself all mortal at sight of Sir-loin, who is as coot and entertaining a knight as any on this side the Welch mountains."

"Excellent, faith! (exclaimed De Clavering;) and you look at him with as much pleasure as a goat would at a field of young grass, or as Edwin at his sister Roseline."

Edwin at this moment was gazing at Madeline with an earnestness that struck the doctor, and he took this method of withdrawing his attention from an object which he considered might prove dangerous to the peace of his young friend, to whom he was most sincerely and affectionately attached.

The day was spent with all that serene harmony which attends the society of friends. Madeline's return to the social party was like that of one having been so long absent, that little hope was entertained of ever meeting again. She retired to her room at an early hour, accompanied by Roseline; and the progress of her recovery, though slow, was so visible, as in a few days to remove all anxious fears from every heart but that of the impassioned Edwin, that no further danger was to be apprehended from the effects of the fever.

For more than a week the young ladies heard nothing to disturb them. They were lodged at a great distance from the rest of the family, and Roseline, having informed her brother of Madeline's fears, he had requested his mother to let him sleep in that wing of the castle, lest Madeline should be taken ill in the night, and his sister under the necessity of leaving her to call assistance. His request was granted, at the same time he received his mother's commendations and thanks for this prudent precaution.

CHAPTER III.

DURING the time that De Willows was cherishing an increasing affection for Madeline, the youthful Edeliza, now in her sixteenth year, was in a situation more distressing. She had long been accustomed to consider De willows in the light of a playfellow, and to be gratified by his almost undivided attention, while to him her's was wholly confined. With Camelford she would sometimes romp, if De Willows were absent, but, as soon as he returned, she would fly to him, and complain of the young lieutenant's having wearied her playing too roughly.

Love even with the inexperienced is generally quick-sighted. Edeliza had observed, with a kind of trembling apprehension, and a fear she knew not how to account for, the attentions De Willows paid to Madeline. She was angry,—she was shocked,—thought her not half so handsome as she once had been, and wondered what the gentlemen could see to admire in so ghostly a figure; her brother, De Clavering, Hugh Camelford, and Elwyn, might make as much fuss as they pleased about the beautiful nun, as they chose to call her, but that De Willows should be so blind, so provoking, she could not bear to recollect; however, as she would soon be obliged to return to the nunnery, she hoped De Willows would then forget she had ever left it, and recover his senses.

Thus was the little blind god, who has been the delight and the torment of all ages, beginning to play cross purposes at the castle, and aiming his arrows at hearts too innocent to guard against or repel their attacks. De Willows had ever admired Edeliza as a beautiful and interesting child; he had been in the habit of seeing her, from the time she was ten years old, every day; therefore her progress toward womanhood had passed in a manner unperceived, and he had indulged himself and his little favourite in the same fond and playful endearments as had taken place from the first of their meeting, and that without forming an idea of there being either danger or impropriety in so doing. Had any one informed De Willows that Edeliza was cherishing a growing affection for him, which, if unreturned, would endanger her future peace, he would have treated it as the idle chimera of their own whimsical brain; but, had he once seriously supposed he was destroying her happiness, and planting the thorn of anguish in her innocent bosom, his heart was so much the seat of true honour, he would have stabbed in his own breast rather than have acted unjustly by the daughter of his friend.

It happened about this period that Sir Philip de Morney was obliged to go to London in order to settle a law-suit which had been long depending, and which had harassed his mind very much. De Huntingfield was to take the command of the castle during his absence, being the oldest officer in the place. De Willows, though of higher rank, was too young to be entrusted with a charge of so much importance, and gladly yielded the honour to one so much his superior in years. Sir Philip departed with reluctance, took leave of his family with tenderness, and promised to return the first moment after the affair was settled.—Lady de Morney was reconciled to the temporary absence of her husband by the important business which had called him away.

The young friends, having slept for several nights undisturbed, had almost lost all remembrance of their fears before the departure of Sir Philip, whose absence happened very opportunely to gratify their curiosity in visiting every part of the castle, Edwin having promised to procure the keys, and accompany them.

Two nights after Sir Philip's departure, having spent a cheerful evening, they retired to rest in unusual good spirits, but were awakened about midnight by a war of the elements, and what made the scene more terrific, though it was in the depth of winter, the thunder rolled in tremendous peals over their heads, the sturdy walls of the castle appeared to shake from their centre to the battlements, and the lightning flashed upon the walls, and gleamed along the vaulted passages, as if to make horror visible. The young ladies dressed themselves, and Edwin tapped at the door with a light, inviting them to go down into one of the lower rooms, to which he would accompany them.

Cheered and revived by the sound of his voice, they readily agreed to his proposal, and in a few minutes opened the door to admit their conductor. They made as little noise as possible, fearful of disturbing Lady de Morney, if she was not already alarmed by the tempest; and, to prevent the possibility of doing so, they agreed to go down a winding staircase that led through one of the towers, and which was seldom used by the family. They crept slowly along, when, in one part of it, which was rather wider than the rest, they passed four steps, which led to a door in the wall, and which appeared so well secured by locks and bars, as if it never was intended to be opened.

"For heaven's sake, (whispered Roseline,) to what room does that door lead? I never saw it before."

"I entreat you (said the trembling Madeline) not to stop in this horrid place to ask questions, (for the humid and unwholesome dews of night and noxious vapours hung on the walls.) Though I am not afraid now Edwin is with us, yet I may take cold by staying here."[10]

Edwin pressed the hand which was resting on his arm to his throbbing bosom, and hurried them into the room the family had left, and they were all truly rejoiced to find an excellent fire still blazing on the wide-extended hearth, round which they seated themselves, and neither Madeline nor Edwin uttered a single complaint at having been so unseasonably disturbed.

The tempest having spent its fury, subsided by degrees into a calm, and the party, entering into conversation, almost forgot it had ever been. Roseline however repeated her question respecting the door they had seen in their way down the staircase. Edwin assured her he knew no more than her self to what place it belonged: he had heard that the restless ghost of some one had been bound in the apartments to which it led, and that orders had been given for it never to be opened. He had once made some inquiries of his father, but was desired by him never to ask any questions till he came to years of maturity, nor to explore any of the secret passages or entrances to the castle.

"Then, surely, (said Madeline,) it would be extremely wrong to disobey the commands of Sir Philip, merely to satisfy an idle and perhaps blameable curiosity."

"At the moment (interrupted Edwin) that I admire the complying sweetness of the gentle Madeline, I must beg pardon for retaining my own resolution of seeing those parts of the castle from which I have been so long secluded. I am now arrived at an age that surely deserves to be trusted, or I must be unfit to live in a situation like this. My father's reasons for the secresy he has observed so long, I am unacquainted with; but I will most assuredly avail myself of his absence to gratify my curiosity. I know where the keys are deposited, and in a night or two will begin my nocturnal search. If you and Roseline are in the humour to accompany me, it is well; if not, I shall certainly go by myself."

"As that might be dangerous, (said Roseline, who rejoiced to find him so resolute,) you must promise to take me along with you."

To this he assented, and Madeline agreed, with some little confusion, to be of the party, concluding, Sir Philip must be wrong in not granting his son's request. This matter settled, they retired for the

---

[10] Madeline's fear of catching a cold, or worse, is well founded. Even as late as the seventeenth century, people suspected bad air, 'noxious vapours' as the major carrier of the black death which, in a little over three years, killed 1/3 of the population of Europe in the middle of the fourteenth century. For more information, see John Kelly's *The Great Mortality: An Intimate History of the Black Death*.

rest of the night, to forget, in the arms of sleep, not only the castle and the nunnery, but the whole world.

The next night they were surprised by an unusual noise, that seemed to be immediately under them. It appeared something like the rattling of a carriage over stones. Groans too they thought they heard; and, after dressing themselves, Roseline called her brother, to convince him their alarms were not the effects of imagination. He heard the same sounds, and, in looking round their apartment, and into an adjoining closet, he discovered a trap-door, that was very curiously concealed under a board, which slided over it. He attempted to lift it up, but found it was secured by a lock which was hid in a small projection of the wall.

Finding it impossible to obtain a passage, they determined to defer their search till the succeeding night, when Edwin promised to secure the keys. He stayed with them till daylight dissipated their fears; they then retired to repose; but sleep deserted their pillows. A thousand vague conjectures occupied their minds, and Madeline, for the first time in her life, wished herself absent from the castle: that there was something to discover appeared beyond a doubt; but, whether the discovery would serve to relieve or increase their anxiety, was as hazardous as it was uncertain; however, as Roseline and Edwin were resolute to make the attempt, she determined not to oppose them.

Edwin revolved in his mind how he might be able to find some clue to guide him, and resolved to apply to an old soldier, whose whole life had been spent in the castle, to give him some account respecting it. He was fond of retracing past scenes, and, when once he began talking, knew not when to stop. From him Edwin learned all he wanted to be informed; by him he was told the use of the keys, and received every necessary direction. The old man, considering himself honoured by holding converse with the governor's son, told him every circumstance he knew or could recollect. The next day was spent in the same manner as usual. De Clavering was uncommonly facetious, De Willows particularly cheerful, Hugh Camelford entertaining, and De Huntingfield busy in the active duties of his important office.

The afternoon being remarkably clear, mild, and serene, the whole party agreed to ascend to the top of the castle, and walk on the ramparts, for the benefit of air and exercise. Edeliza would not quit the arm of De Willows, therefore Madeline was left uninterrupted to the care of Edwin.

The air was reviving, the prospect picturesque and interesting; for, notwithstanding the season, nature had still beauties to catch the inquiring eye, and awaken the gratitude of innocent and cheerful hearts. A few evergreens, scattered here and there among the leafless trees, afforded shelter to innumerable birds. The red breast warbled his artless song, surrounded by a number of chirping sparrows, who seemed gaily to flutter around, making a most uncommon bustle, which was occasioned by a shower that had lately fallen.

"Confound these impertinent noisy little devils! (said De Clavering,) I wish I had my gun, and I would most assuredly put an end to some of this clatter."

"For shame, toctor, (cried Camelford;) what! would you testroy such pretty harmless creatures as these? Rather save your ammunition for the enemies of your king,—that would be coot sport indeed!—then, my man of mettle, we should be better employed; but let the sparrow-family lif, and enjoy their prating."

"I believe you are nearly allied to that same family, (replied the doctor,) and therefore I do not wonder at your being anxious to preserve your relations."

"Petter not provoke me, toctor. I am in a valiant humour just now, and, as Cot shall pless me, I will not pocket an affront from any one."

"Pack it up in your knapsack, (replied the doctor dryly,) and say, as our Saviour did, when tempted, "Get thee behind me, Satan!"—for really, Hugh, I often think the devil has jumped into your skull, and, by kicking about your brains, has made you so hot headed."

"Then the best think I can do (replied Camelford) would be to put myself under your tirection to lay this same tevil, and by the time you had trained me of all my Welch ploot, he would leave my lifeless carcase to be poiled for your improvement; but avaunt, thou cataplasm of cataplasms!—I defy thy incantations, plisters, and pleadings."

"I believe the young dog will live the longer, (cried the doctor, addressing De Willows,) but who among us will deny or defy the sweet influence of these lilies and roses that are now blooming around us."

"I do not pretend to any such philosophic apathy," replied De Willows.

"If you did, your looks would betray you, (retorted Edwin.) To deny the united influence of love and beauty is not the province of a soldier."

"Do all soldiers admire beauty, and fall in love?" inquired the artless Edeliza, looking earnestly at De Willows.

"I believe so, my sweet little girl, (he answered;) love and death are alike inevitable."

"But not equally dangerous, (said the laughing Roseline;) for I never heard of any one dying of the wounds given by the little blind god, though thousands fall victims to the more certain arrows sent from the furnace of war."

"By the crate Cot, (said Camelford,) I had rather tie by the wounds a pair of pright eyes than by those of a cannon, loaded by the hands of an ugly tog, who like a putcher delights in ploot."

"More fool you, (replied De Clavering;) the death in the one case would be glorious and instantaneous,—in the other, foolish and lingering,—"

"Unless I applied to a toctor to put me out of my misery, and then I should get rid of it in a trice."

"A truce with your compliments, good folks, (said Roseline;) suppose we endeavour to reconcile ourselves to the world, and all its strange vagaries, by a dance in the great hall. This proposal met with general approbation; to the great hall they descended, and, surrounded by the rusty armour of their hardy forefathers, they enjoyed in the mazy windings of the lively dance, a pleasure as innocent as it was amusing, Lady de Morney herself being a gratified spectator of the scene.

This hall was decorated, if we may use the term, with a vast number of suits of armour, belonging to the family of Norfolk. One, more light and higher finished than the rest, appeared to have belonged to a youth of Edwin's size. He was prevailed on to fit it; and, armed cap-à-pié, strutted about in bold defiance, and threw down his gauntlet, daring any one to single combat who should deny the balm of beauty being due to the lady he should name.

"Suppose I throw down my glove," said de Willows.

"You would soon take it up again, (replied Edwin, somewhat scornfully,) as I fancy our taste in beauty to be the same."

De Willows coloured,—Madeline appeared uneasy,—and Edeliza declared armour was the most frightful dress she had ever saw, while the younger part of the family jumped round their brother, and with eagerness made many inquiries concerning the use of every part of his dress, and requested their mother to let them wear some of the nodding plumes which hung in lofty state around them.

In the course of the evening, Edwin gave Madeline a hint to retire early to her chamber, having obtained possession of the keys, and gained such directions as could not fail to satisfy their curiosity and guide them in their researches. Madeline silently acquiesced, and imparted, with trembling impatience, the tidings to her friend. She was thoughtful and absent the rest of the evening, and availed herself of the earliest opportunity of withdrawing to her chamber. Roseline very soon followed her, and, as soon as the family had retired to rest, Edwin stole gently to their apartment. They had anxiously expected his arrival, and therefore gave him immediate admittance.

Roseline rejoiced at seeing her brother, and eagerly inquired if he was sure that he had the keys that would enable them to proceed. He then produced a most enormous bunch, with a dark lantern, which was to guide them through the intricate labyrinths of the castle, and advised Madeline and his sister to guard against the damps of the passages they had to go through, and to arm themselves with their whole stock of resolution, lest their terrors should betray him.

Roseline assured him her fears were conquered by her strong desire to explore the secrets of their habitation, and Madeline promised not to let her apprehensions impede their progress. Edwin lighted his candle, and with some difficulty unfastened the trap-door he had discovered in their closet; but, on opening it, a kind of noxious vapour ascended, that almost tempted them to give up their design. A flight of broken brick steps, of amazing depth, carried them into a narrow winding passage, in which it was impossible for more than one person to move forward at once.

Madeline caught hold of Edwin's coat, and Roseline followed her with a lighted candle in her hand. For some time they groped along, frequently stumbling over the stones which had fallen from the mouldering walls, and trembling lest this passage should lead them into danger. Edwin frequently stopped to encourage them to go on, assuring them they had nothing to apprehend. By degrees the path widened, and, on suddenly turning, they entered a kind of square, round which were several doors, but so low, they did not seem made to admit men but dwarfs. Going up to one of them, Edwin pushed it open with his foot, and he was convinced they were the dungeons in which prisoners of war were confined. Some contained only bedsteads, iron rings, and fetters; in one of them they saw a human skull; in another was a coffin, which appeared to have stood their for ages, and with its silent inhabitant was falling to decay.[11]

They proceeded till they came to a door which was so thickly studded over with nails, bolts, bars, and locks, that it impeded their farther progress. Edwin would fain have attempted to open it, but was prevented by his shivering and terrified companions.

"Brother, (cried Roseline,) we have seen quite enough to satisfy us for one night."

"Another time, Edwin, (added Madeline,) I shall feel less repugnance to proceed. But how do you know that door does not lead to some apartment where the restless spirit of another discontented ghost may be confined, by some potent spell, till released by the

---

[11] As evidence of the castle's violent past, Bonhote uses images of imprisonment, torture and death to makes a strong contrast with the current inhabitants gentler demeanour. A common Gothic theme, the past appears barbaric and primitive when compare to the more enlightened present.

intrusion of beings who now wander amid the gloomy scenes of life as he once did?"

"No such thing, (replied the intrepid and resolute Edwin;) that door is an entrance to a subterraneous passage, which leads from this castle to Mettingham, merely to give entrance to troops in any case of emergency, or to cover the retreat of others that may want to escape."

"But, as it has not been used, either for the one purpose or the other, since my father resided here, (said Roseline,) it may now be a shelter for thieves and traitors; therefore, for heaven's sake, let us now return to our apartments."

Edwin, whose disposition was as amiable as his manners and person where captivating, no longer contended with their wishes, but led the way for them as he had done before, and, as he was a fine tall youth, was obliged to stoop as he went along.

Just as they came near the foot of the steps which led to their apartment, they saw, or thought they saw, a faint light gleam across a passage which led to another part of these gloomy habitations, and they imagined they perceived the figure of some one disappear at their approach. This alarmed the whole group, and they hurried up the stairs as hastily as their fears would let them. Having cautiously fastened the trap door, they sat down to recover themselves, and recollected with a degree of horror and disgust the gloomy scenes they had visited; but the light, and the figure they had all caught a transient view of, dwelt most forcibly on their minds. Madeline declared she should never have sufficient resolution to re-visit these abodes of terror, contrived by the stern hands of despotism and ambition.

"When we think, a we surely may, (said she,) with some degree of certainty, how many poor souls have languished out a life of misery in these gloomy cells, can we wonder if they are haunted by all they have entombed? Shut out not only from the world, but from every comfort, nature too recoils and shudders at the cruelties that may have been practiced on the poor victims thus buried in the bowels of the earth."

"All this may be very true, my sweet Madeline, (interrupted Edwin,) but I am determined to re-visit them. Perhaps some poor sufferers may still remain in the castle; if so, it would be delightful to soften the rigours of their fate."

"True, my dear brother, (cried Roseline, her eyes illumined with the soft beams of genuine benevolence and philanthropy,) I will certainly attend you."

"To quiet the fears of our lovely friend, (said Edwin,) I will request old Bertrand, who has lived in this castle from the time we came into it, to accompany and direct us in our search after misery. I am told too, (he added,) there is a passage which leads from this castle into the chapel of your nunnery. If I can find it out, I shall certainly pay you a visit, and steal you from your cell; for, my dear Madeline, whatever may be the truth and the virtues of our holy religion, it is doubtless one of its abuses to shut from the world those lovely works of the creation best calculated to enliven and adorn it. Can it be deemed a greater crime to doom a worthless, or, suppose I say, and innocent, man, to languish in a dungeon, than it is to compel an unfortunate female to waste her days in the austere walls of a nunnery,—kneel to the unfeeling image of a saint,—watch the midnight lamp,—seclude herself from all social enjoyments,—and linger through life in solitary sadness, without a friend, or a lover, to cheer her on her way?"[12]

"Hush, for heaven's sake! (said the frightened Madeline;) if Father Anselm heard you talk thus lightly and profanely of our holy religion, I should before ever debarred seeing you and Roseline again, for life shut out from the world, and compelled to take the veil."

"Never, by heaven! (cried Edwin, thrown entirely off his guard by the tender confusion and agitation of Madeline:) you shall take no vows but such as love and nature dictate. I would parish a thousand times,— lose a thousand lives to preserve you from a fate that would not only make you wretched, but me for ever miserable.—Roseline has long known that you are dear to my heart. Say,—ease me of the torturing suspense I this moment feel,—do you not find an advocate in your bosom that will plead my cause?"

Madeline trembled violently; her eyes were bent to the ground: she would have fallen, had not Roseline not flown to support her. She attempted to speak, but the words died away inarticulately.

"I see how it is, (cried Edwin impassionately;) the happy De Willows has gained by his attentions what I have lost by disgusting you with mine: you hate, you despise me. I will solicit my father to let me join the army: I will for ever remove this detested object from your sight, and pray that the portion of happiness I have lost may be redoubled to you."[13]

---

[12] Though his heart may be in the right direction, Edwin's comparison of torture with religious devotion seems quite extreme. However, many gothic novels feature women who desire to be rescued from evil nunneries. Madeline is just one example of a long line of women trapped by their religious codes. Lewis's novel *The Monk* contains two of the most extreme examples of women trapped within prison-like convents: Agnes and The Bleeding Nun.

[13] Edwin reaches the height of selfless romanticism with this declaration. A frequent theme in Gothic and Romantic novels, many men melodramatically sacrifice their own happiness so the women they love will be able to live happily ever after - in someone else's arms. The sailor aboard Captain Walton's ship in *Frankenstein* sacrifices his home, wealth and career so his fiancé can marry the man she truly loves while the sailor faces an empty and loveless life on the sea. Bonhote, however, uses this trope more frequently as a

Madeline, alarmed by the energy of this speech, was instantly roused from the languor into which she had sunk.

"I hate no one, (said she softly;) but Edwin, you forget it would be a crime in me to love. If, indeed, that had not been the case,—if I were at liberty—"

"You would bless the happy De Willows with your hand."

"Never!—De Willows I regard as a friend: as any thing more I never did,—never could think of him. I am you know banished from all intercourse with the world;—my sentence has been long pronounced; from that sentence there can be no appeal. Would to heaven I had submitted to it, and never quitted the retreat to which parental authority consigned me! At this painful moment my own feelings inflict my punishment."

"Then you do not hate me? (cried Edwin, taking her hand.)–Only say I am not quite indifferent to you, and I will endeavour to rest satisfied, and ask no more; trusting that time may do much in my favour; but, if you attempt to deprive me of all hope,—if you deny me this innocent gratification, I will go to the wars."

"Ah! why will you press me to discover what it would be better to conceal?–why will you tempt me to swerve from my duty to my God and my parents, and make me a perjured, an unworthy sacrifice?—You have, I fear, taught my heart a lesson it ought never to have learned: but it must be the hard task of my future life to atone for the crime I have committed in having suffered a mortal to rival that God, who alone should have occupied all my thoughts and wishes."

Edwin threw himself at the feet of Madeline. His raptures were now as unbounded as the conflict had been severe; and not till she sunk fainting into the arms of her friend, could he be persuaded to quit their apartment.

Happy was it for the party that Roseline had not only a greater share of prudence and understanding than most of her sex, but likewise more fortitude than is usually their portion. She soon recovered, her friend soothed her into some degree of composure, and endeavoured to inspire her with hopes that some plan might be adopted which would remove those difficulties that threatened to divide two hearts love had united, and which appeared formed by nature to make each other happy. Roseline will knew her father would not only be displeased, but shocked, if he discovered this unfortunate attachment, and she blamed

---

threat to the female. Edwin later cries out "if you deny me, I will go to the wars" (72), threatening a passive suicide; his death will be Madeline's fault for not returning his love. Later in the novel, Roseline's father declares that if she refuses the Baron's hand, he will die: the ultimate parental threat.

herself for having been the innocent cause of involving two people so dear to her in such a hopeless scene of complicated distress.

Notwithstanding the agonizing conflicts which had attended the elaircissment, the lovers felt a heavy burthen removed from their hearts. Convinced of being mutually beloved, all other sorrows, all other trials appeared light and trivial: they sunk into a more sweet and peaceful slumber than they had long enjoyed,—dreamed of each other, and arose the next morning with renovated spirits and revived hopes.[14]

Madeline wished the hour was arrived they were to renew their midnight ramble, and thought, if she should meet a thousand ghosts, she should not fear them, while Edwin, who loved her so tenderly and sincerely, was near to guard her. She was eager too, but scarcely durst acknowledge to herself she *wished* the passage might be found which led to the chapel in her nunnery.

---

[14] Even with the lovers isolated and separate, Bonhote emphasizes the restorative power of love with this passage.

CHAPTER IV.

IF there be any so fastidious and unfeeling as to condemn and deprecate the romantic hopes and flattering visions cherished in the buoyant bosom of nineteen, I am sorry for them, and here avow, I wish never entirely to forget the fascinating pleasure of such air-built hopes. Should they be sometimes attended with danger to the weak and frail, they are likewise accompanied with their advantages to the good and virtuous, and often enable us to encounter trials with a resolution and fortitude, which, at a more advanced period of our lives, when time has weakened our bodily frame, and experience deprived us of those gay illusions, we find it difficult and painful to acquire.—The philosophy of nineteen, though not abstruse, is flattering and conclusive; so much the more valuable; for, after all the researches of philosophy, what are we taught to know, but that man is born to trouble as the sparks fly upwards?—that we are merely the pilgrims and passengers of a day,—that our resting place must be found in a better, and unknown world,—that we must encounter innumerable trials on our journey, and at last die and be forgotten, even by those for whom we have toiled, and to whom we are most tenderly attached?—Surely then we may be allowed to snatch, or steal, a few of those innocent enjoyments just thrown in our way, to encourage our fortitude, and clear our path from some of the briars and thorns with which it is so profusely planted.

Happy is it for those in the common walks of life, that all their stock of philosophy is comprised in few words, acquired without study, and retained without study, and retained without taxing their time or burthening their memory,—"it was my fate,—I could not run from it,—it was to be." These trite sentences reconcile them to many distressing events, and sometimes are their excuse for the frailties of their conduct.

When the parties met at breakfast the next morning, any careful observer might have discovered, by the confusion visible on the countenance of Madeline,—the constraint in her manner of addressing Edwin,—his more than usual vivacity, and the pale cheeks and swelled eyes of Roseline, that something had occurred to produce the change; but, suspicion not being a frequent guest at the castle, no such discovery was made: every one employed themselves as usual, and in a few hours universal cheerfulness seemed to prevail.

The only observations made by Lady de Morney were, that her dear Edwin looked remarkably well, was in charming spirits, and had dressed himself better and more becomingly than usual. Madeline coloured, and thought the same. Roseline smiled, and Edwin whispered something in the ear of Madeline that prevented the roses fading on her cheek.

The dress of Madeline, though to her particularly becoming, would to thousands have been totally the reverse. It was the dress of the order of Benedictines, to which she belonged, consisting of a black robe, with a scapulary of the same. Under the robe, nuns, when professed, wore a tunic of white undyed wool, and, when they went to the choir, they had a cowl like that worn by the monks; but the boarders, who were in what we may call a state of probation, were allowed to wear a tunic of muslin or cambrick, and covered their heads with a white veil. This dress, little suited to please the whimsical taste of the present time, was, strange as it may appear, simple and becoming, and proved the truth of the poet's observation, that

—Loveliness

Needs not the foreign aid of ornament,

But is, when unadorn'd adorn'd the most.

Madeline, in the habit of her order, was so captivating a figure, that no one ever thought any alteration or change in it could have added a charm to those bestowed on her by the partial hand of nature. She was tall, and elegantly formed; the expression of her countenance, blended with softness and dignity, conveying an idea of superior virtue being united to superior loveliness.

Just before dinner, the Doctor observed that Madeline looked pale: having felt her pulse, he inquired what had given them cause to beat so much out of time.

"I must examine into this matter, (said he archly.) They are galloping along at a strange rate; either the head or the heart must occasion this revolution in the system of my patient's usual habit. If it be the disease of the heart, I must resign my place to a more able practitioner.—Do not blush, my fair nun, but tell me whom you would have called in."

"I am perfectly satisfied with your advice, my good doctor, and at this time believe I want a cook more than a physician, therefore excuse me if I say you entirely misunderstand my case."

"Don't be too positive (said De Clavering) of my ignorance. You may safely trust me with all your complaints,—even with those of the heart; for I feel myself extremely interested that you should not return to the nunnery with any additional one added to those you so unfortunately brought away."

Ah! (said Madeline,) mentally, advice is now too late. I shall carry back with me a more corroding, a more painful complaint than any I ever knew before; yet, strange as it is, I would not be cured for the world, as my being so would wound Edwin de Morney.

Only Camelford was present when this little badinage passed between the Doctor and his patient. He advised the former to lay aside his wig, and take up the cowl, as the most certain method of discovering the truth; "for, though the laties, (he added,) will not tell all they think to you or I, they will not attempt to teceive their Cot."

"If I thought putting on a cowl would transform me to a god, (said De Clavering,) I would soon hazard the transformation, and then I would place a shield before the heart of every fair daughter of Britain, that should have the property of a talisman, to warn them against the designs and insidious attentions of young men, six feet high, with black sparkling eyes, auburn hair, teeth of ivory, handsome legs, and white hands."

Madeline knew the portrait, and, rising to conceal her blushes, ran hastily out of the room.

Hugh Camelford burst into a violent fit of laughter, and told the Doctor, "so far from being thought a Cot, the young laty certainly took him for the tisel, having discovered his spells and clofen foot, or perhaps for Tafy ap Jones, who, after tying for lof, was thrown into the Red Sea, and had haunted all lof-sick maidens every since, poor discontented tifel!"[15]

"And that will be your fate, Hugh, (retorted the Doctor,) unless you send home the Welch lass whom you betrayed, and then left to starve with your son, a fat chubby boy, very like his father."

"As I hope to escape the toctor and tamnation, (said the indignant Hugh,) I never petrayed a lass in my whole life; therefore, you cataplasm, you plister, you caustic of fire, bring no such scandals on the coot name of Camelford, lest I take a little of your carnivorous plood, and make you drink it!"

The Doctor stole off laughing, and Camelford soon recovered his good humour.

A dance was proposed for the evening, and readily agreed to by the young people, who determined to make the time pass as cheerfully as possible during the absence of Sir Philip and the visit of Madeline.

In those days dancing was the favourite amusement of the youth of both sexes: rich and poor, young and old, one with another, mixed in the animating dance:—complaints of weariness and fatigue were seldom heard. This exercise was not only favourable to health, but the roses it produced on the glowing cheek of youth rendered all application to the borrowed ones of art totally unnecessary. Rouge was

---

[15] Thought to be devilish, corrupt, and the harbinger of bad luck, Davy Jones is the spirit of the sea according to ancient sea legends dating to at least 1751. The treasures of sunken ships and the souls of sailors lost at sea were said to be buried in Davy Jones' locker.

then unknown, and no *Warren* existed to abolish old women, by giving the furrowed features of age and unfading bloom. The plain jacket, with a small quantity of ribbon bound round a cambric cap, were then thought becoming, and few ornaments were worn but on very important and particular occasions; yet beauty was equally admired: the same homage was paid to it, and it held in bondage as many captives, without the adventitious aid of deception and extravagance.

Another preservative of youth and health was their keeping better, that is, earlier hours. Night was night, and dedicated to its original purpose. Day was properly divided, and found of sufficient length for all the useful employments of life. Few young ladies but had seen the sun rise in all its glory, and found their hearts expanded by the grand and awful sight; and, while they welcomed its reviving rays from the portals of the East, it tended to raise their minds to that God who made the sun, and who alone could number the stars by which it was surrounded.

A fine moon-light evening seldom passed unnoticed by these aspiring worthies, eager after knowledge; for, having happily fewer amusements, they had more time to attend to the instructive beauties of nature, the study of which affords an inexhaustible source of pleasure and surprise. Fearless of their complexions, they not only rambled but worked in their gardens. Each had a little spot of ground marked out, and it soon produced the desired effect; every one was emulous to outshine the other in its cultivation, and Sir Philip or Lady de Morney were often called upon as arbitrators to decide the superior beauty of a rose, the size of a carnation, or the snowy tints of a lily.

De Clavering had told them, that, under their feet, they often trampled on plants, in the careful study of which might be found a cure for every disease incident to the climate they inhabited, and that in other climates the earth produced her treasures for the same benevolent purpose; but the careless inattention of mankind to this useful knowledge had rendered the profession of physic absolutely necessary, and given men of learning and genius opportunity of displaying their talents in preserving the lives of their fellow creatures.

In consequence of these hints, all kinds of herbs were planted, and their virtues put to the test by being applied to relieve the diseases of their poor neighbours; and never did a high-bred town belle, at making a conquest, or a hero, after obtaining a signal victory, exult more, or feel greater delight than the having effected a cure produced in the minds of these young practitioners. De Clavering was gratified in giving them all the intelligence they requested, very often inquired when they went their rounds to visit their patients, and offered them his physical wig to give them consequence.

In those days people lived much longer in the same number of years; to rise between five and six o'clock, and breakfast at seven, was their usual custom, the time of taking their meals differing as much as their antique habits. Dinner was constantly on the table between eleven and twelve, and supper regularly served at seven; tea was then but little used. Whether the introduction of that bewitching beverage has been followed by the long catalogue of evils laid to its charge, I am not able to determine; but as I have known many weak constitutions who have never felt any ill effects from taking it, I am inclined to think it has not such dangerous properties as are alleged against it by valetudinarians and their medical advisers.

But what would the antediluvian souls, who compose my dramatis personae, say to the innovations made upon time in these days of delicate and fashionable refinement? They would suppose the world turned topsy-turvy, and be puzzled to know why the afternoon should be discarded, and what part of the twenty-four hours to call night.

The periodical times of taking refreshment are quite different to what they formerly were, and contradictory to the practice of our ancestors, who hoarded their time, and considered it as a treasure of some value. We may now literally be said to turn day into night, and night into day, while the want of time is the source of general complaint. Our people of fashion, and many of no fashion at all, breakfast at three in the afternoon, dine at seven, sip their tea at eleven o'clock at night, and sup at four in the morning; whereas Queen Elizabeth breakfasted at five or six in the morning, and dined at eleven in the forenoon.—She and all her court went to bed with the sun in summer, and at eight or nine o'clock in winter.

The parliament, in the reign of Charles the First, went to prayers at five or six in the morning, and the king dined at twelve; nay, in the licentious reign of that merry monarch, his son, dinner at two was thought a very late hour; for all public diversions were at an end by six in the evening, and the ladies, after seeing a play, went in their carriages to Hyde-Park.

Whether it would not be greatly to the advantage of people in general to revive some old customs, and return to the prudent habits of our progenitors, will not admit of much dispute. Private families, in these expensive times, would undoubtedly be benefited. Morning would again become a theme for the poet, and poor day-light be brought into fashion. Our parliament too would find more time to transact the important business of the nation, on which they so eloquently harangue. Possibly a good dinner would add weight to their arguments, and the not being hungry would prevent their eagerness to adjourn.

But one of its greatest evils, after that above mentioned, is felt by servants, particularly the unhappy cook. She seldom sees the face of day,—never enjoys the enlivening rays of the sun, and can scarcely find time even to change her clothes till the night is too far advanced to render the change necessary. It was formerly the custom for people to walk after tea, and by doing so acquire a redoubled relish for the variegated beauties of nature; but now the table makes its appearance at so unseasonable an hour, and fashionable etiquette, with the love of good cheer, detains them so long, that in fact it appears the chief business of life to study every art and contrivance how to destroy and squander, not how to improve our time; and, instead of people's eating that they may live, they now live only to eat and drink, that the senses, I presume, may be disabled from torturing them with reproaches.—But to return to our tale.

In the evening, as Edeliza was going down the dance, her eyes, with those of Madeline, were attracted by the same object,—a plume of white feathers, placed on a suit of armour, nodded, and the armour moved.[16] This had such an effect, Madeline screamed, and Edeliza, throwing herself into the arms of De Willows, begged he would protect her from the ghost. The dancing stopped, the whole party was alarmed, and Lady de Morney very much surprised; but, on being informed what had occasioned this bustle, Hugh Camelford flew to discover its cause, and, jumping upon a long table, which was placed by the side of the room for the accommodation of large parties on any particular occasion, he without much ceremony caught hold of the haunted armour, when, to the astonishment of the whole company there instantly appeared,—gentle reader, be not alarmed!—not the ghost of a murdered hero, nor forsaken maid,—but the youngest daughter of Sir Philip de Morney, who, skipping from her concealment upon the table, and from thence to the floor, shook her head, decorated with a profusion of flaxen hair, which curled in natural ringlets, and laughed heartily at the fright she had occasioned.

"Of all the chosts I ever saw, (said the delighted Hugh, catching her up in his arms,) this is by much the prettiest and most entertaining. I should like to be haunted by such an one all the tays of my life."

---

[16] The most famous floating suit of armour appears in the opening pages of Walpole's *The Castle of Otranto*, published in 1764. Walpole's symbolic giant helmet, decorated with black feathers, descends upon Prince Manfred's first born son, Conrad, crushing him on his wedding day. Bonhote's use of floating armour is quite different and absent of Walpole's political ramifications. Though worn by the youngest daughter, Birtha, as a practical joke to frighten her siblings, it is worthwhile to note that it is a young woman who wears the helmet in Bonhote's world.

Lady de Morney called the little culprit, and, having severely reproved her, ordered her to bed, to which she had been sent before the party had began dancing, for some fault she had committed, but had persuaded one of the servants to place her as before described, that she might be a spectator, though she was not permitted to be a partaker in the amusement. Lady de Morney reprimanded the servant; and, had it not been for the general intercessions of the company, poor Birtha would have been a prisoner in her own apartment some days.

This incident, simple in itself, happened very unfortunately for the two ladies, who had agreed to accompany Edwin in his subterranean tour. They lingered till the last moment, and then withdrew with visible reluctance; but determined, as soon as they reached their own room, not to say a word to Edwin of their fears, as they knew it would expose them to ridicule, if not to censure, and there was not in the catalogue of human ills or evils any circumstance Madeline would so much have dreaded as being thought meanly of by Edwin de Morney.

Within little more than an hour after the family had withdrawn, and all the servants retired to rest, they were joined by the sanguine and spirited Edwin, accompanied by the ancient veteran, who, though loaded with the heavy burthen of fourscore years, was still active and hearty, his senses unimpaired, and his sturdy limbs still able to carry with firmness their accustomed load. His grey locks hung with silvered dignity upon his aged shoulders, and his eyes retained some of their former expression. He made a profound obeisance to the ladies on his entrance, and was received with that condescending affability which his years and long-tried faithfulness demanded.

Edwin's manner of introducing him, flattered the old man's remaining stock of vanity, and revived, in full force, the remembrance of his former exploits, which, though they had not procured him preferment, secured him attention and respect.

"This is my friend Bertrand, (said Edwin, addressing Madeline particularly on his entrance;) though you had some fears with only such a stripling as myself for a leader, you can have none with so experienced and brave a guide."

The old man listened with delighted attention to this eulogium from the lips of his dear young master, whom he had so often dandled on his knee, whom he had been so fortunate as to snatch from a watery grave, and for whom he restrained a stronger affection than for any other being on earth. Sir Philip had long maintained him in ease and comfort, and excused him from every employment, but such as tended to the preservation of his health. Both ladies held out their hands, which he respectfully kissed, and prayed that heaven might bless and reward them for their kindness to their old but grateful servant.

"Now the ceremony of introducing you into the bed-chamber of these fair ladies is over, 'tis time for us to think of proceeding, my old friend, (said Edwin.) If you will assist me in unfastening the trap-door, we will procure lights, and, putting ourselves under your direction, follow wherever you are disposed to lead us."

CHAPTER V.

IT was the intention of Bertrand to open the door of the subterranean passage, which communicated with Mettingham castle; but, before they proceeded far, something rushed past them several times: it was rapid, and their candle threw so feeble a light on the walls which surrounded them, that they could not discover what it was.

They hurried on till they came to the square leading to the dungeons, when their attention was arrested, and their fears increased by the barking of a dog. They hesitated, looked with astonishment at each other, and stopped, as if irresolute whether to return or proceed. In the mean while, the little animal made its appearance, jumped and capered about, as if it rejoiced at seeing them in its dreary habitation, attached itself particularly to Roseline, and seemed to recognize an old and beloved friend.

Roseline took it up in her arms, kissed and caressed it; but how to account for meeting with so beautiful, fond, and gentle a creature was not only matter of surprise but wonder.

"Are you sure, sister, (said Edwin, slyly glancing a look at the pale face and trembling lips of the terrified Madeline,)—are you sure it is a real dog?—May it not be one of the ghosts, who, in such various shapes, are said to haunt these gloomy regions, and disturb the peaceful slumbers of young maidens, born perhaps two hundred years after they had left the world?"

This gentle reproof restored the roses to the fair cheek from which fear had driven them, while Roseline declared it was really and truly the prettiest dog she had ever seen. Bertrand had looked thoughtful, agitated, and confused, from the moment it appeared.

"This dog must have a master, (said Edwin,) and that master must be somewhere near these cells."

"Perhaps (said Bertrand) some daring villain may have found entrance here, either with the hopes of plunder, or to accomplish designs against the castle; let us therefore, for the present, give up attempting to explore the passage; it might be dangerous to unfasten a door which is now our security."

"Had we not better call for help?" said the again-terrified Madeline.

"Not for the world! (interrupted Edwin;)—how should we be able to account to my mother for being in this place, without burthening her mind with ten thousand suspicions? While, telling her our reasons would most assuredly expose our venerable companion to the certain displeasure of my father.—Do you (said he, addressing Bertrand) know if there is any one a prisoner at this time?"

The old many hesitated.—"I know but little—I apprehend it may be so,—but I—I hope you will excuse my talking on a subject that—that—"

"It must assuredly be so, (said Roseline softly to her brother,) and from that cause proceeded the noises which so repeatedly alarmed us."

Again every one stood for a moment irresolute. Edwin, however, fearful of bringing his father's anger on Bertrand, and scorning to tempt the old man to betray any trust reposed in him, or any secret belonging to another, instantly formed his resolution to act with the utmost caution. He proposed to his sister and Madeline to return to their apartment as soon as Bertrand had pointed out the passage which led to the nunnery.—On being shewn the door which might one day enable him to meet his Madeline, and open to give him a gleam of happiness, Roseline snatched up the little dog, pressed him to her bosom, and vowed to release him from captivity.

As soon as they had reached their own apartment, Bertrand, after promising eternal secrecy, took a respectful leave. Edwin accompanied him to his room, then returned to his sister's, and proposed instantly renewing their search.

"This is doing nothing, (said he;) all is still left to conjecture and uncertainty."

"If you mean to go again, (said Madeline,) why did you suffer Bertrand to leave us?"

"From respect to my father and regard to the old man, (he replied;) for should we, my dear Madeline, make any discovery of consequence, with us the secret will rest secure, and, should we be found out, on ourselves alone will fall the displeasure of Sir Philip; but, by this procedure, we empower no one either to betray his secrets or our own. We will, however, carry back with us this little stranger, (continued he, pointing to the dog, who was sleeping on a cushion which Roseline had placed for him before the fire,) and, when we set him down, we will follow wherever he may chose to lead us: if he be attached to any miserable being confined in one of the cells or dungeons, we may depend upon his returning to his usual habitation."

Once more the trap-door was lifted up; once more the party descended into regions like those of the grave, while the mouldering walls, glittering with the dews of night, and rendered humid with the unwholesome damps of the situation, hung loose and disjointed over their heads, as if to threaten instant destruction.

Turning into a passage which led to a contrary direction to that they had before entered, and which was somewhat wider and less dismal than the other, Roseline sat down the dog, who ran nimbly away, as if well acquainted with the path. They followed with the utmost caution, observing a profound silence. The dog went before them the whole length of the passage, then turned suddenly down a few steps, at the bottom of which a door stood half-open: he rushed in, and appeared to them to stop at some distance. Instantly they heard him growl and bark, and this determined them to proceed.

They passed through two small apartments decently furnished, and, just as they reached an inner door, at which the dog had demanded admittance, they saw it slowly open, and a faint voice appeared to chide the guiltless wanderer for his long, long absence, and then to caress him with fondness.

Edwin, knowing, if he hesitated to proceed, the fears of his companions would increase by the delay, gently tapped at the door. For a minute all was silent; he then gave some louder raps. The same person very soon opened the door, of whom they had caught a transient glimpse when he had granted admittance to the dog. He was evidently alarmed, and in tremulous and terrified accents inquired who was there,—what was the matter,—and what errand brought them? At the same time brandishing a sword, which he had hastily snatched from a chair which stood near him.

"Whoever you are (continued he) that have found a way to this den of misery, you may safely enter, unless you come to add farther oppressions, and inflict additional woes on the head of an injured and guiltless sufferer. If you come with such diabolical intentions, be assured of this,—I will no longer be a passive or silent spectator of such unheard of barbarity, but give up a life in his defence which cruelty has rendered a worthless sacrifice. Forego then your designs, and know he will not long be either a burthen or reproach to his unnatural parent and sordid oppressors."

"We come with no design to injure or oppress, (said Edwin.) We inhabit this castle, and were led by the curiosity incidental to youth into these horrid regions.—Chance conducted us into these apartments, without knowing, they were inhabited.—We wish not to alarm or interrupt any one, but of this be assured, if you will inform us how we can serve you, or render your situation more comfortable, we will gladly contribute all in our power to do so. Your countenance does not appear stamped with guilt, and your determination to protect the injured speaks a noble mind."

The sword was instantly laid down,—the door flew open,—and they were requested to enter by one, who told them his life and courage were only valuable so long as they would enable him to watch and protect the best and most beloved of masters.

Reader, guess, if it be possible, the surprise and astonishment of our trembling and compassionate adventurers, when they beheld an elegant young man, whose countenance was as prepossessing as his situation was interesting, wrapped in a striped-satin morning-gown, which reached to his feet, with his hair hanging in graceful ringlets, and nearly concealing a face pale as death, lying on a kind of couch, and to all appearance in the last stage of a consumption.[17]

On the entrance of Edwin, he took but little notice, but, on seeing Roseline and her friend advance, he looked up, and attempted to rise, but was not equal to the effort, and instantly sunk down in a state of apparent insensibility. Roseline, more agitated and terrified by the whole of this unaccountable and affecting scene than she would have been at the sight of the ghost she had almost expected to meet, flew to support him. She was assisted by Edwin and Madeline, and their united endeavours soon restored the poor sufferer to life and an imperfect sense of his situation.

Having now no longer any fears, he fixed his large blue eyes on the stranger,—wondered from whence they came,—how all this could happen,—and to what blessed chance it was owing that he saw himself attended and consoled by two celestial beings, for as such he actually considered them; while the pure drops of genuine and the gentlest pity fell softly on his emaciated hand, he raised the precious gems of compassion to his lips, sighed deeply, then, looking earnestly in the face of Roseline, with a smile of doubt and anguish once more sunk down in a state of insensibility, unable to bear the weight of his own agitated and contending feelings.

The attendant, who had strictly observed the whole of this extraordinary scene, now approached to assist in recovering his master. Edwin hastened to his sister's apartment to procure proper restoratives; they were applied with their usual success, and the change they produced gave new life and spirits to all around, particularly Roseline, who concluded they arrived merely to witness his dying moments, and hear him breathe his last sigh.

She was still supporting his languid head on her knee; his hand rested on her arm, his eyes were fixed upon her face, his lips moved, and the words "kind, consoling angel" were all they could understand.

---

[17] Associated with tuberculosis, consumption is the generic name given to individuals whose lives waste away due to an unknown or unnamed illness. Manifesting itself in listlessness, loss of appetite and great muscular weakness- consumptive individuals can linger on the brink of death for years. Usually striking women, Cathy Linton in *Wuthering Heights*, Helen Burns in *Jane Eyre*, and most notably Isabel Vane in *East Lynne*, the death-bed scenes of consumptive women and children became the height of the Victorian Sensation novel. However, in *Bungay Castle* the consumptive individual is a male, Walter, the frail and weak youth discovered in the castle's dungeon.

"What can this mean? (said Edwin;) who is your master?—who brought him here? And of what crime has he been guilty that he is sentenced to such a place as this?"—

"I am bound (replied the servant) by the most solemn oath to silence and secresy. By complying with these conditions I obtained leave to attend him. Were I at liberty to speak, I could a tale unfold would tempt you to curse the world, and even detest those claims which bind man to man. You would be ready to forego the ties of nature, and shun society.—Time will, it must develop the whole of this mystery."

"But my father!" said Edwin.

"Your father, sir, like my dear unhappy master, is blameless and innocent: he has been deceived like many others."

"But why (cried Roseline) are you thus shut our from the world, and banished society?—why, if innocent, is not this poor sufferer placed in a situation more likely to restore him to health?—why thus cruelly deprived not only of liberty, light, and air, but of every other necessary comfort?"[18]

"A higher power has willed it should be so," said the stranger, whose unreserved manner, superior language, honest and open countenance, found an instant passport to their hearts, confirmed their belief, and banished every suspicious doubt of his sincerity.

"Are you involved in the crimes of which this gentleman is suspected?" inquired Madeline.

"No, madam; my only crime is my attachment to him. I am here by my own voluntary choice, and were they to convey him a thousand fathoms deeper in the earth, I would not, unless I were compelled, ever leave him till his noble and guiltless soul was summoned to appear before a more just and merciful tribunal than he has found on earth."

"A thousand blessings on you! (cried Roseline, a tear trembling in each expressive eye,) for shewing this care and god-like compassion to one so helpless and oppressed.—Brother, surely we may, without deserving reproach, unite our endeavours with those of this friendly stranger, to soften the pangs of misery and death, be they inflicted by whom they may."

"You ought to do so, (cried the lovely Madeline, whose gentle spirit was awakened into action by the scene before her.)—As fellow-creatures, and the children of the same Almighty Parent, it is our duty to assist each other; but we should do more, nor remain coldly

---

[18] Roseline is being quite melodramatic here- She neglects to notice that though deprived of freedom, Walter is well dressed, living in a furnished apartment, and fed. The peasants of the era have a much harder life. Perhaps Roseline is demonstrating the extent to which the walls of Bungay Castle have protected her.

indifferent to sufferings which, if we cannot entirely remove, we may in some measure alleviate."

"And we will do so! (cried the generous and animated Edwin.)— You too, my honest fellow, (turning to the servant,) shall share in our kind offices. You deserve the thanks of every good Christian, and to be immortalized for your faithful attachment to one so helpless and unable to reward you.—But how is this?" observing the invalid had sunk into a gentle and quiet sleep, like the peaceful slumber of an infant.[19]

"This has been the case for some weeks. His spirits depressed by the corroding anguish which preys upon his mind, his body has become a victim to the conflict, and the soul of my master will soon, by quitting this earthly tenement, escape the farther persecutions of his enemies. Much, much as I love him, I should rejoice at his release."

The words trembled on his tongue, and the tear of manly compassion rolled down his cheek.

"Has he no one to attend him? (said Roseline, looking at him with eyes that beamed with all the heavenly animation which at that moment throbbed around her heart;) has he no advice?"

"Only such as I can give him, madam. Poor and ignorant as I am, he has never been allowed any other physician, or better tutor than myself; but I trust, if the Almighty would again restore him to health, he would now meet with those who would assist in performing a task for which I was never calculated."

"Has he no bed to sleep on?" cried Roseline, gently removing his languid head upon a cushion that laid on a couch, without awakening him.

"There is one in the inner apartment, but this being the most comfortable and airy room, he will not leave it."

"I will fetch some pillows."

She did so; they were instantly placed under his head. Still he slept as if he were never to awake again.

"In the morning, (said Roseline,) at the foot of the stairs, which you will find by turning to the left, at the end of this passage, I will leave some few trifles and comfortable cordials, which I hope will be of service."

"And to-morrow night, at about this time, you may expect us again, (said Edwin.) I hope your master will then have shaken off this death-like slumber, and be able to converse with us."

---

[19] In her descriptions, Bonhote feminizes and infantilizes Walter. Tearful, weak and passive, he is a striking comparison Edwin's robust health. Even his servant sheds a tear of 'manly compassion' while Walter tenderly licks the fallen tears from his hand. Volume II of the novel transitions into a Bildungsroman as it follows Walter's growth into gaining masculinity and adulthood.

"Perhaps he may, (replied Albert, the name of this faithful servant;) but he never talks much. I had taught him to read, but they took away our books, and since that time I am afraid he has lost the remembrance of the little knowledge he had of reading. He has lately learned to play a few simple tunes on the lute,—that sometimes amuses him."

"We will bring you some books, (said Roseline,) and surely, Edwin, you and I can assist Albert in the delightful task of restoring by friendship what has been lost by cruelty."

Albert informed them they were regularly served with their meals, but never saw the person who brought them, all intercourse with any one being forbidden, to prevent the possibility of discovery or escape; but he said, they had better food and more indulgences than had been allowed them in their former prison, which consisted only of one room.

The party now retired with the utmost caution, lest they should disturb the apparently-peaceful slumbers of the prisoner, and deprive him of his only refuge from misery.

Before they parted, Roseline and her brother, actuated by the same generous feelings in behalf of this unfortunate young man, and his equally unfortunate companion, satisfied, should there be found any thing in their conduct to condemn, (which they could not bring them selves to think,) in their present situation there was much to pity, resolved to unite in their endeavours of relieving their miseries, and softening the rigours of a confinement, of which they knew not the cause; but they were told, the object who had most excited their compassion was innocent, and therefore they determined to think him so till his own conduct, or an explanation from any other quarter, proved him otherwise. It is true, they had nothing on which to found their belief but the word of a stranger, and him they found in the humble capacity of a servant; but, though a stranger, he had, by his simple, modest, and unaffected language, given ample proofs in their opinion of his sincerity.

They now left the cells, and retired instantly to bed, —dreamed of the prisoner, and sometimes imagined they could distinguish his groans; in fact, they thought and talked of him, and him only.

Early in the morning, Roseline carried every little nicety she could procure, and left them at the foot of the stairs,—then hurried back to her room, not daring to stop and make inquiries, lest the person who supplied the object of her pity with his daily food should discover and betray her benevolent designs.

Madeline was now making a rapid progress in her recovery, and was every hour in fear of receiving a summons from the abbess to return to the nunnery. Edwin participated in all her fears, and lamented, in the language of tender affection, the cruel necessity which compelled her to leave the castle, protesting neither walls nor vows should long divide them, and swearing to release her from a situation, which, through sanctioned by religion, only bigotry, superstition, and priestcraft, could justify; which he knew would not only destroy all his prospects of happiness, but, as he could not disbelieve the fascinating hopes he had not absolutely been forbidden to cherish, the happiness also of a beloved object, dearer to him than life, without whom fortune, honour, prosperity, and youth, would be robbed of all their value.

The next day, accompanied by Bertrand, Edwin stole by another entrance into the lower recesses of the castle, not mentioning a word of the prisoner, and carefully avoiding that quarter in which he was confined. They first explored the subterraneous passage, leading to the nunnery, and found fewer impediments in their way than they expected. They easily gained an entrance into the chapel, having fixed upon an hour when they knew all the fathers and nuns would be engaged in their cells. They found the opening under the organ, and in that part of the chapel appropriated to the use of the nuns, the door being concealed from observation by a very curious tomb, belonging to the ancient family of De G—.

They entered next the passage leading to Mettingham-castle, and determined to see the whole of it. Here they met with many difficulties: in some places huge stones had fallen from the walls,—in others the arch-way was so low they were almost obliged to crawl,— while toads, snakes, and various kind of reptiles impeded their progress when, at length, they reached the end of this wonderful labyrinth, the production of labour and art, they found themselves close to the ballium of Mettingham-castle, and under a strong machicolated and embattled gate.

They now discovered another short passage, which was terminated by a door that opened to the outer ballium, and through which the cavalry could sally in any case of emergency. They ventured cautiously to look around them. Edwin's mind, however, was chiefly occupied by one dear object, and he secretly rejoiced at having found the means of escaping with Madeline, should the obstinacy of her parents, or the ambition of his own, leave him no other resource.

He likewise, in the course of the day, but unaccompanied by any one, opened the door on the stair-case leading to the South tower. He felt a kind of repugnance at taking this step, but determined, as matters were now circumstanced, to go through the whole of this unpleasant business at once, that nothing might be left to conjecture. He also recollected that it would not only put an end to that restless curiosity which had long dwelt upon his mind, but enable him to judge whether it would be possible to remove the dying prisoner into a more airy and convenient room, without the hazard of a discovery.

This wing of the castle he knew was totally unoccupied, as in his boyish days he had frequently, and at all times gone that way to the ramparts to lodge his playthings in a secret apartment in one of the highest towers, and never in his peregrination had met with a human being.

On attempting first to open the door, he was a good deal startled at the noise it occasioned, and was almost buried beneath the heap of cobwebs and dirt which fell and enveloped him in a cloud of dust.— Some birds too, that had here found a safe asylum, flew in terror around him. Not willing to disturb them more than was necessary, he unfastened a narrow casement, to give those an opportunity of escaping who wished to obtain their liberty. He then stole softly and cautiously across the room to an opposite door, which opened without any difficulty, and he entered a second apartment, much larger and more commodious than the first. It was hung with ancient tapestry, on which time and moth had made many depredations; but, in some parts of it, the full-length figures remained perfect, and the colours retained some of their beautiful shades. He soon discovered that it represented the most striking and interesting scenes in the well-known history of Hero and Leander, from his first seeing her, in the temple of Venus, at Sestos, in Thrace, till the last closing scene of their unfortunate loves.

The figures of the lovers were fine, and in excellent preservation, and the tapestry was of so superior a kind, that it gave as full force and expression to the faces and drapery as the finest painting could have conveyed. The temple, the palace, the turret, and the Hellespont, upon whose waves the rising and setting sun were alternately reflected, with the downy swan, in snowy dignity, which was seen laving on its bosom were admirably depicted.

The nurse, or attendant of the faithful Hero stood at full length on the edge of the water, which gently undulated near the walls of the palace, pointing to the waves, and as if in the act of telling her fond, impatient mistress her lover was coming, while she, with modest sweetness, seemed fearful of stealing a look at the element which contained a treasure dearer to her soul than the whole of her ambitious father's dominions.

In another part, he saw the lifeless body of Leander, and the despairing Hero in the act of throwing herself into the Hellespont, which had unfortunately proved the grave of her lover.

Edwin stood a long time, silently admiring this pathetic tale: it had an instantaneous effect upon his feelings; it served to remind him of the difficulties he should have to encounter in his attachment to Madeline, and he could have kissed the senseless portrait of the old Egyptian woman for her kind and faithful attentions to the persecuted lovers.

In the middle of the room stood a square table, on which were carelessly spread a number papers. Four massy silver candlesticks were likewise placed upon it, each of which contained a wax candle, that had never been lighted, and an old writing, to which was annexed a vast many seals, laid folded up under them.

This he concluded was the mystic bond which held in captivity the restless spirit it was supposed to confine. Edwin opened and attempted to read it. In some parts the writing was defaced, and the whole of the language so unintelligible he very soon replaced it in its former situation, imagining that, if the ghost was not to regain its liberty till the bond could be read, it would rest in peace for ever, and suffer others to do the same.

In the chimney stood an antique grate, that had once been bright, and still shewed some of its brilliant features through the rust by which it was enveloped. A few chairs were standing here and there, but they were falling to decay. He then opened another door, which led him into a vaulted chamber, in which were placed the tattered remains of a bed, that had been handsome, and could be repaired. A book of devotion was lying upon it. The windows were high and narrow, admitting but little light, notwithstanding which they were secured by iron bars of immense thickness, so strongly, that, had they been lower, it would have been impossible for the arm of the strongest man to remove or shake them.

This led him to conclude it was originally designed for the security of prisoners of rank, its distance from the ground precluding any communication with the people on guard; and he shuddered as he recollected how many, like the poor prisoner in the cells, might have lingered away their wretched existence in this very apartment, in the hopeless expectation of meeting with a release.

He next carefully searched in every part of the room, to discover if there was not a more secret entrance, but found none.—He put the key into his pocket, as he had before done that of the trap-door, and in the morning, unobserved by Bertrand, had the precaution not to lock the door of the subterraneous passage, leaving it well secured by the bolts and bars which were on the inside.

He now hastened to replace all the rest of the keys in the repository from whence he had taken them, and was satisfied those he retained in his own possession would not be missed by his father or any one else.

After this he returned to join the family, and said not a word of what he had seen, nor the plans which floated in his own mind, in the consequence of the morning peregrinations he had taken.

CHAPTER VI.

IN the course of the day, Roseline asked a thousand questions, with apparent indifference, of De Clavering, respecting the nature of consumptive cases, their symptoms, progress, &c. and how people ought to manage themselves in regard to diet, who were confined in the damp regions of a dungeon, or immured in the narrow precincts of a prison; to all which she received such plain, direct, and experienced answers, as the cherished hopes would enable her, with the approbation of heaven, to be the humble means of restoring to health, or a more promising degree of convalescence, the interesting object whose secret sufferings had stimulated her to make these unusual inquiries; and what gave new life and added energy to her benevolent hopes was the arrival of a letter from Sir Philip to Lady de Morney, in which he was reluctantly obliged to inform her that his stay in London was unfortunately prolonged, and he was sorry to find his absence from the castle was likely to be protracted a considerable length of time from the slow progress of the law, and the difficulties thrown in the way by his opponents. This account would have given her pain a few days before; it was now a source of pleasure, which produced the most sanguine expectations of preserving, under Providence, the life of a fellow-creature, or, at least, of rendering its closing scene less hopeless and more comfortable.

A sensibility, like that which was lodged in the bosom of the artless and innocent Roseline, I would with all my sex to possess. So far from tempting her to run from misery, it led her in search of it, and, when found, it awakened every gentle passion of the mind into immediate and resolute action; while the fictitious feeling, the affected sensibility of a modern miss is confined to kicking, fainting, or squalling at sight of a wretched object, and the little they may really have will evaporate in the trouble of acting their part so as to impose on the minds of others an unjust and sense of their own delicate and extreme compassion.

How much might men as well as women add to the dignity of nature by never attempting to destroy her! In the formation of man, God lent his own image; how would it astonish, how would it excite the indignation of the almost unenlightened savage, if he met with any one so foolish as to suppose they could improve that image by the ridiculous distortions and grimaces of affectation! And how would he be diverted, could he see the devoted slaves of fashion so disguise the human form, that the head is frequently increased to twice its original size,—the waist sometimes dwindled to a span, at others entirely lost; then again restored with such protuberances as even to render the character suspected;—and at times our modern beaux and belles are seen so completely in masquerade, that it is a matter of some difficulty to distinguish one sex from the other,—a circumstance that might be attended with ludicrous, if not dangerous, consequences.

As the spirits of Lady de Morney were much depressed by the receipt of Sir Philip's letter, every one exerted themselves to amuse her. They sung, they danced, and the tale went merrily round. De Willows and De Clavering appeared unusually animated, and Hugh Camelford fared the worse for their exertions. They roused the fiery blood of the brave Cambrian, and then cooled it again by a well-turned compliment. They likewise so powerfully assailed Elwyn to give a dinner he had long promised them, that the following day was fixed for the treat, and his apartments were prepared for the ladies, the gentlemen with one voice agreeing not to go without them. They also entered into a confederacy to drink till they had emptied the miser's last bottle, determining to have one good frolic, as they despaired of ever obtaining a second at his expence.

Madeline received a few lines from Agnes de Clifford, to inform her, that, by what she could learn from one of the old nuns, the abbess expected her return to the nunnery the following week, as father Anselm had signified his disapprobation of her longer absence. This gave great concern to the young people, which did not pass unobserved by Lady de Morney, who gently blamed them, adding, as they had been so long indulged with the company of their friend, they ought to submit to the will of the father without repining or reluctance.

After a day which appeared to Roseline the longest she had ever lived, the hour arrived in which they were to revisit the dark abode of misery and oppression. They found Albert impatiently waiting for them in the passage, near the foot of the stairs, almost despairing of their return. Every one carried something for the use and gratification of the prisoner. Edwin was loaded with books; Madeline with sweetmeats, wine, and cakes; Roseline with some white meats and soup. She had likewise prepared a reviving mixture from a recipe of De Clavering's, extracted from a variety of healing herbs, admirably calculated to restore health and spirits to the fragile frame of the languid sufferer.

Albert informed them that his master considered the whole of what had passed the preceding evening as a dream;—had repeatedly mentioned the good and consoling angels, who had condescended to visit the couch of a wretch who, almost from his birth, had been an outcast from society; and, notwithstanding he assured him he would see them again, he could obtain no credit to his assertion, nor divert his mind from the idea that it was a warning from heaven, merely to prepare him for a summons before its awful tribunal.

"Hasten, my good friend, (said Roseline,) and undeceive him, by letting him know we wait here to convince him, if he will receive us, that we are mere mortals like himself."

Albert did not stop for a second command to execute a commission he eagerly wished. They followed him; the little dog ran out, and greeted their arrival with every testimony of joy it was in its nature to express, and they were requested to walk in the moment they reached the door of the apartment. They were not only surprised, but highly gratified at observing the visible change for the better which a few hours had made in the countenance of their new friend, whose dependence on their good offices, for many of the necessary comforts of life, and total seclusion from the world, made very forcible claims on their hearts.

He arose on their entrance. Edwin flew to embrace him. Madeline held out her hand, which he gently pressed between his; but, observing that Roseline's was likewise extended, he dropped the hand of her friend, and eagerly caught her's as if he were afraid it should be wrested from him.

"I would fain tell you what I feel at this moment, (said he, faintly and fearfully;) but I do not know a language to make my-self understood.—This I know, that yesterday I wished to die, and be forgotten even by Albert; but now I think, if I could have you always with me, (stealing a look at Roseline,) hear you talk, and see you smile, I could be content to live for ever, even in this sad place. If all other women are like you, how charming must be the world, in which Albert says there are a vast many! I have often told him, and he knows why, that I never should like a woman; (here he smiled expressively on Albert.) I thought they were all very cruel and very ugly creatures, therefore I concluded, when I first saw you, that you were angels, or kind and celestial spirits, who came down from heaven to receive my soul, and carry it to a place of rest."

"Indeed, my good sir, (said Roseline,) you were never more mistaken. We are like the generality of our sex, but much inferior to many. We broke in upon you unexpectedly, and you judged merely from feelings too highly raised, which originated from surprise, and were in part confirmed by the effect they had on the susceptibility of your nature and the seclusion of your situation.—I must now entreat you to take a few spoonfuls of a mixture I have brought you. I am afraid it is not very pleasant to the taste, but I hope and trust it will be conducive to your recovery."

She poured some into a tea-cup, and presented it to him; he drank it immediately. They then produced the more grateful treat they had brought with them; he ate a little cake, and some sweetmeats, with an avidity and greediness that shocked them,—said they were very fine, and much better than the liquor.

Edwin next gave him some books, which he opened with eagerness, seemed vastly delighted with the prints, but shook his head on finding himself unable to read their contents. He turned over a few of the leaves, and seemed a good deal chagrined. Edwin explained their titles, and gave him a few outlines of the works.

"Albert can read them," said he.

"I hope you will soon be able to read them yourself, (replied Edwin:) we will join with Albert in instructing you."

"Ah! (cried he, shaking his head,) you will soon grow weary of one so ignorant, so dull as I am; (his eye glanced at Roseline.)—I belong to no one,—I have no friend but poor Albert; he will not leave me to die alone in such a place as this."

"My dear sir, (said Albert,) talk not of dying the very first hour you are beginning to live, I yet trust we shall see many happy years."

He looked melancholy, whispered something they could not perfectly understand, and appeared wholly lost in his own painful reflections. Edwin again addressed him.—At hearing his voice he started, and gazed on him with a wild and vacant stare, as if he had never seen him before, looked at his dress, then at his own,—seemed struck by the contrast, and a faint smile came over his features, but it was the smile of internal sadness.

It will not be thought superfluous, perhaps, if we stop a few moments, in order to describe, as well as we are able, the face, person, and dress, of this unfortunate young man. His complexion, from never having been exposed to either air or sun, was whiter and more delicate than that of Madeline: his large blue eyes were shaded by deeply fringed eye-lashes, and arched with eyebrows which the nicest pencil of the painter could not have improved. His face was oval, his nose aquiline, and his mouth so exquisitely formed, as to give grace and expression to all the other features: he was much thinner, but some inches taller than Edwin; yet the whole of his appearance shewed that confinement and ill health had stolen, in their thievish and destroying progress, many of the natural graces from his face and person: his hair waved in careless ringlets over his forehead, and hung down some length on his shoulders; he was still wrapped in a loose morning gown, wore slippers, and his linen was of the finest texture.

With some difficulty, but not without the assistance of Albert, they drew him by degrees into something like conversation; but he did not appear perfectly to understand all they said; and, when they mentioned the days beginning to lengthen, the increasing and reviving influence of the sun, the beauty of the moon and stars, he sighed,—wished he could see and admire them as other men did, and inquired if they thought any but himself and Albert were denied so many of the blessings which he had been told God had given for the use and benefit of all his creatures. Edwin replied, painful as it was to recollect, he had no doubt but at that moment thousands of his fellow-mortals sustained even greater hardships and deprivations than himself.

"Must you and these sweet creatures ever do the same?"

He hoped not, but fortune was so fickle in the favours she bestowed, and every thing so uncertain, it was impossible to tell what might or might not happen in the course of a few years.

"It is surely very strange, (said the prisoner,) and I think those people, whose hard hearts and hands contrived and made prisons, are the most proper, indeed the only persons who should be forced to inhabit them."

This observation produced a general smile, which they hoped would pass unnoticed, but it did not escape him, and he said, while a faint colour flushed his cheek, he knew he was very ignorant; but he begged they would not despise him for so great a misfortune. After this he only ventured to ask a few questions, but at the moment of doing so seemed to shrink into himself, and to be astonished at his own temerity. This shyness and reserve they trusted would wear off, as he became familiarized to their visits and conversation; they therefore took no notice of his absence or timidity, but endeavoured by every attention to draw him from his own painful and humiliating reflections, and by a few well-timed praises strove to give him self-confidence.

After staying as long as time and the nature of their visit would permit, and giving proper directions to Albert in regard to the medicines and nourishing restoratives they had brought with them, they reluctantly arose to depart. Observing their design, he held his hands before his eyes, to prevent his seeing them go, and exclaimed, "Don't, don't leave me!—I cannot bear it. I never shall see you again:—you will forget me, you will leave me for ever!"

His extreme agitation alarmed and affected them all. They knew not how to go, and yet to stay longer might risk a discovery.

"Speak, Roseline, (said Edwin,) and if possible quiet these distressing apprehensions."

Roseline, as soon as she could sufficiently command the tone of her voice, took hold of his trembling hand, which was cold as death, and gently intreated him to hear her with composure. He looked at her with passive acquiescence, and she proceeded to assure him that it was their united and determined intention to repeat their visits as often as their own and his situation would permit: but that, for his sake particularly, they were under the necessity of acting with caution, and carefully guarding against the possibility of a discovery.—If he were so much affected when they left him, they must visit him less frequently than they wished.

"Ah! no, no;—do not think of me, or what I may feel: that is of no consequence, only say you will come again and again."

"On my honour we will, and continue to do so while you remain an involuntary resident in this castle."

"I am satisfied, (said he, sighing inwardly as he spoke; then, fixing his eyes on Roseline,)—if you would come every day,—talk to me, and look at me thus gently,—if you would continue to pity my weakness and pardon my ignorance, I should not think this a prison but a paradise, and could be content to end my useless days in this dungeon."

This pathetic address Roseline could not acquire sufficient resolution to answer, and, while her heart felt intolerably oppressed, the silent tears, which stole softly down her cheek, explained the nature of her feelings. Madeline, finding the scene was become too painful, rose, and bade him good night. Roseline gently withdrew the hand which for some moments had been clasped in his, and Edwin, seeing the necessity of immediately retiring, tenderly bade him farewell.—

Finding they were resolute to depart, he dropped on his knees by the couch, and concealed his face in the pillow. They insisted on Albert's not leaving his master, and hurried back to their own apartment in a state of mind difficult to be described, carrying with them a variety of feelings, which, though new and painful, they wished should be retained in their remembrance.

As it was now two hours beyond their usual time of going to bed, the great clock having struck the awful hour of twelve, Edwin, without stopping to make any comments on the scene that had so recently occurred, instantly took his leave. Madeline put on her night-clothes, and, after taking a few minutes, sunk into the leathean arms of sleep. Not so her friend; sleep deserted her pillow: in vain she sought and wished for its approach, to obliterate new and uncomfortable sensations. It was extremely odd that the image of the prisoner haunted her imagination with such persevering obstinacy, that, notwithstanding she closed her eyes, she could not exclude him from her mental sight; and, what was still more strange and unaccountable, though she saw he was less polished than those with whom she was accustomed to associate, without education, and entirely ignorant of the world,—a prisoner for she knew not what, yet still she thought, and was extremely angry with herself for so doing, that he was the most handsomest man, and had the most prepossessing and elegant form she had ever seen. His manner too!—could any thing be more captivating than the manners of this uninformed son of nature, whom cruelty and injustice had immured in the dungeons of her father's castle!

A few hours sleep might, and she trusted would, restore her to a more just and rational way of thinking; if not, he who caused her judgment to mislead her would perhaps be the means of its returning to its proper station.

We will now therefore leave her to try an experiment, which has often produced as powerful an effect, and, stealing the mind by a temporary oblivion from the objects of its sudden partiality, has likewise stolen, by the dawn of the succeeding morning, all recollection of woes, which, in a moment of unguarded susceptibility, had found a passage to the heart. Whether it had this convenient soporific, and benumbing property on the mind of Roseline, we are not now at liberty to declare; but, if it should not, we hope some of our readers will make allowance for the unfashionable taste of a young lady, who lived so many ages before themselves; who was unhacknied in the devious paths of life, with a mind unvitiated by pride or the pangs of envy, and who had seen little or nothing of the world beyond the precincts of the castle she inhabited.

CHAPTER VII.

The next day every one prepared with high glee for Elwyn's promised treat and puzzled them selves with various conjectures as to what kind of feast the miser would set before them. Bertha and Hugh Camelford were very busy after something which those who saw them concluded would be productive of mirth or mischief, no two dispositions being more likely to succeed in a cause for which their humourous talents were calculated; while poor Elwyn, in secret but unavailing regret, lamented too late his yielding folly, in having been prevailed on to comply with what he termed a very foolish and unreasonable request, viz. for so many people to dine at his expence: but this he wisely kept to himself, well knowing, if the party understood his sentiments, it would expose him to their whole artillery of wit and ridicule; he therefore made all the preparations for an excellent dinner, but his caution, busy looks, anxiety, and distress, promised a much higher entertainment than his repast could afford.

The company assembled at the proper time, and were seated in due form and order, Lady de Morney at the head, and Elwyn at the bottom of the table; when, having helped most of the party, Camelford requested him to send him a slice of a large raised pie, which made a distinguished figure.

Bertha cried out with well-affected terror, "Don't touch it; I am sure 'tis enchanted; I saw the crust move."

"Child, (cried Lady de Morney,) what do you mean?"

"What I say, madam, for indeed it was lifted up."

"Take care what you are about, Elwyn, (said Camelford,) or, py Cot, you may cut off the head of a conjurer, who has jumped into the pie in honor of your feast."

"Suppose we let De Clavering dissect him, (said De Willows;) he is undoubtedly the best hand at cutting up his own species."

De Clavering, who suspected some joke, cautiously raised up one side of the crust, when, to the astonishment of the party, out jumped a squirrel. Happy in having regained its liberty, it sprang across the table, and immediately made its way into Edeliza's pocket, where it was accustomed to run for shelter. She was shocked at the danger from which her favourite had escaped, caressed the little stranger, and rejoiced at seeing it unhurt.

Every one was surprised and alarmed at the unexpected appearance of poor Pug, while the terror of the master of the ceremonies was somewhat increased, when he saw a dish of blanc mange, which one of the ladies was beginning to help, fall, and a variety of the most beautiful shapes dissolve into water. This produced a general and hearty laugh.

"Fine teceptions these! (said Camelford.)—I suppose we shall find in the rest of the pies lif cats and dogs, and see little Pertha turned into a pillar of salt ."As to Pug, he declared by Cot, Tavy Jones, and the tisel, he never saw a coat run swifter on his belofed Welch mountains, and he would pet five hundred kuineas he would not be peat if put in podily fear.

The dishes were removed, and those originally ordered now brought on to fill their places, which, if not altogether productive of so much mirth, served to gratify a more craving and importunate sense.— Elwyn however was highly provoked and mortified at the tricks which had been played him, and swore, if he could discover the perpetrator, he would insist on an apology, or compel him to take a little cold iron.

"That (said De Clavering) would be rendering your hospitality too profuse. It would not only produce matter for conversation, but in all probability furnish me with a job that puzzle or improve me in the art of surgery; and, as nature has entailed so many diseases on us poor mortals, methinks no reasonable man would wish to increase them."

"But, were it not for the unreasonable, (said De Willows,) you gentleman of the lancet and gallipot would not find sufficient opportunities to employ your genius, and give such proofs of your chirurgical skill and abilities."

"On my poor poty (said Hugh Camelford) I hope their apilities never will be tried. Petter to eat squirrels, as Elwyn would have tempted us to do, than be cutting up one another for pies and pasties!"

De Huntingfield unfortunately whispered to Roseline that he never saw her so unusually serious, adding, he supposed she was thinking of matrimony, and advised her to begin her attacks against Elwyn, while the generous and hospitable fit was upon him; for, if she permitted it to evaporate, Plutus, in all probability would again render every avenue to his heart inaccessible to the power of love.

This remark brought the roses into her cheeks. She however denied having formed any designs on one whose predominant passion set every other at defiance, and declared herself perfectly guiltless of all such hostile intentions. The hint however was sufficient to put her upon her guard, and she exerted herself to prevent any further observations of the like sort.

Madeline, now satisfied that the heart of Edwin was as much the slave of the tender passion as her own, and beat responsive to her every wish, would have relished the cheerful scene, had she not, in the very moment of enjoyment, recollected it was the last time, for perhaps a long tire-some period, that she should make one of the happy party.

Edwin, who guessed the nature of her feelings, sympathized too much with her to be more at ease. De Clavering, who observed them both, gave humourous dissertation on the powers of sympathy, and execrated its effects. The day however passed pleasantly, and the evening concluded with a dance, in which the lively Bertha was permitted to join, and had her favourite Hugh Camelford for a partner.—Edwin withdrew with the ladies at an early hour. The rest of the gentlemen returned with Elwyn to his apartment, much against his inclination, and did not leave him till they had literally fulfilled their agreement of emptying the miser's last bottle; then, consigning him to the care of his servant, with difficulty found their way to their own rooms.

Neither Edwin nor his sister however had forgotten their unfortunate friends. They former had stolen an opportunity of conveying a few nice things to the dungeon, had delivered them to Albert, and spent half an hour with his master, promising to renew his visit in the evening, accompanied by the ladies. This threw a gleam of joy over the countenance of the prisoner, who assured him he would not again distress them by shewing so much reluctance at parting.

Albert was pressed by Edwin to enforce the necessity of his master's endeavouring to recover all that he had lost of his reading, and by that means acquired a proper and useful knowledge of the customs and manners of the world, which would be absolutely essential to the rendering it pleasant, should he ever obtain his freedom, and become an active member of society.

"I shall find but little trouble, sir, (replied this excellent servant,) in doing that which my poor master has himself been so anxious to accomplish ever since he saw you and the sweet ladies, who have made our situation in comparison comfortable. Nature has kindly done much for him, education scarcely any thing. Now I foresee all will be right; he is roused from his lethargy of desponding misery, and laments his own ignorance in language, that shew him truly sensible of it. He has insisted on being better dressed against the evening, and the book has not been five minutes out of his hand since you left him."

"I will give you all the assistance in my power, (said Edwin,) and fortunately at this time my father's absence renders the design less hazardous. I have likewise another plan in my head, which I hope will not only greatly contribute to his comfort, but do much towards the more perfect reestablishment of his health, which I now begin to think is not quite in the hopeless state the alarming situation in which I first saw him led me to imagine."

Edwin next inquired of Albert how his master's wardrobe was furnished. "I recollect (said he) you mentioned his desire of changing dress. I can supply him with any thing he wants."

"In that respect, sir, my master has not occasion to tax your bounty. Toys and fine clothes were never denied, and for a long time they had their influence, and served to amuse him."

"Good God! (said Edwin,) that this mystery could be explained!"

Albert shook his head, and immediately withdrew.

In the evening, Edwin, his sister, and Madeline, visited the prisoner; but, if they were surprised before at the happy alteration a few hours had produced in his looks, how much more so were they now at observing the still greater progress in the improvement both of his health and spirits.—He was drest in the most fashionable stile of the times, with an elegance and neatness that astonished them: every part of his dress was such as was only worn by persons of the highest rank,— his clothes richly trimmed, his stockings silk, and his shoes fastened with gold clasps.

At the approach of Roseline and her friend, his eyes sparkled with delight. In fact, he appeared like one raised from the grave by a miracle,—new fashioned and created. It was visible to all the party that his chief attention was directed to Roseline. He watched her every look, and the language of his artless soul was easily read in every expressive and animated feature.

They were now tolerably cheerful. His fear, reserve, and timidity, began gradually to wear off. He even ventured to address a question to Madeline, and to gaze with tender earnestness on her friend. Edwin, with an arch smile, reminded them it would be time to retire, when Roseline had given proper directions respecting her patient, from whose rapid recovery he foretold she would reap such honours as would firmly establish her reputation, as the first female physician in the world.

"And as the best, the most gentle of her sex," added the prisoner, blushing deeply as he ventured to express his gratitude.—"I owe her more than life,—more than—"

"A truce with your thanks, my good friend, (cried Roseline, now blushing in her turn,) and prove, your value our endeavours to render you more comfortable by taking the utmost care of yourself, and by not permitting your mind to dwell on any circumstance likely to agitate and distress you."

He promised to be directed by his friends, and to follow strictly all their injunctions. Again they could not prevail on themselves to leave him, till the night was pretty far advanced. On receiving a promise from Edwin to visit him again the next morning, and one from the ladies to be with him in the evening, he saw them depart without any violent agitation; yet a visible gloom and reluctance pervaded his features, not to be concealed by one who never had formed an idea that it was either necessary or possible to disguise the feelings, or disavow the sentiments of the heart.

Happy state of unspotted unsuspecting integrity! When no pangs of guilt harass and corrode the mind with unceasing anguish! We can scarcely prevail upon ourselves (when we recollect its incorruptible advantages) to think such an enviable portion of internal peace dearly purchased even with the lots of liberty; for, amidst all his sufferings, our hapless prisoner could not recall one action that hung heavy on his mind, or that awakened the scorpion sting of a reproaching conscience. His life might justly be compared to the spotless pages of a book, whose leaves no blot had yet defiled, but which remained properly prepared to receive the fairest and most lasting impressions.

The expected summons for Madeline's return to the nunnery arrived. However reluctant to obey so unwelcome a mandate, she was obliged to comply. The parting between the lovers was attended with many uncomfortable and unpleasant feelings.—Melancholy presentiments were encouraged, which increased the distresses of the moment. She could not leave the prisoner without shedding many tears. She even envied his situation, and when she first compared it with her own, it did not appear so hopeless and solitary. He still retained one faithful friend, and had lately met with others, who, if not so long known, were equally attached to him: he would likewise see Edwin every day, while she immured in the horrid vale of a nunnery, as inimical to her felicity as those by which he was surrounded had till then proved to his, would be denied even the soothing influence of hope;—that ignis satious of the mind had deserted its post, and left it open to the sad encroachments of fruitless and unavailing regret.— Most severely did she now condemn herself for ever having quitted the holy asylum, in which, if she had not found happiness, she had never felt such conflicts as those she now endured.

Lady de Morney and Roseline accompanied her to the nunnery, and delivered her up to the maternal care of the abbess, and the protection of father Anselm. They both appeared pleased and satisfied with her ready compliance with their commands, and rejoiced to see her look so well. They had suffered great anxiety on her account, and the father, who had visited her frequently during her indisposition, and had cherished but few hopes of her recovery, now told her he trusted she would no more wish to forsake their holy sanctuary, as he doubted not her illness was a penance inflicted by Providence for leaving it at a season so particularly appropriated to the sacred duties of the church.

Roseline, before she left the nunnery, accompanied Madeline to her cell, the abbess having granted her this indulgence. Here they unobserved gave way to the sad luxury of tears. They wept on each other's bosom, and the sobbing Madeline, deaf to the soothing consolations of her sympathizing friend, requested her to present Edwin with her grateful acknowledgements for his many kind attentions, and which in the moment of parting she was unable to express. She hoped he would not forget her, and begged his sister to assure him, that, if she were compelled to take the veil, she should retain his image in her heart, though her life were dedicated to the service of her God. She likewise cautioned Roseline to beware, and guard against the sly and dangerous intrusions of love, which brought with them innumerable sorrows, and never to encourage hopes, as she had done, which she feared would end in disappointment and misery.

Roseline knew these hints alluded to the prisoner: the blush which tinged her cheek convinced her friend she was perfectly understood. Indeed, she had before ventured to tell her, that, in her attentions to relieve the miseries she commiserated, she might become too tenderly a sharer in them, and, in freeing the captive from his fetters, might herself be enslaved. Roseline thanked her friend, but denied the caution being necessary, and instantly took her leave, in order to put an end to a conversation which now became unpleasant, and gave her more pain than she chose to acknowledge.

The evening, as may be supposed, passed slowly and heavily at the castle. Roseline felt unfeigned regret at the departure of her friend, and Edwin found in her absence the deprivation of happiness; yet, as it was unavoidable, he determined as much as possible to conceal his distress from the prying eye of suspicion, and to employ every hour he could command, in the service of the unfortunate prisoner, to whom he felt himself irresistibly and unaccountably attached; but Edwin, amidst his family at the castle, was not less internally wretched than poor Madeline, counting her beads in her silent and solitary cell.

At the usual time Roseline and her brother revisited the interesting object of her compassion. He expressed such rapture at seeing them, and made so many acknowledgments for their friendship, that their minds became insensibly harmonized, and their attention engaged.

Edwin now for the first time proposed removing his friend from the dungeon to the haunted chamber, which no one dared to approach, and which we before mentioned as having an entrance from the South tower. Roseline obtained permission of her mother to keep possession of the apartment into which she had accompanied Madeline; therefore they thought his removal could be easily accomplished without any risk of a discovery. It was agreed that Albert should attend the cells in order to take away the provision regularly carried there. All these matters settled, the following evening was appointed for the accomplishment of their purpose, at the same time Edwin cherished the most sanguine hopes that, with the assistance of Albert, and by means of the subterraneous passage, he might sometimes obtain a stolen interview with Madeline.

The next night Edwin, his sister, and Albert, accompanied the prisoner to his destined apartment; but to describe his gratitude and joy, at finding himself in a situation so comfortable and airy, would be impossible. Every thing was new and delightful, and in the morning, when the light (which but dimly enlivened his chamber on his arrival) broke in upon his astonished sight, his raptures were alarming, and his faithful attendant, with the utmost difficulty, prevailed on him to confine them within the bounds of moderation, and cautiously to indulge himself in looking at objects so surprising, but to other people so familiar, that they seldom could spare a moment to contemplate them.

When he viewed the sun, from one of the windows of his room, rising in its utmost splendor, had not Albert prevented him, he had fallen on his knees, and worshipped the brilliant luminary.—He observed the birds with ecstacy, as they lightly skimmed through the boundless regions of the air, and listened with a kind of throbbing agitation as the lark warbled forth her morning oraisons, and, not till he had shed tears, could he reduce his feelings to any degree of composure. He admired the trees; his eyes rested on some of the distant hills, and he told Albert he did not think the world had been so large and fine a place. He next amused himself with looking round his apartment, and at every little interval gave way to the effusions of genuine transport.

Can it be wondered that so helpless a being should feel, on experiencing such a change, more than mere language could express! Liberated from misery by the benevolence of strangers,—a thousand comforts bestowed which he had despaired of ever tasting, his gratitude was as unlimited as his joy, and I am sure all my readers will pardon him for still continuing to think his benefactors more than mortal; yet at times he would recollect, with a sigh of trembling regret, the dangers to which they exposed themselves in order to make him happy.—Their parents, too, might shut them in a dungeon for their disobedience. These reflections fortunately abated the fervour of his high wrought feelings, or in all probability he would have brought on a return of those complaints which had so much interested his young friends in his behalf.—In a few hours he became more composed, and endeavoured to remark every thing around him with serenity. As he was now situated, Edwin and his sister could see him several times a day without inconvenience or danger, and, to guard against any surprise, they had taken care to lock the door at the foot of the stairs, strongly fastened it within-side, and concealed the key, that none of the family might wander that way.

In the evening, a new scene presented itself to the sight of the prisoner. The moon and stars were pointed out to him by Edwin. At first he mistook the moon for another sun, less brilliant, but as beautiful. The stars he called little suns, and attempted to count their number; and, while his eyes were raised in silent rapture to the spangled firmament, he inquired why so much more pains had been taken to decorate the heavens for the night, when mortals slept, than for the day, when all nature was awake to wonder and adore. So delighted was he with the sombre beauties of this all astonishing scene, that it was with the utmost difficulty, after Edwin left him, that Albert could prevail upon him to think of retiring to rest. No sooner however was he convinced that his faithful attendant had lost in the arms of sleep all remembrance of those scenes which kept him waking, than he softly stole to the window, where he remained till the dews of night and the cold blasts of an easterly wind drove him again to his bed.

The few necessary articles which had been allowed in his former abode were now removed to his present one, and such added as would tend to his comfort and convenience. As his food in the dungeon had been conveyed to him by means of a turning cupboard, his having vacated it could not be known so long as Albert attended at the proper times to receive it; and, Edwin having shewn him another secret way, which led from under the stairs in the South tower to his old habitation, he would be able to go as often as he pleased, without any danger of being discovered.

It was now two months after the prisoner's removal before Sir Philip de Morney was able to fix a time for his return. A letter then arrived, in which he mentioned, that, by the end of another fortnight, he hoped to reach the castle. He informed Lady de Morney that he should bring a friend with him for whom he had the highest regard, and he trusted she would make such necessary preparations for his reception, as would serve not only to prove the sincerity of his attachment, but the high respect and esteem in which he was held by the rest of the family; telling her it was no less a personage than Baron Fitzosbourne, whose friendship had done him much honour, and in whose society he found pleasure.

Lady de Morney, who perfectly understood by her husband's letter, how anxious he was that his friend should be received with the utmost splendour and hospitality, gave such orders as she hoped would please the one and gratify the other.

In the mean while, the prisoner made such rapid improvements, as astonished and delighted his youthful instructors. He was indefatigable in storing his mind with all the knowledge the best authors could impart. With returning health his memory regained its former power, and all the natural and brilliant faculties of his mind recovered their usual strength, and proved he was endowed with more than common capacity and genius. His elegant form, animated features,—the serene, ensnaring gentleness of his manners, and the mild sweetness of his disposition, unfolded themselves by degrees, and endeared him beyond expression to his friends.

As a curious and rare plant, guarded by the active hand, and watched by the careful eye of the gardener, raises or depresses his hopes at first putting forth its tender blossoms, till a kind of congenial season brings it to maturity, and its beauties, suddenly bursting on the sight, prove an ample reward for his fostering care,—so did the heart of Roseline expand and rejoice at every proof the prisoner gave of the goodness of his disposition, and the superior excellence of his understanding.

It was clearly visible to Edwin and to Albert that a mutual passion united the prisoner and Roseline, while every fleeting hour served more and more to endear them to each other. Edwin, already entangled in the toils of hopeless love, and enduring all the pangs of despair and apprehension, trembled for the fate of a sister for whom he felt an uncommon degree of fraternal affection, but to whom he could not prevail on himself to mention a subject so delicate and distressing. The prisoner made no attempt to conceal his ardent love for Roseline:—it was an effort as far beyond his comprehension as his power, and, though he made no formal declaration, every word, look, and action, betrayed the situation of his heart. Of the world he was totally ignorant; of marriage he had not even thought,—that being a subject on which they had never conversed, and his own situation, desperate and hopeless as it was, now seldom engaged his attention. Roseline, and Roseline alone, engrossed his every idea: while he saw her smile, and heard the sound of her voice, he was contented and happy, and, when she was absent, the wish, of rendering himself more worthy and better able to converse with her, stimulated him to pay unremitting attention to his own improvement, and the instructions he received; but, he had been assured he should see her no more, he would have sunk into the same apathy and indifference for life and its enjoyments from which her kindness had drawn him.

After Madeline had left the castle, and before the return of Sir Philip, Edwin, at the utmost risk of a discovery, which would have involved him and the object of his regard in danger and difficulties, prevailed upon her to grant him several interviews in the chapel of the nunnery. One night, Albert, having agreed to accompany him through the subterranean passage, the trembling nun met them at their entrance, and seated near the tomb which concealed the door, listened to the vows of her lover.—Equally reluctant to part, they sat longer than usual, and heard footsteps in the chapel. Madeline rightly concluded it was one of the friars come to say mass for the soul of a nun lately dead. When the ceremony was ended he departed and, as the door closed after him, the resolution of Madeline revived. She knew if they had been discovered, even the life of Edwin would not be secure, and that she should instantly be compelled to take those vows from which there was no release but death.

Her own imprudence, and the danger to which her lover was exposed, struck so forcibly upon her mind, that after he left her she could scarcely acquire courage to return to the nunnery; and, as she passed the awful and silent receptacles of the dead, she was almost led to think she heard a friendly voice warn her never again to be guilty of so sacrilegious a crime. She glided quickly by the grave of the nun who had been interred but a few days, and even imagined she could perceive the earth move.—She had no sooner reached the cell, (into which she hurried without daring to look to the right or to the left, lest she should see the frowning spirit of some departed sister,) than she fell on her knees, and earnestly intreated forgiveness of the holy virgin. The next morning, far from finding her terrors abate, they gained still greater ascendancy over her mind, by hearing that father Anselm had been making inquiries about some footsteps he had observed in the chapel when he went to early prayers. Recollecting the unguarded warmth of Edwin's temper, and the eager tenderness with which in an hour of yielding softness he prevailed upon her to indulge him with these stolen interviews, she was fearful of acquainting him that it ws her determination to grant no more.—She wrote to her friend Roseline, and entreated her to persuade her brother not to make any attempts in future to see her in the chapel; but to them she left the power of procuring as many opportunities as possible of meeting without danger. She sincerely lamented being obliged to deprive herself of the company of a lover to whom she was tenderly attached, and for whose sake she was become an unwilling votary in the service of her God.

This letter was instantly communicated to Edwin by his sister. He could not at first be easily reconciled to a measure so repugnant to his feelings; but Roseline adding her intreaties to those of Madeline, and pointing out the necessity of it, he became more willing to observe the greatest caution, and to practice the most rigid present self-denial, in order to secure his future happiness. She reminded him that it was now four months before Madeline would enter on her year of probation, previous to which something might happen favourable to their wishes; observing, that their mother could at any time prevail upon the abbess to grant Madeline leave for visiting the castle. These arguments had so much effect, that Edwin promised his sister to make no farther clandestine attempts to see her friend, till all other means were rendered impracticable.

It happened about this time that Roseline was prevented, by a slight indisposition, from visiting the prisoner for four or five days. At first his alarm and distress were unspeakable. It was scarcely possible to convince him that it was owing to ill health he did not see her, and his restless impatience would have now betrayed the secret of his heart, had it not before been discovered. He neither ate nor slept; all his spirits forsook him: the sun was no longer admired, the moon and stars were deprived of their lustre. He wished to shun the light, and, had all nature been lost in universal chaos, it was been a matter of indifference now he saw not Roseline: he wondered what he could have found to admire in anything with which she was not connected.

Albert observed his master was very busy with his pen, and, in removing a portfolio from his writing table, papers containing the following sonnets dropped on the floor. He read and copied them, and gave them to Edwin the next time he saw him.

Though they were written by one who had never drank at the Parnassian fount, love had given such pathos to the language of taste and nature, that he was charmed, and could not prevail on himself to withhold such a treasure from his sister, to whom in justice they belonged, and who like another Iphigenia had in a manner raised a phoenix from the flame inanimate materials of which a Cymon had been formed.[20]

Roseline, as she read the interesting proofs of genius and affection, which she wanted not to convince her she was sincerely beloved, shrunk from the agitated and trembling feelings of her own heart, which too well informed her he had nothing to fear from not meeting an equal return of regard. Absence had been as painful to her as it had proved to

---

[20] In Greek mythology, Mount Parnassus is home to the Muses. Those who drank the waters were gifted with creative inspiration. Apparently Walter's sonnet is not an inspired poem, but because it is influenced by loving Roseline, it rises above academic standards. (Additionally, it must be remembered that Walter has only recently learned how to read and write).

the prisoner, whom love had taught a lesson equally charming and delightful.

SONNETS TO ROSELINE.

SONNET THE EIRST.

Ah! what to me are birds or flow'rs,
The Sun's most radiant light!
I pine away the ling'ring hours,
And sigh for endless night.
Come, Roseline, sweet maid, on roses borne,
Sweet as thyself,—unguarded by a thorn!

SONNET THE SECOND.

Fair Roseline, why didst thou chase the gloom
Which late envelop'd my benighted mind!
Why didst thou snatch me from a living tomb
To sigh my hopeless sorrows to the wind!

Why was I caught in love's bewitching snare,—
Believ'd thee gentle, tender, kind, and fair!
Now thou art absent, my desponding soul
Has lost its wonted pow'rs in sad despair;
Reason no more my passion can controul;
Joy flies with thee, and nought remains but care.
The blessings thou hast giv'n no more have charms,
And my rack'd mind is torn with wild alarms.

With soothing words thou didst my cares beguile,
Taught me the page of learning to explore,
Banish'd despondence with a gentle smile,—
Then left me solitary, sad, and poor.
Would'st thou return, and to my pray'r incline,
Me thinks a dungeon's gloom would be divine!

If I no more thy beauties must behold,
Death soon will free me from this painful smart;
If a proud rival win thee by his gold,
Soon will despair and anguish break my heart.

But, though all cares, all sorrows should be mine,
Heaven shower its brightest gifts on Roseline!

———

SONNET THE THIRD.

No more for liberty I pine,
No more for freedom crave;
My heart, dear Roseline, is thine,—
Thy fond, thy faithful slave.

First taught by thee I own'd love's pow'r,
And yielded to my chain;
Sigh through each sad and cheerless hour,
Yet bless the pleasing pain.

Sweet Roseline, my heart is thine,
It beats alone for thee;
In pity to my vows incline,
Or set the captive free.

Like a poor bird, in his lone cage,
I pine and flutter round,
Sullen and sad, in fruitless rage,
Yet still in fetters bound.

CHAPTER VIII.

THUS stood matters at the castle, when Sir Philip de Morney returned, accompanied by his friend, Baron Fitzosbourne, who was highly gratified by the cordial and respectful reception he met with. Every one vying with each other in their endeavours to amuse him, he assumed the most conciliating manners, appeared pleased and good humoured, paid the most flattering attention to the young ladies, and bestowed the warmest encomiums of their beauty and accomplishments; at the same time admiring, or pretending to admire, and maturer graces of the mother, who had given to the world a race of women fairer than the first daughters of creation, and, to render the gift complete, had stored their minds with a fund of knowledge that could put philosophy to the blush at its own ignorance.

Sir Philip assiduously courted the Baron, seemed to watch his looks, and to make it his whole study to oblige him,—thought as he thought, and, whatever he recommended, was sure to approve. Lady de Morney, seeing her husband so anxious to please, followed his example, not doubting but he had good and sufficient reasons for what he did. She requested her children strictly to observe the same conduct, with which request they all at first readily compiled, and exerted themselves to entertain their noble guest. Edwin was honoured with particular marks of his favour and approbation: he promised his best interest to obtain him promotion in the army, when he found that was the profession for which he was designed.

The Baron was nearly as old as his friend Sir Philip. In fact, they had received the first rudiments of their education at the same school, and under the same masters; and, though their pursuits were alike, they had been thrown into very different situations, but ever retained a pleased remembrance of their boyish friendship, and took every opportunity of keeping it alive, and serving each other. The Baron, though large and robust, was neither clumsy nor forbidding in his appearance. His eyes were penetrating; he looked the warrior, and seemed formed to command and be obeyed. He was tall, and had an air of grandeur about him that bespoke the man of fashion: his voice was not unpleasing; but he was rigid and austere with his servants and dependants; and, though upon the whole they found him a generous master, as he had nothing conciliating in his manner to them, they took every opportunity of abusing him; for, though they durst not venture to speak before him, they made themselves amends when they joined their companions in the kitchen, by giving such traits of his character, as not only shocked them, but made them feel with redoubled gratitude the happy difference of their own situation.

Roseline, while she was compelled to treat her father's visitor with attention and respect, felt an invincible disgust when ever he addressed her, and attempted to give specimens of his gallantry, which was often the case; but, if he took hold of her hand, she shrunk from his touch as she would from that of a snake, and trembled, she knew not why, if she saw him looking earnestly at her face.[21]

Edeliza laughed at and detested him. She slily compared him with De Willows, and wondered how nature could have contrived to form two creatures so different from each other. Bertha wished to pull off his ugly great wig, and to have it stuck upon one of the towers, observing, that, if his frightful face were seen from another, no enemy would ever come near them. How were they all struck with sorrow when they found he was to spend the whole summer at the castle. Roseline, with more earnestness than usual, questioned her mother as to the truth of this report, but received only an evasive answer, that the length of the Baron's stay depended on a circumstance not yet determined.

"I sincerely hope, my dear madam, whatever it may be, that it will a least prove unfavourable to his continuance here. My father may, and I dare say has, just reasons for esteeming him, though no one but himself can discover them. Every one else dislikes him, and I shall most truly rejoice when he takes himself away."

"My dear girl, (said Lady de Morney,) consider the Baron's rank, and the dignity of his character."

"I do consider them (she replied) as the greatest misfortunes that could happen to any one, unless accompanied with good humour and humility; but I think it particularly hard that the other must suffer so many mortifications because the Baron is a great man."

Again she was requested by her mother, who could scarcely forbear smiling at the seriousness of her manner, to recollect that men of his consequence could not bring themselves to act as if they were upon a level with their inferiors.

"The more is the pity, (said Roseline;) therefore, my good mother, it would be unnecessary for me to consider any thing about the Baron's importance, since he thinks so much and so highly of it himself: but I do not see, for my part, why rank and fortune should tempt their possessors to assume so much on merely accidental advantages; or why people, distinguished as their favourites, should have a greater right to

---

[21] Roseline's ability to silently recognize that the Baron is bad news indicates her instincts are sharp and well tuned. She intuitively trusts her interior voice—one that society would have silenced long ago had she been a weaker woman. Her ability to listen to her insight grows through out the novel.

think and act as they please than those less fortunate. We were much happier and more cheerful before he came among us, and my father more indulgent."

"Your father (said Lady de Morney, with the utmost earnestness) is, I have no doubt, perfectly satisfied that he is acting right, and therefore you, Roseline, must be blameable in presuming to call his conduct in question. I insist, as you value his and my favour, that you never again address me on this subject; and let me advise you, if you wish to be happy, to shew no disgust to the Baron, but receive his attentions with politeness and good humour."[22]

On saying this, she withdrew, and left Roseline, struck dumb with surprise, to form what conclusions she pleased. She knew not what to think from this unusually strange and unpleasant conversation, and could not comprehend either her father's or mother's reasons for being so much attached to any one, whatever might be his rank, who was so little formed to excited any feelings but those of disgust in the minds of those unfortunate people with whom he condescended to associate. She saw and lamented that, since the Baron's arrival, neither De Clavering, De Willows, nor Hugh Camelford, came without a formal invitation from her father, while the reserve which prevailed in their parties banished all that enlivening conversation that once rendered them so pleasant. Her sisters too, the dear Edeliza, and the sweet Bertha, were kept under so much restraint before this great personage, they seemed almost afraid to speak.

Roseline, to shake off for a time these uncomfortable reflections, stole into the prisoner's room, in which she seldom failed to find her brother: there she lost all remembrance of the Baron; and, in conversing with friends so dear to her heart, progressively recovered that native cheerfulness which was one of the most engaging features of her character.—The sonnets, which her brother had so recently given her, not only served to raise her spirits, but had made an indelible impression on her mind. She smiled with something more than even her usual complacency on this love-taught poet. Of his tenderness and sincerity she could cherish no doubt. His honour and worth it was equally impossible to suspect. No one knew them better,—no one estimated them so highly as herself. To suppose he could be less amiable, less deserving of her attachment, would have appeared to her a crime of the most enormous magnitude. Thus did the fond effusions of love throw a veil over the eyes of their artless votary, in order to give a

---

[22] Lady de Morney attempts to silence her daughter's voice and instinct due to the gender codes which still hold both mother and daughter prisoners. Roseline and Madeline attempt to break free of this restricting code by rejecting the patriarchal demands placed upon them.

fair colouring, and to reconcile her to a conduct which, in another, her prudence would have taught her to condemn; but thus it is with too many erring mortals: when once they become the hood-winked slaves of any predominant passion, they are not only regardless of the world's opinion, but insensible to the secret admonitions of that silent monitor, which they carry in their bosom. Roseline at first acted merely from the generous impulse of pity and universal benevolence; but, in so doing, she admitted a guest to dispute with them a place in her breast, which neither time, reason, no prudence, could banish thence.

Our artless heroine was unfortunately the darling child of sensibility, and her mind so susceptible of the miseries and misfortunes of others, that, from the moment she discovered them, they became her own. What then must be the poignancy of her feelings, when she reflected on the dependent, helpless, and unprovided state of a lover, dearer to her than life!—who dared not disclose even his name,—whose blameless conduct proved to her partial judgment that he suffered unjustly, and whose virtues could alone reconcile her to herself for having risked so much on his account, and entrusted her heart to the keeping of one whose situation precluded hope,—who had declared he belonged to no one,—a prisoner, a stranger, without fortune or friends: yet, think as she would, these cruel circumstances, after the strictest investigation, acted as a talisman in favour of her lover.

The life, which she fancied, under Providence, she had been the humble means of preserving, she concluded it was now her duty to render happy; therefore, to deprive it of its value, by affecting an indifference she did not feel, was as far from her power as her inclination; yet there were moments when she recollected, with the severest anguish, how much her brother, as well as herself, was acting in opposition to the designs and will of her parents. To deceive such parents was a thought which, in her most impassioned moments, she could not dwell upon, but love and sensibility had woven their webs so close around her heart, that she struggled in vain to disentangle herself from the bewitching snare.[23]

Sensibility I have long thought, nine times out of ten, proves a source of misery to the generous and benevolent, and as often is merely the boast of the ignorant, who pretend to be overstocked with the milk of human kindness, and whose feelings are equally excited by the death of a husband or a lapdog. I am satisfied there is no blessing more earnestly to be wished for than a calm and composed resignation to the

---

[23] Like Walter and Madeline, Roseline is trapped when personal desires come in conflict with social rules and obligations. Like her friends, Roseline must learn to navigate this world to achieve the life she desires with out abandoning her social role—a difficult task.

events of this life, and all its complicated concerns.—It appears rather an Irishism, that to be happy we must become indifferent,—but so it is.

Real sensibility is of all burthens the heaviest to bear. Long experience and careful observation have convinced me too painfully of this truth. A thousand and a thousand times I have shed torrents of tears, and felt the most tormenting anxiety for those who would have seen me with the most stoical apathy begging through the streets for bread. The pleasures attending high-raised sensibility are so much over-balanced by the painful effects they produce, that I protest I had rather be an oak, or a cabbage, than alive to such ever-varying and corrosive feelings, which act upon the human mind as slow poison would upon the body.

When Roseline was going to bed, the servant who attended her, and who, from having lived some years in the family, was indulged in the habit of conversing familiarly with the young ladies, determined to get rid of a kind of confidential secret, which had been entrusted to her by one of her fellow-servants.

"Laws, Miss Rosline, (said she,) what think you that frightful old Baron comed here for?—As I live I should not have dreamed of any thing so ludicurit!"—

"Came for? (replied Roseline,)—why he came to see my father to be sure;—what else could be his inducement for visiting this stupid place?"

"Ha, ha! I thought I should poze you, miss, (cried Audrey, drawing herself up, and giggling at her own consequence,)—why, as sure as you be borned and christened, he come here to pick up a wife, if he can meet with one to please his own superannuated meagrims; and his man, Pedro, thinks as how a person I could name would suit him to a tee, but I thinks otherwise.—Such an old frumpish piece of crazy furniture, says I, will not suit any of the ladies that belongs to the noble genitors of Bungay Castle and its henvirons. 'You may be mistaken, dame, said the fancy fellow;—if they suit my master, my master may suit them sure, for he is as rich,—as rich as Crasus."

"For heaven's sake, (said Roseline,) what nonsense have you picked up? You must not presume, Audrey, to speak of the Baron in so disrespectful a manner. If my father and mother heard you, I am not sure that you would be permitted to stay another night in the castle."

"It would be a good story, indeed, (resumed the talkative Abigail,) to turn away such a servant for such an offence! As I have a soul, which, by the goodness of father Anselm, I hope to get saved, my heart bleeds for you, miss, and I could claw out his ugly, staring eyes for to go for to think that you, who be so sweet tempered, and kind, and

affable, to your unfeerors, should have to nurse his crazy old carcase.—
'Tis vexing to—

Roseline has started up in her bed as soon as she found herself so strangely introduced with the Baron, and seeing that Audrey had taken up the candle in order to leave the room, gently called her back, and begged some explanation of what she had heard, which she declared herself unable to comprehend.

"Mayhap you are;—so much the better, (said Audrey.) – Less said is soonest mended, as I have gone to the end of my line;--I may be turned away if I assume to speak of the beautiful old Baron;--things will all come out in time;—I can be spectful to my betters:--they that like an old husband let them have him;—'tis no bread and butter of mine.—Good night, miss;—the Baron is a fine old Gracian, and will make his lady marvelly happy."

Saying this, she left the room, and Roseline was too much displeased to call her back a second time, but determined to question her still farther the first opportunity. "The Baron came to the castle for a wife!"—It was too ridiculous to be believed; but, if he did, he could not possibly think of uniting himself with her! Servants were ever prying into the secrets of their betters, or forming such stories as only very ignorant people could think of inventing.

She now went to sleep, forgot the Baron, and dreamed of the prisoner, whom her fancy represented as being released from confinement, and eager, with the consent of Sir Philip, to lead her in triumph to the altar of Hymen. To the delusive excursions of the soul we will for the present consign her; but, before we take leave of the inhabitants of the castle for the night, we will just take a peep into the kitchen, where, around a blazing fire, spread on a hearth four yards wide, were seated several of the domestics, earnestly engaged in talking over the affairs of the family, each of them drawing the character of their master or mistress, as the humour of the moment dictated, and giving their opinions of actions, the motives of which they knew so little, that they were just as able to pronounce sentence on them as a judge without a fair and candid examination.

Sir Philip, it was said, was become quite the proud and penurious,— the young ladies troublesome,—and Lady de Morney cross, whimsical, and suspicious. Suddenly the door burst open, and a young man, who had been for some time an assistant in the stables, tumbled into the kitchen, and, with terror depicted on his countenance, exclaimed, "I saw it,—I saw it!—I saw the light with my own eyes!—The ghost followed me up to the door, and then vanished in a flash of fire!—Shut the door, or it may get in!"

This in a moment alarmed the whole set; they all crowded round the terrified man, and with one voice eagerly inquired what ghost, what lights he meant? and when and where he had seen them? After drinking a copious draught of ale, he became able to satisfy the curiosity he had excited, and told them, as he was coming from the stables, just as he passed the gate of the inner ballium, and was within forty yards of the South tower, he saw a light as plain as ever he had seen one in his life, through one of the grated windows, and, after it had disappeared a few seconds, it appeared again at a much lower window, flashed upon the wall, and smelt like sulphur.[24] At the moment it vanished the second time, he saw something all in white, which he thought glided past him, but, on looking behind him, it was there also, and it had actually followed him till he fell into the kitchen.

"Then, as sure as we are alive, (said one of the grooms,) Thomas has seen the ghost of the lady who died for love of the young officer that was put to death in the dungeons. I have heard my grandfather say a thousand times he must have died innocent, for he was as bold as a lion till his last gasp."

"Well, (said one of the women-servants,) I shall be afraid to stir out after dark, if these confounded ghost are again found taking their nightly rambles, and prying into every thing that is going forwards."

"I always knew (said another) this castle was disturbed ever since the great clock struck twelve twice in one night; for what on earth could touch it at that time, if it had not been a spirit?"

"Ah! (said a third,) no doubt there have been sad doings in the castle."

"Not since we came to it, (replied an old grey-headed footman.) My master has practiced no deeds of darkness that would bring the dead from their graves. As to what was done before our time, that can be no business of ours, and I don't see how any ghost can have a right to frighten and interrupt, either by day or night, those who were never acquainted with it."

"Christ Jesus preserve us! (cried one of the maids,) I verily thinks I saw something glide past that door! Surely father Anselm should be sent for to give them absolution.—There! Did you not hear that rustling?"

"I see and hear nothing, (said the before mentioned old servant,) but what I wish neither to see nor hear. You are all a parcel of superstitious ignorant fools, and, if my master should once find out

---

[24] A symbol of guilt, punishment, and the devil, sulphur has long been associated with Lucifer and the underworld. Clearly the scent of sulphur in Bungay Castle forecasts ill omens.

what cowards you all are, he would soon compel you to give place to a bolder set. Come, come, let us go to bed, and leave the ghosts to do the same."

The old man led the way with a candle in his hand; the rest followed, clinging to each other like a flight of bees, not one of them daring to be left behind; and the groom, who had really seen a light from the tower inhabited by the prisoner, was so convinced he had seen a ghost, that neither father Anselm, nor all the fathers in Christendom, could have persuaded him to think the contrary; and so much had it alarmed him, that his terrified imagination had mistaken his own shadow for the ghost following close at his heels, and it was with some difficulty he could be prevailed upon by his fellow-servants to go to bed, lest he should see it again.[25]

The next morning, when Audrey went to call her young lady, Roseline requested she would forgive her for her having spoken so angrily the preceding evening, and with the most winning softness begged to be informed what she meant by coupling her name with that of the Baron.

Audrey, who had never before seen Roseline so much out of humour, and had neither forgotten nor forgiven the affront of being prevented from disclosing a secret with she had for several days found very troublesome to keep, replied, "I couples no one; matches are made in heaven, or in the church, or at wakes; but I think, for my part, some are made in a much worser place, and so she will think to who is tacked in hollybands with the old Baron." "But who do you think, my good Audrey, will ever be so unfortunate?" "Why will you ax me, miss? I must not speak my senterments: we poor servants never knows nothing; but this I do know for certain, if ever I marries, it shall be to a young man, a pretty-looking man,—good humoured ones I loves,--something like Mr. Camelfor;—not to an old crab, sowrer than vinegar, who would not suffer me to see with my own dear eyes, nor believe with my own natural senses,—a crotched faced toad, who would shut me up for life, mayhap, if I liked a better or a younger man than himself,—an accident I think that might happen."

"But how should the Baron find out what you thought?"

"By going to a negromancer. Such old cattle are to the full as cunning as their black master, and might strike one dumb."

---

[25] This moment exemplifies a basic difference between Male Gothic and Female Gothic. Bonhote gives the reader more information than she gives her characters; thus, relieving our own terror as we laugh at those who are frightened. Writers in the Male Gothic tradition would not appear so kind. Their readers would experience the events as they unfold with the characters- creating more suspense and horror.

"That, to be sure, (replied Roseline,) would be a heavy misfortune to those who were fond of hearing the sound of their own voice in preference to that of any other person."

"For my part, (said Audrey,) voice or no voice, I verify thinks something mendusly bad after all will happen to this crazy castle, for Thomas last night saw lights in the South tower, and the ghost of a young woman followed him in such a hurry, that, if he had not ran as fast as a hound, it would have stamped on his heels. It went away like a sky-rocket, and the smell of sulphur almost *sifficated* the poor fellow, who will certainly have a *parletic* stroke."

Lady de Morney's bell now ringing, Audrey left the room, without having said half so much as she intended to do about the ghost, or unburthening her mind of a secret she heartily wished to reveal.

CHAPTER IX.

WHEN the family met at breakfast, the Baron appeared unusually affable, and Sir Philip in high spirits. A walk was proposed to take a view of the town, nunnery, and environs of the castle. Roseline and her sisters were requested to be of the party, and they were very soon joined by De Clavering, De Willows, and Hugh Camelford. This little promenade was so pleasant, that it seemed to harmonize every mind, and so produce a redoubled and grateful relish for the early beauties of the infant spring.

> "Already now the snow-drop dar'd appear,
> This first pale blossom of th'unripen'd year,
> As Flora's breath, by some untransforming pow'r,
> Had chang'd an icicle into a flow'r.
> Its name and hue the scentless plant retains,
> And Winter lingers in its icy veins."

The Baron, who had politely offered the assistance of his arm to Roseline, (which her father bade her accept,) whispered some very fine things in her ear in praise of her shape, beauty, and understanding,— told her it was a reproach on the taste and judgment of his sex that so charming a female had not put on hymeneal fetters;—it was a positive proof of the blindness of the god of love. [26]

"Surely you forget, my lord, (replied the blushing Roseline,) that I have scarcely left off my leading strings, and am but just liberated from the confinement of the school."

Age, he told her, ought not to be reckoned by the number of years, but by accomplishments and good qualities.

"That kind of calculation (said De Clavering) would make your age, Miss de Morney, more upon a par with the Baron's."

"More upon a par, you mean, (added De Willows,) with our first parent Adam."

"What of Atam? (cried Hugh Camelford, skipping to the side of Roseline, and eagerly handing her over a little run of water they were obliged to cross,)—what were you saying about our crate crandfather

---

[26] It is interesting to note the order of importance in the Baron's list of compliments. Praising her figure first, the Baron dismisses Roseline's intelligence by placing it last. Bonhote characterizes the Baron as a sexual threat in Volume I of her novel. Thus, the Baron journeys quite a distance in his shift from threatening villain to paternal grandfather.

Atam? I have often wished to see the old poy, and trink a pottle of pure water with him from the pond in the garten of Eden."

"Why so, sir?" said the stately and mortified Baron, who felt and seemed to shrink from the contrast between the active and lively gallantry of the giddy Cambrian and the slow and cautious efforts of his own.

"Why—why? Pecause he must be a prave fellow to venture matrimony with the first woman he saw."

"How the devil should he do otherwise than take the first, when there was no other to choose!" said De Clavering.

"The tevil however was even with him after all, (replied the unthinking Camelford;) –the old poy had petter have peen quiet."

"I do not see that, (said De Willows;) and, as the mischief was productive of some good, surely we have no right to criticize with severity that conduct which was forgiven by a Being so much more perfect than the creature he had created."

"That is as much as to say, (rejoined Camelford,) that, when we choose to play the fool, cotet our neighbour's wife or taughter, we have only to plame our own imperfect nature, repent, and be forcifen."

"That would be to trust our hopes of forgiveness upon a very sandy foundation indeed, (said Sir Philip,) as determined guilt, or a continuance in error, can have but little chance of immortal happiness."

"And for our mortal share of that same commodity, (replied the lively Hugh,) we must not trust to matrimony, I fear, as I never heard married people found their happiness puilt upon a rock."

This speech produced a general laugh, but Sir Philip, who was by no means pleased with the subject, said with a smile to the Baron, "These young men think they know more than their forefathers."

"By which means, (replied he,) they will most assuredly entail upon themselves the mortification of knowing less."

The conversation, during the rest of the walk, was confined to such objects as occasionally presented themselves to observation. The inhabitants of the town came to their doors to catch a look at the party from the castle. To as many as were known by the governor he spoke familiarly, as did the other gentlemen, and they concluded that Baron must be some very great man, perhaps the king himself in disguise, because he did not once condescend to address them.

Roseline chatted with some young girls who came out to make their best courtesies, while the Baron thought all these attentions paid to such plebian souls wonderfully troublesome. At dinner he scarcely spoke five words, and De Willows was so disgusted with his forbidding haughtiness, that the next day he presented to De Clavering the following satire on pride, saying it was a tribute justly due to the Baron for his supreme excellency in the display of that detestable feature in his character.

Hell's first born exhalation sure is pride!
Who, with its sister, envy, would divide
The various blessings to poor mortals given,
By the kind bounty of indulgent heaven.
What at the last have kings to make them proud!
A gilded coffin and a satin shroud.
The lordly worm on these will quickly prey;
For worms, like kings, in turn will have their day.

What then is man who boasts his form and make?
A reptile's meal,—a worm's high-flavour'd steak.
The epicure, who caters like a slave,
Is but a pamper'd morsel for the grave.

Envy's a canker of such a subtle power,
It steals all pleasure from the gayest hour.
It is the deadly nightshade of the mind;
With secret poison all its arts refin'd;
And, when attended by its vile relation,
Would spread a plague destructive to a nation.
Then send these hags back to their native hell,
With fiends and evil spirits formed to dwell.

No more on worth let man look down with scorn,
And frown on those not quite so highly born;
Nor, as the coaches rattle from his door,
Boast, like proud Haman, of not being poor!
Earth's doom'd to earth, all folly there must end,—
Then read, and own the satirist a friend.

Madeline had been invited, and obtained permission of the abbess to spend the following day at the castle. This gave additional vivacity to the lively spirits of Edwin, who, with his sister, spent as much time with the prisoner as they could steal, without exciting curiosity or suspicion. Roseline gave them with some humour the ghost-story, as imparted to her by Audrey, and cautioned Albert against having any lights seen from the windows, left it should be productive of such inquiries as might lead to a discovery of the rooms being inhabited; but, notwithstanding all her attempts to fly from herself, and conceal from the observing eye of love her own internal conflicts, she was almost tempted to throw aside the mask, and at once confess all her apprehensions.

How were these apprehensions heightened, when, in the afternoon, her father told her in a whisper he wished to see her in his study before the family assembled at breakfast, having some intelligence of the most agreeable nature to impart, which he hoped and believed would make her one of the happiest, as it could not fail to render her one of the most envied, of her sex.

Roseline trembled, turned pale, and took the earliest opportunity of withdrawing, not daring to trust Edwin with her fears, or risk seeing the prisoner for some hours, lest her agitation should betray suspicions of she knew not what, but in which her terrified imagination confirmed all the hints her maid had given her.—Marry the Baron!—it was a thought so unnatural, so repugnant to every wish, every feeling of her heart,—so inimical to the ideas she had formed of happiness, that it was not to be endured.—She wept, wrung her hands, recollected herself, and again sunk into despondency; but at all events resolved to acquire resolution to go through the interview with her father, and give him such answers as should convince him an union with his friend (if such was the painful subject he had to communicate) would make her the veriest wretch on earth. Her heart was no longer in her own possession, but that she must not dare to avow; all therefore that she could determine was, to refuse the Baron, and to love the prisoner, and him only, to the end of her life.

These important points settled for the present, gave to her perturbed spirits momentary relief, and enable her to join the family without creating any suspicion that they were unusually depressed; when, however, she followed her brother into the prisoner's room, it was with the utmost difficulty she maintained any command over her feelings; but, unwilling to alarm or distress her unfortunate lover, till necessity compelled her to acquaint him with her sorrows, the only difference her painful struggles produced was an addition of gentle tenderness to her manner; and, though she had often thought her affection could admit of no increase, yet, at this moment, he was, if possible, still more beloved, still more endeared by the ten thousand uncommon ties which had so wonderfully tended to unite hearts that appeared to be under the directing will of Providence. The next morning, previously to seeing her father, Roseline once more ventured to question Audrey, and so earnestly begged she would explain all she meant by the hints she had given respecting the Baron, that poor Audrey, softened almost to tears by seeing her young lady really distressed, no longer remembered her former petulance, but readily complied with her request, though, in fact, all she knew amounted to little more than she had already told;—namely, that the Baron came to look for a wife to carry home, and shut up in his old castle; —that the Baron's servant had informed her he was in love with her young lady;—that Sir Philip liked him for a son-in-law, and they were soon to be married:—"But, Christ Jesus, miss! he is such an infamy man, he would no more mind ordering one of his vassals to be thrown into a fiery furnace than my master would killing a pig; and Pedro says, he ought to have been put into the spettacle court fifty and fifty times, for his entregens and fornications; for, before his first wife died—"

"What then? (exclaimed Roseline,) has the Baron been married more than once?"

"Bless your heart, miss, he has killed two wives already, and the Lord in his mercy shorten his days, that a third may never fall into the clutches of such a manufactor!—Miss, I would not fortify my word even to gain a gentleman for a husband; and, as I have a Christian soul, which I hope father Anselm will keep out of purgatory, I have told the truth, and only the truth; you must demonstrate with your father, but don't go for to get me turned out of my place for wishing to preserve you from being led to the haltar by such an old imperial task-master."[27]

Roseline, too much alarmed to be as usual amused with the singular oratory of her simple but well-meaning attendant, thanked her for her good wishes, and promised never to mention the information she had communicated.

"Well, then, bless your sweet face! I'll be crucified but I'll municate to you all I can pick up. Pedro is marvelly keen and clever, yet he appears as innocent as the babe unborn, and for all he gets pretty gleanings and pickings out of his old master, he hates him as heartily as I hates fast-days and confessions; for you see, miss, one does not like to tell tales on oneself, and, in my opinion, some of our monks and father confessors don't find in their hearts an ejection to us pretty girls."

Roseline, having dismissed her locquacious attendant, endeavoured to acquire sufficient fortitude to meet her father with

---

[27] First published in Charles Perrault's *Stories or Tales of Past Times* in 1697, 'Bluebeard' is a violent fairy tale focusing on the wedlock as deadlock theme. With seven dead wives behind him, Bluebeard is the ultimate symbol of the life threatening qualities found in marriage. Upon marriage, Bluebeard tested each of his wives and punished them with death due to their independence and curiosity. Roseline's sense of wonder and autonomy has already been established. Clearly she would not pass Bluebeard's perverse test; thus, making her an unwilling victim of a cruel patriarchal villain. Audrey's statement "he has killed two wives" clearly makes the Baron a murderer, for, according to her, he is an active participant in their deaths. Additionally, she states "the Baron came to look for a wife to *carry home*, and *shut up* in his old castle" (italics mine). Roseline's impending wedding will reduce her to a piece of property to be imprisoned in the ancient laws of the Baron's old castle - a horrific end for such a positive heroine.

composure, and to arm herself with resolution to withstand any attempts he might make to compel her into measures from which every feeling of her heart recoiled. She too well knew the warmth and obstinacy of her father's temper, when he met with opposition in a favourite plan, not to dread the contest. She now concluded, from many preceding circumstances, that the Baron was brought to the castle for the horrid purpose of becoming her husband, and unfortunately at this moment recollected with redoubled tenderness the very great difference between him and the man whom, by a chain of the most singular and interesting circumstances, she had been led to regard with a degree of affection she scarcely dared to investigate, and of which she knew not the full force. Her brother, her dear Edwin, too, had formed an attachment equally repugnant to the will and ambition of his father. The painful recollection awakened her warmest sympathy, and increased her own sorrows.

"Ah! (she exclaimed,) how darkly over-clouded is the prospect which a few months back seemed so bright! Well, let the tempest come, let the thunder burst on my defenceless head, I will—"

Here she was interrupted by a summons to attend her father, which she instantly arose to obey; but her trembling limbs were scarcely able to support her, and she was obliged to rest several times before she could sufficiently recover herself to appear in his presence, without discovering the long and severe conflicts she had vainly endeavoured to conquer.

Sir Philip, on her entering the room, eagerly arose to meet her, and either did not, or, what is more probable, would not seem to notice her confusion. He tenderly took her hand, and led her to a chair; then, seating himself by her, observed with a smile, that he doubted not her curiosity had been excited, and told her he would have a kiss before he would disclose the secret; "for the business (he continued) which I have to negotiate with my sweet girl demands secresy."

Roseline, afraid of trusting her voice, bowed in silence, but her manner shewed she was all attention.

"My dear girl, (said Sir Philip,) why all this apparent tremor? I hope you are, and ever have been convinced that my first, my most anxious wishes are to see my children happy."—

(Then, thought Roseline, you will not surely so much mistake the road to happiness as to propose your friend to me for a husband.)

"Baron Fitzosbourne has solicited me to intercede with you in his behalf. Notwithstanding the greatness of his pretensions, he has even condescended to entreat I would intercede with my dear Roseline, that she will in due time permit him to lead her to the altar."

Roseline, extremely agitation, made an attempt to speak, which Sir Philip observing, said, "Attend to me a few moments longer, my dear; I will then give you leave to express your joyful surprise at the good fortune which awaits you.—My noble friend, from the very first moment of seeing you, loved, and wished to make you his own: he, like a man of honour, inquired if your heart was disengaged; I assured him it was, for I knew you too well, my dear girl, to suppose you would ever dispose of it without a father's sanction. Eager to possess a treasure which had never strayed from its own spotless mansion, he then requested my permission to become a candidate for your favour. I readily and freely gave it, and encouraged him to hope he would meet neither with caprice nor opposition; at the same time I candidly told him, that, though my fortune was upon the whole considerable, yet, as my family was large and still might increase, my daughter's portions could be but small,—so very small, that I feared it would prove an impediment to your union. He generously overlooked this objection, and wishes only to gain your heart and hand; while the share you would be entitled to have of your father's property he requests may be given among the rest of my family, and he will make an equal settlement upon you, as if you brought him a large fortune. Indeed, so noble and disinterested were his proposals, that they both gratified and astonished me: they are such as no parent could receive with indifference,—no young woman refuse. The Baron has not only a princely fortune, but a princely spirit, and such unbounded interest, that my Roseline will not only secure rank and splendor to herself, but will prove the fortunate means of obtaining them for her brothers and sisters, and of making the last closing scenes of her parent's days happier and freer from care than they have ever been."

Ah! thought Roseline, and her own irretrievably wretched; for, among all the treasures to be purchased by this unnatural union, happiness is not included. She sighed deeply, and, without looking up, remained silent.

Sir Philip, rather alarmed at the alteration in her countenance, which changed from being extremely flushed to the most deadly paleness; and, observing a tear stealing down her cheeks, still appeared determined to think he should find no difficulty in over ruling any little objection she might venture to make. He put one hand into her's, and the other round her waist, and again addressing her, said, "He did not wonder that an offer so splendid and noble should affect and overpower a spirit humble and unassuming as her's. I always knew the inestimable value of the Baron's friendship, and am equally sensible of the rich prize I possess in a daughter; but I never dared to cherish the grateful hope that I should live to see two persons on whom I depended for so large a portion of my happiness united, or that a child of De Morney's was to repay the noble Baron for his generosity to her father."

"For heaven's sake! My dear dear father, (cried the almost fainting Roseline,) do not thus seem to misunderstand the nature of feelings entitled to your tenderest pity.—I never, never can love the Baron!"

Sir Philip hastily arose; fury flashed from his eyes; every feature was beginning to be convulsed with passion, but he struggled against the rage he wished to subdue, while she continued,—"Consider my extreme youth; contrast it with the age of your friend;—can I be a fit or eligible wife for a man older than my father?—Without feeling any affection on my part, would it be just or right to give him my hand?— Would not that be to punish most severely the man for whom you profess a friendship, whom you call both generous and noble; but for whom, so far from loving, I have ever felt an invincible dislike, which sometimes I have thought, if he stayed much longer at the castle, would increase to aversion."

Sir Philip, who had neither expected to meet nor was prepared to encounter an opposition so determined, was no longer able to keep his passion within bounds.

"Roseline, (cried, he, striking his clenched fist on the table, and looking with the wildness of a maniac,) dare not presume to cherish, or to avow, a dislike which will not only plunge a dagger in your mother's heart, but rob you of a father. What business can a girl of your age have to like or dislike but as your parents shall direct?—Give them up for ever, or accept the Baron!—How will you reconcile yourself to become an alien to your family?—how relish spending your days in a nunnery, instead of enjoying liberty and every pleasure in the gay sunshine of a court, glittering with diamonds, surrounded by admirers, equal in rank and superior in fortune to many of our most ancient nobility?— Consider well before you determine. To enable you to conquer your diffidence, or caprice, one month I will give you;—one month I will allow to the struggles of maiden bashfulness, or the wayward humour of your sex. Yet bear at once my final resolution. If, during that period, you either alarm or disgust the Baron by your folly or ignorance, so as to make him repent the noble overtures he has made to secure an alliance with my family,—or if you attempt to damp the ardour of his passion by your coldness,—if at the end of that period you do not, without any visible reluctance, accept him as a lover, and promise to give him your hand, I will instantly send you into a convent of the severest order, and compel you to take the veil."[28]

---

[28] Roseline's options are very bleak at this point. She will either be trapped in a loveless marriage or will be imprisoned in a strict convent's cell. Mr. De Morney sees his daughter's role in a very limited way: she is either wife/mother or nun. With these male

Roseline, overpowered by his manner, fell on the floor in a state of insensibility.—Her father now saw he had gone too far; he was alarmed; but, much as he felt himself distressed, he too well knew what he was about, to call for assistance; he therefore, by the usual methods, endeavoured to recover her as well as he could, and, and soon as he saw her revive, soothed her hurried spirits with every fond attention, addressed her by the tenderest appellations, and begged her to have pity on him and on herself.

Roseline, too much terrified to contend farther at that time, heard him with silent despondency, and hoped the cruel contest would be ended by her death; for, as she never before had fainted, she imagined it was a prelude to her dissolution. Sir Philip, to reconcile her, if possible, to his ambitious views, argued the matter with that sophistry and art which in all ages have been practiced with too much success; assured her of every flattering indulgence that a youthful heart could desire,— painted her future prospects in colours most likely to captivate the attention and ensnare the senses; and even went so far as to promise, till the end of the month, he would not mention the Barron's name to her again, but insisted on her receiving his attentions with complacency, and desired her not to make a confidant of any one in a matter of so much importance: he likewise informed her, he had forbidden her mother's talking to her on the subject, and concluded this painful interview with telling her, he trusted her gentleness, duty, and affection, would determine her to oblige and gratify her anxious and tender father in the first and most prevailing wishes of his heart.[29] He recommended her to retire to her own room, and promised to find a proper excuse for her absence. After leading her to the door of his apartment, he embraced and left her.

Sir Philip de Morney, though in many respects a kind father and a good husband, was proud and aspiring. These passions, as he advanced in years, gained additional ascendancy over his mind, and as he saw his children approaching that period when it became necessary to think of an establishment for them, he was more and more anxious to see them placed among the great.

---

dominated options, we can perhaps gain more insight in Lady de Morney's motives in attempting to kill her first born son. It can be seen as retaliation against the patriarchal order which perpetuates the subjugation of women restricting them to very limited roles. Lacking the means to change her life, and dizzy from her post delivery fever, she subconsciously attempts to destroy what holds power over her: men.

[29] Knowing she'll attempt to help her daughter, silencing his wife's voice reveals Mr. de Morney's fears of losing control over the women in his house. Thus, the men of Bungay castle become the key-pers of women's' lives. However, the younger generation begins to heal and reverse this limiting theme, for Roseline holds the key for Walter's life - leading him to freedom instead of perpetual entrapment.

His lady, equally attached to the fascinating influence of birth and splendor, had neither inclination nor power to counteract his designs, nor to dispute with him on a point to which her own wishes tended. She was too partial, too fond of her children not to think they were calculated to shine in the most exalted situations, and that they deserved every blessing, every indulgence which rank or fortune could bestow. She had married a man much older than herself, and was happy; therefore she saw no reasonable objection in the difference of age between her daughter and the Baron, whose birth carried an irresistible passport to her heart.

Sir Philip has talked the matter over with her, and, with that prevailing influence he had ever retained, brought her not only to consent to any measures he should find necessary to adopt in order to carry his point, but obtained a solemn promise from her to conceal from Edwin, and every one else, the sanguine hopes they entertained for the splendid establishment of their daughter.—The fact was, Sir Philip had at different periods of his life received many favours, and some of a pecuniary nature, from the Baron, which had never been settled, and had it not been for the assistance of the Baron's purse, he must have deeply mortgaged his estates to carry on the law-suit, which, without the interest of his friend, would at last have terminated against him. It was in consequence of their unexpected meeting in town that he prevailed upon him, with some difficulty, to return with him to the castle.[30]

What ensued was so much beyond the most flattering expectations he had ever dared to cherish, that the feelings of the parent were sacrificed to ambition, and he instantly determined to carry his point, let the consequence be what it would; and, though he had observed, in the whole of Roseline's behaviour to his friend, convincing proofs of that dislike which she had in her interview with him avowed, yet he did not despair of gaining his purpose: he was aware that he might find some little opposition to his wishes, and therefore, to guard as cautiously as possible against disappointments, he had more than once represented to the Baron the youth, inexperience, and extreme timidity, of his daughter, and the terror she would feel at being separated from a mother from whom she had never been absent.

By such wary precautions as these he had prevailed upon his friend to postpone making any proposals to Roseline, till he had paved the way for a welcome reception. To such a plan a lover could not make any reasonable objection, particularly one who wished to have as little trouble as possible in the gratification of his desires.—Too proud,

---

[30] Roseline is reduced to a commodity—her father sells her to repay old debts.

haughty, and fastidious, to pay his court, or make any sacrifice to the wayward humours of a young beauty, he secretly rejoiced that her father would take the whole upon himself; and, knowing how agreeable the offered alliance was to him, he had no fears but as soon as the young lady's consent was asked, she would be happy to comply; he therefore looked forwards with less impatience than he would have done, had any doubts rested upon his mind.

CHAPTER X.

NO sooner had Roseline reached her own apartment, and fastened the door, than she sunk on her knees, and having for some minutes given way to the severity of her feelings by tears and lamentations, she recovered sufficient resolution to supplicate her Maker to support and direct her in this trying hour of distress. By degrees she became more composed, and sat down to reflect on her situation with less agitation and terror. Her father had promised her, and she knew his promise would be held sacred, that she should be indulged with one whole month to determine whether she would or would not accept the Baron: she was already determined, but she would avail herself of the few weeks allowed her to struggle with her feelings, and preserve the peace and tranquillity of her family; besides, it was placing the dreaded evil at some distance, and that to one so wretched was obtaining a great deal. After the month was expired, (but to that dreadful moment she had not yet acquired fortitude to look,) she should still persist in her resolution; till then she would oblige her father all she could by quietly receiving the Baron's attentions; but she was resolved not to deceive him by appearing to receive them with pleasure.

Madeline came to spend the day as had been proposed. Edwin found many opportunities of renewing his vows, and of marking some tender reproaches for her not seeing him so often as he wished by the subterranean passage, for which she assigned such prudent reasons, as served in some degree to quiet his apprehensions, which, however, were rather increased than abated by observing the marked and particular attention which was paid her by De Willows, who, it was but too visible, cherished a growing passion in his bosom, which equally tortured Edeliza, Edwin, Madeline, and himself. Roseline generously determined not to interrupt the few hours of happiness and tranquillity which her friends seemed to enjoy, by giving them the most distant hint of her own internal misery.

They took an opportunity of visiting the prisoner. Madeline was received by him with the cordial affection of a brother, for she was the adopted sister of his beloved Roseline,—the choose friend of her heart. With him they partook that soft intercourse of soul which gives to the human mind its highest and most perfect enjoyment. Without fear or restraint they addressed each other in the pure and unadulterated language of genuine tenderness, indulging in the innocent and fond endearments which the sincerity of virtuous love will claim, and with which its purest votaries might comply without a blush.

But how short and transitory appeared these fleeting moments (on which she thought old time had bestowed an additional pair of wings) to the agonized mind of the half distracted Roseline! who, notwithstanding her father's prohibition, determined in the course of the month to inform her mother and brother of every circumstance that had occurred. She dreaded, more than she would the stroke of death, imparting to the unfortunate Walter (she had prevailed on Albert to tell her his Christian name) that he had a rival, who, authorized by her father, would endeavour to separate them for ever; and more, much more for herself, she trembled for that hapless, persecuted, unprotected lover, at whose bosom fate had already aimed some of its most pointed arrows, whose life would be endangered, should her partiality be discovered—that life on which her own seemed to depend: his happiness, which was dearer to her than her own, rested with her only to preserve; if they must be parted, the contest could not be extended beyond the confines of the grave, and in the friendly grave they should both find shelter.

The visible change, which appeared the next morning in the countenance and manners of Roseline, was such as those only who determined not to see could have avoided observing. Edwin, who met her as she was going to enter the breakfast-parlour, eagerly cried out, "For heaven's sake, my dear sister, what, in the name of ill-luck, has happened to you?—how long have you been ill?"

With tender earnestness she begged him not to mention her altered looks, promising to acquaint him with the cause the first convenient opportunity. He agreed to comply with her request, and neither Sir Philip nor Lady de Morney took any notice; and, when the Baron joined the breakfast-party, every thing passed as usual. He was very attentive to his fair enslaver, who, seeing her father's eye sternly fixed upon her from the moment the Baron entered the room, dared not to repel his odious gallantry with the coldness and contempt she knew not how to suppress; but she thought it better to yield submissively to the mortifications of the present hour, in order to secure to herself the short respite from certain misery, which upon such painful conditions had been allowed her.

As soon as breakfast was ended, the Baron and Sir Philip ordered their horse, and rode out to spend the day at some distance from the castle. Lady de Morney withdrew to give directions respecting some domestic arrangements, and the younger part of the family retired to go on with their usual employments. Edwin followed his sister to her own apartment, and eagerly requested her instantly to relieve his mind from the anxiety he could not help feeling on her account, as he was certain something unpleasant must have happened.

Gratified by this proof of his tenderness and attention to her happiness, Roseline, after a few painful struggles to suppress her agitation, and having obtained a solemn promise from her brother, that, however provoked, or whatever indignation he might feel when he became acquainted with her internal and hopeless misery, he would not betray by the most distant hint that she had disobeyed the positive injunctions of her father, informed him, with many tears, of the Baron's views in coming to the castle.

Edwin had long suspected something would arise from the frequent conferences of the Baron and his father, and the unusual reserve of his mother. He had likewise observed, with some degree of surprise, the very flattering and uncommon attentions paid to their noble visitor; he therefore was not so much astonished as his sister expected he would have been. He carefully avoided filling her mind with unnecessary alarms at the moment he felt a thousand fears on her account, and could not restrain his indignation at hearing a tale confirmed which appeared too absurd almost to be believed. He tenderly embraced, and vowed to protect her from such cruelty and oppression, should his father continue obstinately to insist on her giving her hand to a man she disliked.

He had long known her extreme partiality for the prisoner, which, though he could not approve, his own clandestine engagements with Madeline prevented his attempting to condemn. They had innocently and mutually assisted in bringing each other into situations which threatened them with many sorrows; they must now in this trying moment as resolutely determine to extricate themselves, and those they loved, from distresses which otherwise would in all probability overwhelm and destroy them.

Edwin, at Roseline's earnest request, was to inform Walter of the dangers which encompassed them, and of the formidable rival who had appeared to interrupt their happiness; but she insisted on his concealing from him the name of that rival, begging him not to give a hint of his fortune or consequence. Eager to save her lover from feeling such pangs as she herself had endured, she entreated he would soften the sad tidings he conveyed, by assuring him he had nothing to fear from herself, as her affection was equally tender and sincere.

When Edwin had imparted the unwelcome news to the prisoner, though he observed the strictest caution, and worded the heart-wounding communication in language best calculated to sooth and quiet those tormenting apprehensions, to which it would unavoidably give birth, the effect it had on the unhappy sufferer was dreadful. His agonies disclosed to the astonished Edwin the strength of an affection which, while it alarmed him, demanded the utmost pity; and, at that moment, had he possessed the power of disposing of the hand of his sister, he would sooner have presented it to his unfortunate friend than to the greatest monarch upon earth.

Roseline dared not venture to see him for several succeeding hours, and no sooner were his watchful and impatient eyes gratified by her entrance into his solitary apartment, than he hastily arose; and, throwing himself at her feet, almost inarticulately entreated her to pronounce his doom.

"Tell me, (cried he,) if you, my only earthly treasure, must be wrested from me for ever?—if I must no longer hear the soft sound of that gentle voice, sweeter and more melodious than celestial music? I can die without reproaching, but I cannot exist without seeing you; and I will never, never live one hour after you have given your hand to another.—Madness and torture are united in that thought!—Let us fly,—let us leave this horrid castle!—The world is all before us: love shall be our guide. Surely we can find one little sacred spot that will shelter us from persecution and tyranny; if not, we can wander, beg, and at last die, together."

"Have patience, my generous, my beloved Walter, (cried the weeping Roseline;)—I yet trust we shall not be reduced to the hard, the degrading necessity of taking such desperate and improper steps to preserve our faith unbroken. Be assured of this, and endeavour to rest satisfied with a promise I will ever hold sacred,—that, while you continue the unrivalled possessor of my heart, only actual force shall compel me to give my hand to your rival; and I think I may venture to say, if I know any thing of my father's disposition, unkind as it appears at present, he will never go to such unwarrantable and unnatural lengths to gratify an ambition I never suspected had found place in his mind."

"Ah! (said the prisoner) you little know, you cannot suspect to what lengths pride and ambition will carry unfeeling people. I am their victim, and if I thought you were to suffer as I have done—"

"Attempt not to think about it," interrupted Roseline.

"Consent then to escape this very night. If we stop to deliberate we are lost,—we are separated for ever! You know not what such love as mine, when called into action, and blest with liberty, would enable me to do, to preserve a treasure so dear and estimable. Albert would go with us: with his direction and assistance, surely we could procure sufficient from the bowels of the earth to support you in ease and plenty, if not in affluence."

The entrance of Albert luckily put an end to a conversation which was become to tender and painful for Roseline any longer to have kept up that appearance of composure which was absolutely necessary to quiet the tormenting apprehensions of her lover; she therefore immediately availed herself of the opportunity to quit his apartment, and retired to her own.

Within rather less than a week after Roseline's interview with her father, the alteration which took place in her was such as could not pass unobserved, but it was wholly imputed to indisposition. She became much thinner; the rose of health was fled from a countenance no longer marked with animation. She had no spirits, and was seldom seen to smile; even the playful fondness of her sister Bertha ceased to interest or entertain her.[31]

Lady de Morney, who was a tender mother, became alarmed, and imparted her fears to Sir Philip, who endeavoured to laugh her out of them.

"The poor child (said he) is only a little mother-sick. She is pining, I suppose, at the thoughts of leaving mamma: you must therefore take no notice, for I so well know the softness of your disposition, that a few tears will mould you to her own wayward purposes, and deprive you of all your resolution. The unfortunate girl will, to be sure, be sadly hurt at becoming a baroness, and being placed in a situation to which even the proudest ambition of her parents could not have aspired. We, therefore, have only to remain silent spectators for a time, and leave the natural vanity of her sex, united with the sanguine wishes of youth, to operate for themselves. We will invite company to the castle; I mean to give a ball in compliment to the Baron:—Roseline will reign queen of the ceremony; assailed by flattery, softened by music, exhilarated by exercise, she will forget to sigh in the midst of gaiety, and cease to disapprove the Baron, when she begins to feel that consequence which the being noticed by a man of his rank will give to her."

"Let us then try the experiment as soon as possible, (replied Lady de Morney;) for I cannot help thinking, unless some change takes place for the better, our sweet Roseline, instead of bridal finery, will want only a winding sheet, and that she will be removed from the castle to her grave."

Sir Philip was displeased; he instantly left the room in order to avoid returning an answer which he well knew would have been succeeded by an altercation with his wife.—She saw he was angry, and therefore, though she was extremely anxious on her daughter's account, she determined for some time to remain a passive observer, let what would be the consequence; but she did not experience that serenity of mind at forming this resolution which she had done on some former occasions, when she had sacrificed her own will to that of her husband;

---

[31] Predating the symptoms of vampiric infection, Roseline wastes away as the agency of her life is given to the hands of others. The Baron becomes the Gothic demon lover, draining his victim of life.

for, aspiring as she was by nature, and much as she was always attached to the gaudy trappings of grandeur and the alluring sounds of title, she felt the life of her daughter, when put in competition with them, or even the throne itself, was of infinitely more importance.

De Huntingfield was at this time absent from the castle. Elwyn very seldom mixed with his brother officers; therefore De Clavering, De Willows, and Hugh Camelford, were often left to mess by themselves, the Baron not appearing to like being much in their society. They were too young and too pleasing in his opinion, and, as he could not help sometimes making comparisons not much to his own advantage, it was natural for him to think the young ladies might do the same. As the three gentlemen were returning from a walk, they saw the Baron, Sir Philip, his son, and daughters, going out for one. Observing the apparent reluctant step and pale countenance of Roseline, as she walked by the side of her stately and venerable lover, and having picked up some hints which had been dropped at different times of the projected alliance, De Clavering, with some little indignation, exclaimed, "It will never do;—I see it will never do:—the girl's spirits are too low, her uncorrupted mind too pure, and her stomach too weak, to digest so much pride and acid as that old fellow has in his composition. His love seems to have operated on her feelings as being so nearly allied to misery, that she has already caught the infection, and I wish in the end it may not prove an incurable disease. Upon my soul I do not wonder at it, for he acts upon my nerves like a torpedo, or rather as the Greek fire did upon our armies, exciting both fear and indignation."

"By heaven! (said De Willows,) the folly and ambition of parents, in respect to their children, are, in my opinion, the most unaccountable of human absurdities. They form plans from their own passions and feelings, and then expect that young people can adopt them at their command, without making any allowance for the material difference between the sentiments, opinions, and inclinations, of nineteen and fifty."

"Suppose we all talk to the governor, and toss the Paron into the rifer. A cood tunking might trive all the flames and darts of lof out of his pody, and restore the poor cirl from the crave, to which the toctor is for sending her like a tog, without giving time for Christian burial!"

"To argue, or contend with such characters (said De Clavering) would be like opposing a fiddle against thunder, or a squirt against a cataract in Switzerland."

"Then, on my soul, (replied Camelford,) you must take the Paron's bpody under your own tirection. With your regimen, and a few of your tevilish experiments, you will, Cot willing, soon dispatch him and his lof into another world."

"That, indeed, Hugh, would prove an effectual cure; but, in respect to the Baron, it would not be quite so easily accomplished; for I look upon him still to possess a constitution that would set physic and even the doctor himself and defiance.—He seems formed to wrestle sturdily with death before he will be vanquished, or yield to the contest."

"If you can once lay hold of him, and cif him some of your pills and potions, he would soon be clad to gif up the chost."

"What, then, (said De Clavering) you think me more dangerous than love?—That little, subtle, and revengeful god will one day bring you upon your knees before his shrine for the affront put upon his all subduing influence."

"He had petter let me alone, (replied the Cambrian;) I am not so plind as his tivine highness, and will nefer worship any cot put the creat Cot of heaven. Eteliza has taught you petter, De willows: that girl's tell-tale eyes petray that lof has been pusy with more than one person."

De Clavering laughed at this unexpected attack upon his friend, who felt a painful consciousness that Camelford had more reason for his observation than he wished, the partiality of the artless Edeliza being too visible to be longer mistaken. On his own part, he had, from the first seeing Madeline, cherished an increasing affection for her, while her uniform and unaffected coldness, with the preference she had shewn to another, too well convinced him he had nothing to hope; neither could he any longer affect to be blind to the mutual attachment which subsisted between her and his friend Edwin, the latter having made no attempt to deny it; but, being satisfied of the honour of De Willows, had in part entrusted him with the wishes he determined to encourage, notwithstanding the insurmountable obstacles that appeared to preclude the most distant ray of hope.

"That same love, of which you are thinking and talking, (said De Clavering,) has so many devilifications in its train, I am determined to have nothing to do with it, till it becomes more rational, and can be reduced into a regular system, by which we poor short-sighted mortals may find directions how to act, without exposing ourselves to ridicule or disappointment. I am inclined to think I shall one day or other be tempted to marry, but it shall be to a woman who will take care to keep such ear-wig sort of fellows as you at a proper distance.—You tell fine tales, are all smoothness and deceit,—like a snail can give a gloss to the path you crawl over, and then leave such traces of your deceptive and invidious progress as cannot be concealed. Let the subject of your next satire, De Willows, be the male flirt,—an animal more dangerous than a tyger."

"Why so?" asked De Willows, determined not to apply the hint which he well knew was designed for him.

"Can there (said De Clavering) be found a character more deserving satire?—a thing that borrows the form of man to disgrace the name,—an adept in mean stratagems and mischievous devices,—insensible to the admonitions of conscience,--well versed in all practices of refined cruelty,—working like a mole in the dark, in order more effectually to ensnare the youthful heart of unsuspecting innocence, and that merely to gratify the vicious vanity of the moment; and, after he has sacrificed the health, happiness, and perhaps the life, of a young woman, who, by her tender nature, he has beguiled of peace, he laughs at her credulous folly, and boldly declared he had never any thought of making her his wife. That there are such men, who, under the sacred semblance of honour, can act thus despicably, I have, in the form of one once dear to me as life, unhappily experienced, and from that moment I became the friend and champion of the sex, and in bold defiance to all such deceivers, I throw down my gauntlet."

"How, in the name of Cot, came you to be so valiant, (cried Camelford,) as to think of fighting tuels for other people's pranks?"

"Because many of the fair sex are to gentle to vindicate themselves, too artless for suspicion, and too lovely to fall a sacrifice, without arming the hand of courage to avenge their injuries; for I think the man, who can trifle with the peace of a fellow-creature, may be justly compared to one of the exhalations of hell, sent to destroy and lay waste the small portion of happiness allotted to our mortal pilgrimage."

"You are warm, (said De Willows, confusedly;) perhaps I have undesignedly given you pain, without knowing I interfered with the wishes or pretensions of any one. On my honour, I never had any; but, on a subject so important, I cannot speak coolly, or canvass it with indifference. I will be frank, and own I admire Edeliza; and, were her heart as much in my power as I fear it is in your's no man with impurity should wrest it from me. "

"Well said, my prave toctor, (cried Camelford;) little tan Cupid must next take care of himself, or you will be after tissecting his cotship; and, though the poor cot is as plind as a peetle, you will be for couching his eyes, till he can see as clear as yourself."

A servant came to invite them to sup with the governor and his party, which luckily put an end to a conversation that was become unpleasant. It made De Willows rather uncomfortable and small in his own opinion, and compelled him to reflect more seriously on the subject than he had ever done before. Of Madeline it was folly to think any longer. If Edwin, who was beloved, dared not hope bring blest with her hand, without the interference of a miracle, what chance could there be of his succeeding, for whom she felt only the coldest indifference? He determined to take his heart severely to task, and to—but it was impossible for him at that moment to tell how he should dispose of a heart which had received so many wounds, that it scarcely retained any of its native unmutilated form; but, on a more serious examination, he found a something lurking in it that made him feel very reluctant to give up his pleasant and interesting intercourse with the tender and artless Edeliza, which long habit had rendered more necessary to his happiness than he was aware of.

CHAPTER XI.

THE design of Sir Philip, in giving a ball, was this evening made known, and the next day messages were sent out to invite the company for that day week. Preparations were instantly begun, and new dresses ordered. Madeline and Agnes de Clifford obtained leave to be of the party, and several of the inhabitants of Bungay were highly pleased by receiving invitations. Roseline, on whose account, as much as the Baron's, it was given, was the least gratified. Any scene of cheerfulness to her was become a scene of misery. Her spirits depressed, her mind, itself a chaos of contending passions, could not admit a single ray of hope or comfort to chase away the gloom which there prevailed. She no longer felt either pleasure or consolation in her stolen interviews with her beloved Walter, which once afforded her such indescribable satisfaction.

They now saw each other with a tender despondence, with served to deprive them of that resolution which could alone support them in those trials which no longer appeared at a distance, and Roseline, sinking under the burden of her own sorrows, felt herself totally unable to share in those which equally overpowered her unfortunate lover, from whose prison she never went, but he concluded it was the last time he should be indulged with seeing her.

Walter heard of the ball, which was to be given in compliment to his rival, with that kind of contempt of trembling indignation which a brave officer feels at seeing some upstart stripling stepping over his head to preferment, and, by dint of mere adventitious events, obtaining authority to lead those whom he dared not have followed. It has always been said that the sincerest love could not exist without hope. In this instance, however, the assertion did not hold good; for, though hope was lost, love maintained its empire, and, environed with despair, lost none of that tender energy which had united two hearts under circumstances the most extraordinary, and in a situation the most alarming and distressing.

The conduct of Sir Philip de Morney surprised all those who were let into the secret of the projected alliance. The Baron's pride appeared to have infected him with a mania of the same kind; and the unpleasant change it produced was not more inimical to the happiness of others than he soon found it proved to his own. He was now seldom greeted with the smile of affection: he saw looks of distress, and heard the sigh of discontent vibrate on his ears and, whilst he condemned the obstinacy of others, determined resolutely to persevere in his own.

How much it is to be lamented, that, with all the knowledge he acquires, man knows so little of himself! How astonishing that a sudden and unexpected change in his prospects, or situation, should instantaneously work so unaccountable a revolution in his feelings, that he scarcely retains any recollection of his former dispositions!—and, still more strange it appears, that, while adversity serves to exalt the mind and purify the heart, prosperity should harden and debase them.

About forty of those who had been invited to the ball returned answers that they would do themselves the honour of accepting the invitation. Roseline became so much changed in her looks, appearance, and manner, that at length the alteration struck the Baron, and he mentioned it to Sir Philip. This produced a second warm altercation between him and Roseline, which ended as the former had done, namely, in the want of resolution, strength, and spirits, on her part, to contend longer on a subject so painful to her feelings, and so inimical to all her hopes of happiness; for Sir Philip now insisted, and that with a degree of unfeeling ferocity, that she should give her hand to the Baron within ten days after the month was expired which he had so foolishly allowed to perverse folly and caprice.

Of this interview Roseline said nothing to her brother or the prisoner, but felt that her fortitude deserted her as time stole away, and, with the deprivation of health and spirits, threatened to leave her an uncontending and helpless victim to the authority she began to doubt having power to resist. Still she determined, if dragged by force to the altar, she would resolutely and openly, before its sacred front, declare not only her unwillingness to become the wife of the Baron, but her repugnance and aversion to the monastic life.[32]

At length the anxiously-expected, the long wished for evening arrived, and produced an assemblage of as much elegance, grace, wit, and beauty, as had ever been collected together in so confined a circle.—From the social town of Bungay some very lovely young women made their first appearance at the castle, decorated to the utmost advantage, and justly entitled to dispute the palm of beauty with many found in the higher ranks.

On this occasion, it is not to be doubted but they cherished hopes that their charms would conquer some of the young officers appointed to guard the fortress, on which the safety of themselves and the town depended.

---

[32] This is a very strong moment in the text. Bonhote has created a female character who breaks the stereotypical mould of a Gothic shrieking female. Roseline's voice is loud and clear in her refusal to become what men what her to be. Not only does she stand up to her father and future husband, but she also rejects the patriarchally enforced religious codes as well.

From the earliest ages of the world, the old adage prevailed,—
"None but the brave deserve the fair," while the military dress, shining
sword, and becoming cockade, were ever found useful auxiliaries in
assisting their wearer to find easy access to the female heart.

When the dancing was ordered to begin, the Baron, arrayed most
superbly, took out Roseline, and led her to the upper end of the room.
De Willows followed, leading Edeliza, who was drest in the most
becoming and captivating stile, and looked so enchantingly beautiful,
that he wondered he had ever beheld her with indifference, or preferred
another. Her expressive eyes told a tale so correspondent to the feelings
of his own heart, as completed its conquest, and the captivity was found
so pleasing and easy, it never afterwards wished to regain its freedom.
Edwin danced with the gentle Madeline; Hugh Camelford with Bertha,
and the rest of the party disposed of themselves as their vanity or
inclination prompted.

The dancing was begun with avidity and spirit, which some very
excellent music served to heighten and keep up. The Baron not
ungracefully exhibited his well dressed person, and this great personage
had the satisfaction of seeing that the eyes of the company were chiefly
fixed upon him who had procured them this unexpected indulgence,—a
circumstance unusual in an age when expensive pleasures were
confined to the higher ranks of life, and by that means less coveted by
those in inferior stations, which certainly tended to the good of society
in general, as it served to render all parties contented with their lot. We
now often see, with pity and regret, if young people are thrown by
chance into a walk of life some degrees higher than their habitual one,
they seldom know how to return to their former humble path without
discontent and regret, which will too often lead them to sacrifice virtue,
and every real good, for the frivolous nonsense of dress and the parade
of ceremony, while, to obtain the enjoyment of pleasures destructive to
time and real happiness, they will give up their peace of mind, nor
repent the poor bargain they have made so long as they can live in stile.

Some few pitied, but a far greater number envied Roseline for
having made so important a conquest, and were surprised to see how
little she was animated amidst the exhilarating scene of gaiety and
splendor, wholly occupying the attention of one of the first barons in
the kingdom, whose smile by most people would be reckoned an
honour, and whose frown among many was destruction from which
there was often no appeal.

Every rarity that could be procured was set before the party.
Hospitality and festivity went hand in hand, and, to a careless and
uninterested spectator, it would have seemed that universal happiness
prevailed; but it was far otherwise. Happiness is seldom found amidst a

crowd. In the more retired scenes of serene unambitious enjoyment, we have a much better chance of finding that rara avis, and of retaining it in our possession, if possible to be found.

Sir Philip de Morney was tormented with fears that the obstinacy of his daughter would disappoint his ambition, while the tenderness of her mother had so far subdued the influence of her pride, that, to see her daughter restored to her former health and spirits, she would gladly have yielded up the honour of an alliance with the Baron.

The artless unaspiring Roseline, before she was brought into notice by the proud attentions of her noble admirer, was a far happier being than she found herself at the moment she was looked up to as an object of envy; but the simple dress she had been accustomed to wear was more conformable to her own unadulterated taste than the splendid habiliments with which she was now loaded, and which the pride, or design, of her father had procured to throw a veil over her senses, and tempt her to purchase those still more brilliant at the expence of her peace; yet, notwithstanding all the fascinating allurements with which she saw herself surrounded, the court, adulation, and respect, paid to her, the eagerness of the company to obtain a share in her notice, her heart remained with Walter, the unknown stranger, who belonged to no one,—who was without fortune, and deprived of that freedom which is the birthright of the poorest peasant; nevertheless Walter, in a gloomy and solitary prison, was an object more captivating and far more valuable in her eyes than the lordly Baron in a stately castle.

When they had danced about half an hour after supper, the Baron apologized to Roseline for withdrawing to make some alteration in his dress, which he found unpleasant. She felt herself gratified by this temporary absence, and took the opportunity of chatting with some of her young companions. Deeply engaged in conversation with Madeline and Agnes de Clifford, she did not observe that her father was suddenly called out of the room, and requested by the servant in a whisper to hasten with the utmost speed to the apartment of his friend.

Too much surprised to inquire the cause, he instantly obeyed the summons. On his entrance, I will leave my readers to guess how much he must have been alarmed and shocked at seeing that friend extended on the floor, with every appearance of death on his countenance. After trying various methods to recover him without effect, he ordered one of his people to call De Clavering to his assistance, who, by some powerful and proper applications, soon produced signs of life, but it was near an hour before any of sense returned. He neither seemed to know where he was, nor why he saw so many people about him. At length, however, he recovered his recollection,—said he had been very ill, but found himself better, and requested to be left a few minutes in private with Sir Philip de Morney, whom he beckoned to sit down by the side of the bed on which he was laid.

The room being cleared, and the door fastened, to prevent interruption, the Baron grasped the hand of his friend, and in a hurried tone, at the same time looking around him with terror, informed him that he had seen a spirit. "It stood there!" pointing with his finger to a particular part of the room. Sir Philip appeared incredulous, and his looks were not misunderstood.

"Believe me, (continued the Baron,) it was no delusion of the senses. I actually saw the ghost of my first wife as surely as I now see you, and as perfectly as ever I saw her when alive. She glided out of the apartment the moment I entered it to change my dress, which I found too heavy for dancing. She looked displeased, frowned sternly upon me, and shook her head as she disappeared. Her countenance was as blooming, and retained the same beauty and expression as when I led her in triumph to the altar twenty years ago."

"Surely, my lord, (said Sir Philip,) this supposed visionary appearance must be the effects of the disorder which attacked you so violently, that it led De Clavering, as well as myself, to tremble for your life."

"Say rather, (replied the Baron,) and then you will say right, the disorder was occasioned by the terror, which, in that moment, indeed deprived me of my senses.—If I see you at this time, I then beheld the face, form, and features, of my once loved Isabella, of whom I was deprived by death in the infancy of my happiness, six months after she had given birth to a son, of whom the same inexorable tyrant robbed me in the fourth year of my second marriage."

Sir Philip found it was useless to contend with his friend on a subject in which he so obstinately persevered; and, though he was satisfied that the fright was merely the effect of disease, he thought it wisest to confine his disbelief to his own bosom, and drop the conversation as soon as possible. He insisted on remaining with him the rest of the night, and cherished hopes that by the morning this unaccountable vagary would be forgotten, or only remembered as a sudden delirium, occasioned perhaps by heat, and the unusual exercise in which he had been engaged. His offer of sitting up was cordially accepted, and the two gentlemen agreed it would be right and prudent to say as little about the ghost as possible, Sir Philip secretly trembling lest the Baron's unfortunate whim should operate so powerfully upon his feelings as to prevent his fulfilling at engagements with Roseline.

This strange circumstance occasioned so much confusion and hurry in the castle, that the party separated much earlier than they wished, and every one accounted, as their own humour dictated, for the sudden indisposition of the Baron. One or two, mortified by their pleasure being so unseasonably curtailed, said the old man had better have gone to bed at eight o'clock, or not have attempted dancing in a ball-room when he was dancing on the verge of the grave.

Sir Philip, with two servants, sat with the Baron during the night, and in the morning De Clavering found him so much recovered, that he advised him to get into the air, as that, with moderate exercise, he ventured to pronounce would perfect his recovery, and he would have nothing to fear from a relapse, if he kept himself composed; but that same composure the Baron did not find quite so easy to acquire as De Clavering imagined.

The awful appearance he had seen was not one moment from his remembrance: it still flitted before his mental sight, and his tortured mind presented only Isabella to his view. She had frowned upon him, shaken her head, and vanished with a look of anger and contempt: with this regretted and beloved wife he had passed by far the happiest moments of his life. She was the first, and indeed the only, woman he had really loved, notwithstanding the world had unjustly branded him with being an unkind and morose husband. It had in that respect dealt by him with the same injustice it had done by a thousand others. The delicate frame of Isabella was wasting in a rapid decline, from the moment she became a mother. He had adored her, and watched her as his richest treasure during the few months she had lingered with him, after having presented him with a son: she expired in his arms, and the severest pang she felt was being torn from them for ever. Why she should rise from the grave, why she should frown upon him, who had loved her so sincerely, he could neither comprehend nor reconcile to his feelings.

With his second wife he had lived several years; but all the happiness he had found in the course of them was not to be compared with that which he had enjoyed with his gentle Isabella, in the short time he had been indulged with the pleasure of calling her his own.

By the second lady, he had several children, and it was the death of an only surviving son, at the age of sixteen, on whom she had doated with an almost unpardonable fondness, which had occasioned her own.

Having thus been deprived of two wives, and bereaved of his children, without having any near relations for whom he felt those prevailing and powerful affections which could lead him to practice self-denial on their account, he justly considered himself at the liberty to endeavour to find happiness in the way to which his ideas of it were annexed, and therefore made choice of the daughter of his friend, Sir Philip, to share his fortune, and inherit such a part of it as he should find her worthy to possess, if she did not bring him those who would have a more rightful claim to it.

He had no sooner recovered the shock and terror which he had so awfully and unaccountably experienced, than he determined to persevere, and accelerate all the necessary preparations for the completion of his marriage.

He was now eager to quit Bungay Castle, and to return with the most convenient speed to his own, as he could not entirely divest himself of apprehension, that he might receive another unpleasant visit from his Isabella, whom, much as he had sincerely loved and admired when living, he did not now wish should leave her grave to interrupt those pleasures which he anticipated from the nature of his present engagements.

Sir Philip, who from the first had suspected the Baron's alarm and subsequent terror to have originated from a more natural (however unaccountable) cause than that to which he so obstinately imputed it, made all the inquiries he dared risk, without giving his reasons for so doing; but, notwithstanding his most artful endeavours, the mystery remained unexplained, and he was obliged to leave it to time, or chance, to develope.

END OF VOL. I.

VOLUME II.

CHAPTER I.

THOUGH every means had been made use of to render the ball given at the castle pleasant and agreeable to all the party, they did not succeed so well as we could wish. There were several of the company, as it is to this day found but too customary on all such important and interesting occasions, distressed, mortified, and discontented, who returned to their habitations with more cares than they had carried out, more pangs than they well knew how to bear, or than the pleasure, if unalloyed, could have repaid. One or two young ladies had actually fainted at seeing others better dressed and more noticed than themselves. Another was wretched, and out of humour at observing the Adonis, for whom she had long cherished the most romantic affection, pay his whole attention to the beautiful Edeliza, who was rendered wild by the gaiety, novelty, and splendour of the scene, while her little head was nearly turned by the fine things said to her, and the admiration she excited.

Edwin secretly repined that, as soon as the evening closed, Madeline would be again for an age, in the calculation of a lover's calendar, secluded from his sight, and compelled to count her beads in the cheerless and solitary cell of a nunnery, from which he knew not whether it would be in the power of art or stratagem to deliver her, and how dreadful would be the consequence, both to himself and the woman he loved far better than himself, should the project, which he had long cherished in his enterprising and enamoured heart, be discovered! These distressing thoughts threw a cloud of despondency over every surrounding scene, and in some degree deprived him of that vivacity which had endeared him to his friends, and rendered his society both pleasant and entertaining, while the cause of this unaccountable revolution was suspected but by few.

De Willows had never before felt himself so forcibly struck with the charms of the fond and artless Edeliza, which blazed upon him with unusual lustre, from the stile and manner in which she had adorned and heightened her modest beauties by the artillery of a dress admirably chosen to captivate; and so well did she succeed, aided by the little blind god, under whose banners she had ventured to enlist, that a change took place in the heart of her favourite, against whom alone her designs were levelled, as sudden as it was to himself surprising.

Madeline was almost forgotten, and as little regarded as his grandmother would have been. Every thought, every wish now rested with Edeliza,—the little girl whom he had so long considered and treated as a mere playful child. He even felt himself angry with every gentleman who paid her any attention, or appeared as well pleased with her as himself, and his bosom actually throbbed with jealous indignation while he observed her animated look and sparkling eye at the various compliments addressed to her; but when she bestowed her smiles on another it was agony. Those enchanting smiles, those engaging looks, till this ill fated evening, had been wholly engrossed by himself, nor, till he knew the value of what he might lose, did he think he had anything to fear;—the delusion was ended, and he felt himself engaged in a new passion at the moment he was disengaged from an old one, which, having never been cherished by hope, was the more easily subdued.

He observed (for love, though said to be blind, is at times amazingly clear sighted) that De Clavering, the insensible, the fastidious De Clavering, appeared like himself, particularly attentive to Edeliza, condescended to say some civil things, hovered as near to her as possible, and followed her with an approving eye, as she gracefully exhibited her light and elegant figure in the dance, which, in his opinion, by no means proved him so indifferent to her charms as he had pretended to be in some of their unreserved and confidential conversations.—He had declared to De Huntingfield, as she glided past them, that she had a mine of harmony in her head, a troop of Cupids lying in ambush round her eyes and mouth, and an army of virtues encamped for life within her bosom.—De Willows heard him, and was convinced De Clavering had designs against his peace, and was as much in love as himself. The same charms which had so much influence on him might have made a captive of his friend.

Thus seriously in love, thus tortured by the sudden impulse of jealousy, De Willows sullenly cursed the folly of giving balls, execrated the misery of being obliged to mix with a crowd, and the unpardonable levity of permitting young women of delicacy and fashion to exhibit their beautiful persons and fine attitudes in the dance, to amuse a parcel of unmeaning and designing fools, and wound those who loved them,—while such robust amusements were only fit for Indian girls or Hottentots. He almost determined never to go to another ball, and to persuade Edeliza to form the same resolution.

Thus, with doubts, fears, and jealousies, was marked the beginning of a passion in the mind of De Willows, which ended but with life, and which every succeeding day, month, and year, served to strengthen and confirm.

The tragical tale of two lovers, who had been present at the ball, and who seemed to happiest of the party, appeared to make a deep impression on all who heard it, and had so much influence on De

Willows, that he determined no part of his conduct should ever give a moment's pain to the susceptible heart of Edeliza, if he should prove so fortunate as to be entrusted with the precious deposit, and obtain he consent of Sir Philip and Lady de Morney to bless him with the hand of their lovely daughter. The tale we have alluded to, though melancholy, being a real fact, we hope it will not be unacceptable to our readers.

Mr. and Mrs. Blandeville were the respectable parents of a numerous family, whom they educated from the produce of a well established and profitable business. They had several daughters; the eldest, who was both lively and handsome, was unfortunately admired by a young gentleman of the name of Narford. The attachment had been cherished by both parties from the time they went to school, and so marked were the attentions which, even at that early age, they had shewn to each other, that it had often excited the jokes and ridicule of their young companions, who were in the habit of frequently addressing the timid and blushing Lucy by the name of Mrs. Narford.

Her lover had the irreparable misfortune to lose both his parents before any plan had been formed for his future establishment.—He was likewise, unhappily for his interest, left to the care of inexperienced and careless guardians, who permitted him, as his fortune was genteel, to follow the bent of his own inclinations. His disposition being lively in the extreme, led him into innumerable eccentricities, and his juvenile indiscretions wasted a part of that fortune which should have been kept for his maturer age.

When his clerkship was just expired, (for he was articled to an attorney,) he made application to the parents of Lucy for leave to address their daughter. Mr. Blandeville was no stranger to some part of the vices and follies of which he had been guilty, but, as he likewise knew that enough of his fortune still remained to secure his daughter as comfortable an establishment as she had any right to expect, he promised, if his future conduct was irreproachable, that, when he was fixed in life, and able to provide for a family, he would give him the hand of his daughter, and from that period he had permission to visit Lucy as a lover, and was received at Mr. Blandeville's house as one of the family.

Lovers, it is too well known, will say and promise any thing. This observation was unhappily verified in the giddy and erring Narford, who, though he sincerely loved the daughter of Mr. Blandeville, and could not be ignorant that on his part he was equally beloved, very soon broke his word, and ran in to some glaring excesses, which could not be long concealed from those whom it most materially concerned. The gentle Lucy often ventured to reproach her lover, but his repentance and promises of amendment very soon procured his forgiveness.—Not so easily was the father to be softened. After repeatedly hearing of his intemperance and consequent riots, he forbade him his house, and prohibited his daughter from holding any further intercourse with one so unworthy of her regard, who had given such frequent proofs of his libertine disposition, had already wasted part of his property, and was in a way to squander the whole.

Unfortunately the prudent prohibition of the father was disregarded by the daughter, whose attachment to the unthinking Narford neither his vices nor follies had been able to conquer. She lamented his failings, but she could not subdue that attachment which had from so early a period of her life been implanted in her heart. From him only she had heard the tale of love, and he alone had obtained any interest in her affections. Love had bound her in his silken fetters, and she and not power to shake them off.

Many stolen interviews did the proscribed Narford obtain with his believing and inexperienced mistress by means of that all prevailing traitor, gold, whose influence few of the needy children of dependence can long withstand; nor could all the reproaches of a duteous and uncorrupted heart prevent Lucy from listening to the beguiling flatterer.

At the time they met at the Castle they had not been able to see each other for some weeks, and the pleasure was as great as it was unexpected. Their present situation and past sorrows were forgotten in their mutual joy, and the young lady easily prevailed upon to accept the hand of her lover for the evening, as she still hoped it was the hand destined to guide her through life.—Too happy in enjoying the society for which she languished to recollect the causes which had prevented their more frequent intercourse,—her spirits exhilarated by the gay and cheerful party, and the enlivening sounds of music, she listened to his vows with believing tenderness, and in a fond conceding moment of unreluctantly agreed to his proposal of a private marriage:—the day was fixed, and the hour for escape appointed.

The plan once determined, they indulged themselves in all that innocent fondness the prospect of being speedily united seemed to claim and authorize, but their happiness was as unstable and visionary as their plan. Some one that was present, either actuated by friendship to the parents, or envious at seeing the exulting transports which sparkled in the eyes of the lovers, and excited a suspicion of design, obtained sufficient intelligence from some broken sentences (conveyed in rather loud whispers from the lips of Narford, who was too much intoxicated with his unexpected success to be guarded by prudence) as to betray their intention.

The next day a letter was sent to Mr. Blandeville, to inform him of the plan, that he might take such steps as would prevent the threatening mischief. In consequence of this unpleasing intelligence, the young lady was so strictly confined and closely watched, that it was impossible she could either receive or send any letters with out being discovered, and Mr. Blandeville was too much enraged at finding the disobedient trick his daughter would have played him, to relax one moment in his rigour or care to prevent her eloping.

Narford, in the mean time, not able either to see Lucy, or convey any letter or message to her, became madly desperate, and ran into innumerable excesses, which, in the opinion of the prudent and thinking part of the world, justified the conduct of the lady's father, who commanded her not to see him, nor attempt to leave her own apartment till she could prevail upon herself to give him a solemn promise never again to hold intercourse, by word or letter, with that base, designing, and vile scoundrel, Narford.

The mother and sisters were equally offended with the unfortunate lover, whose conduct, previous to the time he had been forbidden the house of Mr. Blandeville, had in too many respects been highly blameable; but, as is frequently the case, what in his behaviour was worthy of praise had been concealed, while every deviation from prudence and rectitude was basely and maliciously exaggerated, Narford not having the happy art of concealing his frailties, or marking himself friends, by that bewitching softness of manners which, in our more polished days, will recommend the most libertine characters, and procure them a favourable and cordial reception in polite and even virtuous circles.

After trying, by every art and stratagem to bribe, or elude, the vigilance of Lucy's attendants, and making many attempts to soften the displeasure of her parents, Narford, in a fit of despair and intoxication, obtained by force an entrance into the house, and, falling on his knees, in the most humiliating manner, and most intelligible language he could command, begged they would permit him to see and converse one hour with his beloved Lucy, who he had heard was ill, and confined to her bed.

Though Mr. Blandeville fortunately was not at home, his request was peremptorily denied; but Mrs. Blandeville, somewhat softened by his agony, which, in spite of her anger, she could not help commiserating, promised, that, as soon as her daughter was in a state of convalescence, he should be indulged with seeing her in the presence of herself and one of her daughter; at the same time she could not help gently reproaching him for the inconsistency and unpardonable levity of his conduct, which not only compelled Mr. Blandeville to adopt these severe measures, but had involved her whole family in distress, as well as the unfortunate girl he pretended to love, and had attempted to draw aside from the paths of duty.

With great difficulty he was prevailed upon to leave the house, but not before the sound of his voice had caught the ear of the unhappy Lucy. She raised herself in the bed, and insisted on being informed what had occurred to bring poor Narford, and why she had not seen him.—It was now too late, (she added,) to run away; the danger of that was over; therefore surely she might be allowed to speak peace to his mind, and once more see him whom she had so long and so fondly loved, before the hand of death should close her eyes for ever, and in that sad moment shut our every bright ray of hope from his earthly prospects.

On being made acquainted with what had passed, and told the manner in which her lover forced his way into the house, she burst into tears, and exclaimed, she should never see him more in this world; "but he will not survive me long, (she continued.) I know he cannot live in peace when I am gone, and therefore we shall soon meet in a better, and I hope a happier, world."

These conflicts brought on a return of fever, which a frame so emaciated and weak as her's could not long sustain: it was succeeded by a delirium. The grief she had long cherished had preyed upon a constitution, always delicate, with so much violence as to render strength unequal to the contest. In a few short days her life was pronounced in the utmost danger, and hope was almost precluded.

No sooner was this sentence made known, than it was recommended to Mr. Blandeville to send for the lover of his daughter. At length he yielded somewhat reluctantly to the proposal. Narford came, and was admitted into the darkened apartment of the dying Lucy, who laid totally insensible of what passed around her. He heard her call upon his name, yet could not prevail upon her either to look at or speak to him.—Her eyes, glazed and obscured by the shades of death, and robbed of their former lustre, were no longer able to distinguish the beloved object for whom they shed so many tears, but, fixed on vacancy, seemed still bent in search of something they wished to behold. Her lips moved, and she appeared as if holding conversation with some one her disordered imagination fancied near her. The unhappy young man was so much shocked, that it was with the utmost difficulty he could confine his agonizing feelings from breaking forth into loud lamentations.—Somewhat recovering from the first stroke of seeing the ruins which grief had made on her with whom he had rested all his hopes, in whom were centered all his wishes, he knelt by her bedside, and, tenderly clasping between his own the burning hand of his almost dying mistress, he softly begged she would once more speak to her distracted Narford.

The voice seemed to be understood; she suddenly turned her face toward him, and feebly pressing his hand, in broken and hurried sentences said something to him.—Only the words, "Dear Narford, we must part, and part for ever!" were understood; and, after making a feeble effort to draw him closer to her side, as if afraid he should leave her, she was seized with convulsions, which obliged the terrified lover to quit the room. He rushed out of the house in a state little less alarming than that in which he had left the fair cause of his distress.

The whole night he wandered before the habitation of the dying Lucy,—for that she was dying the horrid scene he had witnessed, the countenances of those around her, and his own feelings, too well informed him. During the long and gloomy night, in which he remained exposed to and unsheltered from the wind and storm, he frequently stopped to listen at the door. All within was silent and cheerless as the grave, and in every sound that reached his ear from without, he imagined he could distinguish groans and sighs. Every object he could see brought to his tortured imagination the distressing, the convulsed figure of the once-animated and lovely Lucy, whose distorted features and painful struggles were ever before his mental sight, there to remain fixed as long as his existence should endure; for was it possible he could ever forget or wish to lose the remembrance of that persecuted and innocent sufferer, who died for the unworthy, the unfortunate Narford?

At length the day broke. The sun arose with its usual splendor, but appeared to him dark as Erebus. All nature wore one universal gloom, and had all nature been at that moment annihilated, (as were his hopes,) the change had been scarcely perceived; for Lucy, who gave to life its brightest tints, and to all things animate or inanimate, grace, beauty, and value, was seen no more!—No longer the soft tones of her voice vibrated on his ear to lull his soul to peace, or, if seen, she had lost all recollection of the poor forlorn wanderer, who now felt ten-fold every pang she suffered.

Late in the morning Narford saw a female servant slowly open the door. He ran, or rather flew, to make his trembling inquiries. She was in tears, and totally unable to tell him that all was over,—that the loveliest of women, the favourite child of nature, was no longer the victim of pain and sorrow, and that her freed spirit now soared beyond the reach of persecution, "the mortal having put on immortality;" but her emphatical silence unfolded the sad tale.—A freezing chillness ran thrilling to his heart, and with a groan of despair he sunk upon his parent earth. In that happy state of insensibility he was conveyed to his lodgings by some people who were passing by, where we will for the present leave him to the care of his sympathizing friends.

This unfortunate young man, notwithstanding his unguarded conduct and numerous eccentricities, was beloved by many for his generous disposition, cheerfulness, and unceasing humour.

In the house of Mr. and Mrs. Blandeville all was distraction, despair, and self-reproach. The illness and subsequent death of a beloved and amiable child laid heavy at their hearts, and overwhelmed them like the sudden bursting of a torrent; for, though prudence forbade them to unite their daughter to a man whose conduct threatened her with many sorrows, at the moment they wished to put an end to so unpromising an union, they had no idea that any fatal consequences would have attended the separation, and they too late regretted not having granted Narford's request of being permitted to see their daughter at a more early stage of her illness.—Mr. Blandeville drooped under his own painful reflections, his wife felt more than she either could or wished to express, and the younger part of the family were for a time inconsolable.

The tale spread rapidly abroad, and in all its various shapes excited the compassion of those who heard it. Lucy had been as generally beloved as admired, and Narford, who had once appeared deserving of contempt, was now the object of pity. Such are the rapid changes which take place in the human mind.

Mrs. Blandeville, unknown to the rest of the family, sent several times to make inquiries after the unhappy Narford. The accounts she received were as various as the melancholy changes which succeeded each other. He was sometimes in a state of actual distraction,—at others in a sad and silent despondency the most determined and alarming, refusing to take his food, or to hold conversation with any one.

At length the day for the interment of Lucy arrived. The procession, sad and slow, was followed by almost every inhabitant of the town and adjoining villages. A solemn dirge was sung as they went along, and a number of young maidens joined in the chorus. Flowers were strewn into and around the grave, as emblematical of the charming flower that like themselves was untimely cut down, and doomed like them to wither and to die.

The service began;—the coffin was carefully let down into the grave, and, just as the earth was thrown upon it, and the priest pronounced that awful and humiliating sentence,—"Earth to earth, ashes to ashes, dust to dust," a figure, with dishevelled hair, and a face pale as that of the victim just deposited in her last sad resting place, rushed past them all, and quick as lightning, before anyone could suspect or think of preventing his design, threw himself with the utmost violence into the grave, and, clinging with agonizing frenzy to the coffin, cried out, "I have found her now, and no one shall ever again tear her from me, for she was mine,—mine by her own consent! Proceed, (added he, in a shrill and distracted tone, for the surprise and confusion that this scene occasioned had prevented the service from going on,)—be quick, and hide me in the friendly earth!—I come to sleep with Lucy:—this is our bridal bed!—Why do you hesitate?—here I shall find rest for ever:—this is my home, and here shall be my heaven!"

The priest endeavoured to persuade him to quite the grave, and let the ceremony be concluded, telling him, time and patience would, he hoped, reconcile him to the will of heaven, and convince him that all things were ordered for the best and the wisest purposes.

"Avaunt, deceiver! (cried the enraged maniac.)—I tell you that Lucy was unfairly robbed of life,—stolen from my arms, and forced into this place, and where I will watch by her and protect her from farther violence;—therefore say no more, lest my daring hand should attempt to pluck the sun from its orbit, or call upon the stars to fall upon your head, and mine for permitting a star more brilliant than themselves to fall.—Go on, I say,—bury me deep and sure!—I wish to become a worm, that I may crawl to the side of Lucy.—She will own her poor distracted Narford, even in that most loathsome and degraded form."

It is impossible to describe the scene that followed. Many attempts were made before the poor young man could be dragged from the grave of his lamented mistress.—At length, he was forcibly taken out,— guarded, and carried home by some of the weeping spectators.

It was many months before any hopes of his recovery could be cherished. His reason was still more endangered, and, from that period to the end of his unfortunate life, he was deranged at times, and by his conduct appeared as much a lunatic in his intervals of reason. He very soon squandered all that remained of his fortune, and became a wanderer upon the earth, never having a settled home, and seldom going into a bed.

He was frequently absent so long, that his friends concluded he was no more.—He would then return to those scenes which never failed to bring on a renewal of his unfortunate malady, and would lay whole nights by the side of Lucy's grave, talking to her with the same ardour and enthusiastic affection as if she had been living.

At length Mr. Blandeville, whom he would, as frequently as he saw him in his fits of insanity, attack with the most pointed and virulent abuse, took compassion on his sufferings, and settled a sum of money upon him, to be paid quarterly, sufficiently competent to procure him the necessaries and many of the comforts of life; placing him in a family who had been long attached to him, and who continued to take the utmost care of him to the end of his wretched existence, and by every tender attention softened, as much as it was in human power, those sorrows which could only terminate in death.

CHAPTER II.

A tale so sad and interesting as that we have recited soon found its way to the inhabitants of the castle, particularly as De Clavering had been called in to the assistance of the dying Lucy.

The melancholy scene he witnessed, as we may imagine, made a lasting and forcible impression upon a heart so tender and susceptible as his, and he did not fail to make such comments upon it, as he hoped would have some weight on the minds of those to whom they were addressed; but he did not succeed in his design; for, whatever Sir Philip de Morney might think, he chooses, and took care to keep to himself, and the Baron not even condescending to make any observations on a subject in which he did not appear to feel the least interested, and which he considered as being too romantic and childish to merit the attention of a person in his high station.

Lady de Morney and the young people wept for the fate of Narford and Lucy, while the latter wondered any parents could be so cruel as to separate such fond and faithful lovers.

Notwithstanding the utmost pains had been taken to conceal the cause of the Baron's sudden indisposition, it had in part transpired, owing, as we may presume, to the irresistible propensity, and restless curiosity, the Baron's servant felt to know all his master's secrets, and his great eagerness to impart them when known. Some words, which had dropped from the Baron to his friend Sir Philip, the evening of the alarm, just as Pedro was ordered out of the room, unfortunately caught his ear, which was instantaneously applied to the key-hole of the door to obtain farther intelligence; and, though he could not so exactly understand the story as to connect it with accuracy, he picked up enough of it to make him desirous of knowing the whole; and, having heard the word ghost uttered more than once with great emphasis, it gave him some suspicion that his master's illness originated from a fright, and the more than usual earnestness, with which he asserted the truth of what he had been saying, confirmed Pedro in this opinion.

Thus the half-formed tale was whispered under the most solemn promises of secresy from one to another, till every servant in the family had gleaned up something, without any one of them knowing what it meant.

A few nights after, as Pedro was attending his master, when he was going to bed, he determined to make one effort to discover the whole story, and try whether he could not prevail on the Baron to entrust him with a secret he would have given some part of his wages to find out. He opened this important business as follows.

"I shall be heartily glad, my lord, when we get from this castle, and return to your own."

"Why so? (inquired his master:)—my friend, Sir Philip, is very hospitable, and his family infinitely charming."

"Yes, yes, I dare say, my lord, in your opinion the young ladies are charming creatures, and I fancy they are not a whit less pleased with your lordship."

"Do you think so, Pedro? (said the Baron, in one of his most harmonious tones, his pride and self-love being gratified by his servant's observation.)—Why, indeed, I had never much reason to complain of the ladies' coolness."

"It would certainly be surprising if you had, my lord. A man of your rank, fortune, and figure, is not very likely to meet with coldness; it is only such a poor ugly dog as I am that must expect to be frowned upon by the women."

"Oh! then, Pedro, (said the Baron smiling,) a disappointment in love makes you wish to quit this place."

"No, my lord. I complain of nothing in the day; *that* generally passes off very well; but, in the night, there are so many cursed ghosts clattering about, with such confounded noises at their heels, both within and without doors, that a man can neither sleep nor move with comfort or security."

"Psha! (replied the Baron,) let me hear of no such idle and improbable tales.—I did not suppose you so great a fool or so dastardly a coward as to mind the nonsense of women and children."

"As to that, (said Pedro, nettled by the contemptuous manner of the Baron, and the epithet of coward,) I have as much courage as most men among *men*; but, when I am forced to mix with ghosts and evil spirits, I want a little spice of that courage with which your lordship is so bountifully endowed. I dare say, my lord, you never saw a ghost, and were never frightened either by the living or the dead."

"What should I be frightened at? (cried the Baron impatiently;) let me hear no more such impertinent nonsense."

"I hope (muttered Pedro) the next time they come, they will pay you another visit. It is an honour due to your dignity, and we servants can very well dispense with their company;" but this said in so low a voice, as he shut the door, that it was impossible to be understood by the imperious master to whom it was addressed. "As much a coward as I am, (continued he, as he went along,) I was never frightened into a fit as some folks have been with all their boasted courage and great knowledge."

Notwithstanding the Baron was so much alarmed by the appearance of his Isabella, that he could scarcely shake it from his mind a moment, and remained in a state of anxiety and terror, yet it was impossible he should be any longer blind to the dejection of Roseline, or insensible of her cold indifference. If she met him with a smile, it was visibly the smile of anguish. She sometimes appeared to avoid him, and more than once had made an effort to leave him at the very instant he was addressing her in one of his fondest and most impassioned speeches.—Sir Philip was his friend; on him he had conferred many favours: it was both his interest and inclination to bring about an union between him and his daughter. It was possible he might have deceived him as to the real situation of her heart;—the thought was too alarming to his feelings and his pride to be easily got rid of. Roseline was often absent, and that for several hours together: it looked suspicious. He would no longer trust either the father or the daughter; but, with the assistance of his man Pedro, who was a shrewd fellow at finding out a secret, he would endeavour to discover whether he was not right in his conjecture of having a rival. Sir Philip had certainly promised more for his daughter than he supposed him authorized to do, or than the young lady herself was able or willing to ratify: he determined therefore to get rid of his doubts as soon as possible, and either obtain the prize he had in view, or withdraw himself for ever from the castle.

Audrey, who had in the mean while picked up a vague unconnected account of what had happened in respect to the ghost, was eager to tell the wonderful tale to Roseline, who, though incredulous as she had ever appeared to all the marvellous tales she had imparted to her, ought to be informed of this, she thought, as it was so connected with the history of her intended husband. She luckily met her young lady on the stairs, put her finger on her lips to impose silence, and, with much solemnity in her look and manner, beckoned her to follow her into the gallery, when, stepping into the first room she came to, she thus eagerly began.

"Well, miss, it was as I said; the Baron is no better than he should be. I have waited successfully these three days to tell you so; but you are grown so preserved and so shy, a body can seldom catch a moment to speak to you."

"What is the matter, my good Audrey?"

"Matter enough on my conscience, if one believes all one hears! Only think, miss, of a ghost, that should have been minding its business at the Baron's own castle, having taken the trouble of following him to this upon some special business it had to municate. However, travelling three or four hundred miles is nothing to a ghost, that can, as I have heard, go at the rate of a thousand miles in a minutes, either by land, sea, or water, it matters not to them; but we could have expenced with such visitors, God help us! For we have enow such that go with this castle, and, 'tis said, must do so till the day of judgment."

Roseline, who paid but a little attention to Audrey's tales, smiled at this, and gave her a sly look of incredulity, which convinced her of her unbelief. This was a kind of claim upon her to confirm it more strongly.

"Well, you may think as you please, Miss Roseline, the Baron was actilly scared into a fit of arpaplexy at seeing his own wife, all in white, the very moral of herself when alive; and, what is more, she held a knife and a lighted candle in her hand, and shewed him the wound in her bosom which casioned her death; and she sneered at him, shaked her ghostly head, grinned, and, as he was found upon the floor, 'tis supposed she knocked him down, and then went away in a sky-rocket, or a squib, or some such thing, as belong to those sort of hanimals; for the noise she made at going off was so great and amendous, it broke the drum of Pedro's ear, and left the Baron in a state of sensibility."[33]

"I would advise you, Audrey, (said Roseline,) not to give credit to such improbable tales, and never again to repeat this which you have been telling me."

"'Tis genevin, miss, I assure you. I had it from Pedro's own mouth; so, if you are determined to marry a man haunted by the ghost of another wife, you must abide by the incision. She was certainly sent out of the world unfairly, or why should she not rest in her grave as quietly as other folks?"

Roseline, much as she disliked the Baron as a lover, had too much respect for her father's friend to permit her servant to speak of him so freely, and to lay so dreadful a crime to his charge, which she concluded, like the story of the ghost, was merely the invention of evil-minded people.—She therefore reproved Audrey with a seriousness that alarmed her, and assured her, if she ever again presumed to mention Baron Fitzosbourne in terms so disrespectful and degrading, she would instantly request her father to send her from the castle.

The prating Abigail, finding her young lady really displeased, chose to alter her tone.—To be sure she might have been wrong informed; the world was a wicked place, and some people were sadly entreated in it:—the Baron was a gentleman,—a powerful fine gentleman it was successively hard to be belied;—no one could expence with that:—he was a lord into the bargain, and, notwithstanding his methodicalness, had some good qualities, and, for

---

[33] This ghostly image recalls a frequently repeated motif in gothic literature: the Bleeding Nun. Matthew Lewis's novel *The Monk,* written in 1794 and published in 1796—a year before publication of *Bungay Castle,* contains the most extreme application of this frequently used character.

certain, was as fine as pice of 'tiquity as any that hung up in the great hall, and looked as antic as the old walls covered with ivory.—Roseline made no answer to this curious eulogium, and Audrey very soon took herself away.

The Baron was not long in determining how to proceed. He became resolute to satisfy his doubts respecting his having a rival. It was neither improbable, nor unlikely, that some of the young officers, stationed in or about the castle, might have designs inimical to his. The lady herself might have favoured their pretences unknown to her father; and, if so, he should run some risk in making her his wife.—The thought was too painful and degrading to be supported, and the critical situation of affairs would not admit of longer deliberation.

The month was on the very eve of terminating, at the expiration of which Sir Philip had promised him the hand of his daughter; yet the young lady was not more conciliating, or less coy and distant in her behaviour to him, than she had been the first day of their meeting. Pedro was summoned, and for some time was closeted with his master. He was promised a liberal reward if he could get into the good graces of the female servants, and make himself master of the young lady's secrets; luckily for our heroine, she had not made a confidant of any one of them.

This Pedro undertook, as he had already began to make love to Audrey, who, in her moments of conceding tenderness, had told him all she knew, making some additions of her own; but the whole amounted to but little more than—her young lady was strangely altered: it might be, her love for the Baron had produced this change; but, for her part, she could not think it possible for any one to like such an old frampled figure.

The Baron next proposed that Pedro should accompany him, in taking a ramble about the castle, after the family had retired to rest, to reconnoitre the premises, and learn, if possible, from what quarter they were most exposed to danger. He determined to explore all the secret passages, for he could not help cherishing suspicions that lovers might be admitted, and intrigues carried on, unknown to the most watchful and careful parent; and to what but the prevailing influence of a favoured rival could he impute the uncommon and increasing coldness of Roseline?

It was not to be wondered at that the Baron ws alarmed, for the conduct of his daughter had not escaped the eyes of Sir Philip, who, chiefly displeased with what he termed her obstinacy and caprice, in order to compel her to his purpose, had notwithstanding he promised to drop the subject for a month, found it necessary to caution her to be more guarded and respectful in her behaviour, and that same time assuring her he would not survive the disappointment of his hopes, in seeing her united to his friend; adding another horrid threat, that, if she betrayed his design, in that moment she would terminate her father's existence.

This dreadful sentence at once determined the fate of the unhappy Roseline, and, having no alternative left, she instantly promised to give her hand to the Baron, and sacrifice her own happiness to preserve the life of her father, on which she knew that of her mother depended. Her brothers and sisters too! how could she support the thought of depriving them of a father's protection, and become herself a parricide!—Her own sufferings would be but short;—their's might be continued through a long and weary pilgrimage.

Her father, satisfied with her promise, retired and left her to recover herself. Then it was she recollected her engagement, and thought of the prisoner. Her resolution faltered, and reason tottered on its throne.

The dreadful fate she was preparing for him,—the distress her loss and inconstancy would inflict on the interesting object, dearer to her than life, or ten thousand worlds, tortured her to distraction, and shook her whole frame: the blood of life receded from her heart for a few moments, and she fell to the earth.

Soon however she recovered to a more perfect sense of her miseries: she wrung her hands;—she would see her Walter;—she would continue to do so till she became the property of him whom she detested, and could never love, and who, she fervently prayed, might be deprived of claiming the rights of a husband, by her being snatched from his embraces by the friendly hand of death, a rival, which if he did not fear, he could neither injure nor subdue; and she should have the delightful, the soul-consoling satisfaction of descending to the grave a spotless victim to her love of Walter. Her spirit would perhaps be permitted to guard him from danger, and watch his footsteps, while he remained on earth, and in heaven she could meet and claim him as her own.

These thoughts, romantic as they appear in the eye of reason and experience, had a wonderful effect upon her mind, and restored in it some degree to its usual tone and composure. She became more resigned to her fate, and to the above-mentioned determinations added another, namely, that, before she became a wife, she would write to her unfortunate lover, and explain the motives that had induced her to break her engagement with him, sufficiently to exculpate her from blame, prevent his execrating and hating the name of Roseline, and if possible still to preserve his esteem. Edwin should be the messenger she would entrust with her letter. These weighty matters settled in the only manner that could make them conformable to the present state of her feelings, she resolved silently and without complaining to yield to a sentence from which, however unjust and arbitrary, she knew there could be appeal, no chance of a reprieve.

Her determination and unconditional consent were soon made known to the Baron by his delighted and exulting friend, who now ventured a few gentle reproaches for the little confidence that had been placed in his word, and the injustice which had been shewn to his zeal. The Baron received this intelligence with unaffected pleasure,— apologized for his lover-like doubts, which had originated from the superior merits of the beloved object, and the disparity of years, which some ladies might have considered as an objection to an union taking place.

Superb dresses were to be ordered for the bride, new carriages built, and the lawyers set to work with all possible expedition; for, as Roseline had stipulated for no certain time being allowed her, to prepare for the awful change which was to take place in her situation, her father, eager to put it beyond the power of any earthly contingency to disappoint his wishes, availed himself of the omission, and determined to hurry matters as much as possible. In fact, the horror of her father's vow had impressed itself so deeply on the mind of Roseline, and introduced such a train of distracting images, as lessened the apprehension of what might happen to herself.

It was now publicly said, that the important event was very soon to take place, and the joyous bustle which succeeded plainly shewed, the report was not without foundation. The surprise and consternation of Edwin are not to be described: he sought and obtained an interview with his sister, who, without absolutely betraying her promise to her father, or explaining how her consent had been extorted, said enough to convince him that compulsion, in some shape or other, had been made use of to force her into measures so entirely repugnant to her feelings, that he feared would involve her in irretrievable wretchedness, and he took his resolutions accordingly.

The enamoured lover, after hearing such unexpected and pleasant intelligence from his friend, requested an audience with the lovely arbitress of his fate. He was accordingly admitted.

Roseline made no attempt to deny having given her consent to become his wife; but the freezing coldness of her manner, and the continued dejection still visible on her artless and expressive countenance, served to increase his doubts; and, so far was it from exciting his compassion, it awakened his pride, confirmed his suspicions, and roused them into action: but, as he had no clue to guide him, and could make no discovery sufficiently conclusive to fix his jealousy on any particular object, he was under the necessity of trusting to chance, and his own unremitting endeavours, to unravel the mystery he suspected. Actuated by a sullen kind of resentment, he determined at all events to avail himself of the power thrown into his hands to obtain his desires, resolving, if ever he discovered she loved any man in preference to himself, to sacrifice the detested object of her regard to the just vengeance of an injured husband.

A few nights after, a favourable opportunity presenting itself, the restless Baron, accompanied by his man Pedro, who had undertaken to conduct him about those parts of the castle contrived to defeat the designs of men when they came with any hostile intentions, but which might be favourable to those of an artful lover, began his silent perambulation.

After descending from the battlements, which he had cautiously paced over, looking into every place he thought likely to conceal the rival he expected to find, he returned by a different route, and accidentally went down the winding stairs of the South tower. The door, leading to the prisoner's apartment, he passed in silence, supposing it a lodging-room belonging to the guards, or some of the domestics.—When, however, he came to the bottom of the stairs; turning to look under a kind of arch-way that seemed to communicate with some other apartments, he was startled, and his doubts received farther confirmation from seeing a door, which led to the dungeon, standing open,—a circumstance that served to convince the Baron all was not right, as those places were in general kept well secured, not only to guard against danger, but to prevent their being seen, as it often happened the safely of the castle depended entirely upon the secret contrivances for their internal defence being unknown to all but he governor.

It happened unfortunately, that Albert, who, after he knew the family were in bed, had descended from his own room in order to fetch something which his master wanted from his former habitation, not supposing he was in danger of being followed by any one, had incautiously neglected to shut this door after him. The Baron, not doubting but he was on the eve of making some important discovery, ordered his man to guard the door, to prevent any one escaping while he proceeded in his search.

Albert, luckily hearing some one enter the passage after him, had likewise his suspicions, though of a very different nature. He concluded no one could come to that place with any good design, and trembled lest some discovery had been made respecting the removal of his master, which might expose him to farther persecutions, and bring on a renewal of his former miseries. Who ever it might be, he determined, if possible to find out their intention.

Edwin had acquainted him with every circumstance he knew in regard to the distressing situation of his sister, and they had agreed not to inform the unfortunate Walter of the impending storm which threatened him with the deprivation of a treasure far dearer to him than his own existence, and which they concluded would at once fatal blow rob him not only of every hope that he had so long and fondly cherished, but even of life itself.

Albert was soon convinced that the person who has followed him was no other than the haughty imperious Baron, the rival of his beloved master, and the destroyer of that fabric on which he had rested his security for happiness. He carried a lighted candle in one hand, and a drawn sword in the other, and appeared wonderously curious about something which Albert, not in the humour to put the most favourable construction on his actions, concluded must be mischief.—Thus put upon his guard, he cautiously locked the door which led to his master's former apartments, and, as he was well acquainted with every avenue, each turning and winding in the curious labyrinth of these cheerless regions, he had no fear for his own safety, knowing that it was easy to elude the search of one who was a stranger to them; but, as he did not suppose the Baron (or the business which brought him there be what it might) came entirely unattended, it behoved him to act with the utmost circumspection.

In a little time he observed the Baron had entered the damp unwholesome square that was surrounded by the still more gloomy and unfriendly habitations contrived to render life a worse punishment than the most cruel death. He looked carefully into every one of them, and, coming to that in which stood the coffin before mentioned in this narrative, and seeing the black cloth, by which it had once been covered, now hanging in mouldering and tattered fragments around it, a silent memento of that destroying hand which spares neither the dead nor the living, urged, as we may suppose, by one of those sudden and irresistible impulses which we are often actuated to obey against the dictates of sober reason, he stept in, and in an attitude of thoughtful meditation, struck with the horrid scenes which till now his eyes had never encountered, unknowing what he did, he placed one foot on the top of the sad receptacle, on which his looks were bent in serious reflection, when, awful and dreadful to relate, a deep groan issued from the coffin, and a voice exclaimed,—"Forbear, you hurt me!—you will crush my bones to powder!"

The Baron started, and flew back so violently, that he struck his head against the opposite wall.—A moment's reflection, however, served to inspire him with more resolution, and to convince him that this could not be real;—it must be the wild effects of his own distempered imagination;—the dead were never heard to speak, and why a voice from the grave should be sent to him he could not comprehend. He determined therefore not to be alarmed but firm in his purpose; when, in the next instant the same voice, as if it knew the thoughts which floated in his mind, addressed him another time in a rather louder and more authoritative tone from another part of the dungeon and warned him not to interrupt the peaceful slumbers of the dead. Again called upon, it could not be delusion. Some one, a lover perhaps, was concealed in that tomb from which he was to be frightened like a school-boy. In an instant, with one violent blow, he crushed the mouldering abode of its insensible inhabitant to pieces, and a heap of bones were then presented to his sight, which had once belonged to a creature like himself, endowed perhaps with feeling, more generous and humane than those which dwelt in the bosom of the man who had thus insulted its humble remains.

"Cause my bones to be decently put in the grave!" said the voice issuing from the coffin,) and tremble for yourself! The Baron rendered desperate by terror, and his recollection of the scene he encountered, the Baron eagerly wished to get from a situation so calculated to instill every kind of fear into the mind, if unaccompanied by the still greater horrors which had so wonderfully occurred to increase them; but, well knowing, if he were discovered in such a situation, it must subject him to various suspicions, among which those of a treasonable nature might probably be numbered.—He determined to brave it out, and retire without making any alarm, not doubting but an explanation would equally expose him to censure and ridicule.

As a last effort, however, he mustered courage enough to inquire in a tremulous tone, "What is it I hear?—If a man, let him come forth, and declare his wrongs; I will undertake to defend and right them."

"Can the man (replied his mysterious companion, who now appeared to be close to him) expect being believed when he offers to revenge wrongs of which he never heard a complaint? Can he who oppresses others, and is deaf to the sufferings of innocence, think to purchase pardon by the appearance of mercy?—Mend your own heart:—leave this castle:—then the living and the dead will sleep in peace."[34]

The Baron now shook with terror, and called for no farther explanation, but, as quickly as his trembling legs could carry him,

---

[34] Accentuating his villainy, the Baron, like the vampire, disturbs both the living and the dead.

began to explore the same way back by which he had gained admittance. Just as he reached the bottom of those stairs which Edwin and his fair companions had so often descended to make their benevolent visits to the prisoner, his ear was again arrested by the same invisible monitor. "Rob not his castle of its treasure:—search to find one more dear, whom you may render happy, who long has suffered imprisonment and wrongs."

Again he stopped. The words vibrated on his ear, and then all was silent. At length he proceeded in his miserable progress, and distinguished the distant sound of footsteps, which he concluded were the centinels on guard, and was soon afterwards revived by hearing the watch proclaim the hour of night. He now eagerly rushed onwards, and found, though Pedro had not deserted his post, he was fast locked in the arms of sleep, and snoring as soundly as if his weary limbs had rested on a bed of down. He was awakened by a hearty shake from his master, and ordered to lead the way to his chamber.

Pedro, glad to be released from an employment for which he had no great relish, rejoiced at hearing the welcome mandate, and humbly inquired if he had made any discovery. The answer he received was,— that all was safe and quite in the castle, and that he believed his fears and suspicions had been hastily formed, and had not foundation.

The Baron, however, was not exactly in that state of serenity and composure of which he endeavoured to assume the appearance.—That voice!—what could it mean?—from whom, and from what quarter could it come?—It might be the echo of some one confined in a cell over his head, or beneath his feet. It could not allude to him, or it might be a contrivance to alarm him from his purpose; yet, if he mentioned it to his friend, he would treat it as the delusion of a distempered fancy.

All he could determine upon doing was to hasted the preparations for his marriage, and, if Roseline should be over-ruled by her father, and give him her hand with reluctance, the fault would bring its punishment upon their own heads; but he still hoped that, when once she became his wife and saw herself surrounded with splendor, her coy airs would be done away: she would set a proper value on his love and generosity, and as Baroness Fitzosbourne be the happiest of her sex.— With such consoling and fallacious hopes he endeavoured to banish his doubts, and compose himself to rest, and, soon forgetting Isabella, and the warning voice of his invisible monitor, he sunk into the arms of sleep.

CHAPTER III.

NOT so soon, nor so easily, did the artless, the devoted Roseline lose the remembrance of her heart-felt sorrows. Every hour, every moment, as it fled, brought with it an increase of anguish to her agitated mind. The most distant idea of an union with the Baron was scarcely to be borne, as the certainty of it no longer admitted of a doubt, she shrunk from her own reflections as she would have done from the stroke of death. To be for ever torn from Walter—to see him no more,—no more to converse with and soothe the sorrows of that oppressed and solitary sufferer,—was by far a more insupportable trial than that she was doomed to endure in her own mind and person.

From the world and its unsatisfactory pleasures she could expect no resource:—friends she had none whose power could remove her distresses: her only hope therefore rested on death to release her from persecution, and the reflection most tormenting to the giddy and happy children of prosperity, who consider life as their greatest treasure, and over whose minds a thought of its termination will throw a gloom in the midst of their gayest moments, proved to our heroine her only consolation. She now considered the shortness and uncertainty of life as its greatest blessing, and feared that time, of whom she had often complained for being so rapid and unmarked in its flight, would now torture her by moving in a slow and sluggard pace to the close of her days. She continued, as usual, to make her stolen visits to the prisoner as opportunities presented themselves; but these visits were no longer attended with pleasure or satisfaction. In her own mind she formed a resolution, even if the consequence should prove fatal to herself, to attempt obtaining the freedom of the prisoner as soon as she had lost her own. This she considered merely as an act of humanity and justice, and would have thought no sacrifice too great, could she have restored that peace of which she knew her loss would deprive him.

Walter, notwithstanding much pains were taken to prevent his making any discovery of what passed in the castle, observed so alarming an alteration in the manners, countenance, and spirits, of Roseline, as led him to puzzle himself with various conjectures respecting the cause; but, as he had been often told by Albert many things occurred in the world to harass and give uneasiness to those who were engaged in its busy scene, of which he could form no idea, being a stranger to their nature, it was impossible for him to judge of their effect. He therefore determined not to enter on a topic which might wound the feelings of Roseline, and could not fail proportionably to distress himself; and as he would, had it been in his power, have prevented her knowing the slightest pang of sorrow, to her he resolutely remained silent on a subject in which his heart was so much interested, as seldom to allow his thinking on any other. To Albert, indeed, he ventured to make known his tormenting apprehensions; but, as Albert was now guided by the direction of Edwin, he only returned such evasive answers to his questions and complaints, as just served to keep hope from sinking into absolute despondency.

Edwin had reposed an unbounded confidence in De Clavering, De Willows, and Hugh Camelford, in regard to his sister, and without reserve informed them of his own engagements with Madeline, who had received the positive commands of her father to enter on the year of her noviciate. His situation was now become desperate; the crisis had arrived which admitted of no alternative. He must either give up the connexion, or make some effort to secure the prize he had taken such unwearied pains to obtain. His friends promised secrecy and assistance in whatever way he should find it convenient to put their sincerity to the test. He had likewise separately introduced them into the apartment of the prisoner, and if, before they saw him, they found themselves disposed to pity and respect him, they were now actuated by the personal regard they could not help feeling in his behalf, which his manners and understanding failed not to inspire in such liberal minds. Hugh Camelford declared himself ready to tie in his defence, and to encounter a host of tevils to procure his freedom.

Preparations were now began, and the day fixed for the wedding. The marriage ceremony was to be performed in the chapel of the nunnery by father Anselm, and, as Roseline made no effort to stop or postpone the proceedings, none but the parties most intimately concerned had an idea that she felt any reluctance to become a bride.

Edeliza and Bertha were half wild with joy: they were to be met at the altar by the abbess, Madeline, and Agnes de Clifford; the two latter intended to officiate as bride-maids with the Miss de Morneys.—To describe the various feelings of the parties would fill a volume. Suffice it then to say, that Lady de Morney, far from engaging in the necessary arrangements with pleasure and alacrity, never looked at the dejected countenance of her daughter without feeling a severe reproof from the silent monitor which she, like every other mortal, carried in her bosom. Sir Philip exulted in having managed matters so cleverly as to carry his point (a point to which the necessity of his circumstances reduced him with less difficulty than he expected,) and the Baron, resting satisfied that no woman in her senses could dislike him, or be insensible to the advantages that an union with a man of his rank and character would procure her, determined no longer to encourage either doubts or fears as to her shyness and reluctant compliance. It might, as her father had asserted, proceed from her inexperience, her lover for her parents, and her ignorance of the world. In this delusion we must for the present leave him, in order to return to those for whose happiness we confess ourselves more interested.

Roseline, who was obliged to confine her conflicts chiefly to her own bosom, saw the preparations going forward with that settled and silent despair, which, at the moment it evinced her fortitude, would have shewn to those acquainted with the nature of her feelings that every hope was precluded.

Edeliza and Bertha were astonished that their sister could see the rich clothes, and all the paraphernalia of her bridal dress, with such indifference. The former secretly thought she should not be able to shew so much composure if she were as soon to give her hand to her favourite De Willows.

The passion, which this young beauty had cherished in her innocent bosom, had "grown with her growth, and strengthened with her strength," and, lately encouraged to hope meeting an equal return from the increasing attention of the beloved object, it remained no longer in her power to conceal her partiality, and De Willows, attached and grateful for being so flatteringly distinguished, only waited till the marriage of her sister had taken place to make known his inclinations to Sir Philip, not less anxious than his lovely enslaver to have his pretensions authorized by the approbation and consent of her father; but he was not without his fears that the ambition, which had of late taken such full possession of the governor's mind, might disapprove his aspiring to unite himself with a descendant of the De Morneys.

The day before the marriage was to take place, Roseline made several attempts to enter the prisoner's apartment without being able to accomplish her purpose. At length she sent to speak with her brother Edwin in her chamber, and begged of him never to forsake the dear, the unhappy Walter, when she should be far distant. She then gave him a letter to deliver to her unfortunate lover as soon as she had left the castle. Of Madeline she proposed taking leave in person. On her brother's affairs she dared not trust herself to converse, confessing that her own distresses rendered her unable to talk, or even think, of his being as wretched as herself.

Edwin in reply said but little; his mind seemed agitated and employed on something he did not appear inclined to communicate. He readily agreed to comply with her request to accompany her for the last time to the apartment of Walter.

They found the solitary sufferer more composed and more cheerful than they had seen him for some time; Albert too appeared lively and active. Roseline was welcomed by her lover in a language far more expressive than words, and as perfectly understood: his eyes rested on her pallid and death-like countenance, with a fond, yet chastened delight, which she thought she had never observed in them before; he took her hand, pressed it to his lips, and looked up to her with that kind of adoration which he would have felt in the presence of an angel. He did not seem to notice the dejection which Roseline every moment expected would have occasioned some tender inquiries. Edwin began to converse on in different subjects; but the silent anguish he saw his sister vainly endeavouring to conceal rendered him very unfit for the office he had undertaken. The lovers were never less inclined to talk. The prisoner had taken the hand of Roseline on her first entrance, and retained the willing captive without its making one struggle to regain its freedom, till she was startled by a tear that fell upon it.

Nature, how powerful, how all-subduing, is thy simple but prevailing influence! The tenderest speech could not have said half so much as this precious and expressive tear.—Till this moment our heroine had preserved the appearance of fortitude; but now the mask fell to the ground, and she could no longer keep up the character of heroism she had assumed. By a kind of convulsive pressure of his hand, he perceived she noticed his silent agitations, and it acted with the rapidity of electricity on feelings which he found could no longer be restrained.

"My dear Walter, (said Roseline, giving him a look that penetrated to his heart,) why will you thus distress yourself and me? You know not, you can never know, how dear you are to the ill fated Roseline de Morney, whom ere long you will perhaps execrate, and wish you had never seen; but forbear, in pity forbear to load me with a curse, that would indeed destroy me." Suddenly recollecting herself, she added,— "Walter will not be so unjust!—He will pity, pardon, and respect, her, who will not be able to forgive herself if she make him wretched."

"Wretched! (exclaimed the agitated lover,)—Can I ever be wretched while you thus kindly condescend to sooth my sorrows,—thus generously confess that I am dear to you, and possessed of your heart?—Can it be in the power of fate to make me otherwise than blest?"

It was too much. Roseline sunk on the bosom of her lover, and at that moment secretly wished to breathe her last sigh, and yield up her spotless life, in those arms which now perhaps for the last time encircled her.

The situation of Roseline caused a general alarm. Walter, frantic with terror, clasped her tenderly to his heart, and called upon her to speak. It was some time before she recovered, and Edwin, who saw the necessity of putting an end to an interview so dangerous and painful, in a voice between jest and earnest, exclaimed, "Indeed, my good friends, I have no relish for seeing such scenes as these performed, particularly when they do so little credit to the performers. These high-wrought feelings may be very fine, but excuse me for saying they are very silly. Recollect, my dear Walter, that our Roseline advances but slowly in her progress towards convalescence; therefore, in her present state of weakness, an interview like this must prove very prejudicial to her recovery."

"Take her away, (cried Walter,) that I may not become a murderer; only before we part, let me hear my pardon pronounced."

He threw himself at the feet of his weeping mistress, who, giving him her hand, said, with a convulsive sob, "There could be no doubt of pardon where no offence had been committed."

Edwin availed himself of this moment as the most favourable to withdraw. He took the reluctant hand of his sister, and with a gentle compulsion drew her away, saying, he would not tax his feelings by staying any longer.

Roseline, again, and almost unknowing what she did, grasped the hand of her lover, and, in a voice too low to be perfectly understood, murmured some tender admonitions, which we could not were intelligible to the ear of the love, but, to an indifferent person, they might as well have been expressed in Arabic.

Till the door shut Walter from her sight, her eyes were fixed immovably upon his face, with such a look of anguish, as may be easier imagined than described; and, when she could see him no longer, she thought the deprivation of life would have been the greatest blessing heaven could bestow on one so hopeless, and, had it not been for her father's dreadful threat of destroying himself, she would have thrown herself at the Baron's feet, and informed him how little she deserved to be his wife who had bestowed her love upon another.

Edwin accompanied his sister to her apartment, but had too much consideration, too much respect for her sorrows, to break in upon moments sad but precious. Happily however for this amiable unfortunate, she was not long permitted to indulge her heart-breaking reflections in solitude.—Her mother and sisters requested her presence to consult her taste, and hear her opinion on some of the preparations going forwards.

Sir Philip, from the time he had extorted her unwilling consent, had carefully avoided another private interview, but had taken every opportunity of caressing her in the presence of her friends, frequently making use of various pretences to get the intended bridegroom out, in order to draw off his attention from Roseline, constantly trembling lest she should appeal to his generosity, or disgust him with her coldness.

Prohibited by her father's cruel vow from applying to any one, she had no alternative but to yield to her destiny, and combat her sorrows, unconsoled and unsupported, except by her distracted brother, who was unfortunately nearly as hopeless as herself. Thus environed with misery, thus entangled in the subtle toils of cruelty and oppression, she was at times led to think she should be less wretched if her fate were determined, concluding, from the torturing sensation of her present feelings, she could not long support them.

The bustle, hurry, and confusion, which pervaded every department of the castle, afforded none of its inhabitants much time for the reflection or conversation. Lady de Morney wished to question her daughter, but was afraid of making the attempt.—She found it difficult however to obey the mandate of her husband, which, though unnatural and unreasonable, was absolute; therefore, after some few conflicts with herself, she thought it better not to contend a point of much consequence.

She saw the internal wretchedness of her daughter with the tenderest regret, and shuddered whenever she remarked her cold and freezing manner as soon as the Baron approached to pay her those attentions due from a lover. She took every opportunity of giving her approbation of her conduct, and by a thousand nameless proofs of tenderness shewed a commiserating sympathy, which did not pass unobserved by Roseline, who, though she received these marks of affection in silence, determined to avail herself of her mother's tenderness by endeavouring to interest her in favour of the man to whom she had given her heart.

The dreaded morning came, but it came enveloped in a gloom which exactly corresponded with the feelings, spirits, and prospects, of the mourning bride. The sun arose invisible to mortal sight, as if unwilling to witness a deed his brightest rays could not enliven. Dark lowering clouds threatened to touch the turrets of the castle. The rain descended in torrents. It appeared to the disconsolate Roseline that the very heavens wept in pity to her sorrows; the thought was romantic, but it was consoling.

Melancholy, and even madness itself, are said to have their pleasures, and the most wretched sometimes steal comfort from the delusions of imagination. Happy is it that such resources are found to sweeten the bitter draught so many are compelled to drink!—

Roseline submitted to be dressed as the taste of her attendants chose to direct. She was silent and passive, and made no remarks on the elegance of her attire, or the brilliancy of the ornaments with which she was decorated. When summoned to breakfast she attempted no delay, and on her entrance was met by the Baron, who addressed her in a very tender and respectful speech, as he gallantly led her to her seat. She would have assumed a smile had she been able to command her features. She would have said something, but speech was denied. Indeed, none of the company appeared in a humour to converse. Lady de Morney was sad and sick at heart, and Sir Philip himself, in the very moment he saw the gratification of his wishes in so fair a train to be realized, felt neither satisfied nor happy.

CHAPTER IV.

A message arrived from father Anselm to say he was ready, and waiting their pleasure in the chapel of the nunnery. The carriages were instantly ordered to the door. Roseline, more dead than alive, was handed into the first, and followed by her mother and two sisters. The Baron was accompanied by Sir Philip and Edwin in the second. They soon arrived at the chapel, and were met there by the abbess, Madeline, and Agnes de Clifford. Several of the friars and monks also attended. After stopping a few moments to pay and receive the proper compliments, the Baron took the trembling hand of his intended bride, and led her to the altar. Father Anselm opened his book, and began the awful ceremony, when the whole party were thrown into the utmost consternation by the door, which led from the subterranean passage to the castle, being suddenly burst open, and Walter, with drawn sword in his hand, his eyes flashing fire, followed by Albert, instantly rushed up to the altar, and, calling to father Anselm in a tone of frenzy, bade him desist, or proceed at his peril.

"The hand of Roseline (he cried) is mine, and mine only! I come to claim my affianced bride, and accursed be the wretch who shall attempt to wrest her from me!"

The Baron sunk down, exclaiming,—"Again that dreadful spectre!—Save me, save me, from it!"

The book dropped from the hands of the venerable priest, and the terrified and astonished Roseline fainted in the arms of her mother, while the countenance of every one assembled was marked with surprise and consternation, but the attitude, the expressive face of Walter, as he stood gazing on the party, caught every eye, and excited universal admiration. His dress was scarlet, richly laced: in his hat he wore a plume of white feathers, fastened by a clasp of diamonds, his tall elegant form and fine-turned limbs presenting a subject for the statuary, which few could copy in a stile that would have done justice to the original.

Roseline for some minutes remained in a state of total insensibility, but the Baron soon recovered sufficient recollection to look around him; his eyes were again fixed on the prisoner with a look rather of tenderness than displeasure.

"Tell me, youth, (he cried,) whence comest thou?—to whom dost thou belong? Those features are as familiar to my astonished sight as they were once deeply engraved on my heart. Hadst thou worn any other countenance but that of my once-loved Isabella, my sword ere now should have taught thee to respect those sacred rites thou hast so rudely interrupted; but that is the shield which still protects thee, and by some invisible influence withholds my arm from punishing thy daring intrusion."

"Then hesitate no longer, my lord, to execute your purposed vengeance!—(said Walter, gracefully bending one knee to the ground, and baring his bosom, as if to receive the uplifted sword of the Baron.)—Roseline is mine, and were there ten thousand swords ready to pierce my bosom, I would thus publicly proclaim my right."

"How!—what is the meaning of all this? (said the Baron, looking with indignation at the astonished Sir Philip;)—truth appears to dwell on the tongue of this youthful stranger.—But why have I been thus grossly deceived?—why brought into this sacred place to be made a fool of by a boy and girl?"

"You must inquire of that same boy, (replied his friend,) of whose very honourable pretensions I never heard till this moment. Why do you hesitate, my lord?—why vent your rage on me, when it would be more justly and properly employed in punishing a madman who has dared to dispute your claim to the hand of my daughter?"

"His countenance still protects him, (said the Baron.)—Order some of your people to take the youth into safe custody till this matter can be investigated."

Father Anselm now inquired if he might go on with the ceremony.

"Not till I have been heard, (cried Walter,) though you tear me piece-meal, shall you proceed!"

Roseline had recovered, but she was still surrounded by her female friends. The voice of Walter operated like a charm. She gently raised her eyes to his face, and begged he would be patient: then, addressing her father, entreated he would not permit any one to hurt him: "I, and I alone, (said the generous maid;) ought to suffer.—My dear Walter, (cried she,) contend no longer for me: think not of risking a life which is too precious to be so madly thrown away. Let every circumstance which led to the painful occurrences of this morning be openly and candidly explained, and let us rest our cause on the justice and humanity of the Baron, father Anselm, and Sir Philip de Morney. I wish not to make my appeal before any other tribunal."

The Baron, who now for the first time discovered Albert among the crowd, (for the contest had brought all the inhabitants of the nunnery into the chapel,) started as if he had seen a spectre. He became more agitated than before, and requested they might return to the castle, that an investigation of this strange business might instantly take place, for his own heart informed him there was some awful mystery to be explained.

Albert approached him: "My lord, (said he,) till this moment I have supposed you cruel, unjust, and unfeeling: my heart reproaches me for my injustice. I begin to see through the cloud which has too long enveloped me. I suspect we have been equally deceived,—alike the dupes of artifice and guilt."

"Art though not Albert? (exclaimed the Baron,)—the confidential servant of the Lady Blanch, and the favourite of her brother?"

"I am the same unfortunate person, my lord, (replied Albert;) and am not only ready to account for my being here, but to give you all the intelligence in my power respecting some very interesting circumstances with which till this moment I never supposed you unacquainted. My dear sir, (said he, turning to his agitated master,) endeavour to be more composed:" for the countenance of Walter was too faithful an index to his mind to enable him to conceal the conflicting passions which tortured his bosom, and, while his attention was divided in observing the Baron and Roseline, he seemed sinking beneath his own agonizing emotions.

Father Anselm, the lady abbess, and two bride-maids, were requested to return with the party to the castle. A guard was ordered to take charge of Walter and his servant, but he informed them the order might be countermanded; for, being a prisoner, he had requested three gentlemen from the castle to attend him, lest he should subject himself to the suspicion of designing to escape.

De Clavering, De Willows, and Camelford, were now summoned from the passage, where they had impatiently waited to see how this strange and unaccountable business would terminate. This occasioned further surprise to Sir Philip, who refrained his rising displeasure with only desiring them to take charge of the gentleman they had chosen to escort, and to be ready to appear when called upon.

Before Walter left the chapel, he approached the Baron, and presented him his sword. "To you, my lord, (said he,) I am impelled to yield a weapon which never yet was stained with human blood, and at this moment I feel a grateful joy that it was not aimed against your life. Most ardently do I desire to prove myself deserving of your friendship, and worthy of your esteem."

The Baron returned his sword, and requested him to wear it. "You have already obtained your wish, (said he, smiling,) and that I must confess against my inclination; but there is something about you speaks a language I find difficult to explain, and cannot comprehend."

Every countenance was brightened up with hope and expectation at this reply of the Baron, except that of Sir Philip de Morney. Even the cold and frigid father Anselm, who, in his long seclusion from the world, had as it may naturally be supposed, lost many of those generous and tender feelings which a more unrestrained intercourse with his fellow-creatures would have helped to cherish, seemed animated and enlivened. It was agreed that Walter and his friends, accompanied by Edwin, should return the same way as they had entered, and the rest of the party be conveyed in the carriages.—After proper apologies being made to father Anselm, and some of his brethren, for the unnecessary trouble they had so undesignedly occasioned, they returned to the castle,— with what different feelings than those they carried with them to the chapel I must leave my readers to imagine.

No sooner were the party assembled in the drawing-room, than the Baron requested that the young man and his servant might be summoned to give some account of themselves, and explain their motive for their daring and unprecedented proceedings; at the same time, observing in the countenance of Sir Philip de Morney indignation, resentment, and disappointment, he addressed him in the following words.

"I should not, Sir Philip, presume to take the liberty I have now done, did I not from the nature of the intended connexion, consider myself as authorized to act in this castle as if I were in my own. I am afraid some very dark transactions have been carried on which it is necessary should be investigated, and be brought to light. A mysterious cloud hangs over us, which I am impatient to disperse. Woe be to that man who has assisted to deceive me!"

"If you doubt my honour in what has passed between us, (retorted Sir Philip,) you do me injustice, and I shall, at any time and in any place, be ready to meet you upon whatever terms you please. If my daughter has deceived me,—if she has dared to encourage the hopes of an adventurer,—a maniac,—a traitor,—let her remember that her crime will not be her only punishment, nor will the sacrifice of her father's life be a sufficient atonement for the disgrace and dishonour she has entailed on the name of De Morney."

Roseline burst into tears, in which she was joined by every one of her female companions, who trembled lest some dreadful catastrophe should close the heart-rending scenes of this eventful morning.

"It may be happy for us both, (said the no longer haughty Baron, whose complicated feelings had produced an instantaneous revolution among his contending passions,) that at this moment I do not find myself inclined to engage in any farther hostilities, till I am better satisfied the affront and disappointment were intended for me. If I have been meanly and wilfully deceived, my sword shall revenge me upon those, and those only, who are found guilty, and dearly shall they atone for the injustice they have practiced; therefore, till matters are cleared up, I am content to be silent on a subject which, I hesitate not to declare, appears to me inexplicable."

Roseline, who would have given the world to have obtained permission to retire during the awful investigation which was going to take place, dared not make an attempt to withdraw, as she saw by the eyes of her father his rage and indignation were only kept from breaking out by the determined manner and authoritative tone of the baron, who did not appear in a humour, notwithstanding his language spoke the spirit of peace and candour, to put up with any contradiction. Again he expressed the most restless impatience to be confronted with the parties, who had so unaccountably deprived him of his young bride, by stopping the marriage-ceremony.

In a few moments the painful suspense was ended by the eager and intrepid entrance of Walter, the three companions of his enterprise, and his humble friend: they were desired to be seated. Walter and Albert, however, continued standing, requesting they might be permitted to do so, till they should be acquitted or condemned. The Baron instantly called upon Albert to perform his promise, and, if he were really the honest man he pretended to be, to step forwards, and without fear or prevarication, before the present party, inform them who it was he acknowledged as his master, and prove the justice of those claims which he had made to the hand of his elected bride, and what were his inducements for preventing a marriage, sanctioned by the lady's own consent, and the unequivocal approbation of her parents."

"I am happy, my lord, (replied Albert, in a firm, manly, and unembarrassed, tone of voice,) to be thus generously and publicly called upon. Unpractised in either guilt or deceit, and having nothing to fear from my own self-reproaches, I hail this moment, awful as I own it appears, as by far the happiest of my life. But, before we proceed any farther in this important business, I must entreat your lordship to perform an act of tender and atoning justice, for which I trust you will find an approving advocate in your own heart, and require little farther testimony than the receipt carried in a countenance which you have already confessed has stamped its validity upon every tender feeling of your soul.

"My dear, dear sir, (continued he, addressing himself to the trembling Walter,) throw yourself at the feet of the noble Baron; for, as sure as you now live to claim that distinguished honour, you are his son, his only lawful heir!—the darling offspring of the Lady Isabella Fitzosbourne, who, to give you life, yielded up her own."

Walter in an instant was at the feet of the Baron, and in another the interested and astonished party saw them locked in each other's arms, at the same moment the agitated Roseline sunk into those of her mother. In a little time every one became more composed, and the Baron, resolutely struggling to acquire a greater degree of firmness in order to obtain farther information, exclaimed, in a tone of voice that evinced the nature of his feelings, "You are, you must be my son!— Nature, at first sight of you, asserted her just, her powerful claims: yes, you are the precious gift of my sainted Isabella,—the only pledge of a love that was pure and gentle as her own heart and mind! but how, where, by what cruel policy and unfeeling hand have you thus long been concealed from my sight?—how prevented from enjoying the advantages of your birth-right, while I was tortured with the belief that death had robbed me of a son?"

"Of all these matters, my lord, Albert can fully inform you, (said Walter.) He is much better able to explain them than I can possibly be, who till this hour did not know I should ever be folded in a father's arms; yet to me Albert has been a father, a friend, and a guardian. For my sake he has voluntarily buried himself for years in the gloomy and narrow confines of a dungeon; for my sake suffered the punishment of the most atrocious offender without being guilty of a single crime. If you therefore condescend to love and acknowledge me for a son, you will feel for him the affection of a brother. To you, my lord, I am indebted for life,—to this, my second father, I owe its preservation."

"Generous man! (cried the enraptured Baron, who was charmed at hearing the noble sentiments of his son,) come to my arms, and command my power to serve you!"[35]

Albert would have knelt at his feet, but was prevented by a warm embrace from putting his design in execution. Walter was now seated by the side of his happy father, who, observing that his eye wandered in search of something, with anxious tenderness, soon guessed the cause, and, instantly rising from his chair, took his hand, and led him to the weeping Roseline, who, smiling through her tears, instantly proved how warmly she participated in his happiness. Walter, though the acknowledged son of Baron Fitzosbourne, was still the son of nature: he sunk at her feet, and in the unadulterated language of rapture and affection, exclaimed,—"For a moment like this, who is there would not suffer years of anguish! Look down, my gentle friend, my benefactress and protecting angel,—my first, my last, and only love, and let me in your smiles find a confirmation of my bliss! Let them convince me that

---

[35] Upon regaining family- his son- the baron suddenly becomes humanized. In a twist on the 'Beauty and the Beast' fairy tale, the Baron transitions from his Beast-like domineering control to a loving father who understands the renewing power of love. Ironically, it is his son, Walter, who stands in Beauty's shoes for he is disguised as a beautiful woman- his mother. Confronting his Ogre-ish patriarch allows magical transitions to occur.

all I see and hear is real; for I am almost tempted to think it must be the effects of enchantment, or the delusions of a distempered imagination."

Roseline, no longer awed by the presence of her father, no longer able to conceal the joy which revelled in her bosom, gave him her hand, which he instantly conveyed to his lips. Albert, who carefully watched every change in the countenance of his beloved master, trembled for the consequence of such new and high-wrought feelings, lest they should be attend with danger to a mind which had so recently been sunk in a state of the lowest dejection. With the approbation of the party, who saw the necessity of the design, he prevailed upon him to retire for a few minutes, in order to acquire sufficient fortitude to hear his own story recited with composure. This request being seconded by his father and Roseline, he immediately complied, leaving the company so much charmed with the whole of his behaviour, though the interesting scene we have described, and so captivated with is figure, good sense, and sweetness of manners, that surprise was lost in admiration. As soon as the two friends had withdrawn, (for, if ever any one deserved the name of friend, that title belonged to the worthy Albert,) Sir Philip de Morney approached the Baron, and with some little embarrassment congratulated him on the wonderful discovery which had so recently and unexpectedly taken place.—He then entered on his own defence, with the candour and ease of one, who, if he had erred, it proceeded from ignorance.

"That I have undesignedly been made an agent in the diabolical injustice practiced against your son, by keeping him confined in this castle, I beg your lordship's pardon, and entreat you would use your influence to procure the forgiveness of him whom I have innocently injured. He was brought to this place under a fictitious name, and, with the false pretence of being at times deranged in his intellects, I was told he was the illegitimate offspring of a person inimical to the plans of government, and easily wrought upon by his associates to enter into any scheme which the enemies of his country might throw in his way; at the same time it was asserted that he was particularly disliked by a great person in high office. All that was required of me was to keep him and his servant in close confinement,—to suffer no one to see or converse with them, and to convey no letters nor messages beyond the walls of the castle. This request came from one with whom I had lived in habits of intimacy, and whom I looked upon as a respectable character. He had previously obtained permission of the noble owner of the castle for the use of its dungeons, but who, as well as myself, must have been led into the practice of so glaring a piece of tyranny by the designs and misrepresentations of those whose interest led them to keep your lordship in ignorance of your son's being alive. In justice I ought to inform you, that I was ordered to supply them liberally with every necessary accommodation the nature of their situation would admit, and was not restricted, if I found them quiet and submissive, from allowing them some occasional indulgences. I take shame to myself when I own, that, after I had seen them safely lodged in their dungeon, and had forbidden any one attempting to go near or hold conversation with them, I never visited them more than once, concluding they were two dangerous and worthless people, who were receiving the reward of their base actions, and contenting myself with only making such inquiries as the duties of my situation imposed. Indeed I thought very little about them, and waited with composure for the farther explanation promised by my friend, when we met to settle the accounts for their board, &c. How the youthful prisoner became acquainted with my daughter, or by what means he obtained an introduction to her, I am to this moment totally ignorant."

"If it can be as well accounted for (said father Anselm who for some time had remained silent with surprise,) as you have accounted for the part you were prevailed upon to act, I think the most rigid judge will find but little to condemn."

"I have no fears (replied the Baron) but their actions will stand quite as clear; the sparkling eyes of my affianced bride are at this moment telling tales of their own beguiling influence, and testifying by their intelligent language that I am right in my conjectures. No wonder, as she conquered the father, she should have wounded, and rendered the son doubly a captive: but here comes the fortunate culprit. Let us hear his defence before we venture to pronounce whether he is entitled to forgiveness and an honourable acquittal, or merits condemnation for daring to fall in love while sentenced to languish in a dungeon."

Roseline, having now shaken off that languor and despondence which for so many days had depressed the generous and active feelings of the gentlest of human minds, impelled by justice and the unbounded affection she had long felt for Walter, exclaimed, "If every virtue merits reward, if every good and engaging quality be entitled to happiness, your son, my lord, will be the happiest of men; for, to the long list of virtues he inherits from his noble ancestors, you will find added all the bounteous gifts which nature could bestow on her most distinguished favourite."

The artless eulogium was not made without a blush, and the rose which blossomed on her cheek gave to her face an expression which, in the eyes of the Baron, exceeded that of the most perfect beauty. Walter, followed by Albert, now returned into the room.

"Come here, young man, (said his father, in a tone of gratified affection,) come and prove yourself worthy of the character I have heard given of you by a very lovely historian. Sit down by me, and endeavour to keep your mind free from agitation, and your spirits composed, while our friend Albert gives us the promised narration, which is to establish your claim to my name as firmly as your merits and conduct have already done to my regard; for, though you played me a sly and mortifying trick before I had the happiness of knowing you, I find in myself little inclination to resent it. Take notice, however, that perhaps I shall not be quite so favourably inclined to excuse any deviations in future, should a certain young lady be in the case. "This was spoken in a tone that proved the Baron was far from being dissatisfied at having found arrival, so long as he had regained a son.

General congratulations now took place, and the merry, good-humoured Hugh Camelford, after jumping up and cutting a few capers in the true stile of Cambrian hilarity, declared he could dance a fandango with his crandmother; or the toctor, round the topmost pattlements of Pungay Castle, for he never lifed a happier moment since he was porn. Every eye spoke the same language, and De Clavering said, though he dreaded the oyster-shell devilifications of a woman's mind, he had a pretty widow in his eye, whom he should entreat to take care of him for life. Sir Philip, with a smile, whispered Lady de Morney, telling her, he thought after all women catered the best for themselves in the choice of their husband: for, prejudice out of the question, the Baron's son was certainly the finest young man he had ever seen.—As all the party were impatient to hear the tale Albert had to communicate, he was requested to begin, which he did in the following manner.

CHAPTER V.

"YOU cannot but recollect, my lord, (addressing himself to the Baron,) that, when you married the Lady Blanch, I came into your family. I had been brought up in her father's house, and from a boy was appointed to attend her person, no one being allowed to command or employ me without her permission. When all preliminaries were settled for your marriage with my lady, I was informed that I was still to have the honour of attending her; as favour so great, and voluntarily conferred, rendered me not a little vain. You soon after married, and I became a resident in your family: my lady still distinguishing me with her approbation, made me grateful and happy, and, though I was frequently reproached by my fellow-servants, with ill-humour and acrimony, for being so great a favourite, I endeavoured all in my power to convince them, I wished not to deprive them of any advantages they had enjoyed before I came among them, and this in a little time made them more reconciled and obliging.

My dear young master was then in his infancy, and my place not being one of the busiest, I had many hours of leisure, which I was allowed to dispose of as suited my inclination: these hours I chiefly spent in the nursery, and, being remarkably fond of children, I soon became so strongly attached to the young lord, that I often regretted the necessity of leaving him, which I was sometimes obliged to do for weeks and months together, either when your lordship took my lady to town, paid visits to your friends, or went to any other of your estates; and once, if you recollect, you were absent a long time, when you carried my lady to Montpellier whose declining health led you to adopt this plan for her recovery, which the physicians said would perfectly restore that bloom a slow and nervous fever had stolen from her, and alarmed every friend who saw the ravages sickness had made in a countenance formed to captivate.—Ah! that unfortunate excursion!—I have wished with an aching heart a thousand and a thousand times it had never been made.

During our absence my lady lost her fever, and gave birth to a son, who very soon engrossed so much of her time and affection, that your lordship had just reason to complain of the change it produced. There was another, change which you did not so soon discover.

During our residence among a parcel of jabbering foreigners, my lady learned to despise the blessed manners and customs of her native country, and all those feelings which once made her so charming. We must eat, drink, sleep, dress, and do every thing after the French fashion.[36] I was often reproved for retaining more than any of my fellow-servants my clumsy English manners. She frequently expressed her satisfaction that her son first saw the light on the Gallic shore, where, if she could have persuaded your lordship, she would have continued to reside.

After an absence of eighteen months, which appeared to me the length of as many years, we returned to England, and found my young lord just recovered from the small pox, of a very bad sort, which had so much altered him, that my lady believed, or rather affected to believe, that your son had been changed during our absence, or that he might have died, and some designing artful people had imposed their own offspring upon you, to usurp his rights, and rob her little daring of his title and estate. The boy she found in your castle could not be the sweet creature she left:—*he* was beautiful and finely formed;— *this* was ugly to a degree, robust, clumsy, and half an ideot."

I know not what arts were used to make your lordship give any credit to so fallacious and improbable a tale; but I observed, with unfeigned regret, from that time your affection was continually decreasing, till at last your son was seldom admitted to your presence, and never indulged with those fond caresses which, previous to your departure from England, were frequently and tenderly repeated. He was generally dismissed with epithets of beggar's brat, foundling, and idiot."

"I feel deep contrition for yielding belief to such infernal tales, (said the Baron,)—for being so long the dupe and tool of a designing malicious woman, and neglecting the son of the most amiable and best of wives. Ah! my Isabella! if you are permitted to look down on this lower world,—if you are acquainted with the conduct of him to whom you entrusted your virgin-heart, and made the chosen lord of your destiny, how must you despise and detest the mean, the forgetful wretch, who deserted the sacred, the precious charge you so tenderly committed to his care! May my future penitence atone for the cruelty of my past conduct, and my sainted Isabella intercede with her Creator for the pardon and forgiveness! Then may Fitzosbourne hope her spirit will in the grave find a place of rest. No wonder my crimes have robbed her even of that asylum."

The tears of remorse stole down the Baron's cheeks, and he gave Walter a look of tender regret, that said as much as volumes could have done.

---

[36] This detail seems remarkably xenophobic, especially when considering that Walter is the foreigner at this point, for he is travelling in a foreign land. Many Gothic and sensation novels place foreigners in the racist role of antagonist—most notably are Stoker's *Dracula*, Du Maurier's *Trilby*, and Marsh's *The Beetle*.

"I know to what your lordship alludes, (said Walter,) and I am happy that it is in my power to remove a tormenting delusion from your mind, which, all circumstances considered, I cannot be surprised, made so forcible an impression on it. The striking likeness which I bear to my ever-regretted mother had often been remarked to me by Albert, and was undoubtedly designed to be the means of restoring me a father."

Every one being impatient to hear the remainder of the prisoner's story, the explanation was deferred, and Albert went on.

"Before my young lord had recovered his former complexion, or his features began to reassume some traits of what they had been, till attacked and disguised by that baneful distemper, so often the grave of beauty,—the enemy of love, I was one day summoned into my lady's dressing-room. After desiring me to shut the door, and take care our conversation was not overheard, she bade me sit down; I obeyed reluctantly, as I never before had been allowed the honour of sitting in her presence. She then inquired if I were in reality as much attached to her as I had frequently pretended to be, and whether, if she should have occasion to place a confidence in me, and require my assistance, she might trust to my fidelity?

"I assured her she might command my services to the utmost of my power, as I must be the most insensible and ungrateful of men not to be ready to yield my life, if necessary, for so generous and kind a benefactress."

"As to your life, my good Albert, (cried her ladyship, rising, and putting her purse and picture into my hand, which she compelled me to take,) I hope that will long be preserved to do me service. The request I shall make will neither involve you in difficulties nor danger; and if you faithfully perform what will be asked of you, rely upon my word, it will not only free you from labour and servitude, but be a certain means of procuring you a comfortable independence for the rest of your life,— an income that will enable you to marry the woman you love, with whom you may live to see yourself surrounded with a numerous offspring. (The picture was drawn in the most flattering colours,—the back ground was not quite so pleasing.)—But you must, to obtain my good opinion, and secure to yourself those enviable comforts, (continued her ladyship,) unconditionally and without knowing the nature of the service required of you, take a solemn and sacred oath never to betray, by thought, word, or deed, the confidence reposed in you. I will give you three days to consider of my proposal, and at the end of that time shall expect your answer."

"I was now ordered to withdraw, which I immediately did, in a state of mind not to be imagined. What could my lady mean?—what was the business in which I was to be employed that demanded the solemn prelude of an oath? Oaths were sacred things; they were not to be trifled with, and were thought necessary only on the most important occasions. I next recollected that I had known my lady from a child: she had ever been my friend, had frequently given me good advice, and was religious, generous, and charitable. It could not therefore be any wicked or unjust action she wanted me to accomplish; *that* was contrary to her nature. What then had I to fear from taking an oath which could do no one any harm, and might make my fortune? Independence was promised me. I was young, sanguine, and aspiring, yet I had never dared to hope being placed in a situation above that I at present enjoyed. The lure was thrown out by a hand I could not resist, and I was caught by the tempting bait, with I swallowed to the destruction of my own peace."

"But, by your fortunately having done so, (exclaimed Walter,) my life was repeatedly preserved to enjoy the present moment of exquisite happiness and soul-enlivening hope."—He fixed his eyes tenderly on the blushing Roseline, as he uttered this affecting exclamation.

"When the appointed time was expired, (continued Albert,) I was admitted to a second conference with my lady, and without making any terms, being, as I thought, well assured I might safely rely on her virtue and rectitude as trust to her generosity, I took an oath, which was tended to me by father Paul, her confessor and domestic chaplain, to obey such orders as were given me with secresy and fidelity, for which I was to receive in quarterly payments eighty pounds a year, and to have clothes, board, and every other necessary, allowed me.—Father Paul bore the character of a just and pious man; therefore, had I retained any reluctance, receiving the oath from so sacred and important and personage would have rendered any doubts an unpardonable offence against our holy church. In compliance with my earnest request to be informed what was expected to be done by me, and when I was to enter on my task, father Paul himself, after some little hesitation, opened the business.

"Her ladyship (he said) was convinced, and he was of the same opinion, that the child, (meaning my young lord,) which passed for the son of the worthy and unsuspicious Baron, was in all probability the spurious offspring of some low-born peasant, the fruit of an illicit and illegal amour, imposed upon the noble family, for base and artful purposes, by some designing wretch, after the death of the lawful heir, which, by some very wonderful means, has so far been brought to light as to confirm the fact. This child was so totally different from that left in England, it could not possibly be the same. He was beautiful, sensible, lively, and active; this was an ugly brat, dull, and stupid, and as much the child of King Solomon as of the Baron.—It was become necessary for the honour and comfort of the family to sent it away: it was to be removed into some distant and healthy county for change of air, and placed with a country woman to be nursed. After he had been absent a few months, I was to withdraw myself from the Baron's service, take the boy from his ignorant nurse, and accompany him to whatever place I should be directed. Till he came to a certain age, I was to have the occasional assistance of a female in rearing him up, and was desired to do all I could for the poor stupid creature, who, to be sure, in the eyes of impartial justice, had not yet been guilty of a crime; but, to prevent his being so, by monopolizing the rights of another, this plan was adopted.

"I was next commanded never to presume to give the most distant hint either to himself or any one else, that he had ever been suspected, or even thought of consequence,—never to mention the name of Fitzosbourne to him, or to say that he or myself had resided in the family. When he arrived at the age of fifteen, I might, if I were so inclined, give up my task, and should have proper security for receiving my salary during the rest of my life, even if the boy should luckily die before the age fixed upon to release me from my engagements. If I chose the trouble, I might teach him to read and write; but it was a matter of little consequence:—the less such people knew, the better,— ignorance to them was happiness, and knowledge only a burthen, of which it was better not to be possessed.

"I had been unwarily drawn into the snare from which I now wanted judgment, courage, and resolution, to disentangle myself. The influence and unbounded power my lady ever held over me,—her consequence, and my humble station, arose to my terrified imagination, and I dared not venture to expostulate against such a plan sanctioned by the Lady Blanch, and approved by father Paul, with whom it was equally dangerous to contend.

"Of the identity of the young lord I never cherished a doubt; and, if I had, the restoration of his sweet features to their former beauty and expression, which was now beginning to take place, would have banished them as soon as they arose; yet the fear of offending kept me silent: the oath I had taken hung over me with a terror;—it was a heavy weight upon my spirits;—every struggle I made with conscience was over-ruled by worldly motives. I would not be perjured, but I consented to be ten times worse. Alas! I little suspected, when I took that sacred, yet unhallowed oath, that I was sentencing myself and a helpless innocent to years of hopeless imprisonment,—to a kind of living death, and burthening my conscience with the heavy crime of being the vile agent in assisting to rob the best, the most amiable of all God's creatures of his title, a noble estate, and even of that freedom which the poorest of his father's vassals enjoyed."

"Dear Albert, (cried Walter,) do not abuse yourself so unjustly: represent not your actions in colours that do not belong to them. If I suffered, you did the same; the barbarous hands which robbed me of liberty, and the all-cheering light of heaven, deprived you also of your's. Had it not been for your unremitting and watchful care, your more than parental tenderness, I had long ere now been numbered with the dead, and my existence and injuries lost in eternal oblivion."

"My noble boy, (exclaimed the Baron,) there spoke the soul of your angelic mother! Just so would she have shewn her grateful sense of benefits received.—Go on, my friend, regard not the feelings you excite; they are due to the sufferings of this injured youth, and to the virtues of his generous guardian and protector."

Albert proceeded.—"A plan so deeply laid and artfully contrived, supported by such authority and power, succeeded but too well. I was, in due time, form, and order, dismissed from your lordship's castle, and very soon the precious charge was delivered into the hands of the villain who had been aiding and abetting his ruin; but the degrading, self-reproving feelings, the horrid conflicts I endured, in the moment when the innocent victim ran joyfully into the arms of the Judas who had betrayed him, shouting, jumping, and skipping with pleasure, to think I was come to live with him, and be his nurse, were such as I would not have encountered for ten thousand worlds, could I have foretold the scorpion stings with which I found them armed at all points. It was judged necessary that we should speedily remove from the house of the poor, ignorant woman to whom my young lord had been entrusted, and under whose fostering and maternal care he had entirely recovered his looks, and found more happiness than in the habitation of greatness. I took care she should not go unrewarded for her kindness, and received at the expected time my instructions for our removal.

"After a long and tiresome journey, we arrived at an old ruinated castle, on the borders of ——, and there I found a woman, who was appointed to assist me in the care of my important charge. We had a small, gloomy, and inconvenient apartment appropriated to our use; our table was tolerably well supplied: we had plenty of what the country afforded, were never denied any addition I requested should be made to our wardrobe, and at times books and toys were sent unsolicited; my salary was likewise punctually remitted me.

"Here we lingered away some time, and were afterwards removed to two places before we were brought hither, owing I suppose to some circumstance that rendered our removal necessary, for the better secreting of our persons. Long before the time expired in which my engagement was to end, and I should be authorized to demand my freedom and continued reward, I found myself so strongly attached to my young lord, felt such pity for his situation, and such corroding regret at having lent my assistance to his cruel persecutors, I could not support the most distant idea of forsaking him, and would have suffered torture rather than have left him in a state so desolate and unprotected.

"I hinted in my letters, that, if any attempts were made to separate me from my beloved charge, I should consider the oath which had hitherto kept me faithful to their secret as no longer binding. I heard by chance of the death of Lady Blanch, but never till very lately that she had lost her son. I for some months cherished hopes that her death would procure our liberty, and release me from my oath, but I was soon given to understand, that to her brother she had discovered the secret; that, in future, our remittances were to be sent by his order, and we were to be guided by his direction.

"Finding things thus settled and arranged, after we had lived so many years in confinement, I concluded that the whole plan had been contrived and executed with your lordship's consent, and no longer doubted but it was your wish that the son of the Lady Blanch should inherit your titles and estates."

"Good God! (exclaimed the Baron,) how awful and mysterious are thy dealings with us erring mortals! I was told, and supposed the tale was true, that my poor boy died suddenly, in a few months after he was sent from the castle, on the pretence that change of air was necessary. I gave orders for his interment in our family-vault, went into mourning, and knew not till this ever blessed day that a son of mine existed.— Unhappy, mistaken, guilty Blanch!—the untimely fate of thy darling boy is now fully and solemnly accounted for! It was doubtless the just judgment of heaven for thy unpardonable crimes in depriving the son of my Isabella first of his father's love, and then of his protection. The agonies of thy dying moments are now explained: they were the direful effects of unavailing contrition; for, when thou wouldst have relieved thy mind of its heavy burthen, speech was denied thee: I hope thy anguish, in those moments of terror, have in part atoned for thy unheard of cruelty.

"Father Paul has found a shelter in the grave from my resentment; but the man, I will not call him brother, who must have been tempted to take an active part in this iniquitous business, in the hopes of obtaining some of my fortune for his children, still lives to feel my anger. What could induce one of his exalted rank to persecute and rob the innocent, if from his sufferings and seclusion he had not expected to reap considerable benefit!"

"Perhaps the fear of punishment and exposure might prompt them to continue the deception, (said Albert;) what occasioned our removal to this castle I could never learn; it was sudden, and conducted with secresy and caution, for we were guarded as if we had been prisoners of state, owing, I presume, to some attack being made, or meditated, against the castle we left; but, whatever was the cause, we had reason to be thankful for the change it produced, as we had more liberty, and better accommodation, than we had experienced in any other prison."

"I shall ever reproach myself, (said Sir Philip,) for having been led into an act of unpardonable oppression, for which I can never stand excused to my own heart. I trusted too implicitly to the account which was given me, not doubting the honour or veracity of the parties concerned. I must now entreat, the worthy narrator would proceed with this story, for I own I am very impatient to know how the son of my friend obtained an introduction to my daughter."

"I trust, my father and indulgent friends will excuse my absence, (said Roseline,) during a recital, that, in my present agitated state of mind, would be too much for me to support."[37]

"No, no, no!" was echoed from every part of the room. Walter, rising, and seating himself by the side of Roseline, whispered something in her ear that instantly reconciled her to a compliance with the general request of the company.

Albert then proceeded, and gave an account of their first interesting interview, and of the dangerous state to which long confinement and a slow fever had reduced his master. He dwelt with delight on the tender attentions of the charming Roseline to the poor, forlorn, helpless, and dying prisoner; described her unremitting care, and mentioned with what joy be marked their growing affection, which was soon visible to all the parties but those most interested.—The friendship of Edwin was not forgotten, nor were the polite and sisterly attentions of the gentle Madeline passed over in silence. Nothing was omitted in the narrative but the Baron's fright in the subterraneous passage, and that for reasons which will hereafter appear, he dared not venture to explain.

"Your alarm, my lord, (continued Albert,) on the night the ball was given by Sir Philip de Morney, and which occasioned so much bustle and confusion, originated from a cause more natural than you, misled by terror, could suppose. To explain things in their proper order, we must go back to the day previous to that of the ball.

"Miss De Morney and her brother had informed my master of what was intended; in consequence of this intelligence, he became more

---

[37] Considering how brave and confrontational Roseline has been in the past, it is strange that she leaves the room at this point allowing a female story to be told through male voices.

restless and wretched than I had ever seen him, and felt the miseries of his situation so severely, that I trembled for the consequence so irritable a state of mind might produced on a constitution sufficiently injured already by the unsparing rigours of oppression and confinement. I therefore, without giving him a hint of my intention, formed a plan in my own mind to relieve his sufferings, little suspecting the surprising and happy effects of which it would be productive, or once supposing, that, in his successful rival, I should see Baron Fitzosbourne.—Never was I so puzzled as in the moment I made that discovery, to conceal the feelings by which it was attended, from giving any alarm to those which had already harassed and half destroyed my dear master.

Without much difficulty I prevailed on Mr. De Morney to procure me two female dresses, telling him for what purpose they were intended. He was at first astonished at the singularity of my request; but, finding no ill consequences likely to attend it, readily complied, and with the assistance of his sister the matter was easily accomplished.

"We helped each other in putting on female attire as well as we could, and took as much care as possible to make such an appearance as was not likely to attract attention. At the time appointed we sallied forth in our female habiliments, slipped through some of the forsaken apartments, and joined without any suspicion a vast number of people who had obtained permission to witness the festival, and see the company dance.

"The eyes of my young lord were feasted by beholding the beloved object who engrossed his every thought, and constituted his every wish, exhibit her elegant person in the mazy windings of the dance, which till now he had never seen. With a kind of saddened delight, he was soon convinced, that, though her person was engaged, her heart appeared to have no share in the pleasure which was legibly depicted on the countenance of her youthful companions; but, on that which his eyes alone delighted to mark, he saw a silent uncomplaining sadness, which, at the time it wounded, cheered and revived his soul with the sweet hope that, had he been present, had he been her envied partner, no sadness had clouded her brow,—no regret found entrance to her bosom.

"She frequently withdrew her eyes from the company to fix them on the humble crowd, in which she concluded her lover was numbered. He likewise felt his spirits relieved by the coldness and indifference with which he saw she received every flattering attention that was paid her.—When he had sufficiently satisfied his curiosity, and I observed he was weary of being incommoded by the number of people which continued to increase, I whispered him that I thought it time to retire, while the coast was clear, and we could steal away undiscovered.

"He desired me to go first, saying he would follow me in a few moments. I instantly obeyed. My master, by taking a wrong turn, was passing through your lordship's bedchamber as you entered it. He saw it was his rival, and, in the instantaneous indignation of the moment, forgot every thing but the resentment which was rankling in his bosom.—You perceived him,—looked alarmed, and trembled: he frowned, and shook his head, while the face on which you gazed with terror was flushed with passion.

"On seeing you fall, unable to account for the cause, and fearful of being discovered, he hurried out of the room, and hastened to inform me of what had happened.—Hearing a vast bustle, I instantly disrobed my master of his female attire, having already gotten rid of my own disguise.—I was next day informed by Mr. De Morney that your lordship had been alarmed by something in your own room, and was much indisposed. I soon collected sufficient proof to be assured that it was the appearance of your son which had occasioned this confusion, and imparted enough of my sentiments to make myself understood. From that moment, having no alternative, no other method to adopt, in order to bring about a discovery, we agreed to enter the chapel, and these gentlemen, at the request of their friend, hesitated not to be of the party."

To confirm more fully, and to remove every doubt from the mind of the Baron, Albert produced many of the clothes and trinkets which had been sent by the Lady Blanch. The mark of a bunch of currants on the arm of Walter, with which he was born, and which had been occasioned by one of nature's strongest freaks, was perfectly recollected by the Baron, and was a fact not to be controverted.

So many corroborating and convincing testimonies of his identity would have banished doubt, had any doubt remained; but truth and nature were too prevailing to be disputed; the countenance of Walter was, unsupported with farther evidence, sufficient to prove him the son of Lady Isabella.

This narrative contained so many interesting circumstances, cold and unfeeling must have been the heart which could have heard it with disbelief or indifference: no such heart was enshrined in the bosom of the delighted audience; every eye readily paid the tribute of a tear. The conduct of Roseline and her brother was generally applauded and admired; all were eager to praise, and De Clavering slyly observed, that, if any young lady should fall in his way who had a mind to study the use of herbs, he should conclude she had something more in her head than a wish to learn physic or botany.

"Perhaps 'tis a sign of luf, (said Camelford,) when people pegin to study potany, and that is a reason De Willows thanks so much apout it himself; for I heard him in his sleep call out, that he must die, unless some palm could be tiscovered to heal the wound in his heart, which was a pig as a parn door."

De Willows called him an incorrigible miscreant for betraying the secrets he pilfered from his friend, and vowed to be revenged in his own way. This little sally gave an enlivening turn to the conversation, but it was not possible that a party, circumstanced as the present, should be able to converse on any subject but that in which every heart was interested: it had even bereaved father Anselm and the abbess of many tears.

Sir Philip de Morney avowed that the gentle and benevolent virtues of his children made him blush at the failure of them in himself. The Baron still shed tears, but they were tears more calculated to provoke envy then excite compassion. He embraced his son again and again, led him to Roseline, and entreated she would make the youth her captive for life, and bestow on him the only treasure which could reward him for his long confinement and uncomplaining fortitude. He called upon Sir Philip to accept him for a brother instead of a son, saying, as he should now certainly never think of marrying again, the settlements, with a few alterations, might stand as they did. This proposal was too agreeable to meet with any opposition. Upon Albert the Baron proposed settling an annuity that would enable him to live in a stile equal to that of the most respectable country gentlemen; but this good man instantly declined accepting the generous offer, declaring, that if they compelled him to leave his dear young lord, and deprived him of the pleasure of attending him, life would lose its value, and he should pine away the remainder of his days in discontent and misery, though he were possessed of the most unbounded affluence.[38]

"And I, (said Walter,) though blessed with my gentle and lovely Roseline, should appear despicable in her eyes, and contemptible in my own, could I ever consent that my preserver, friend, and preceptor, should live under any roof but mine. I hope and trust he will permit me to repay to his declining age the mighty debt I owe him for his tender care, his unceasing attentions to my helpless and persecuted youth."

---

[38] Bonhote stresses Albert's devotion to Walter beyond the basic role of a devoted servant into that of the unrequited lover. Albert's devotion to Walter is more emotional than servile. Furthermore, upon Walter's declaration that Albert must stay with him, "Albert burst into tears, and, suddenly throwing himself at the feet of Walter, found, in the eager and cordial embrace with which he raised him, an ample reward" (184). Clearly in a subordinate female role, Albert lives to serve and to please Walter. I do not claim Albert is a gay character; however, I do think it is important to point out the homoerotic bond between the two men. For more information on Queer Theory in British literature, see Sedgwick's *Between Men: English Literature and Male Homosocial Desire*.

Albert burst into tears, and, suddenly throwing himself at his feet of Walter, found, in the eager and cordial embrace with which he raised him, an ample reward for his long tried fidelity.

Edeliza, Berth, and their youthful companions, were no longer able to confine their joy in silence. Bertha crept to the side of Walter, and looked at him with an expression of countenance so good humoured and arch, that he took her on his knee, and inquired if she would give him leave to be her brother.

"That I will! (said she.)—You are so tall and handsome, and by seeing you I have found why my sister Roseline shed so many tears, had so many fainting fits, and went about without singing the pretty songs she used to do;—it was all owing to you;—therefore you must be very good, and very entertaining, to make her love you better than she does Edeliza, brother Edwin, or myself."

Lady de Morney, father Anselm, the abbess, Madeline, and Agnes de Clifford, were severally introduced. The abbess, as she expressed her approbation of her niece's lover, told her sister that she saw in his animated and expressive countenance a likeness of her regretted Henry. De Clavering and the rest were not silent. Never can there be found a happier party than were at that time assembled in Bungay-castle. The gloom, which had so long enveloped them, disappeared with every threatening cloud, and was succeeded by the brightest sunshine. Various reports were in rapid circulation respecting the circumstances which had so wonderfully concurred to promote and secure the happiness of Walter and Roseline; and, while some were pitying, others blaming the bride that should have been, the parties themselves were congratulating each other on account of that very disappointment which had been productive of joy as great as it was unexpected.

Roseline, eager to disrobe herself of her bridal ornaments, which, in spite of herself, carried her reflections back to the agonizing conflicts she had endured when putting them on, retired with her young friends, and then in the fullness of heart, as she embraced them with delight, unmixed with self-reproach or doubt, informed them of her long and tender attachment to the poor, helpless, and unknown prisoner.

Edeliza declared he was almost as handsome as De Willows. "But not half so merry and good humoured as Mr. Camelford, (said Bertha;) but I will try to make him romp with me, and then perhaps I shall like him as well."

Roseline smiled with complacency at her sister's artless observations, in which she read the sentiments of hearts which had not yet learned the art of concealing what they felt, and which already yielded to the influence of the same blind god who had conducted her through such varying scenes of hope, despair, and misery, to a prospect of the most enviable happiness.

The whole company were invited to spend the remainder of the day at the Castle, notwithstanding the purpose for which they came had been defeated. Father Anselm, who, though a very pious and rigid Catholic, had no objection to good living, very readily accepted the invitation. The doors of the Castle were ordered to be thrown open; every one that chose was permitted to partake of the hospitality and good cheer, and, though the company were disappointed of being at a wedding, it would have been impossible for an indifferent spectator to imagine any matter of such consequence could have happened, as mirth, pleasure, and satisfaction, revelled in every eye, and every countenance was drest in the serene and placid smiles of joy and contentment.

Roseline was closeted half an hour with her mother and aunt; she received their congratulations and caresses with that pure delight which ever attends the heart when duty and affections are united. Lady de Morney could not withhold her praises; yet once or twice gently adverted to the dangers which might have arisen from the duplicity of her conduct in concealing an attachment of so much importance to her future peace, had not the holy virgin condescended to watch and guard her. The abbess bestowed her the most pious benediction on her lovely niece, who, she pronounced, had acted under the influence of her guardian saint, and was entitled to the ample reward which appeared to wait her acceptance.

CHAPTER VI.

WHEN the party met at dinner, the simple elegance of Roseline's engaging figure, divested of those ornaments which a few hours before had been so lavishly put on by the fingers of taste, appeared far more captivating: her eyes were illumined with an expression of joy and satisfaction to which they had long been strangers; the change conveyed a train of the most enchanting sensations to the heart of her admiring lover, and did not pass unobserved by her friends. To Sir Philip they carried a silent reproach for having so long robbed them of their lustre.

Roseline was seated between the Baron and his son, and, though this was the first time Walter had ever dined with so large a party, or witnessed the comforts of a plentiful table, laden with the rarities of art and nature; for his friend Albert, to fill up the heavy hours as they slowly crept away during their long and tedious imprisonment, had described to him the manners and customs of the world, among all ranks of people, with the utmost accuracy and care, and by these means prepared him for scenes which must otherwise have astonished, and in many instances alarmed, him.

The good Albert was placed between De Clavering and De Willows, who took this opportunity of shewing him their utmost flattering attention, and, in consequence, he was encouraged to hold a very respectable part in the conversation. As he had before given undeniable proofs of the goodness of his heart, he now unfolded to the company the excellence of his understanding, and convinced them, that, if the prisoner had been educated amidst the bustle of the world, he could not have found a better preceptor as to sound judgment and useful knowledge.—Thus honoured and happy, he found in part a reward for the integrity and humanity of his conduct, while the approving eye of his grateful master spoke a language which conveyed a joy to his heart that is rarely felt, and cannot be defined.

Edwin and De Willows paid every attention to their fair enslavers, no longer fearing the penetrating eyes of the governor, who was too much taken up with the éclaircissement of the morning to suspect any other lovers were present.

After the company rose from table, at the Baron's particular request, they went to look into those dreary apartments to which the prisoner had been consigned at this first coming to the castle. Edwin produced the key of the trap-door, and conducted them down the same stairs which he and his trembling companions had descended when they were alarmed by the unusual noises they heard in the lower part of the castle. Every minute circumstance was interesting to the company; but to the Baron they were connected with a tale that awakened every feeling of his heart. Few therefore can be at a loss to guess his sensations when he entered the cold, gloomy, and unwholesome dungeon in which this darling son, the child of his Isabella, had lingered so many months, and was told by Albert, that it was far more comfortable and commodious than the one he had been inclosed in many long and tedious years.

The Baron shuddered with horror, sat down on the humble and uneasy couch which had been Walter's only bed, during a long and dangerous indisposition, and again called upon Albert to describe his first interview with Roseline; the tale was again repeated, and lost none of its effect by repetition.—Walter, the tear trembling in his eye as it was fondly bent on Roseline, grasped her hand, and poured out the warm effusions of his grateful and enamoured heart.

To trace the progress of nature, unvitiated by false taste, and uncorrupted by guilt, is, in my opinion, (said De Clavering,) the most entertaining and instructive history we can read, and far more useful is the language it contains than all the crabbed and unfeeling documents of the most studious philosopher, who loses the gentle propensities of his nature by snuffing up the dust of ancient libraries, till the spiders have woven their cobweb-looms in his head, and left no space for nature to creep in, and shew her unadulterated face; but, in my opinion, the chief happiness, both of man and woman, consists in the knowledge and practice of all the social affections."

The Baron, struck with these observations, held out his hand to De Clavering, requesting to be better acquainted with him, and apologizing for his former neglect, which was chiefly owing to the singularity of his situation, which made him behold every man younger than himself with envy and suspicion; "but now (added he) I have resigned all my pretensions to the prior claims of my son, wishing to atone for my past errors, and to prove myself worthy the esteem of all those to whom he owes an obligation."

"To me, my lord, (replied De Clavering,) your son owes nothing: till a few days back I knew not of his residence in the castle: to my respect and esteem I considered him as having a just claim. From the first hour I had the honour of being introduced to him, I felt a desire to serve him; but all I ever did was to accompany him from the castle to the chapel, for which I never expected to be pardoned by your lordship."

"But, as his lordship offers you his friendship, (said the giddy and spirited Hugh Camelford,) you had petter accept it now he is in the humour. Lorts are not always in the mind to be coot friends with teath and the toctor."

This essay of elocution obtained the Baron's notice, and, by making every one smile, succeeded to his wish. Camelford, thus encouraged, gave way to the unbounded cheerfulness of his disposition, by again renewing his attack upon his friend De Clavering, telling him it was high time for him to be prushing away the cobwebs of old patchelorship, and pecome a man of the world, otherwise to laty, maid, or witow, would undertake the care of his old pones, and the pones of those he had pought out of their craves. De Clavering, who seldom felt himself in the humour to be displeased with his young friend, owned that he was as singular in his sentiments as the ladies, he was afraid, might think him in his manners and appearance.

"You must endeavour to become more modern, and like one of us, (said De Willows.) To be better known cannot fail to secure you a most favourable reception."

"A piece of advice I have often given myself, (said Sir Philip.) To make our progress through life with credit and advantage to ourselves, we must so far become men of the world, as to seek for those favours it is not willing to bestow unsought or unsolicited."

"But, for a man to be able to get through it with uninterrupted success, (replied De Clavering,) I have sometimes thought he must be brought up a rascal from the first. I own I should find so many places that would tempt me to halt in my way, that I should certainly be prevented reaching the envied and contested goal; for, before I would submit to have my house crowded with a succession of what might be called good company, I would take an inn, and, in the character of mine host, play a safer, and as pleasant a game. I should not then be under the necessity of sacrificing my sentiments, or more of my time, than I found answered the purpose of keeping house to accommodate all comers and goers."

"What! (said Camelford,) would you be peat py a prother toctor, because you would not apply a strengthening plaister of goot and smooth worts to make it stick close? would you not gif the laties a healing cordial of compliments or reconcile them to heir loss of peauty, their lap-dog, or their lofer? Fie, man, they would not suffer you to toctor their cat!"

"What I might be tempted to do, or how far I might relax from my system, to please the ladies, (replied De Clavering,) I cannot tell till I become more *a man of the world*, and feel myself more attached to many of its customs: but this I do know, there are a set of patients to whom I could not sacrifice my own sentiments to obtain the command of their purses. For instance,—can the man, who has wasted his youth in vice and debauchery, justly complain of a premature old age? or ought he to excite the pity of any one who knew the source whence his miseries originated? Can we sympathize with the man of business, who has brought upon himself the torturing paroxysms of a fever by the disappointment of some monopolizing plan, the success of which must have been productive of distress and misery to many hundreds of their fellow-creatures. Can the voluptuary and the drunkard think themselves entitled either to flattery or compassion, when their sufferings have been occasioned by eating till they gained a surfeit, or by drinking so hard as to make a kind of turnpike-road from their stomachs to their bowels."

"All in the way of business, (said Edwin.) Instead of quarrelling with the cause, you have nothing more to do, my good friend, but to turn their follies to your own account, and do as thousands have done before you—make them contribute in some way or other to the good of the community."

"If we were disposed to quarrel with vice and folly every time we encountered them, (said Camelford,) we should be engaged in a perpetual contest, and should only ket proken pones and the plister of contention for our pains."

"True, (replied the venerable father Anselm, who till now had observed a placid silence as he listened to the above conversation,) we should all agree to make the same allowance for the failings and frailties of others as we are inclined to do when we sit in judgment upon our own, and rather strive to find excuses than causes to condemn; like the blessed master we all unite to serve, whose precepts and practice were calculated for the good and happiness of mankind."

"Just so would mine be, my dear father, (said De Clavering,) so far as an erring mortal can be supposed to copy a divine original; but I would not flatter people with a belief that I could feel for the miseries entailed by vice as I would for those which originated from any other cause. There are moments when I see the patient and virtuous sufferer looking up to me for health and life, that I would compound with pleasure to be any thing rather than what I am."

"Rather (said Sir Philip) endeavour to rest satisfied with being what you are,—the true Samaritan, the friendly physician, who assumes the appearance of misanthropy, without having a grain of it in his composition."

"In order to conceal feelings that do honour to his profession and to human nature."

The Baron, having looked at every thing and asked innumerable questions, the party next visited the rooms where Edwin and Roseline risked so much in daring to remove Walter, and in which he had so long remained undiscovered by the family. Here Walter himself described, in his own artless manner, the delight he felt when he, for the first time, saw the rising sun, and contemplated the brilliant scene which the moon and stars presented to his astonished sight; he mentioned likewise his rapture when first convinced that the fair Roseline felt for him a mutual passion. He then described the conflicts he endured on the morning when he knew she was really gone to give her hand to another, and owned the miseries of that moment surpassed those of his whole life, and, if thrown into a scale against them, would have weighed down all. He then adverted to his feelings when he approached the altar, and to the awe and respect he felt at sight of the Baron.

In the evening it was proposed to take a ramble through the gardens belonging to the castle now profusely decorated with all the variegated beauties of the soul-enlivening spring, which were on the eve of giving place to the succeeding charms of summer. Here it was that the happy, the grateful Walter met such a succession of wonders and delight as rendered the scene doubly pleasing to those who partook in his raptures.

Every flower, plant, and shrub, every tree, leaf, and vegetable, excited his admiration and gratitude. The distant fields,—the rising hills,—the water,—the numberless houses,—all, all were admired in turn, and became the theme of his praise.—It was a charming world,—it was the paradise of which he had read,—the very garden of Eden, such as our first parents possessed, and Roseline the magnet which gave such sweet attraction to all he saw, and all he should enjoy in it.

So much was he delighted with the scene, it was not till the shades of evening began to approach, and throw a gloom over the face of nature, that even the gentle admonitions of Roseline could prevail upon him to return to the castle. Like another Cymon, he found liberty too great a blessing, too pleasing to be willing to part with it when once he had tasted its soul-reviving influence.[39]

Many of the following days were spent in making excursions round the country, and in shewing him every thing worthy of notice. He visited the neighbouring towns and villages, looked into the churches, saw the sea, and was conveyed on board a ship, whose wonderful construction, and the vast world of waters on which it so majestically floated, awakened every sensation of astonishment. He was next indulged by sailing on the river Waveney in an open boat, rowed by

---

[39] A fitting comparison for Walter, Cymon is an unattractive and uneducated young man who transitions into a sophisticated and successful gentleman upon falling in love with Iphigenia in Boccacio's *Decameron*.

some of our old English sailors, whose rough and cheerful humour gratified and entertained him.

A horse was likewise procured for him: he soon learned to ride, and became so fond of the exercise, that few days passed without his going some miles about the country. His fine figure, expressive countenance, and conciliating manners, his gentleness, and unceasing good humour, made him an universal favourite, and all the inhabitants of Bungay welcomed his appearance among them with every testimony of respect, joy, and satisfaction.

The Baron and his friend, Sir Philip, had many consultations respecting the intended marriage of their children, whose youth and total ignorance of the world, of which Walter could scarcely be called an inhabitant, rendered it absolutely necessary that he should be properly introduced at court, in order to have his birth made known, and his rights and titles ascertained. It was equally necessary that he should become more conversant with the customs and manners of that world, on whose stage he was now to make so distinguished a figure; and, as he had been prevented seeing foreign countries, it was a duty the Baron thought incumbent upon him to take care he should be well acquainted with his own, and instructed in the value of its just and equitable laws, which, he had cause to lament, were sometimes abused by the designs of artful and wicked men, though the envy of every other nation in the world.

When these designs were made known to Walter, the distress it produced is not to be described. To be separated from Roseline!—the thought was agony;—without seeing her every day, without being in the same place with her, it was not to be borne. He should never be able to acquire any knowledge unless the gentle maid, to whom he was indebted for life, was near, and by her soul-enlivening presence animated his endeavours, while in her smiles he should find a bright reward for the unwearied pains he should not shrink from encountering for her sake.

Roseline was not at all better reconciled to the plan, nor more at ease than himself. She was apprehensive he might in the great world see some one he liked better than herself. She had heard men were inconstant and prone to change. The heart she had gained in the dungeon of Bungay-castle might perchance, when engaged in the great world, surrounded by pleasure, and besieged by the bright eyes of beauty, stray from her bosom to that of a more lovely and accomplished mistress;—to a more fond and faithful one it could not be entrusted; but, as no one, she supposed, could refuse the attentions of Walter, she trembled at the idea of being separated.

These timid fears were not kept from the ear of her lover, who, in some degree, quieted them with that persuasive eloquence which love never fails to bestow on its faithful votaries. He inquired if she thought it possible he could be so great a villain as to prefer the beauties of a court to the lovely Roseline of Bungay-Castle,—the gentle being who not only preserved his life, but taught him to enjoy it, whose unwearied attentions smoothed the bed of sickness, removed the veil of ignorance, and gave to his unfortunate life the first bright moment it had ever known. He vowed, if he thought any thing he might find in the world could tempt him to forget her, or love her less than he did at that moment, he would voluntarily return to his dungeon, and never leave it more: he earnestly and pathetically petitioned his father and Sir Philip de Morney not to compel him to leave his adored Roseline till he was blest with calling her his own.

With this request, however, they could not with prudence comply: it was not only right, but absolutely necessary he should be publicly acknowledged as the Baron's son before his marriage took place, to prevent the establishment of his rights being subject to suspicion or litigation. Against reasons so weighty and just there was no contending, and therefore they were obliged to submit, though these untaught children of simple nature yielded very reluctantly to a plan which was to secure in their possession all those fascinating enjoyments which the inhabitants of our busy world are continually pursuing, and to obtain which, without any necessity or compulsion, they often make more important sacrifices.

Albert was no long considered or treated as a servant. The Baron generously determined, as soon as he reached town, to give such orders to his attorney as should secure him a genteel independency; and, as he was no longer distressed with the apprehension of being separated from his beloved master, he enjoyed all the comforts, with a grateful heart which the liberality of his benefactors bestowed, and met with that unfeigned respect, from every one who knew the worth and integrity of his character, to which he was so justly entitled.

As Audrey was attending her young lady, in her apartment, after she had been at the chapel to be married, and returned from thence without becoming a bride, she, as it may be supposed, was too full of the occurrences of the day to be silent on a subject every one was talking about, but which she did not, on her part, by any means approve, knowing what her own feelings would have been on a similar occasion.

"Well, to be sure and certain, miss, (cried she,) the like of this was never heard since the mencement of the world; for to go to church to be married, to take the bride's groom in your hand, as a body may say, and then to come back as you went, without being married at all! As I have a vartuous and Christian soul to be saved, if I had been volved in such a quandrary, I would never have left the chapel without a husband, young or old, let what would have been the consequence.—People sleer and jeer so about misventures of this kind, and asks one for brides's cake, and talks so indellorcatly on this subject: however, don't fret, miss; it seems you may be married still, but, for my part, I likes it best as it is."

"I think in this instance as you do, Audrey, (replied Roseline, with difficulty keeping herself from offending the honest-hearted Abigail, by bursting into a violent fit of laughter,) yet the Baron is certainly a fine-looking old gentleman."

"Fine feathers make fine birds, (said Audrey,) but as to his being fine-looking, Christ Jesus, miss, to be sure master Cuford, the blind god of love, has made you blinder than himself."

Roseline could no longer preserve her gravity.

"Blind or not blind, (said she,) I assure you, Audrey, I thought the Baron looked and talked like an angel after we returned from the chapel; and, what is more, ugly as you think him, I love him dearly, and cannot help looking at him with pleasure and delight."

"To be sure, (said Audrey aside,) the disappointment has turned her head, and arranged all her interlects.—As sure as God is true, miss, (said she,) you have taken strange vaggaries into your head: it was but yesterday I thought you were going into vapid recline, as I have heard you mention, and now I verily thinks Bedlam will be your potion instead of a husband."

"As far as I know I am now in my proper senses, (cried Roseline, laughing,) notwithstanding your prognostics, and taking so much pains to convince me of the contrary."

"Well, well, it may be so, miss, (replied the mortified damsel;) I know but little of nostics; but this I do know, there is no recounting for the humour of quality people. The young Baron however, it must be said, if poor folks can see the judge, is to the full as good as his father. Handsome as you think him, and though he cannot speak to make himself understood, and do not know his right hand from his left, or the moon from a green cheese or young gosling, he may soon be taught to know what's what. He was monstrously frighted when he saw his father, and took him for a negromancer it seems."

"You have been strangely misinformed, Audrey, (interrupted Roseline,) the young lord is neither so ignorant nor so soon alarmed as you have been taught to believe. I have known him long, and therefore, if you will rely upon my word, I assure you he is one of the most amiable and best of human beings."

"Well, miss, (again continued Audrey,) I must think that your brain is cracked, or that love has overset your understanding; for I am told by Pedro, who knows every thing about every body, that, till this very blessed day, the sweet young gentleman have been chained down in a dungeon, and never looked upon the face of man, woman, or child, not even the mother who bore him. It was tirely on his account, we all thinks, that the bustle, fuss, and disturbations in the castle riginated, and I dare say if the old Baron had refused to own him for a son, we should every one of us have been witched into the Red Sea, and drowned as the Gyptens were. I hope now, however, the spells will be taken away, and we shall see only men and women, made of flesh and blood like ourselves, for I hate ghosts."

"Amen! (cried Roseline;) I trust we shall be very quiet and happy, and that neither witches nor evil spirits will have any thing to do with us."

"I say amen again, (replied Audrey,) for I always likes to pray whenever I see any one else set about it. Thank God you escaped the claws of the Baron: I verily thinks I could not have found courage enuf to have married him myself."

Roseline rejoiced when her prating attendant bade her good night, and she hoped soon to forget in the arms of sleep both the painful and pleasant events of the day; but she now found joy as great an enemy to repose as grief had been the preceding night. To find her lover, the acknowledged son of her intended husband; yet to have his consent,—the consent of her parents to love Walter, and be loved by him,—to know he was restored to liberty, rank, and fortune, to the protection of a father, and herself released from an engagement to which she never had consented,—it was such a sudden, such an unexpected reverse of fortune, as she could scarcely prevail upon herself to believe real. She had been assured too she should one day be the wife of Walter,—be permitted to live with him;—see him always, and without fear or controul be allowed to study and contribute to his happiness,—it was rapture, it was felicity far beyond her hopes.

Having once entered on a train of thinking, so delightful to a fond imagination, it effectually precluded sleep from shedding its poppies over her pillow; besides, to have slept would have been for some hours to have lost the pleasure of thinking of Walter.

No sooner did she see the god of day break forth in all his glory from the portals of the East, than she quitted her bed. Never before had she observed the sun so brilliant,—never before had the face of nature looked so charming: every tree which she saw wave its branches had acquired new beauties, and even the sturdy and impenetrable walls of the castle seemed to be wonderfully improved.

With spirits harmonized by love and expectation, and a mind enlivened by hope, she bent her knee in humble gratitude to that God who said, "Let there be light, and it was so," With a heart truly sensible of the blessings she enjoyed, and thankful for those she was permitted to behold at a distance, she fervently prayed that neither Walter nor herself might be tempted, in the midst of prosperity to forget the useful lessons they had learned in the school of adversity.

CHAPTER VII.

AS the dreaded day of separation drew near, the dejection which appeared on the countenance of the lovers was too visible to escape the observation of their friends.—The Baron felt himself particularly hurt: his son had already endured so much misery by his neglect and unpardonable compliance with the wishes of an artful and designing mother-in-law, that, to inflict any farther mortifications or sufferings on him, was in reality to inflict them more severely upon himself: he therefore promised to return within six weeks, or two month, to unite the young people.

This period of time, reckoned in the usual way, was not long; but lovers are not guided by the same rules, nor can bring themselves to calculate hours and days, weeks and months, like other people. To repeat the tender adieus, the fears, tears, cautions, and promises, of everlasting truth, would perhaps be tiresome to some of our readers, as it would be merely a repetition of the same fine and tender things which have been said by ten thousand fond lovers, upon ten thousand interesting occasions; suffice it then to say, the Baron and his son departed from the castle at the appointed time, and left the disconsolate Roseline in a state none could envy, and all were inclined to pity; and so much was the heart of her lover afflicted at being the cause of distressing her, he could not be prevailed upon to join in any conversation, and scarcely looked up till he entered the great and busy city of London, the noise and bustle of which drew him in some measure from his reverie, which had been nearly as painful to his friends as to himself, and the Baron, eager to disperse the gloom from the countenance of his son, pointed out some of the most striking objects to engage his attention, as they were whirled along to a very noble house in——square, where we must leave him for the present, in order to return to the castle.

From the moment of Walter's departure the disconsolate Roseline sunk into so absolute a state of dejection, as not only distressed but alarmed her friends. She shunned society, seldom joined in conversation, and, if left a few moments by herself, fled to the apartments once inhabited by her lover;—there, and there only, did she assume the appearance of cheerfulness; every place in which she had seen him was endeared to her remembrance. The chairs on which he had rested, the table on which he had written, the window at which he had stood to listen for her coming,—all were interesting objects, and loved by her for his sake; and, in being deprived of seeing him, of hearing no longer the sound of a voice so long endeared to her fond imagination, she felt so total a deprivation of all that served to render life or fortune of real value, that she determined in her own mind, if this regretted lover should prove forgetful or inconstant, if he should return no more to the castle, to end her days in his forsaken apartments; for what would be the world to Roseline de Morney, if she should see Walter Fitzosbourne no more?

Pompey, the little dog, which she had seen the second time of going to the dungeons, and which had been the favourite and faithful companion of her lover during some years of his confinement, she would scarcely permit to be out of her sight: to him she talked of his master, and in caressing the grateful little animal felt pleasure and consolation.

Sir Philip and Lady de Morney were distressed beyond measure at seeing the despondency of their daughter, which they feared would put an end to all their flattering hopes. They endeavoured by every soothing and tender attention to reconcile her to this temporary separation, and in a short time succeeded so far as to prevail upon her to resume her usual employments. They advised her to dissipate her fears, and try to regain her spirits for the sake of the lover whose absence she lamented, reminding her how much it would harass and distress him, if, at his return to the castle, he found she had brought upon herself an indisposition which might still preclude him from enjoying her society.

But their cares and anxieties were soon increased, and their minds occupied and thrown into the utmost consternation, from a circumstance more unaccountable, inexplicable, and alarming, than any thing they had ever encountered.

Madeline had escaped from the nunnery, and Edwin had left the castle. No one could tell what was become of them, but all supposed they were gone off together.—A general confusion took place; messengers were sent in pursuit of the fugitives, and a very considerable reward was offered to any who would bring tiding of Madeline. Sir Philip de Morney joined in the search, and sent out large parties of his men, in hopes they would be able to discover the place of their concealment.

Roseline, though less surprised, was extremely shocked at the dangerous step her brother and friend had ventured to take.—The abbess was angry, the fathers enraged, and the youthful offenders threatened with the utmost severity the laws could inflict, should they be found out. Lady de Morney was wretch beyond descriptions, and Roseline, who almost lost the remembrance of her own sorrows at seeing the agonies of her mother, and in fears for her brother, was alarmed at the return of every messenger.—These affectionate relatives trembled lest they should bring tidings of the unfortunate lovers. A week however elapsed, and no discovery being made, Roseline secretly cherished hopes that they would be able to escape their pursuers.

She accompanied Sir Philip and Lady de Morney to the nunnery: they soon removed the displeasure of the abbess, and dispersed the gloom, which had long hung upon her brow, at their first entrance: they likewise softened the asperity of father Anselm, and the rest of his brethren, who had written to inform the father of Madeline of the occurrence which had taken place, and had received an answer dictated by the spirit of malice and revenge, vowing to renounce her for ever, unless she returned to the nunnery, and instantly took the veil; at the same time adding every thing that passion could suggest to rouse the vengeance of the fathers for the indignity offered to their sacred order by the flight of a wretch he never again would acknowledge as a daughter.

This cruel and unfeeling letter operated directly contrary to what it was intended, and awakened feelings in the bosoms of men who had long been strangers to the world and unpractised in the habits of social life,—too unpleasant to be encouraged. They felt a kind of trembling horror at the denunciations of a parent against a daughter, whose interesting features, sweetness of disposition, and gentleness of temper, had endeared her to every one in the nunnery.

Nearly a fortnight had now elapsed, and no tidings being heard of the fugitives, Lady de Morney began to revive, and she cherished the soul-reviving hope that her beloved Edwin would escape, and remain undiscovered till a pardon could be procured for him and his fair companion, for the crime they had committed in robbing their holy church of a votary designed for its service; and she lingered with impatient fondness to clasp her son and the lovely Madeline to her maternal bosom. Sir Philip was much hurt by this affair; and, though he said very little on the subject, it was very visible to every one that his mind was very deeply wounded.

It may now be necessary that we should give some account of the means made use of to escape, and the cause which drove the young people to take so desperate a step.

The abbess, who felt an almost maternal regard for Madeline, had observed with affectionate regret that there was something which preyed deeply upon her spirits, but had not the least suspicion of the affection which she cherished for her nephew; and, being too much bigoted to her religion, too much attached to the habits of a monastic life, to suppose any one could long remain unhappy after having given up a world which she had voluntarily quitted and never regretted, she confined her observations to her own bosom, and, in drawing her conclusions, forgot the melancholy and distressing cause which had determined her seclusion from the world. Time had likewise in some degree blunted those tender feelings which would otherwise have taught her to make more indulgent allowances for the feelings and conflicts of nineteen, when sentenced by an arbitrary parent to the unsocial and rigid rules of an order that precluded the soul-enlivening, the enchanting influence of love.

The abbess, on receiving a letter from the father of Madeline, with a peremptory command for her instantly taking the veil, summoned her into the presence of father Anselm and herself, and the letter was put into her hand, without any kind of preface that could discover or soften its contents.—The effect this horrid mandate had on the mind of their youthful charge could not be concealed: she was instantly obliged to be conveyed to her cell, and remained for some hours in a state that threatened distraction.

The alarming situation of Madeline distressed both the good father and the sympathizing abbess; but, circumstanced as they were, they could only pity; for they would have considered it as a crime of the most sacrilegious nature to have assisted in depriving their holy institution of a votary so likely to be an ornament and acquisition to it; and, as the father of Madeline was determined she should embrace a monastic life, they had neither any right nor inclination to contend against a decision which operated so much in their favour, and would add so lovely a sister to their society: they agreed therefore that it would be better to take no notice, unless she herself should voluntarily impart the cause of her distress.

It is now become absolutely necessary to inform our readers that Edwin had for some weeks conquered the fears of Madeline, and prevailed on her to grant him frequent interviews in the chapel. He had also extorted a promise from her, when matters came to the last extremity, to fly with him, if her escape from the nunnery could be effected, in order to avoid a fate which her love had taught her to think of all others the most miserable, and to accept his vows instead of taking those which would separate them for ever.

On the one hand, happiness stood pourtrayed in its most captivating colours;—on the other, wretchedness, solitary wretchedness grinned with ghastly horror and meagre aspect. At her age, I am inclined to think, few young ladies would have hesitated how to choose, particularly if, like the artless and gentle Madeline, they had given away their heart to an amiable and impassioned lover.

Edwin, in his stolen visits to the chapel, had usually been accompanied by his trusty friend Albert, and once or twice Walter had been of the party. On the promises and intrepid firmness of Albert they rested their security of not being discovered. Madeline's situation was likewise becoming so alarming and distressing, she no longer yielded to those timid fears which had formerly deterred her from meeting her lover. She found herself so encompassed with dangers, that it required both resolution and spirit to disengage herself from the fate which threatened her; and, as no farther time could be given either to deliberation or doubt, and no alternative remained but to escape from the nunnery or take the veil, she hesitated no longer, but met, fearlessly met her lover, in order to settle a proper plan to secure the success of their design, which, as it drew near being put in practice, appeared both hazardous and dangerous.

Their meetings in the chapel were frequently interrupted by the friars or nuns, who had generally some sacred duty to perform either for the living or the dead, in the execution of which some of the fathers had been extremely alarmed, and it was whispered throughout the sacred walls, and by some means the report crept into the world, that the chapel of the nunnery was disturbed by an invisible agent, which was considered as a miracle in favour of its holy institution.

It was an age of bigotry and superstition, when every plan was adopted to impress on the minds of the people that reverence and awe which would prevent their finding out the various arts made use of to impose on their belief. Hence that reverence and enthusiasm for relics shewn in almost every church and chapel, and applied to for aid on all important occasions.

Yet it sometimes happened that impositions were discovered, but the power and influence of the priests prevented, as much as possible, reports so dangerous gaining any credit, and the minds of the common people were kept so much in awe by fear, and so hoodwinked by superstition, that thousands resorted daily to one repository or another, in order to feast their eyes with its sacred treasures.

"At Reading they shewed an angel's wing, that brought over the spear's point which pierced our Saviour's side, and as many pieces of the cross were found as joined together would have made a big cross. The rood of grace, at Boxley, in Kent, had been much esteemed, and drawn many pilgrims to it. It was observed to bow and roll its eyes, and look at times well pleased or angry, which the credulous multitude, and even some of the inferior priests, imputed to a divine power; but all this was afterwards discovered to be a cheat, and it was brought up to St. Paul's cross, and all the springs were openly shewed which governed its several motions.

"At Hales, in Gloucestershire, the blood of Christ was shewn in a phial, and it was believed that none could see it who were in mortal sin; and so, after good presents were made, the deluded pilgrims went away well satisfied if they had seen it. This was the blood of a duck, renewed every week, put in a phial, very thick on one side, as thin on the other; and either side turned towards the pilgrims as the priest were satisfied with their oblations.—Other relics were shewn as follows:—God's coat, our Lady's smock, part of God's supper, our Lady's girdle of Bruton; red silke, a solemn relic sent to women in travail; the parings of St. Edmund's nails, relics for rain, for avoiding the weeds growing in corn, &c. &c."—[40]

It happened one night, when our young lovers were deeply engaged in a most important and interesting conversation, in which they did not recollect there were any other beings but themselves in the world, they were terribly alarmed, and very near being discovered by the abrupt and sudden entrance of father Anselm, and one on the monks, into the chapel. The hastily approached the altar, being summoned to attend a dying monk, and to perform the ceremonies which the necessity of the case required. They were however informed by a voice, which appeared to rise from the earth on which they stood, that they might return in peace to their cells, for the soul of their dying brother was in no danger of being lost, their prayers and pious oraisons having already had a salutary effect.

It so happened, that the monk, having conquered the crisis of his distemper, was sunk into a profound sleep at their return, which promised a happy change in his favour. The whole society were summoned into the chapel the next morning, and informed of this miraculous communications. All the proper ceremonies were ostentatiously performed which such an honourable attestation of their sincere piety required, and the sick monk considered as worthy of canonization.

A few nights after, a monk, who had forgotten to place one of the consecrated vessels on the high altar, which father Anselm had particularly requested should be left there against the following day, on which the sacrament was to be administered with the utmost solemnity, on recollecting the omission, rose from his bed, and stole softly into the chapel to obey the orders he had received. This unfortunately was a night on which the lovers had agreed to meet. Before he had reached the altar, he was somewhat startled at seeing one of the oldest and most austere of the nuns kneeling by the grave of a father lately deceased, and with uplifted hands praying that pardon and peace might be extended to his soul.

---

[40] Vide Gross's Antiquities, copied from an original letter, written by R. Layton. (Bonhote's original note.)

The monk, when he came to the altar, instantly dropped on his knees before it, unwilling the old nun should suppose he came upon a less pious errand than herself; but he was soon frightened from his devotions by a soft voice, which seemed to descend from behind a very fine painting of the crucifixion.—He was desired to return to his cell, no longer to act the hypocrite, and in future to perform more punctually the duties of his office.

The monk no sooner heard this alarming address, than he hurried out of the chapel as fast as his gouty legs and the numerous infirmities of age would permit him; but the nun, who was at too great a distance from the monk to hear the cause of his terror, went on with those devotional rights which a particular regard for the departed father rendered so gratifying to the feelings of her pious and affectionate heart, that she was in no hurry to conclude them; when the same mysterious agent, whose voice appeared to rise from the grave of her deceased favourite, near which she was so devoutly kneeling, shivering with age and cold, roughly warned her to have done, advising her to go to rest and sleep in peace, as he did, who no longer could be disturbed by her tongue or benefited by her prayers.

The poor frightened nun scampered off as fast as she could, muttering something against the ingratitude of man, who, dead or alive, was unworthy the attentions of her pious sex. Yet, as she crossed herself, she secretly rejoiced at having, as she thought, obtained leave of heaven and father John to abstain from such great and unreasonable demands upon her oraisons in future.—She took care, however, the next morning to inform the monk, with seeming exultations, of her being so highly favoured as to hear a voice from heaven, which excused her from praying at those hours appointed for mortals to be at rest.

This was a night calculated to alarm the lovers; for no sooner had the nun left the chapel, than another entered to fetch a solemn relic, to send to a woman who was in travail, from the chest near which they were seated. As she was looking for the precious treasure, they were trembling at the danger they were in of being discovered; for there was but just time to step into the tomb which led to the subterraneous passage, when they were thus the third time disturbed.—The nun, as she closed the chest, was addressed in the following words.

"Wear Mary Magdalene's girdle twice a week:—place the scull of St. Lawrence at the East corner of your cell, and live on bread and water every fifth day; or neither you, nor your father-confessor will escape purgatory."

Down dropped the relic, and away ran the nun to repeat to her cher ami the warning which had been given her; but, whether he was as much terrified as herself we do not know, as the lovers very soon effected their escape, and the voice was heard no more.

No longer to puzzle our readers, excite their fears, or keep them in suspense, respecting his miraculous voice, which had alarmed the Baron in his visit to the cells, and had likewise been the occasion of much surprise, and some exultation, to the pious inhabitants of the nunnery, it is necessary to inform them that it proceeded from Albert, who was himself a ventriloquist, or person possessed of the power of using a kind of artificial hollow voice, in such a manner, as to make the sound appear to come from any part of the room, wherever he happened to be, or from any animal that was present in it.

This uncommon power, rarely known in that age, Albert had frequently exercised to amuse and entertain the solitary hours of his master, in his long and painful seclusion from the world, and afterwards to serve him and his friend.

It may not perhaps, in this place, be improper to mention, that, a few years since, a person came to St. Edmund's Bury, in Suffolk, whose uncommon and wonderful powers of throwing his voice to any distance, and into whatever place he chose, alarmed some, and surprised all who witnessed this strange and almost unaccountable phenomenon of nature; therefore, in an age so much more prone to indulge the idle chimæras of superstition, so much under the dictatorial bigotry of priestcraft, it is not to be wondered that a circumstance so uncommon should be considered as miraculous, particularly among a set of men who had recourse to such various arts, and took such wonderful pains to instill into the minds of the people a firm and unshaken belief that miracles were shewn on some important occasions, in order to confirm the truth of the religion they professed.

CHAPTER VIII.

BY following the cautious directions of Albert, Madeline escaped from the nunnery undiscovered, and, accompanied by her lover, lost, in the happiness of the present moment, all remembrance of the trial she had sustained, and all apprehensions of what she might encounter in future. Edwin, from a principle of honour, did not inform his friends, De Willows, De Clavering, and Camelford, of his intention; the only tax he levied on their friendship was to borrow a small sum of money of them to supply present exigencies, and procure such accommodations on the road as would be most agreeable and convenient to his fair companion.

About midnight he led the trembling agitated maid, unattended by any one but himself, to the entrance of the subterraneous passage. With difficulty and danger they made their way through this scene of desolation and terror. Having opened the door which led them through the same gloomy paths Edwin had formerly traced, they narrowly escaped being discovered by the centinels who guarded Mettingham-Castle.—Alarmed at their danger, they made not a moment's delay, but hurried on till they came to a retired and almost unfrequented road, where they found a man and horses waiting their arrival. These horses had been hired of a countryman, who agreed to send for them the next morning to a neighbouring town.

Though money was undoubtedly very scarce in the age in which the characters lived that furnished us with these memoirs, yet the necessaries of life were all so cheap, and the people in general so extremely hospitable, that it required but a moderate sum to procure accommodations for a journey to the most distant part of the kingdom, and, as there was then no marriage-act in force, the road to the temple of Hymen was more frequented, because it was neither found so difficult nor so thorny as it has been to too many of the present age.

As to the vulgar and old-fashion habits of eating and drinking, they are matters in general but little thought of in expeditions under the directions of a god who is too sublime to be satisfied with common food. Our lovers felt so little inconvenience from either hunger or thirst, that they determined to make no delays on their journey, but such as were absolutely necessary. They were epicures only in love, and, till they arrived in London, were perfectly satisfied with such repasts as were to be procured from any of the humble cottages on the road, by which prudent precaution they escaped undiscovered, notwithstanding the clamour their elopement had occasioned.

The morning after their arrival in London, a priest joined their hands in marriage, and rendered indissoluble those tender ties which had long united their hearts in love's most pleasing fetters. Too happy for reflection to interrupt their nuptial joys, too inexperienced to look forward to the consequences of an union thus inauspiciously commenced, and too sanguine to think the fond delusions of love could end but with life, they lived for many days in what might be called the delirium of the senses: in each other they saw and possessed all that constituted their ideas of pleasure. Madeline was the wife of the enamoured Edwin, and he was blest.—Edwin was become the husband and protector of Madeline, what then could she have to fear, for Edwin was the world to her?

Alas! what a pity that so few, so scarce, and so short, are the hours of mortal happiness! and that the fallacious foundation on which we rest such innumerable pleasing hopes, which present to our deluded imaginations the most lovely and inviting prospects, should so soon fall to the ground, and humble our air-built expectations in the dust!

As long as their little fund of worldly wealth held out, our new married lovers never recollected it must come to an end, or bestowed a thought on what steps were to be taken to secure the continuance of that felicity they had gone such daring lengths to obtain; but an empty purse soon compelled them to recollect, that two people, however tender their attachment, or superlative their abilities,—however lovely their persons, or captivating their manners, require more substantial food than the god of love will condescend to furnish them with.

Accustomed to affluence, and not knowing what it was to be deprived even of the luxuries of life, they shuddered at the poverty which stared them in the face, and threatened them with absolute starvation: they blushed too at their own inability to procure for themselves the common necessaries of life, and felt some very uncomfortable sensations at being in a stranger's house without the means of paying for their lodging or accommodations. To declare their poverty they were ashamed, and to make themselves and situation known was to run the risk of being separated for ever, as Edwin had no doubt but Madeline would be torn from him, and compelled to a monastic life, if discovered before his friends were reconciled, and would use their interest to procure his pardon.

Luckily, Madeline, amidst her new born fears, recollected it would be no difficult matter to find so great a man as Baron Fitzosbourne, and accordingly, Edwin wrapped up and disguised as much as possible, sat off to find his residence, and to obtain an interview with his two friends, Walter and Albert. He fortunately found the latter at home, and in a few hours was by him secretly admitted to Walter, who flew to embrace and welcome him to his father's mansion, making a number of tender inquires after Roseline and the rest of his friends at the castle. He was both shocked and astonished when informed of Edwin's distressed and perilous situation, gently reproached him for not applying to him before, and for not having giving him the slightest information of his intention before he married.

Edwin made the best excuses he could for his reserve. Vague and unsubstantial as they were, the generous Walter was soon reconciled to his friend, put his purse into his hand, and insisted upon being immediately introduced to his lovely bride. They returned with Edwin to his lodgings, and found Madeline in a state of the most painful and restless suspense, which their presence instantly dispersed. After the compliments and congratulations were over, they sat down to consider seriously what could be done, and what steps were most proper to be taken to secure the persons of the new-married couple. Albert strenuously advised them not to attempt seeing the Baron in their present situation, but to wait patiently till some plan could be adopted for their farther safety. Walter promised in the mean time to supply them with money for all necessary expences.

The meeting of these friends was cordial and tender, and more cheerful than could have been supposed. Walter repeatedly protested, notwithstanding the difficulty sand dangers with which they were surrounded, that he envied more than he pitied them,—complained of his own situation, as being more distressing and uncomfortable than their's, and declared himself unable to support a much longer separation from Roseline, without the deprivation of reason being added to that of all his other enjoyments.

On reflection, it was thought better that Walter should make the situation of the young couple known to the Baron without farther delay: this he readily undertook; for, as the danger was great, rewards having been offered for the person of Madeline, procrastination would have only served to increase the difficulties they had to encounter.

Walter succeeded in his embassy beyond his hopes, and soon prevailed upon his father to comply with a plan they had thought of for the better security of Madeline; namely, retiring secretly for the present to the environs of one of the Baron's castles, at a great distance from the metropolis, and concealing their real names and persons under the habits of peasants. To this scheme the Baron readily agreed, and promised not only to exert his utmost interest to procure a pardon for them both, but instantly to write to Sir Philip and Lady de Morney to inform them of their safety and situation, and intercede in their behalf. He likewise called upon them the following day, presented them with a supply of cash for present exigencies, and sent them in one of his own carriages to the place of their concealment, where we will for a short time leave them, only observing they were as happy as our first parents before their fall: they sometimes indeed recollected the danger of being discovered, and trembled at the thought; but so much did they depend on the friendship and power of the Baron to protect them, should the dreadful misfortune ever befall them, that they determined not to let uncertain apprehensions of what might happen in the future prevent their enjoying that portion of happiness which was now in their power, and the author would wish every one who peruses these pages to adopt and encourage the same useful philosophy.[41]

Walter, from the time of his arrival in London, till a few days previous to his seeing Edwin, had been restless and uncomfortable. The first masters of the age had been procured to instruct him. He was presented to his sovereign, and his introduction was attended with the most marked and distinguished honours.

Many fair ladies in the higher circles were lavish of their smiles, and many parents would gladly have seen him added to the trains of their daughters' admirers, and, to lure him to their purpose, solicited his friendship, and sent him repeated invitations to their houses.

Pleasure courted him in a thousand varying forms, but he beheld her most seducing blandishments with disgust and stoical indifference. Neither the novelty of the scenes with which he was surrounded, the flattering attentions of beauty, or the variety of amusements, of which he was in a manner compelled to partake, could for one moment detach his mind from the fascinating Roseline. With her dwelt every wish,— on her unshaken tenderness rested his every hope of permanent felicity; for her society he pined and languished; and, to have heard the sound of her enchanting voice, he would voluntarily have bidden adieu to London, and all its pleasures.—If he attended to the instructions of his masters, he was actuated by the same motives, and he wished to be as wise as Plato, that he might be more worthy to possess a treasure he estimated beyond the wealth of worlds.—Noble young man!—would love operate on all youthful minds as it did on thine, it would be entitled to universal praise, and might justly be called the guardian-friend of innocence, the patron of every virtue.

At length, both the Baron and Albert were not only surprised, but alarmed at the visible alteration they observed in Walter, who often absented himself, and when questioned where he had been, and how he had been amusing himself, hesitated in his answers, and appeared at a loss what to say.

---

[41] The Baron has made quite a transition. He has become kind and loving, the protector of lovers rather than the Bluebeard destroyer of his past. Bonhote stresses her theme of the restorative power of love through his gentle and compassionate actions.

One evening the Baron particularly requested he would accompany him to some public place; but he pleaded a prior engagement, and, on being asked the nature of it, gave so trifling and unsatisfactory an answer, that the Baron was seriously displeased, and left the room, telling him he did not like to be treated with reserve, recommended him to recollect how much he had already been made a dupe to mysterious transactions, and not to forget that he had likewise been nearly a victim to artifice before he knew guile in his own heart or person.

As soon as he left the room, Albert approached his beloved master, and, with a tear trembling in each eye, told him he was to blame, begged he would follow his father, and do away his displeasure, by going as he requested.

"My dear fellow, (cried Walter,) my father's anger I could bear unmoved, because I do not feel myself deserving of it, but your gentle reproof has in a moment found its way to my heart. Perhaps I may be to blame, but surely, Albert, it is a little hard upon me to be compelled to stay in this place without being sometimes allowed to amuse myself according to my own inclinations!"

"What on earth (said Albert, with a sigh,) can on a sudden have made this change in you, who so lately had an invincible objection to going among strangers, lest you should fall into the snares that are so frequently spread to entangle the unwary!—I thought—"

"Allons, my dear fellow, (replied the impatient Walter,) don't just now attempt to think;—you are a good creature:—but I can stay no longer to listen to you; I will hear you as early as you please in the morning. Would to God my sweet Roseline had accompanied her brother to London!"

"Would to heaven she had! (sighed Albert:) Here is something wrong going forwards. I must be on my guard how I proceed, or my young master will be drawn into some scrape that may lead to mischief, while the fair maid of the castle may be left to wear the willow.—Now, or never, must be the moment of action.—A thought has struck me;—it must be so."

Away went Albert, and I hope none of my readers will have any objection to accompany him in his friendly expedition.

He instantly hurried out of the house, attended by a stout and faithful servant.—They were so quick in their proceedings, that they very soon perceived the object of their pursuit walking before them. After following him through many streets, they saw him stop at a very good-looking house, the door of which was opened by a servant in a rich livery. Albert hesitated for a moment what to do:—to follow him would have been both daring and imprudent, and, instead of setting matters to rights, might have brought on greater difficulties; he therefore stepped into a jeweller's shop nearly opposite the house into which the young Fitzosbourne had entered, desiring his servant to keep a watchful eye. He spent a few shillings, and then carelessly inquired of the shopkeeper who it was inhabited the handsome house in which he saw so many lights.

The man smiled, looked at him very earnestly, and then replied, "If I did not think you were a stranger, sir, I should have supposed you were joking with me, by asking that question, for I thought all the world had known the Jezebel who lives there."

"You have raised my curiosity to a higher pitch, (said Albert.) I have so long been absent from this city, that I know but little of what has been doing in it, and would thank you to answer my question with sincerity, while I am looking over the things I want to purchase."

"No man (replied the complaisant shop-keeper) is happier to please his customers than I am, or more grateful for favours received; but, as one person's money is as good as another's, and as I take a pretty round sum every year from the fair inhabitants of that house, I have no business to be telling of their frailties: however, if I can oblige you, sir, and you will promise me to be secret, and not bring my name in question."—

Albert now became more and more eager to obtain the wished-for intelligence, and not only promised all that he had requested, but to reward him for his trouble, by recommending his shop to some friends who had it greatly in their power to serve him. This at once put an end to the honest jeweller's reserve; for, though he would not voluntarily have told a scandalous tale of any one, yet he saw no objection to speaking the truth when he could serve himself by so doing.

"Please your honour, (he began, for he took it into his head at that moment that Albert was a great man,) in that house lives the noted Mrs. C——, who keeps so many fine young women, that all the fine young men of the age are fond of obtaining admittance, though for that indulgence they often sacrifice health, fortune, and even life itself. Ah! God knows, I have seen sad doings, and many a one have I wished might escape the plans laid for their destruction; but, if the devil himself were to fall into her clutches, I think he would be puzzled to effect his escape."

"Has she many visitors just now?" interrupted Albert.

"As to their number, that is impossible for me to ascertain; but of this I am positive, she is never without some, and at this very time I think there is something extraordinary going on, for one of her nymphs came this morning to purchase a wedding-ring, and, on my joking her a little on the subject, she said it was not for herself but Miss C——, daughter to the old hag, who is a very lovely girl, and well known upon the town. On my expressing myself happy to hear she was going to marry, and become an honest woman, the girl burst into a violent fit of laughter, and called me a puritanical hypocrite."

"Let Catherine once become a wife, (said she,) and then we shall see who will dare to call her virtue in question. She will, I hope, before to-morrow night be married to the only son of one of the wealthiest barons in the kingdom,—a young nobleman who knows so little of the world, that it is absolutely necessary he should have a wife who can instruct him, and I know no one better able to undertake the task than the daughter of Mrs. C——."

Albert with difficulty concealed his agitation at hearing this alarming tale. Recovering himself, however, he inquired of his informer if he recollected the name of the young gentleman.—After a moment's hesitation, the jeweller replied, "the name was twice repeated, but it ran so glibly off the lady's tongue, that I have since forgotten it."

"Should you know it again?" asked Albert; who, on the jeweller's answering that he thought he should, mentioned several, to all of which a negative was given. At length Fitzosbourne was introduced.—"The very person, (cried the jeweller:)—the Baron has but one son; and him, as this girl told me, he has but lately found: but he is such an ideot, and so easily imposed on, that, upon my soul, were I his father, I should think him better lost than found."

The jeweller might have gone on with his observations as long as he pleased, had not his distressed auditor recollected the danger in which, perhaps, his beloved young master was at that moment involved. He started up, and, catching hold of his companion's hand, told him, he must that moment go with him. The man drew back: Albert perceived the folly of his abruptness, and, making some apologies, informed the astonished jeweller, that the business on which he was going would admit of no delay,—that if he would accompany him, lend his assistance, and procure two or three spirited young men to be of a party, he should be well rewarded for his trouble, and would have reason to bless the day chance directed him to his shop.

This promise was a sufficient temptation to a tradesman who had a large family, little money, and few friends. He summoned some of his men from an adjoining workshop, and, thus attended, Albert sallied into the street. His servant, who was in waiting, informed his master a priest had been just admitted into the house he was watching, and that he had seen the young lord at the window with a beautiful woman hanging on his arm, who appeared to be in tears.

This intelligence made them hurry on.—Albert rapped at the door, requesting the others to keep out of sight till he was secure of obtaining admittance. A servant soon appeared; Albert inquired if his mistress were at home. The fellow replied that his lady was then particularly engaged, and could not be spoken to, adding, he might call again in the morning.

"The morning will not do, my friend; I must see your mistress this evening, (said Albert;) my business is quite as particular, I believe, as that in which she may be engaged, therefore make way, and let me come in."

The fellow attempted to shut the door, but the posse in waiting, on being beckoned by Albert, came to his assistance, and they all rushed into the house. Albert, the jeweller, and the rest of the party, except one, who was left to guard the fellow at the door, went as gently as possible up a spacious staircase. They heard voices at a distance, and were directed by the sound to the door of the apartment which contained the party, who appeared to be engaged in a warm dispute.

At time they could distinguish female voices, and very soon Albert heard that of his beloved master exalted to its highest pitch.[42] This at once determined him to open the door, but he found it fastened within side: he then loudly demanded admittance; a female scream was all the answer he received. Again he called: some one then asked what was wanted, adding, whoever it was that intruded on them so rudely must wait till another opportunity.

"Wait no longer, (cried Walter,) but force the door; I know not but my life may be endangered."

The door was instantly burst open. What a scene presented itself! Walter, with a face pale as ashes, and apparently in the utmost confusion, was endeavouring to disengage himself from the embraces of a young woman, who had fallen at this feet, and clasped her arms around him. The priest held a prayer-book in his hand, which was opened at the matrimonial service.—A fierce looking man in the naval uniform, the old procuress, and another of her nymphs, completed the group.

The instant Walter saw his friend enter the apartment, by a desperate effort he disengaged himself from the syren who had held him captive, flew to Albert, and brandishing his sword, called upon the

---

[42] The episode in the whore house reveals an important recurrent theme in Gothic and Victorian sensation literature. Sexual women are frequently demonized due to their power over weak men who "[o]ften sacrifice health, fortune, and even life itself" for sexual indulgences (209). Matilda in Lewis's *The Monk*, the three wives of Stoker's *Dracula*, and Le Fanu's *Carmilla*, are vividly described as sexual predators, for they are able to destroy through their sexuality, not muscular strength. (For more information, see Bram Dijkstra's *Evil Sisters The Threat of Female Sexuality in Twentieth Century Culture*). Additionally, Walter is an easy target for these women simply due to his ignorance of sexuality and the world outside his dungeon. Ironically, the only reason Albert is able to locate and rescue Walter is due to his high pitched, woman-like screams.

wretch who had endeavoured to inveigle him into a forced marriage to draw, and receive the reward of his treachery; but Albert ordered the culprit to be secured, and requested Walter not to stain the purity of his sword with the blood of such a villain.—During this contest, the women and the priest sneaked out of the room unobserved, and, though the strictest search was made throughout the house, not a creature could be found in it that belonged to the family, but the servant who admitted them, and who had been prevented following the rest by the person left to guard him.

Albert insisted, before he left the house, on sending for proper officers to take the prisoners into custody; but Walter, who wished this affair to be kept as secret as possible, entreated, with so much earnestness, on the villain's making a promise of amendment, and leaving the kingdom, to have him liberated, that his friend, after a little hesitation, complied, on condition that the two fellows should be left bound in different apartments till the vile mistress of the house or some of her associates, should venture to return.

The honest jeweller was entreated to be secret, and promised an ample recompense. His people were liberally paid, and Albert, with an exulting heart, attended home his agitated friend, who, after recovering his spirits in some degree, gave him the following account of the circumstances which had drawn him into a situation that might have been as fatal to his peace as they would have been disgraceful to his character, had not his guardian-friend arrived in time to prevent the threatened danger, the whole of which he was now convinced had been planned for the purpose of drawing him into marriage, resting their hopes of success on his ignorance of the world.

"I take shame to myself, dear Albert, (said the grateful Walter,) for not informing you this evening of my engagement, which you, who know the strength of my attachment to the charming Roseline, will not suppose was meant to be of the nature it proved. I knew not that the worthless woman, whose daughter it has been my ill luck frequently to meet at several public places, was of so despicable a character.— Chance, or, as I now suspect, design, has likewise frequently thrown her in my way in my morning rambles: but what induced me to visit at her mother's house, was the having found her one evening in the passage of the play-house, waiting the arrival of her carriage, in the greatest distress; and what served to add to it was the behaviour of two or three young men, who said some very rude things to her in my hearing, for which I chastised them with my cane, and the frightened fair one fainted in my arms as soon as I had driven them away. I supposed they had been led to insult her by having made too free with the bottle; but they doubtless knew her well enough to discover her designs against me.

"When she recovered from the fit into which I imagined they had terrified her, I could do no less than see her home; and, when I called the next morning, I was introduced to her mother, whose unbounded gratitude and flattering acknowledgments, for the trifling service I had rendered her sweet and amiable daughter, overwhelmed me with confusion, and convinced her I was a fool exactly suited to her purpose.

Being always received with the utmost politeness, and seeing nothing in the conduct or behaviour of either mother or daughter to excite suspicion, I continued to call upon them whenever I chanced to pass that way, and was in the humour to wish for conversation. They boasted of being of an ancient family in the North of England, appeared to live in credit and affluence, treated me with the utmost hospitality, and pressed me so warmly to make them frequent visits, that I promised to comply with their request, because I suppose by so doing I was removing a weight of obligation from their minds which seemed to give them pain.

Once or twice it happened when I called, that the young lady had walked out, and the mother said a good deal about the mortification it would be to her to be told at her return I had called upon them in her absence; but this, till about two days ago, I considered as being the effusions of gratitude.

"And how (inquired Albert) were you at length undeceived?"

"By her mother," continued Walter, who, after some little hesitation, with an appeal to my honour and humanity, to excuse the weakness of a fond parent, informed me of the passion I unfortunately, and as she feared undesignedly, had inspired in the bosom of her daughter, a passion she much doubted she would never be able to subdue, adding, that, just before my arrival, she had by mere force compelled her to walk out for air, as she saw with heart-felt distress the ravages despair had made in the constitution of her inestimable child.

I lamented the consequences of my introduction, and added, I would no more venture into a family whose peace I had disturbed, acknowledged a prior engagement, and was about to quit the house, when the old lady entreated me earnestly not to adopt a measure so cruel and unjust: I therefore promised to call again; and, receiving an invitation for his evening, accepted it, but did not suppose them the kind of people they have proved.

"Had you no suspicion of their character?" asked Albert.

"None, by heaven! (replied Walter.)—I never saw the least appearance of indecency, or even levity, and heard no conversation that would have offended the nice ear of a Roseline de Morney."

"The scheme was deeply laid, (said Albert.)—Pray proceed; I am impatient to know how you were received this evening."

"First by the mother, (continued Walter, who appeared in the greatest distress.)—On my inquiring the cause, she said she had informed Catharine of what had passed between us; that, on being told I was engaged, she fainted several times, and, before she recovered, her nephew, who was just returned from abroad, called at the house. This young man, she said, had been long passionately attached to her; that, on seeing the situation of his cousin, he was necessarily informed of the cause,—was now with her, and had so earnestly entreated to have the honour of being introduced to me, that she could not find resolution to deny his request.—

"I will confess to you, my dear Albert, I now began to suspect some design was formed against me; but of what nature I was still at a loss to conjecture. I luckily had put on my sword, and I determined, if they attempted to confine or ill treat me, to sell my life as dearly as I could. However, it was not my life they wanted; they had a more ambitious and less dangerous scheme in view. In a little time, the lady, drowned in tears, and with well-acted distress, entered the room, accompanied by her cousin, as the mother had called him. The gentleman chose to put on a fierce and threatening look, and swore I should do justice to his charming cousin, whom he loved more than life, or that moment settle the matter with him as a gentleman ought to do.

I laid my hand on my sword: Catharine flew to me, fell at my feet, and begged I would not terrify her to death by exposing a life so dear to the risk of fighting with her cousin. She then lamented her weakness, and entreated me to compassionate the sorrows in which I had involved her.

I loudly demanded what all this meant,—declared I had no design against her heart, nor any desire to be favoured with her hand, my own having been long engaged to the best and fairest of her sex, and to whom alone all my wishes were confined. The gentleman again approached me; the lady chose to fall into a fit, and was supported by her female accomplices. A priest at that moment entered the room.

"You are come in good time, (said the pretended cousin,) to assist us in performing an act of justice."

The young lady at that instant recovered, and, seeing her coming to me, I flew to the window, with an intention of opening it to call for assistance, and, on finding it fastened, had no longer any doubts of their premeditated designs against my peace. I therefore shook off the fair syren, (who had clasped her hands around my arm, and, with tears, and all the blandishments of artful beauty, besought me to have compassion on her sufferings,) and made an effort to get out at the door; that was likewise fastened. I then eagerly inquired for what base purpose I was thus forcibly detained, and what it was they wanted with me.

"Justice, (replied the bully;)—justice only!—Reverend father, (said he, addressing himself to the priest,) this fair damsel has been robbed of her peace: her virgin fame must be lost in consequence, unless that youth (pointing to me) will make her reparation, by giving her his hand in marriage. It is to join them in holy wedlock we sent for you."

"I was now enraged too much, (continued Walter,) to have longer any command over my passion.—I drew my sword, and vowed to sacrifice any one who should dare to prevent my leaving the infamous house into which I had been so artfully and basely trepanned.

The women now clung about me, while their bully endeavoured, but in vain, to wrest my sword from me. He then commanded the priest to do his office, and I know not, at that moment, what act of desperation I might not have committed, had not you, my guardian friend and preserver, luckily burst into the room, and prevented my ending that life in a brothel which you protected so many years in a dungeon."

Albert embraced his young lord with tears of gratified affection.

"Long, very long, (cried he,) may your life be guarded from every danger, and never experience a fate so disgraceful! I will inform the Baron of what has passed: he will very soon bring these wretches to the shame and punishment they so justly deserved."

"Not for worlds, my good Albert, would I have the story transpire! (said Walter.)—I already know enough of human nature to be satisfied that the recital of it would not only bring my father's displeasure upon me, but likewise the ridicule of the world. Be assured of this, I will never again run the risk of being drawn into danger by forming an acquaintance with people, however specious their appearance, without their being well known to my father or yourself. All I beg of you is, to join with me in interceding with the Baron for permission to return to Bungay-castle. I will there wait his pleasure, without murmur or complaint, for the accomplishment of all my wishes. With Roseline de Morney I cannot be unhappy;—without her my soul can know no peace."

Albert promised to do what he could with the Baron, but requested his young lord not to be too sanguine in his hopes of prevailing on him to consent to his leaving London, till the time was expired that he had fixed for his stay, and on his promising not to offend him by disputing his will as to the length of his continuance in town, he agreed to conceal this unpleasant adventure from the Baron, strongly recommending him to be more guarded in future, and never to let his own unsuspecting nature lead him to conclude that the people he mixed with were as good and as artless as himself.

CHAPTER IX.

FROM this time Walter became more and more dissatisfied with his situation. He no longer contended with the Baron respecting the length of his stay, or refused to accompany him whenever he was requested to any public amusement or private party. But he became so restless and internally wretched, that it became impossible to conceal entirely how much he was distressed.—He wrote many letters to Roseline. The following is a copy of that which he sent a few days after his being so fortunately saved by Albert from the diabolical plan laid to render him miserable during life, and at the same time would have made the innocent Roseline as unhappy as himself.

My ever dear and charming Roseline,

I CANNOT live much longer in this detestable place, where the women are artful, the men base and designing. I am pointed at as being a fit dupe for vice to ensnare: my ignorance often leads me into error, and my own unsuspecting disposition exposes me to ridicule. If I must learn to be like the people with whom I often associate here, I shall grow in a little time so weary of existence, that I shall only wish it preserved on your account.

The immense distance between this place and the castle you inhabit renders it doubly detestable. It is a scene of bustle, confusion, and design: its amusements are all frivolous and trifling; its pleasures are joyless unsocial, and unsatisfactory, and I a mere cipher, dull and alone, amidst a crowd of beings, for whom I feel neither respect nor friendship. In fact, I am never more alone than when I am surrounded by hundreds of people, not one of whom cares for my happiness. I had rather be with you in one of the gloomiest dungeons of Bungay-castle than in the palace of our king, unless you were by my side.

I have seen a great many young ladies that are called beauties; but I think none of them half so beautiful as my gentle Roseline; neither do they appear so good humoured, nor is their dress so becoming, though they wear as many diamonds as you did on the fortunate morning you went to be married to my father. And would you think it?—one of them actually endeavoured to draw me in to marry her; though I repeatedly told her I could love no woman but you.

I have neither spirit nor appetite; I can neither laugh nor sing, and, if the Baron have a mind to make me polite,—if he wish me to acquire knowledge,—if he be desirous I should become what he calls an useful member of society, he must no longer keep us separate. It is your company only that could give a charm to that of other people, and, if I could see you, I should love the world for your sake. I shall die, dear Roseline, unless they permit me to come to you.

Madeline, though she wept, was happy, and looked handsomer than ever; and Edwin,—ah! how I envied your brother Edwin! He may be thankful he was not the son of a Baron, compelled like me to go through the tiresome drudgery of unmeaning ceremonies, and all the disgusting and nonsensical forms which they tell me belong to rank.—I am sure rank would be more valuable and happier without them, and dignity far more pleasant to its possessors, if they could divest themselves of pride.

Commend me cordially to your parents.—Tell your sisters I love them as a brother, and make my respects to De Clavering, De Willows, and the honest Cambrian, to whom I hope one day to be of service.

Sweet Roseline, think of me, dream of me, and love no one but me. My father is very kind, very indulgent, and Albert very good, for he will hear me talk of you for hours together; but neither the Baron nor Albert can guess at the sufferings they inflict on me by this tedious absence from you, to whom I am indebted for life, hope, and happiness.

Your's forever,
WALTER FITZOSBOURNE.

When the above mentioned letter reached the hands of the dejected Roseline, it alarmed and distressed her. It was however accompanied by one from the Baron to Sir Philip had no longer any fears but his friend would succeed in procuring a pardon for the fugitives. Again the family of De Morney were restored to their accustomed cheerfulness, and their friends admitted as usual; and, though Roseline shed some tears over the fond impassioned letter of Walter, they were tears of grateful tenderness, and she took care that her sighs and unceasing regret for the absence of her lover should be concealed from those to whom they would have given pain. Edeliza too was no longer under the unpleasant necessity of concealing her love for the worthy De Willows. The heart of Sir Philip was softened by the trials he had encountered, and all the parent was awakened in his soul. He therefore consented to the union of his second daughter taking place as soon as her lover could command an income sufficient to maintain a wife and family; and, as he had many friends in power, every one cherished hopes of his soon obtaining some distinguishing preferment.

Audrey, who was still a great favourite with her young lady, was now solely retained to attend her person, and wholly at her command. She considered herself therefore of some consequence, and gave herself airs accordingly. She did not choose to mix with the common class of servants,—truly a lady's maid's place was a place of too much extinction to permit any familiarity with inferiors.—No sooner did

Audrey see the family restored to their usual good humour, than she herself became more lively and chatty than ever, and all her fears of ghosts and hobgoblins were lost in her own self-importance and newly-acquired dignity. She afforded high entertainment not only to her fellow-servants, but to all the rest of the family, and, to make her character appear more ridiculous, her dress was as absurd as her sentiments.

Whenever chance threw Mrs. Audrey in their way, it was become a matter of course to enter into conversation with her, and the vain Abigail was too proud of this flattering distinction not to make the most of it.

De Clavering, who was fond of the humourous, laughed at the absurdities of Audrey, and took every opportunity of shewing her off. One day, while he was sitting with Roseline in the apartment to which Walter had been removed, when released from his dungeon, Audrey came abruptly into the room, bringing in her arms the little dog frequently mentioned in the foregoing pages. She laid him on the lap of his fond mistress, and exclaimed, "There, madam, take the little wandering rascal. I have been in a fine quandrary about him, and have had a blessed rambulation to find him, and drag him from his low-bred wulgar companions. To my thinks, he is as great a rake as the king himself, God bless his majesty; but the young Baron ought to have given him a better eddication than to keep company with his infeerors."

"I am sure, Audrey, (said De Clavering,) you are much indebted to the young rascal, as you call him; for the rambulation you complain of has given so fine a glow to your complexion, so much animation to each expressive feature, that may I die if I did not take you at first for a painted lady, and, had I met you in the passage, am afraid I should have been tempted to see whether those roses so fascinating and so blooming were borrowed or natural."

"Don't talk to me of hannimation or sansenation, (cried Audrey, indignatly drawing herself up several inches higher;) I can assure you, Mr. Doctor, I don't choose to be consulted. I neither buys, borrows, nor covets, roses; I neither wants to tempt or be tempted by any one; but if I was by chance to captify a sweetheart, I dares to say I should soon become pale enough; for I thinks love is as bad as a 'potticary shop."

"I hope I have not offended you, Mrs. Audrey, (said De Clavering, laughing,) I only meant to be civil, and pay the tribute due to the bloom I observed upon your countenance."

"Fended or not, (replied Audrey,) it little matters. Servants, some folks thinks, must not look like other people, and their blooms must be suspected truly. However, as father Anselm often says, God made us all.—You might as well have been silent as to the matter of my looks. I don't want or wish gentlemen 'poticarys to ax me questions, or trouble their heads about me."

"You would not have been half so angry with Camelford, (said De Clavering,) had he said ten times as much to you as I have done, or had he kissed you as often as I once saw him, when you ran to him under the mulberry tree."

"I don't think she would, (said Roseline, smiling,) for I know our friend Hugh is a great favourite with every female in the family."

"Wery vell, miss, (replied Audrey, blushing as red as scarlet at the story of the mulberry-tree,) you have a mind I see to join with the malicious doctor to dash and confound me; but I defy his satarical talons, and can ashure you, miss, though Mr. Camelfor is so cetious and merry, he never proffered to kiss me more than half a dozen times in his life."

"Take care how you reckon, Audrey, (cried De Clavering, humourously,) remember I saw you under the mulberry-tree."

"Well, what if you did?—You might as well have said nothing about it, (replied Audrey.)—I was frightened almost into highsterricks by an ugly black cat jumping from a lilac bush, and I ran to Mr. Camelfor without knowing what I did, and he was so civil and perlite, God bless his good-humoured heart, one must have been a savage to quarrel with him for a civil kiss or two: he does not sleer or jeer people about their looks, or tells what he sees them doing."

Neither Roseline nor De Clavering could any longer refrain from laughing, and Camelford that moment entering the room, Audrey was so much displeased, and in so great a hurry to be gone, that, in running to the door, she almost beat down her favourite.

"Fat, in the name of Cot, (cried Hugh,) is the matter with the girl? She has as many freaks and fancies in her head as a mountain coat, and is as frolicksome too."

"You had better follow her, and make your inquires, (said De Clavering;) I am satisfied the damsel would tell you what brought on her present disorder sooner than any body else."

"I am no toctor, (said Camelford,) therefore don't be playing tricks upon me, by sending me after the tamsel and pringing little Pertha's anger upon me, which, may I tie in a titch, if I know how to bear."

"Oh! if you are enlisted under petticoat government, (replied De Clavering,) I give you up as incurable,—a deserter from the thorny paths of glory, and foresee the sword will be changed into a distaff or a ploughshare."

"Luf (cried Camelford) must not be apused; it is the best stimulus to creat and noble actions, the parent of pold atchievements; but of that same luf you know nothing: there is no heart in your pody, and you are mortified to think you cannot find a nostrum to cure the disease in others: you must therefore be caught in luf's snares, in order to learn the nature of those treadful tribulations it brings upon a man. May I go to the tevil in a high wind, if I had not as hef face a canon's mouth as meet the fire of Pertha's pright eyes, when they look indignantly upon me!"

"Don't talk so much of the devil, Hugh, (interrupted De Clavering,) but request him to do you the favour of kicking about your brains a little, till they return to a more useful station in your pericranium: in my opinion, you are in a fair way of becoming fit for the government under which you think yourself enlisted."

"May the vengeance of all womankind fall upon you! (cried Camelford:)—may you be tragged apout like a tancing pear, to make sport!—may you lead asses in the tark regions of Peelzebub, for your plasphemies against woman! and may—"

But all his farther denunciations and wishes for vengeance on De Clavering were now interrupted by a loud screaming. Soon the door was thrown open, and in bounced Audrey, her cap on one side, and her face as pale as ashes.

"I have seen him, (she exclaimed,) with my own dear eyes!—his ghost, or happorition!"

"Whose cost? (cried Camelford;) where is it?—I will teach a cost to frighten a pretty cirl, and trive her tistracted."

The manner and appearance of Audrey were such as served to confirm the suspicion in the mind of Roseline, and even De Clavering, till, offended by the supposition of her being insane, she called out in her usual peculiar stile, "Thank God! some folks are no more a lunatic than other folks. I have all my seven senses as perfect as ever I had in my life;—but, Christ Jasus, these are sad times, when one is not allowed to believe their own precious eyes.—Down dropped his horse, poor beast, all in a foam, and down tumbled the young Baron arter him, as dead as my dear great grandmother."

"Who are you talking of? (cried Roseline, rising with the utmost emotion.)—Is the Baron?—is Walter?—is he dead?"

"He only died for a few minutes, (answered Audrey,) and then he came to himself—"

She had time for no more. Roseline heard the well known step of her lover.—Walter rushed into the room, threw himself at her feet, and the next instant caught her in his arms.

"This moment (cried he) is that for which my heart has languished! this is a reward for all my fatigue, all my fears and anxieties!—Look up, smile upon me, and say, my sweet Roseline, that my return gives to you an almost equal pleasure as myself; but, first, let me inform you that I have left London without the knowledge and permission of my father."

That Roseline rejoiced to see her lover her eyes informed him, but for a few minutes surprise and agitation kept her silent. Sir Philip, Lady de Morney, and the whole family, were soon assembled in the apartment to which Walter had been directed by Audrey.

The young Baron, it may be supposed, found a cordial reception, and its is not to be doubted but *that* he met with from the fair object of his affection was such as amply repaid him for his fatigue, and in his own mind even, for the risk he had hazarded of disobliging his father. This step, however, was owing to a hint dropped by the Baron, that it would be agreeable and convenient, to himself, and necessary for many reasons to his son, that they should prolong their stay in town some weeks beyond what had been proposed, or intended on their departure from the castle.

On this plan being opposed by Walter, the Baron not only appeared displeased, but resolute to carry his point. A circumstance so distressing to his son rendered him equally determined not to submit to such arbitrary, and, in his opinion, cruel authority; therefore, early the next morning he sat off, without being attended by a servant, or informing any one to what part of the globe he meant to go, and the next day reached Bungay castle in the manner before described.

Sir Philip de Morney, on learning these alarming circumstances from his daughter, immediately sent off an express to inform the Baron of his son's unexpected arrival, and of his apprehensions that the step he had so unguardedly taken would bring his displeasure upon himself and family, whom he seriously assured him knew nothing of his intention.

Walter, in his conversations with Roseline, told her, he found himself so disgusted with the customs and manners of the world, and met with so few people in it to whom he could attach himself, or for whom he felt either respect or affection, that he determined no longer to be detained from her in whose care his happiness was intrusted, and with whom alone he was satisfied it could rest secure.

"And, as you condescended, (he continued,) to love and attend to me when immured in a dungeon,—kindly smiled on me, and endeavoured to instruct me when enveloped in ignorance, and was my friend when I appeared to have no claims,—a solitary outcast from society, I thought you would not be very much displeased if I forsook the world for you, who gave up more, much more, for me, and quitted its gayest and most cheerful scenes for the solitary gloom of a prison.

"Whatever I may still want of polish, address, and what fashionable people stile politeness, love and my gentle Roseline can easily teach me. From a world that I neither like nor approve, I could learn but little, while the chosen mistress of my heart may at her pleasure make me any thing she wishes. With her, and for her amusement, I may be sometimes tempted to live in a crowd; without her, the world itself is only a wide extended dungeon."

Roseline, at hearing this impassioned language from lips which, she was satisfied, knew no guile, was too much gratified to express all she felt. She smiled on him through her tears, and, in the softest language affection could dictate, gently chid him for being so impetuous as to run the risk of disobliging his father on her account, expressing a few timid apprehensions that the Baron might be offended with her has being the innocent cause of his son's proving refractory to his wishes; yet she could not help secretly rejoicing in the strength of his attachment, on which all her happiness depended.

Every thing was done by the family to give this amiable and singular lover a reception not only suitable to his elevated rank, but satisfactory to his feelings,—such an one as the sincerity of his regard for Roseline demanded and deserved, while the joy which appeared upon the animated countenances of the lovers convinced every one who saw them, that they had fixed their hopes of felicity on a basis which the hand of death only could shake from its foundations.

Walter, in his moments of unreserved, expressed his surprise, dislike, and contempt, of many things, persons, and customs, which he met with in the high circles to which he had been introduced, and concluded with wishing that the Baron could be prevailed upon to excuse his farther attendance, adding, it was his determined plan, so far as it met the approbation of his beloved Roseline, to spend as much of his time as the nature of his situation would permit in the placid bosom of retirement, in which he hoped to make himself as useful and worthy a member of the commonwealth as he should be if engaged in more bustling and busy scenes.

"One would think (said De Clavering, who happened to be present when this conversation occurred) that the young Baron had been educated by some of our wise and ancient philosophers, and, taught by their precepts, was convinced by them that happiness was too timid and modest to be found in the confines of court, or the splendours of a ball-room. It reminds me of Enthymenes, who, speaking of the pleasure of solitude to a man of the world, makes the following observations.

"You are compelled to a continual restraint in your dress, demeanour, actions, and words:—your festivals are so magnificent, and our's so mirthful!—your pleasures so superficial and so transient, and our's so real and so constant! Have you ever in your rich apartments breathed an air so fresh as that which we respire in this verdant arbour?—or can your entertainments, sometimes so sumptuous, compare with the bowls of milk which we have just drawn, or those delicious fruits we have gathered with our hands?

"Ah! if happiness be only the health of the soul, must it not be found in those places, where a just proportion ever reigns between our wants and our desires, where motion is constantly followed by rest, and where our affections are always accompanied by tranquillity, breathe a free air, and enjoy the splendour of heaven.—From these kind of comparisons we may judge which are the true riches that nature designed for men."

"Such were the opinions and sentiments of Enthymenes, and such I find are those of De Clavering, (replied Walter,) or he would not have retained and repeated them with so much facility and satisfaction.— Were my fate united with that of Miss de Morney, and had I two such friends as De Clavering and Albert, to direct my conduct and enlarge the small portion of knowledge I have yet been able to acquire, I should think myself the most fortunate as well as the happiest of mankind, having already experienced a long series of oppression from the baneful arts of stratagems of ambition, I have learned to despise it, and, in the gloomy and trying hours of adversity, have been taught, that fortitude, with humility and untainted honour, can harmonize, but can never degrade the most exalted stations, and, while they are the brightest jewels that could adorn a crown, they enrich and ennoble the lowest peasant."

In a few days, the Baron, accompanied by Albert, arrived at the castle. The frown which appeared upon his brow, at his first entrance, was instantly dispersed when the trembling Roseline sunk at his feet, and entreated him to pardon the eccentric flight of her lover, of which, as she was the cause, if his displeasure continued, it would inflict equal distress upon herself as upon his son.

To resist so fair a supplicant was not in the Baron's power. He tenderly raised her from the ground, and the next morning embraced her lover. The utmost harmony and a general cheerfulness soon prevailed, and, before the parties separated for the night, the Baron candidly and generously acknowledged, that, at the same age, and under the same circumstances as his son, he believed he should have acted as he had done. "And upon the whole, (said he,) I was not very sorry when the obstinate sighing boy took himself away; for I was grown weary of having to introduce, and make such frequent apologies for so absent, lifeless, and refractory a being."

What served to reconcile matters the sooner was, that Albert, after the sudden disappearance of his young lord, had informed his father of Mrs. C—'s infamous stratagem to draw him into a marriage with her artful and abandoned daughter. He was so much enraged at hearing the lengths to which these wretches had dared to go, that strict search was made after them, but without effect.

Walter, too, told Roseline of the designs which had been formed to entrap him, and, while she looked at him with increased delight, she secretly rejoiced that he had left a place which harboured a set of people who gloried to destroy the peace of their fellow-creatures.

To make the happiness of the friendly party more perfectly complete, the Baron informed Sir Philip and Lady de Morney that he hoped very soon to procure a pardon for Edwin and Madeline, and to be able to restore them to their protection.

Preparations for the marriage very soon began, the Baron humourously observing, that, till his son was again deprived of his freedom, there would be no knowing how to secure, or what to do with him, and declaring he should be very glad to delegate the care of him to one whom he had no doubt would supply his place much to the advantage of the charge he was ready and willing to give up.

Every appendage, that wealth could purchase,—rank require,—or youth and ambition wish to possess,—was liberally provided to grace the nuptials of Walter Fitzosbourne and the happy Roseline de Morney.

Ah! how different were the feelings,—how delightful the prospects of the intended bride, on this occasion, to what they had been on a former one, when she prepared with such agonizing terrors to give her hand to the Baron!—yet, though she could now think of approaching the altar without reluctance, she could not entirely divest herself of those timid fears which every gentle and virtuous female must experience when she recollects the number of the new duties upon which she is going to enter, and that, from the moment she becomes a wife, her happiness, no longer dependent on herself or parents, rests only on the man to whom she has given her hand.

Walter seemed to tread on air; he was all vivacity and joy, and appeared to have assumed a new character. The world, and every thing belonging to it, wore a different aspect:—all, all was charming. He wondered how he could ever have felt disgust, or cherished discontent. To his father he was attentive and affectionate,—to his friends cordial and complacent,—to his Roseline all that an affectionate lover could or ought to be.

Albert was almost as happy and joyous as his master. The Baron, serene, grateful, and contented, while Sir Philip and Lady de Morney, who found their own consequence and comforts so much increased by this fortunate and splendid alliance, united in blessing the hour which sent their intended son-in-law a prisoner to Bungay-castle.

CHAPTER X.

AT length the happy day arrived which was appointed for the celebration of these long expected nuptials. We presume that the morning, to the world in general, was exactly like what other mornings had been, and that the sun shone without any perceptible brilliancy being added to its rays, except in the eyes of the now happy lovers.

The company assembled in the breakfast-room, and for some time waited for Roseline. She soon made her appearance, led by her beloved Walter, who had stolen unobserved to the chamber-door of his mistress, to chide her for so long delaying his happiness. On this occasion he was splendidly attired, and the bride, elegantly but simply dressed, wanted not the borrowed aid of ornament, but, arrayed in maiden bashfulness and artless purity, appeared all native loveliness.

As she received the congratulations of her friends, a tear, which stole from her expressive eye as it trembled to escape, appeared the spotless harbinger of gratified affection, struggling to conquer the becoming fears of unaffected modesty.

As soon as breakfast was over, they were accompanied to the chapel of the nunnery by a numerous train of friends and dependents. On their arrival, they were met by the Lady Abbess, the venerable and worthy Father Anselm, and almost all the inhabitants of the nunnery, who were allowed to assemble in the chapel on this joyous occasion, while every face wore the appearance of cheerfulness.

A select party went back with them to the castle, where all who chose were permitted to partake of the happiness, and share in the social satisfaction which universally prevailed.

Mutual congratulations and good wishes were exchanged. Sir Philip and Lady de Morney, happy as they were in the completion of their ambition, could not restrain the sigh of heart-felt regret at the thoughts of soon being separated from their beloved daughter.

Roseline was some time before she recovered her usual serenity, till Edeliza, on observing her shed a tear as she looked at her mother, said to her, in a whisper,—"I cannot imagine, my dear sister, why you should weep. I do not think I should be so dejected if I were married to De Willows,—though he never said half so many fine things to me as the young Baron has done to you."

Roseline, smiling, pressed the hand of her sister, and, returning her whisper, assured her she was indeed the most enviable of her sex:—but (added she) it requires more fortitude than I possess to support such happiness as mine with equanimity and composure; and the natural regret I cannot help feeling at leaving his place, and soon being separate from the best and tenderest of mothers, convinces me that Providence never intended we should enjoy bliss without alloy."

The next day the party sat off in new and splendid carriages, attended by a numerous retinue of servants, for the Baron's castle in the North of England. Their grand cavalcade brought a number of people to take a farewell look of the lovely bride, whose departure was generally regretted; and she was followed by the good wishes of all who ever had the pleasure of enjoying her society.

Sir Philip and Lady de Morney, her two sisters, De Willows, De Clavering, and Hugh Camelford accompanied her. Audrey had likewise the honour of attending her lady as fille de chambre, and never felt herself of such infinite consequence as she did when handed into the travelling carriage by the Baron's gentleman, who did her the honour to assist in packing her up to the chin amidst the boxes and luggage entrusted to her care.

The party travelled slowly and pleasantly, stopping to see every thing on their route that was worthy observations; and, as they were now in the humour to be easily pleased, they were consequently amused and gratified with almost every thing they saw.—It is a kind of humour so extremely convenient, that I hope we shall be excused for recommending the adoption of it to travellers of all countries and denominations,—good humour, and serenity of mind, being the best companions at home, are equally eligible to carry with us when we go abroad.

On their arrival at Fitzosbourne-castle, they received a considerable increase to their happiness by meeting Edwin and Madeline in perfect health and good spirit.—Sir Philip and Lady de Morney's cup of joy was filled to the brim, when they found themselves folded in the arms of their long absent children, for whose lives they had so often, and indeed at this very moment inwardly trembled.

The happy bride of the exulting Walter felt such a torrent of added felicity, on being folded in the arms of her brother and Madeline, that she was very near fainting. Observing this, the Baron, to call off their attention, desired them to permit him to come in for some share of their embraces, and in his turn to welcome them to Fitzosbourne-castle. This had the effect it was designed to produce, and the cordial welcome every one received from the Baron gave additional satisfaction to the hours thus marked with joy, happiness, and love.

After they had taken some refreshment, Edwin surprised them all by approaching the Baron, and in the most submissive manner begging him to pardon the liberty he had taken in introducing a guest to the castle, whom, as yet, he knew not of being there,—a guest old and weak, but who was, he hoped, slowly recovering from an attack of illness so severe, as to have threatened his life, and which, in all probability, would have terminated his moral existence, but for the unremitting attention he received from the Baron's domestics.

"No apology is necessary upon such an occasion, (said the Baron.) Had my people been wanting in care to any one who required their assistance, I should have instantly dismissed them.—When may I be introduced to your friend? (added he.)—I am impatient to assure him that this house, and all that it contains, are much at his service."

"Pray, my dear Edwin, (said Lady de Morney,) who is the person for whom you have ventured to tax the Baron's hospitality thus largely, and for whom you appear so much interested?"

"The father of this lady, (replied he, taking the hand of Madeline, and leading her to his mother.)—To her I will refer you for an account of our meeting, and the revolution it has fortunately produced in our favour."

Madeline was instantly called upon to gratify the curiosity of the company, and without any delay, informed them, that Edwin and herself having one day agreed to take a ramble, they told the people with whom they lodged that they should not return till the evening.

Disguising themselves more than usual, so as to avoid the possibilities of being discovered, they sat off; and, being tempted by the extreme fineness of the day, wandered till they came to the great road which led to a large town, not five miles distant.

"In fact, (said the blushing narrator,) my dear Edwin, was grown weary of solitude, and wished perhaps to see more faces than those which he met in the obscure little cottage to which we were confined."

Every one smiled,—Edwin looked confused,—and Madeline thus proceeded.

"We had not walked more than half a mile in the great road, before the number of people we met, and the curiosity our strange appearance excited, determined us to choose a more private walk; but, just as we were going to turn into a lane which led to a neighbouring village, our attention was caught, and our design prevented by a carriage being overturned within a hundred paces of us.

"The horses, proving restive, had drawn it up a high bank, which occasioned the accident. One of the servants, seeing Edwin, beckoned him, and begged him to assist in lifting it up, and liberating his master from his perilous situation. He immediately ran off, telling me to sit down on the bank till his return.

"Thinking, however, that I might possibly be of some service, I walked slowly forwards; but guess my terror, when, just as we arrived at the carriage, they were dragging from it a man to all appearance dead.

"I instantly flew to lend my assistance; but no sooner did I distinguish his person, than I was nearly as lifeless as himself.—It was my father,—my father dying on the road![43] The sight, however terrifying to my fears and torturing to my feelings, gave me strength, and inspired me with fortitude to help in preserving the life of the author of my being.

"I took an opportunity to inform my dear Edwin who it was that claimed our care and attention. After chafing his temples, and rubbing his emaciated hands, some faint signs of life reanimated our endeavours.

"We found, by the conversation of the servants, that their master had been recommended to try what change of air and travelling might do, as medicine had failed in removing a disease which had long preyed upon his constitution, and which had been increased by some domestic sorrow.

"Alas! of that sorrow I knew myself to be the cause, and the tears which I shed upon his almost lifeless hand, as I saw him extended at my feet, atoned I hope, in some measure, for the grief I had inflicted.

"When life was more perfectly restored, we moved him upon a grass plat, till the carriage and horses could be got ready.—He took no notice of any one, and appeared to be totally insensible of the accident, and of every thing around him.—This at once determined us to intrude on the Baron's goodness, and convey him to this castle.

"Having dispatched a messenger for the best advice we could procure, one of his attendants and myself accompanied him in the carriage. His head rested on my bosom, but he knew me not, nor once attempted to speak. On our arrival here, we found every thing prepared for our reception, Edwin having taken one of the horses, and rode full speed to inform the Baron's servants a sick gentleman was coming, for whom he requested their care and assistance.

"My father was taken from the carriage, and instantly put to bed. Two medical gentlemen very soon arrived, who, on examining the state of their patient, from the violence of the contusion and the total deprivation of sense in which they found him, seemed to think there was a concussion of the brain. They assured us, however, that his life would not be endangered by the accident, but said, they saw he was far

---

[43] Bonhote creates remarkably strong women in her novel for this is the second instance of a daughter saving the life of her father. Two daughters, Roseline and Madeline, reject patriarchal orders yet they are still able to become heroines when they save their fathers from death.

advanced in a decline, from which they apprehended more fatal consequences.

"We continued our disguise, and, as our real names were totally unknown in this neighbourhood, having passed for a Mr. and Mrs. Danbury, we were under no apprehensions of being discovered, should my father recover his senses. After remaining in the most painful state of suspense many days, he began to take notice of those who attended him, but made no inquires after his own servants, how he came into a strange place, or the accident which had befallen him. One day, as I was sitting by him, and holding his head, which I had been rubbing with vinegar, he looked earnestly at me.

"If I did not think, if I did not know it was impossible, (said he, in hurried accents, looking first at me, and then at Edwin, who was standing at the foot of the bed,) I should almost be tempted to believe that the hand which has so gently given me relief was the hand of Madeline de Glanville, and that face the face I once fondly doated upon; but it cannot be!—I am a poor, wandering, old man, whose eyes must be closed by strangers, and I deserve it should be so. I once had a daughter, but I banished her my sight:—I had a son, but he perhaps is no longer an inhabitant of this world."

Here he stopped, and burst into a violent flood of tears. By a sign from Edwin I understood he wished me to take this favourable opportunity of making the discovery, for which he knew I languished. Falling therefore, on my knees, in the most supplicating attitude, and pressing his hand to my lips, I exclaimed:

"I am your daughter,—your Madeline, and there is the amiable, the beloved husband for whom I dared to disobey my father, and for whom at this moment I stand trembling victim to the just laws of my country and my religion!"

"The scene which followed it is not in my power to describe. Suffice it to say, that, from that interesting period, my father has not only been reconciled, but renovated with health and strength. He frequently laments the obstinacy which reduces us to the necessity of taking such steps to prevent our separation. He has written letters to every one he knows that has any interest with the higher powers of the church, but his hopes of success are rested upon Lord Fitzosbourne, to whom he is impatient to pay is respects."

"This moment I am ready to attend him, (said the Baron:) the father of Madeline is entitled to every attention that has, or can be shewn him."

After his lordship's visit had been paid, the rest of the party followed of course, and a general harmony prevailed. Mr. de Glanville was instantly placed wholly under the care of De Clavering, and soon obtained as perfect a state of convalescence as the nature of his constitutional habits would admit.

Now again hospitality and festivity took their turn to reign, and the happy and distinguished Walter, after languishing so many years in misery and confinement, found himself in the situation for which nature had designed him.

Restored to his rank in the bosom of affluence, and surrounded by tender and admiring friends, he soon lost that timid shyness which had once rendered him averse to society, and discontented with the world. United to the only woman he had ever loved, and possessed of domains more extensive and fertile than those of many a petty prince, with a mind calculated to promote the happiness of his fellow-creatures, he was beloved by all, and envied by many.

In a few months a full and free pardon was procured for Edwin and Madeline, and Mr. de Glanville, having recovered, contrary to the expectation of every one, from the indisposition which threatened him with death at the time his daughter escaped from the Bungay nunnery, on being convinced she had made so respectable and worthy a choice, gave her a considerable portion, and afterwards, having the fears of his son's death realized, she inherited his whole estate. Edwin also rose to high rank in the army, and was an honour to his country.

Edeliza was happily married in due time to her beloved De Willows, and, about six years after, the worthy Hugh Camelford led the blooming and unrelucant Bertha to the altar.—To these young men the Baron uniformly remained a bountiful and steady patron, and Sir Philip and Lady de Morney lived many years to be grateful and happy spectators of the felicity and prosperity of their children.

The Baron and his son became so sincerely attached to De Clavering during his visit at Fitzosbourne-castle, that, in compliance with their urgent and repeated entreaties, he consented to remain in their neighbourhood.

He very soon afterwards married a lady of respectability and fortune, and his practice became so extensive, and so much esteemed, that his superior knowledge proved a general blessing, of which many hundreds of his fellow-creatures in a few years experienced the benefit.

The Baron was highly delighted with the society of De Clavering, and it was with the utmost reluctance he ever consented to his being a day absent from the neighbourhood.

It was the intention of the Baron, after he had seen his son fixed, and his household properly established, to have resided in another of his castles, about twenty miles distant, but neither Walter nor Roseline would consent to the proposal.

They reminded the Baron of the long and cruel separation which had divided him from his son in the early part of his life, and so earnestly entreated him not to interrupt their happiness, by withdrawing himself from their society, and refusing to reside with them, that, pleased and gratified by the tenderness with which the request was mutually urged, he yield to their persuasions, and a proper suite of rooms, with a large retinue of servants, were set apart for the immediate use of the Baron.

He continued to live with them many years, without any interruption to his happiness; and, in seeing the harmony and felicity they enjoyed, surrounded by a number of lovely and healthy grand-children, he found, amidst the increasing infirmities of old age, sufficient attractions in life to make it pleasant and desirable, while the cordial affection and exemplary conduct of his son, joined to the endearing attentions of the gentle and beloved Roseline, made him remember with joy and gratitude the day in which he saw their hands united.

Albert never left his beloved master, but was faithfully attached to his children as he had been to himself. He had apartments appropriated to his use, a servant to attend him, and met, in the kind and unceasing attentions of his grateful friends, the just reward of his long tried fidelity.[44]

Often, in the dreary winter evenings, having drawn all the younger part of the family around him, he would recite the incidents of his life from the period of his confinement with Walter. To the young Fitzosbournes it was a high treat to hear Albert tell the tale of their beloved father's life.

Sometimes he would excite their wonder, and entertain them with the surprising effect of his double voice; and, when he became a very old man, he was as much beloved for what he had been, as he was respected for his age, grey hairs, and universal philanthropy.

Though many overtures were made by the worthless brother of the Lady Isabella to bring about a reconciliation, neither the Baron nor his son could ever be prevailed upon to see him, and its was with some

---

[44] True to fairy tale form, Bonhote reunites the lovers and family members while pairing up the remaining single daughters with the merry band of De Willow's men. All of her characters rise in class and wealth. (This denouement is representative of Female Gothic fiction. All hurts are mended and all live happily ever after compared to Male Gothic fiction which would emphasize the violent punishment given to the wicked). Even Albert rises in class. Though he is the only male to remain single, he too is rewarded—with his own servant. As new children are born and Albert ages, he becomes the beloved wizard-like grandfather. Like the wise old story-teller, it is Albert who passes on the story of Roseline and Walter to their children-emphasizing the transformative power of love.

difficulty the former was persuaded to give up bringing him to justice for the crime he had committed.

The good abbess and the venerable father Anselm had the pleasure of seeing their favourite Madeline as happy in the arms of her worthy husband, as they had hoped she would have been in the bosom of their church. Walter and his Roseline paid them many visits before they were removed from their exemplary calling on earth to receive the reward of their purity and virtue in the regions of immortality.

The hero and heroine of our tale retained the virtues of their youth, the gentleness of their manners, and the sweetness of their dispositions to the end of their lives; and, what may be thought more rare and singular, they never lost their humility, tenderness, and unbounded affection for each other; but when age, that grave of beauty, had robbed them of those outward graces, which nature with an unsparing hand had bestowed upon their youth, love maintained its empire in their faithful bosoms, and survived every change, till death summoned them to meet the bright and unfailing recompense of a life spent in the practice of religion, justice, and virtue.

FINIS.

Further Reading

Andriano, Joseph. *Our Ladies of Darkness: Feminine Daemonology in Male Gothic Fiction.* University Park, PA: Pennsylvania University Press, 1993.

Davenport-Hines, Richard. *Gothic: Four Hundred Years of Excess, Horror, Evil, and Ruin.* New York: North Point Press, 1998.

Dijkstra, Bram. *Evil Sisters: The Threat of Female Sexuality in Twentieth Century Culture.* New York: Henry Holt, 1996.

Ellis, Markman. *The History of Gothic Fiction.* Great Britain: Edinburgh Press, 2000.

Kelly, John. *The Great Mortality: An Intimate History of the Black Death, the Most Devastating Plague of all Time.* New York: Harper Collins, 2005.

Meyers, Helene. *Femicidal Fears: Narratives of the Female Gothic Experience.* New York: State University, 2001.

Sedgwick, Eve Kosofsky. *Between Men: English Literature and Male Homosocial Desire. New York: Columbia Press, 1985.*

Showalter, Elaine. *A Literature of Their Own: British Women Novelists from Bronte to Lessing.* New Jersey: Princeton Press, 1999.

Williams, Anne. *Art of Darkness: A Poetics of Gothic.* Chicago: University of Chicago, 1995.

Breinigsville, PA USA
03 October 2010
246568BV00001B/13/A